The
Blackheath Séance
Parlour

The Blackheath Séance Parlour

ALAN WILLIAMS

Cutting
Edge
Press

A Cutting Edge Press Paperback Original

Published in 2013 by Cutting Edge Press

www.cuttingedgepress.co.uk

Printed and bound in Great Britain by CPI (UK) Ltd, Croydon, CR0 4YY

ISBN: 978-1908122-51-3
E-PUB ISBN: 978-1-908122-52-0

I dedicate this book to my mother, who has waited long enough.

Chapter 1

Heaving dark clouds collected above the blustery expanse of Blackheath as if they meant to cause immeasurable damage. Pulsing and turning, they crashed into each other like great battleships fighting for space in overcrowded waters that they refused to leave. Beneath them, thrust into the strange darkness, people panicked. Never before had clouds of such blackness and weight visited London. Indeed so spectacular was the scene that people gathered in large numbers to marvel at it.

The lull before the storm announced itself at four o clock precisely, although it appeared to be midnight. In an instant, everything changed. The winds fell and an unnatural warmth rose from the ground, rushing away from the exposed land down into the basin of the village. The heath was quickly abandoned, left empty except for the large black rooks that congregated in sinister numbers at the approach of every storm. Today their numbers were as troubling as the skies above them.

There was silence – a sticky, heavy pressure. Everything and everyone was waiting, as if a countdown had begun.

Under the oil lamp that hung outside the Hare and Billet public house opposite the willowed pond at the bottom right of the heath, a spindly figure came hurrying into view. She was cloaked in black, pulling the swirling material close to her body and moved with determined strides, hurried along by the threat of what stirred above. Illuminated by the orange glow of the pub windows, she stopped suddenly, distracted by a noise at the pond. Beyond the curtain of dark willow branches that dipped down into the water something was moving.

Quietly, and against her better judgement, she crossed the road and stepped softly onto the grass. It was most likely a trapped animal, a duck perhaps or something she could take home to cook. Inside the branches there was a struggle, a sleepy confused cry and the sound of something being dragged through a crisp blanket of dry leaves. The woman reached out, parted the leafy curtains with her cold, nervous fingers and peered into the darkness. Across the pond, a shadow moved and then with a cry of angry exertion a stark white face, violent with rage, turned sharply towards her. She jumped, her heart hammering in her chest, her feet staggering back. She was turning, hurrying away, her body moving her independently of her frozen, panicking brain, striding urgently into the blackness that stretched out endlessly in front of her.

The clouds stirred, as if turning to view her, flashes and glows rippling beneath its belly, warning her as she watched her path darken to blindness around her that it would be claiming her. And as she stepped further from the light behind her, not daring to look back, the whole sky creaked and groaned and lowered.

Further into the dark open expanse, the deafening slams of thunder shook the ground under her feet. She pulled her cloak tight, clutched the bottles swinging in her deep pockets and lowered her head to battle the wind. She was too far across to run for cover and could see nothing, but she knew the way well. Walk straight ahead, stop for nothing, talk to no one, hurry. At the halfway mark she would turn, see the lights of the Hare and Billet fade into the darkness. After thirty-four broad steps, in the distance ahead, the house lights of Dartmouth Terrace would pinpoint her own corner of the heath.

On her right, across the emptiness, Greenwich Park with its giant telescopes and prestigious observatory of the skies was barely visible. Further along, the Ranger's House, grand and imposing and forever refusing to send her an invitation to its annual ball, was being illuminated.

She strained to see Dartmouth Terrace's house lights, hurried forward – thirty-six, thirty-eight, forty steps – peering through the darkness but seeing nothing. Then the chance of seeing anything was gone. There was a howl and the heavens thrashed at her without mercy. She felt lost at sea on some great rocking ship that dug down into giant waves and rose up hurling one and all overboard to the mermaids and sirens. The gale tore at her like a hurricane, pushing her forward, then sideways, lifting her skirts and her long greying hair, reaching inside her lungs and pulling out her breath. She held tight, gripped the bottles, wiped away the water gushing down her face and felt it worm beneath her collar, running down inside her clothes, down her back, soaking her undergarments, running in twisting rivulets down her legs. She lowered her head, focused on the ground and ran, counting her steps, catching her breath between the great powerful gusts that tipped her backwards, inhaling through gasps as she fought to remain upright in the cold icy rain.

The lightning was her concern now. It struck the heath ferociously around her. She held her hand to her frantic heart. It was all around her. She would not escape this. This would be how she died; struck by lightning, burned to a black charcoal statue, still smoking as people peered at her face and said, 'Isn't that Maggie Cloak?' She pushed on, hardly daring to let her feet touch the ground, still unable to see the houselights up ahead through the dense swirling storm. Putting her trust in fate and the unlikelihood of lightning striking the same place twice, she forged ahead, dancing right and left, wiping rain from her eyes.

A sudden and violent flash illuminated something moving quickly alongside her; a figure, a man, long limbed, jumping across the puddles and mounds of slate, his arms outstretched to balance himself, his steps wide and exaggerated like those of a giant spider, his horrible white face searching. Then it was dark once more and she moved quickly, her fingers slipping around the neck of one of the bottles in her pocket. A second flash almost made her scream. The figure was closer, heading in her direction, his furious eyes fixed upon her.

Racing up the old Dover road from the coast two large black carriages pulled by four muscular black horses attempted to outrun the storm that had kept pace with them since their arrival into the country. Finally Blackheath opened up to them, the storm a dramatic black sea above it. The carriages veered and swayed as their wheels hit verge and pothole, turning the corners too fast and at alarming speeds. They threatened to topple as they approached the Princess of Wales public house that marked entry into the village. The sky groaned and let out a heavy roar as the carriages settled and dipped down into Blackheath village following the road that curved right and led back up onto the heath proper.

At the centre of the heath, the large house, kept private by tall walls, was in upheaval. Staff wrenched the gate open. Inside, the butler – an elderly man, obsessed with order – closed window shutters, lit the oil lamps and candles, made last-minute adjustments to flower arrangements, all the time waiting for the whistle from the front gate, which at last sounded. The maids rushed to the hall, he to the drinks cabinet to wipe a bottle of vintage Barolo with a stiff cotton napkin and set it on a silver tray next to two crystal glasses at the only unshuttered window. He looked around the room, inspecting it, enjoying the ambiance before closing the double doors with a bow, pleased with his efforts. Then he joined the staff that had formed a line in the hall for the formal welcome.

The wheels made a final turn into the grounds, pulling to a sudden halt in the light that shone out from the open front door. From the second carriage stepped a small elderly governess who, brushing herself down irritably, opened an umbrella. From beneath it she surveyed the property and its surrounds. Then without any further hesitation, she strode inside.

'We will not need your services this evening' she told the line of eager and apprehensive staff who greeted her with assorted bows and curtsies. 'The count and countess are tired from their long journey and would like to greet everyone tomorrow afternoon, so please, take your coats and return in the morning.'

Disappointed or relieved, the staff moved in different directions, vanishing into rooms and cupboards before reappearing in their overcoats and venturing out into the storm, each casting a nervous glance at the carriages which kept the occupants hidden from view. When the grounds were at last empty, the carriage doors opened. Beneath umbrellas, out onto the sodden, puddled ground stepped two tall elegant figures, young and immaculate and strong. The skies howled, pushing them forward, up the steps, into their new home. Blackheath was about to experience change to a horrifying degree.

Suddenly, ahead, a light flickered. Maggie peered through watery eyes, startled to find herself closer to home than she had anticipated. The light she had assumed to be Dartmouth Terrace's faraway beacon was little more than a flickering candle in a window. She turned her head, dared to seek the figure out, saw him lifting himself up from the ground, staring around as he rested a hand on his knee and straightened his spine. She darted inside her gate before his face turned her way, not daring to consider that he might have seen where she lived. Then throwing herself at the door she burst inside with a cry.

A scream from within made her throw up her hands in horror, shocked to see someone in her home.

'What are you doing here?' She demanded angrily, surveying the dark roomy kitchen, in which her younger sister sat at the table using up her paper, consuming her port.

'They've arrived!'

'Who have?' she asked, slamming and locking the door before peeling off the heavy sodden cloak and letting it drop to the floor. She put the large green and red bottles on the shelf above the unlit stove, tutting as she leaned to light it with a spill.

'The count and countess!'

Maggie wasn't listening, her heart was still racing. She rushed to the window, peering out through the dirty glass. Whoever he was, he was gone. The heath was empty. She kicked off her shoes, undid skirt after skirt and rolled down her stockings. Then she moved into the pantry to dry her cold wet body.

'Shall I pour you a . . .' the younger woman examined a bottle, 'gin?'

'I'll have a port. That is not gin. Put it down.' Nerves and rattling teeth undermined her authoritative tone, so she reiterated; 'Put it down.' She pulled herself into a thin vest and a thick, heavy housecoat, wrapping herself tight, and hurried to light the kitchen fire, taking the glass of port as she passed. It would take both fires to keep out the cold tonight.

'What are you doing here so early? And why didn't you turn on the window lamp? Why are you sitting in the dark?'

'Because,' began her sister topping up her own glass and pulling her chair to the warmth of the fire, barely able to contain her excitement, 'they were about to arrive and I needed to be in the right atmosphere to welcome them.'

'Who?' her sister demanded irritably.

Judy, her junior by seven years, making her thirty-three or thereabouts, relished a big sip of port then began.

'They escaped their father. He was mad, psychotic, insane. He lived in isolation in a large Russian castle in Siberia after the war because he was worried they would find out about his experiments.'

'What experiments? What war?' Maggie wrung out her stockings and turned irritably to her. 'Who?'

Judy rolled her eyes at her sister. 'The count and countess have arrived in Blackheath, tonight!' She reached across the table and picked up a modest pile of handwritten sheets. 'My novel has begun.'

Her sister sighed; she had no time for nonsense like this. Her heart was still thundering from the ordeal of being chased, and although she felt the need to tell Judy, she did not want to frighten her, so she took stock of her emotions, calming herself with deep breaths, using the time her sister's annoying ranting allowed her.

'Read it. Please, please read it.'

'Not now.'

'Oh please, Maggie.'

'Not until it's finished. It's bad luck, or something along those lines.'

'But I worked so hard!'

'When it's finished,' she said firmly, then noting her sister's disappointment, reconsidered. 'I will read it when you have completed chapter six.'

'Very well.'

'After all, you don't want to feel the satisfaction of a novelist before you actually are one. It would spoil it.'

'Yes. You are right. Again you are right.'

'Besides, we have something much more urgent to discuss this evening.'

Outside, the storm was unabated, shaking the ground as it grumbled overhead. It rattled the windows and hammered with angry gusts at the door, lighting up the room with sudden stark brightness, drawing the women to the window to watch the magnificent light show.

The roads were deepening with water, great swells of it tipped from the flooded banks of the ponds and raced down the sloping incline into the village, turning its low-lying heart, Blunt's Hole, into something akin to a lake. It had lifted above the pavements and above the steps of shops and was now surging under the door of Maggie and Judy's sweet shop and cascading down into the cellar. And still the heavy, pregnant black clouds came, queuing until they reached the village and its heath before emptying.

Against the glow of the fire the two sisters got down to business, uncorking more port, pouring large swirls into oversized glasses, flexing their toes above the flames. The shifting orange glow on Judy's face drew Maggie's attention. Familiarity, as was often the case, had made the everyday invisible. She had not noticed how much weight Judy had lost over the summer and now, startled, she questioned her memory as to whether it had been a sudden loss or a gradual shift. They were both hungry and thin but Judy's plump, pleasant face had become gaunt, her beautiful brown inquisitive eyes lost in dark, sunken sockets. Her button nose had narrowed, giving her a sharper profile, even her hands seemed little more than skin and bone. Maggie shifted uncomfortably in her chair and offered a contented smile when her sister looked at her. Even her girlish smile, she noticed, was changed by thinning lips and made her look much older.

'You look tired,' she said, selfishly hoping that her sister would not agree and suggest ending the evening's drinking prematurely.

'Do I?' she replied, her happy demeanour still naturally inclined away from complaint or drawing attention to her own needs.

Maggie leaned forward and topped up her glass. 'There is some bread if you are hungry.'

Judy shook her head and returned her gaze to the fire, wittering happily about the imminent arrival of an elephant to the new London Zoo and how since they couldn't afford the entry price, they might stand outside to see it arrive. She put down her glass and rubbed warmth into her fingers, resting them on the shabby brown skirt that of late had become her daily uniform.

In the mirror, Maggie studied her own face. She was not as pretty as her sister. She had been set in her father's mould rather than their mother's, as Judy had. She had more austere features: a longer nose; smaller, sharper, darker eyes that had the disadvantage of appearing to dart impatiently rather than look interested. A hard life had taken its toll, and numerous lines around the eyes and mouth had proved to be permanent, despite a decade of harsh, abrasive scrubbing. But she had stopped caring about lines years ago, they seemed a minor obstacle in comparison to the rest of her face.

Maggie had always been the taller and thinner of the two but in comparison to her sister, she now looked the better fed. Perhaps the occasional broken chocolates she set aside and nibbled on when the coast was clear did, after all, count. She took a bottle of home-made potato wine from the pantry and carried it through. From the table where she set it down to uncork it, Judy looked tiny, a shadow of her former self. Maggie shook the thought away. There was nothing to be done about it this evening. Tomorrow she would find the money with which to feed her up, encourage more people into the shop instead of sitting passively as she did every day.

'Well,' Maggie began, 'since you are here far too early, we might as well begin. Though I do wish when I stipulate a time you would stick to it. Rules, Judy, are there for a reason.'

'You have too many rules for everything.'

'As your elder and therefore more –'

'Yes, Maggie,' she sighed. Although it frustrated her that her sister seemed determined to carry her self-proclaimed wisdom and authority through until death, there was little to be done about it now. For too long she had been allowed to become set in her ways. Instead Judy bore the lecture with the usual mask of dutiful attention, knowing that an issue of much more significance was up her sleeve.

'Still such a lot to learn,' Maggie said, sniffing the cork of the bottle which had turned a dubious black but was not an entirely unpleasant odour. She dabbed the dark mould with her tongue and considered it. 'Rather like a strong cheese,' she mumbled. 'Well? Let me hear it.'

'Well,' her sister enthused, barely able to hide her excitement at what she had brought to the meeting. 'I am confident that I have the solution . . .'

Maggie choked, steeling herself against the sourness of the wine that still filled her mouth and numbed her tongue. She swallowed with watery eyes. 'Well obviously we cannot continue selling sweets that nobody wants to buy. We can't go on starving.'

That morning in the cold dark, Maggie had found herself, as usual, hurling her bodyweight against the swollen wooden door of their village shop. Her mother, grandmother and countless generations of Cloak women before them had done the same each winter and the same women, come spring, cursed themselves for not remembering that the summer shrinkage which made the door unpredictably light was yet again the cause of the broken glass pane that had smashed against the interior wall. It was said that if all else failed, a Cloak woman could move a stubborn cow and install windows.

In the darkness of the dreary old wood-panelled shop, she tottered for a moment in its bareness, then with determination opened the shutters, wiped down the counter and took the greaseproof parchments off the sugar mice, marzipan ladybirds, liquorice snails and white-chocolate owls. Finally she moved the *pièce de résistance*, a rather aggressive-looking, life-sized and lifelike black chocolate gorilla into the window.

Animal-shaped chocolate oddities, unconvincing antiques from foreign lands, herbal potions, dusty stuffed toys and, of course, a table where tea and cake was served, came together to create the uninspiring and rarely-ventured-into Cloak's Chocolates – the latest incarnation of the family business that had run for over a century.

During the summer, even with the influx of tourists visiting Greenwich Park and local families out for their walks, the shop made barely enough profit for them to survive the customerless winter. Past September, barely a soul set foot inside it from day to day. More often than not, Maggie considered it somewhere she could spend the day sheltering from the rain. She read, attempted knitting, talked with shopkeepers who popped in to complain about other shopkeepers, but mostly she worried about the unpaid bills and affording enough fuel and food to see herself and her sister through the winter.

Often Maggie imagined running away, starting anew in dusty exotic lands – Marrakech, Egypt, India – where she would dart down narrow passages, her face covered in silks, her little store thriving, her abrupt, aggressive lover demanding she give it up so her attention was used solely on him and she wanted to, because she loved him and he her, but no, the exotic life was not to be, her duty was here. Generations of Cloaks had passed the shop from one to another, first as a millinery, then one of London's finest dress shops and eventually as a magnificent shoe shop, each incarnation eclipsing the previous one's success and profit. But when the shoe shop passed from their grandmother to their mother and finally to Maggie and Judy, neither of whom had an aptitude for shoemaking, Maggie had her own ideas and Cloak's Chocolates was born. Steadily and stealthily it dove deeper into debt and disaster. The sisters both remembered uttering the phrase 'going from bad to worse' but that was a very long time ago.

Maggie tasted the potato wine again and grimaced, studying her sister's excited face and pulling her chair closer to the fire. 'Well,' she said, 'as the eldest I think it only fitting that I should tell you of my decision . . .'

'Decision, Maggie?'

Maggie's eyes widened. 'I didn't say decision, I said suggestion.'

'You said –'

'My suggestion is that we should abandon chocolates and open a curtain shop.'

Judy's face fell.

'Judy, there is not a single curtain shop in Blackheath. Blackheath needs a curtain shop!' She waited, pleased with her stroke of genius.

'You look as if you have made your mind up already,' Judy replied.

'No.' Maggie steadied herself; it was crucial at this stage that she was not being seen to be taking over –again, 'No, but that is the suggestion I put forward.'

Her sister nodded. 'It's not a bad idea, but I have a better one.'

So Maggie listened as her sister put forward her own master-plan, the horror on her face barely disguised despite the wine glass held purposefully in front of her lips. She had expected some ridiculous flight of fancy, an art gallery, perhaps, or a hat shop – but this! She swallowed, attempting a smile.

'You have been silent for some time,' Judy said.

'I don't think I fully understand your meaning, Judith.'

The use of her full name indicated quite the opposite but Judy's enthusiasm was unstoppable so she began again, but in a more temperate tone that her sister would find less alarming. She had barely spoken more than two sentences when Maggie began coughing and rose from her seat.

'This wine is . . . No, I shall open the burdock. Here, let me tip that away. It's gone off. The burdock is just ripe.'

Judy watched her and felt the subject close.

'Maggie? It is a very, very good idea.'

'It's different, I'll give you that, but if you walk from one end of Blackheath to the other during the early evening, you will notice just how desperate every house is for new curtains. I was only saying this morning to Henry Morton Stanley how nice his new house would be with a darker curtain. And he agreed with me. Apparently in his house in Africa they use a very light cotton. Now, I'm afraid there's not much to eat. Put another log on that fire, let's get some warmth in here.'

Judy sighed. 'Maggie!'

But her sister was busy washing a pot and did not respond.

Chapter 2

Judy dipped the quill in the inkwell and thought quickly. Time was not her own; soon the morning would pass and Maggie would be back and she would need to appear to have just returned from the task she had set her. She tried to remember the name she had invented in bed the previous evening, the one she had repeated over and over before sleep so she wouldn't forget. But as predicted, she no longer . . . no, she had it. She grinned; that was the one, it was perfect.

During the wars he had been at the forefront of medical science. Countless prisoners entered his buildings and left via the incinerator, in liquid form or in the stomach of one or more of the various wild dogs that were always encircling the mountain hideout.

Money was no object. He was recognised as a leader in his field. The hierarchy above him was often too intimidated or too excited by their association with him to refuse any request he made. All were happy to glow in his success and provide, in abundance: surgical equipment, blood, ice-rooms, animals, heat, prisoners, research students, staff, owls – he went through an extraordinary number of those. And while legitimate experiments with cures, serums and advanced skeletal repair yielded great success and acclaim with exciting frequency, his private experiments, shielded from the eyes of those around him, went unnoticed.

Klaus Van Dayne had a vision that he was determined to achieve. And at his death, by firing squad, he stood focussed solely on the fact that during his lifetime he had achieved it – the impossible. He had created something never before seen on the planet. He was a genius. No one could dispute that now. He was one of the most important men to have ever walked the earth, and these men standing before him, posturing nervously in the Siberian snow, shivering, stamping their feet to keep their toes intact while pointing their guns at him, they would be remembered as the men who made one of history's most idiotic mistakes.

There had been no court case, no explanation; justice had been swift. They had discovered all of the bodies, found the living still clinging to life, crazy and wild-eyed, like specimens in a strange zoo, capable only of being observed.

What had incensed them the most – the one thing they all lost their heads over – was the use of children. This confused him. He could not understand for the life of him why children were viewed so differently from the adults they would become, adults like the soldiers pointing their guns at him now, put to death en masse almost daily and without remorse. There were pond-sized graves all around the mountains and deep within the forests. Hundreds lay upon hundreds, baking and freezing under the ground as the weather dictated.

Why, he wondered, should two dozen children dying during experimentation be such an outrage? Perhaps, he thought, as he looked at the line of soldiers biding their time, rubbing their faces and hands against the freeze of the salty air, it was the simple need to draw a line, to define the unacceptable. To kill the mother and father and ignore that starving child crawling around their dead bodies in war was acceptable but to kill the child, that was barbaric.

And . . . he pondered patiently, unlike soldiers he was not killing mindlessly. He had not intended to kill at all, not one of them. Each death had been a disappointing blow and knocked back his research almost six months at a time. With each operation he prayed with all his heart for each life to bloom and he knew, through trial and error, that that success would come, and it had come, but not for twenty whole years. And not one had been some waif or stray plucked from the roadside with begging hands, they had been his own children, a part of himself. They had been selflessly bred for experimentation.

He watched the man in charge – young, in his twenties – assuming a hesitant control as he marched into the quarry in which Van Dayne stood, buffeted before them by the icy sea wind of the Chukchi that lay beyond the cliff edge. The young man had nothing to say. He was just making his presence felt. The soldiers blew on their hands and stamped, mumbling to each other. They wanted him dead, over with. Why was there this wait? It was winter. It was Siberia. They were freezing.

The front door swung open and Maggie, eager with enthusiasm, appeared a whole hour earlier than she had ever taken lunch before in her entire life. Judy looked up from the page, horrified at being caught and disappointed to be back in reality.

'What are you doing?' Maggie demanded.

'My novel.'

'You were supposed to be out assessing curtain shops, seeing how busy they are, getting prices, estimating profit, not scribbling out some silly little romance.'

'It's not a romance!' Judy replied irritably. She wanted her sister to leave so she could return to Klaus Van Dayne and the firing squad but Maggie would have none of it, so she pulled on her coat and they hurried across the heath towards the gates of Greenwich Park.

'You do realise, as you waste time with your new hobby that we have no money?' Maggie scolded her. 'Soon we will be out of everything, including firewood.'

'Firewood can be collected.'

'And food? Can that be collected too? Oh, this cold weather. Why can't it be summer? I am not ready for winter, Judy, not this year. I cannot afford it.'

They stopped for tea, as was customary, and for gossip, at the Blackheath Tea Hut on Shooter's Hill Road.

The proprietress leaned through the hatch and with an excited confidence whispered, 'They found a body!'

'Who?' Maggie asked peering into the dark tiny space.

'This morning. The rain flooded the pond outside the Hare and Billet and dislodged it, rope around the middle but up it floated.'

'No!' Judy said horrified, blowing the steam from her teacup.

Maggie felt herself shudder and looked to see if the women had noticed. She swallowed and felt herself swoon a little but her fingers squeezed the counter hard and she ordered herself to snap out of it.

'Young woman, they said.' The proprietress looked around and lowered her voice in confidence. 'She'd been murdered – strangled or something. Something about the neck.'

Maggie was pale. Judy watched her with concern and made their excuses, ushering her away on the pretext of an appointment.

'A murder!' she said at once when they reached the seclusion of the park.

Maggie nodded, opening the gate to the rose garden, which lay empty. 'It could have been an accident,'

'It doesn't sound like one! Oh Maggie, you walked past the pond last night, did you notice anything?'

Maggie shook her head. Admitting to it would bring all sorts of complications. Her ordeal would be gossiped about in the tea rooms, and the new policemen, whom she was still growing accustomed to and didn't wholly trust, would visit her, and in turn the murderer would know who it was that had revealed him.

'It was dark and the storm had begun. Besides, you know my rule about the heath after dark.'

'Head down, keep walking, stop for nothing, talk to no one.'

'And under the circumstances I think you can see that it works. If that poor girl had only done the same, perhaps . . .'

They stopped for a moment to inspect the last of the roses, not yet ready to bid summer goodbye. They nodded like bright sparks of light amongst the grey skeletons of their peers already beheaded and cut back to sit out the dark months.

'I always think it's such a sad sight in winter. It reminds me of the seaside towns when they're out of season and everything is closed.'

'I rather like it,' Maggie countered. 'It reminds me that the park belongs to us and not to the tourists.' She paused, wrestling uncomfortably with her thoughts then reached for her sister's hand, watching her startled surprise. 'I have something to tell you.'

Judy was alarmed.

'Last night, as I came across the heath in the storm, there was something, someone. He was hiding at the pond and I went to see what the noise was and he saw me. Later, as I approached the house, he was there, on the heath, seeking me.' She closed her eyes and put her trembling hand to her lips, 'And now it turns out he is a murderer!'

'Maggie!' Judy gasped. 'Why did you not tell me?'

'I didn't want you to be afraid, but now it seems great precautions must be taken. You must not walk alone until he is captured.'

'You must tell a policeman.'

'*No!*' she replied defiantly, 'I do not like them, I do not trust them. And you must tell no one. Promise me.'

Judy nodded.

'Did you recognise him?'

She shook her head. 'His face was painted, like a doll.'

'Like a doll?'

'Like the devil.'

'The devil!'

'And that is another reason why your idea is doomed.'

Judy sighed.

'No, I am convinced of it, Judy. It is a sign.'

'You do not believe in signs.'

'That is because until last night I had never received one.'

'I fail to see the connection.'

'My poor dear Judy, thank goodness I am here to save you.'

They took the steep path down into Greenwich where they spent the remainder of the afternoon covertly watching the every move of the town's leading curtain shop from the comparative luxury of the public house opposite. Here they deduced that the shop's takings amounted to approximately the same as the dozen ports they had consumed while observing. They were further put off by the revelation that skill in sewing and altering would be necessary.

Swaying back up to Blackheath via the Great Observatory, fired up by the port and ready for the evening's rum and conversation, they noticed, across the heath, police activity around the pond at the Hare and Billet. A considerable crowd had gathered to which they added themselves. As well as the murdered girl, it now appeared that a second victim had come up for air.

'Prostitutes,' Maggie whispered.

'Why prostitutes?'

'It's always is.' She turned to the others. 'Prostitutes.'

Some of the women shook their heads.

A policeman turned to face the crowd. 'Spread word. Warn others. Women should not venture outdoors unaccompanied.'

'Ridiculous!' Maggie grumbled.

'Perhaps, madam, you think these two girls aren't enough of a warning. Perhaps you would like to be his third victim.'

'Or perhaps, as it's a man doing the murders, men should be kept indoors.'

The policeman eyed her irritably and turned to the others. 'If you value your lives you will stay away from the heath.'

Maggie took her sister's arm and walked defiantly out towards the centre of the vast, empty expanse under his stare.

'And that is why I do not trust these new policemen. It is just more men who think they are right. London is already full of them. No, if they are to do something about it then let them realise that women will not be staying indoors while they idle away their hours talking nonsense.'

In the kitchen as Maggie took the blunt knife to the doorstep to sharpen it, Judy slipped a fresh sheet of paper from a drawer and set up her ink. It would be some time before her sister noticed she was otherwise engaged. The sharpening of one knife, inevitably led to the sharpening of others, followed by the cleaning of the step and a walk around the garden to see what could be unearthed to be eaten. She pressed the oily nib against the paper and began.

A short distance away in the large house in the centre of the heath, the count was awake. He had slept for over twenty hours. His sister, still exhausted from their long journey, slept on still.

The sound of his movements had alarmed the young housemaid, Anna, who rushed off to warn the kitchen and set dinner in motion. On her return she found the count's door open and the room empty. She slipped inside to make the bed and air the room, then, hearing a noise, turned to see, inside the small adjoining room, a mirror in which the count, shirtless, pulled down over his head a large black sack with belt buckles on it. Her eyes moved down the man's broad, dark muscular chest to a tight sinuous stomach, as he stretched up into the garment that fell down around him. Anna shrunk back, watching him struggle to find the arm and neck holes. It was almost comical. Then her eyes fell to his powerful, muscular legs and broad, masculine feet and she took an involuntary deep breath. The man froze, hearing her creep out of the room as he stepped back out of view.

For the rest of the day Anna felt something new was waking inside her, something overwhelming that she could not and would not even try to control. She felt excitable and light. A nervous tickle in her belly swept her through her morning chores with a cheerfulness that the other members of the household had not witnessed in her before.

'Are you still writing that bloody book?'

'You *have* to read it now!' Judy insisted, offering up the still damp sheets.

'Did you not hear me talking to Piggot the grocer? There's a problem.'

In the sweetshop the two women, armed with oil lamps, prepared themselves for the worst. Heaving open the heavy trapdoor that led down to the cellar, they set foot on the steps. Other shops were reporting water ingress, flooding even. On the third step down they encountered the first inch. The cellar and their supplies now lay under almost seven feet of water. They closed the trapdoor.

In the Hare and Billet they forewent their customary early evening port and moved directly to the whiskies, first the blended then the Irish variety, before arriving at the single malt to which they remained loyal until ten o'clock. It was impossible to take the correct course of action while in shock, they agreed. The matter needed consideration, distance, a period of calm.

'Perhaps now you have had time to consider my suggestion we can . . .'

Maggie's sighs began immediately.

'I will be heard, Maggie.'

'You have been heard and I have said no. We just have to find the right idea. Perhaps a pet shop.'

Judy sighed.

'Then if all else fails at least we will have something to eat.'

Because of the murders, the publican, keen to maintain custom, was offering oil lamps to those venturing onto the heath. 'Lanterns to help warn off attackers, ladies?' he called.

'All lamps will do is illuminate the next victims for him!' Maggie confided to her sister as they queued and took one each. They stepped out into the cold and extinguished them immediately. The oil would come in handy, that was for sure. They set off.

At the best of times the heath could play games with your mind. It had, after all, been the haunt of Dick Turpin and Thomas Rowden who terrorised the Bleak Heath in their grandparents' time. Pitch-black and vast, it was best, when frightened, to maintain one speed, not to allow imagination or fanciful thought and never, ever begin a run unless you could maintain it all the way to the front door. Once you began running, and the heart and adrenaline began to pump, there would be no controlling the emotion or imagination, the demons would already be in your head, and even with palpitations of the heart and exhausted lungs it was unwise to stop. To stop meant listening, looking behind you, staring into the darkness all around you, suspecting that the predator that hunted you could be within arm's reach and your outstretched fingers might press against its face, or touch the back of its head, causing it to turn and make short work of you. Or it could be some distance away, wild eyed and listening, waiting up ahead, or maybe catching up, creeping silently, or maybe it had caught your scent and was galloping through the dark, howling and salivating, or perhaps there were many of them, encircling, watching your frightened face, waiting for those ten more steps before you put yourself at their mercy.

The sisters moved quickly, heads down, silent, each wondering who had put the two girls in their watery graves but not daring to consider possible answers. When they reached the house, Maggie paused before putting the key in her lock. Why was it, she wondered, that for the past two nights, her sister had not returned to her own home? And, more alarmingly, when inside, Maggie began to notice that a lot of Judy's possessions were accumulating around her

When she returned to the kitchen to ask, Judy was asleep in front of the fire, so Maggie poured herself some hot tea and made her way back upstairs to her room, where she sat waiting for the bed to stop being quite so cold beneath the many sheets and patchwork blankets and slowly came to terms with the fact that a curtain shop was not the answer, that the cellar was flooded, that they were broke, and life, already unaffordable, was about to become a lot harder.

The sweetshop could not continue, they could not sew or chop meats or grow vegetables or bake cakes or design gowns. They had no skills or bankable qualities that the men and women or children of Blackheath wanted to purchase. But they did have one thing with which to make a living – that confounded shop with its cellar full of water and its bloated front door and its giant black chocolate gorilla.

Staring at the candle on the dresser, she let her mind wander to Judy's ramblings at the pub, where, full of excitement and enthusiasm, she had suggested again that they open . . . She couldn't bear to think about it and shook the thoughts from her mind, worried that the mere idea of it might fill her mind with nightmares that would keep her awake, too frightened to move and too poor to afford the comfort of unnecessary candlelight. But the more she tried to push it aside, the more forcefully her sister's argument rose again.

'We must open the Blackheath Séance Parlour.'

Chapter 3

'This séance parlour idea,' Maggie said at breakfast, picking stray tea leaves from her lips and wiping them on the chipped edge of her saucer while Judy wrestled a steaming loaf from the oven and slammed it noisily on the table before her. 'Tell me more about it.'

Judy's eyebrows rose. 'Get up. Up! Get your coat.'

'What?'

Judy was looking at the clock, already pushing her arms into her own coat.

'If we hurry we can just catch them.'

Bleary eyed, Maggie followed her sister across the top of the heath and down into Hyde Vale towards Greenwich. She had agreed to nothing, she reminded herself, lifting her skirts as she navigated the pavement. Her sister had stopped some distance ahead and was calling her urgently, undoubtedly taking advantage of her delicate early morning state.

'Maggie. walk quicker. Please! If I don't see them today it will not be until next Sunday.'

'See who? Where are we going?'

'To church.'

Maggie stopped. 'Oh no. No, no, no. I'm not going to any church.'

Judy turned angrily. 'Maggie, we are late! I need you there for moral support.'

Convincing her sister that they need not actually step inside, she watched Maggie take reluctant steps forward, worried that at any given moment she would stop, refuse to go any further and change direction, as was her habit. Maggie was a firm believer in the word no. It was, Judy suspected, by far her favourite word of all.

Reluctantly, however, Maggie followed and they turned out onto Greenwich High Road. St Alfege's, bold and baroque, stood like a battleship towering above everything else around it. Its church bells made Maggie even angrier.

'Such an ugly building.'

'Isn't it?'

They bustled through the crowd at the gate, smiling and nodding with exaggeration, which they took to be customary, although no one else did it, Maggie noted, and slid past the raised eyebrows of the vicar who was surprised to the point of alarm at their presence. Not since they were girls, with the exception of their mother's funeral, had they been back inside the church. And they had been such devout children, too. His smile was greeted with quickly distracted eyes, Judy craning her neck to hunt out the group of ladies that could change everything, while Maggie ignored him.

The vicar hurried everyone inside, and with both sisters caught up in the crowd and unable to fight their way free, closed the doors and walked to the pulpit with an air of satisfaction and triumph. His two most lost sheep had found their way back into the fold and his sermon was full of it. Phrases like the open arms of the Lord, the prodigal son returns, finding strength in admitting you were wrong and coming full circle were thrust so often in their direction that many of the congregation began to turn to see who he was addressing.

Maggie glared down at her feet, wringing her gloves in her hand.

'What,' she hissed, 'are we doing here?'

'We have to see Gloria. I don't know where else to find her.'

'We could have waited outside!'

'It won't take long.'

'It's already taken too long.'

'Hymn number 123. "Here I am, Lord".'

'Oh for God's sake!'

The women stood, and Judy, catching Gloria's eye, motioned that she wanted to talk. Gloria, ever aware of the vicar's watchful eye, gave her a nod then threw back her head to make her high-pitched contribution.

At communion, the vicar awaited the cherry on top of the pudding.

'I will not go!' Maggie warned.

'People will think it odd!'

'I think they are odd for doing it in the first place. Besides, it's not like I'm ever coming here again.'

'Get up, Maggie!'

'No, I shall not.'

Judy pushed past her in a huff. 'You're like a child, you really are!'

'And you are too easily led, my girl.'

Maggie's abstinence was noticed. Not so subtle over the shoulder looks caught her eye but she greeted them defiantly and watched her sister submit to the priest who put bread in her mouth and the chalice to her lips relishing the moment that told onlookers that he, Father Henry Legge was right, yet again.

Before the service ended, he had made a dash for the door while the organist strung out some dismal arrangement of long, depressing notes to keep everyone seated. And finally everyone was standing, gossiping, pushing their way out of the building to hurry off or to crowd around the vicar, basking in his small-town celebrity.

'Margaret!' he called as she stole her moment, pushed out into the street and hurried in the direction of the river. She ignored him, pretending not to hear.

'Margaret!'

It was too loud, she could not pretend; people ahead of her were turning to look. She closed her eyes and turned.

'Oh hello there,' she said, omitting the need that everyone else had to put the word 'Father' in whenever possible.

'How wonderful to have you back. But I notice you did not take communion. Is there a reason?'

There was so much she wanted to say but she took a breath and kept it inside, watching her sister and Gloria talk excitedly inside the doorway until she remembered she was expected to answer. She decided not to give him the pleasure and changed the subject.

'Will the funerals for the murdered girls take place in this church?'

He shook his head. 'A terrible affair. There were plans to hold them here, but I think it is more suitable to hold them at my church in Lee.'

'Your church?'

'St Margaret's.'

'What does one have to do to be handed your very own church?'

He smiled. 'St Margaret's is bigger, and the new priest arriving here at Greenwich will be perhaps a little . . . fresh, for such a significant event. And your shop, how are things there? I noticed it has been closed a lot lately.'

'It's closed down. We are changing direction.'

'Oh? And what direction would that be?'

'A different one.'

Judy, noticing Maggie and the vicar in conversation, rushed to them in a state of panic, pulling her sister quickly away and excusing themselves by mentioning that they were late for an appointment.

'I look forward to seeing you next Sunday,' the vicar called after them.

Maggie turned to reply but Judy's '*Don't!*' whisked her away.

They hurried to the river, Maggie seething, Judy barely able to contain her excitement.

'We're in!' she blurted.

'In what?'

'We have a place at the séance. We're on the list. It's tonight.'

'Tonight! Judy, I need to think this through. I have not agreed to anything.'

They turned onto the path leading down along the Thames and battled against the blustering wind until they reached the Trafalgar Tavern, where they took a window table and ordered German sausage and ale.

'There is no fixed place, so they take it in turns. One week at Gloria's, the next at someone else's, and that's not all.'

They froze as two ales were put before them.

'There are guests, travelling guests, from all over the country and sometimes from around the world. There is a circuit you see, a network, word of mouth that links together spiritualists from as far away as Cardiff and Edinburgh. In June they had a gentleman medium from India who could draw the faces of the dead.'

'Oh good lord!'

'That's nothing! There are others who –'

'We're making a big mistake. I'm not a religious person, Judy, but even I can see that this is tampering with the supernatural. It's wrong. It will bring us harm.'

'You are getting hysterical. If the dead exist and we can communicate with them, it is natural. It was meant to be.'

Maggie listened. 'Where is the meeting this evening?'

'It's at ours.'

'Ours?'

'Your house.'

'Judy, no.'

'They arrive at seven.'

❧❧❧❧❧❧❧❧❧

While Maggie dusted and swept, Judy placed the candles around the room as instructed; while Maggie scrubbed the stone floors, Judy arranged the table and chairs; and while Maggie cleaned the kitchen, Judy put out the best crockery and glasses and opened some port. At six-thirty, they were ready and nervous, fully aware that although the house had once been expensively furnished and well decorated, it was now something of an embarrassment.

'I want to watch. I do not want to be included,' Maggie warned.

'That's not how it works, Maggie. If the spirit knows you it will contact you.'

'I don't like it! Perhaps that was just a very overpriced curtain shop. Perhaps ours will be different.'

'We're not opening a curtain shop. We need to earn money. Lots of it. Maggie, please, let me have a try before you refuse it.'

A knock at the door drained the colour from Maggie's face. Her immediate instinct was to head for the stairs but the idea of being alone worried her equally. She tottered in the middle of the room, moving from foot to foot, contemplating running, staying or perhaps letting out a scream. Then the door was opened and the women were bustling into her house, and before she'd made up her mind she was seated at a table with the other women in semi-darkness.

With tilted heads, the women, like big old swaying birds, listened to the sounds of the house and waited for the spirits to draw near. Maggie's heart was racing, her expression was frozen, her eyes scanning the room nervously. Judy squeezed her hand in an attempt to reassure her but even she could not control her own breathing or take her eyes from the medium, a stern, blubbery woman with a frilly collar and a lolling head who groaned and moaned while the others nodded in appreciation with their eyes closed.

Maggie's kitchen looked eerily unfamiliar in the rapid flickering of the candles. The milliseconds of darkness divided by the sharp glare made movements seem disjointed and sudden. Nasty shadows appeared here and there – a head in the doorway, something lurking in the corner, a shadow reaching out from behind the armchair at the far end of the room.

The medium was swaying dramatically, first right and then so far left that for a moment both of the sisters expected the chair to fall over. Maggie looked in alarm to the other women but they were so enthralled by it all that for a moment the devil in her wanted to let out a deafening scream to amuse herself. Now the woman was rocking backward and forward, her head nearly touching the table, the back of the chair creaking loudly as she pressed against it. Maggie leaned irritably to the right, peering at it, hoping it was not one of her best chairs. It was. She wrung her hands in annoyance and mumbled under her breath.

Judy's reproachful glare snapped her back into focus immediately and she adopted a look she thought suited to deep and fervent prayer. She held this look for several seconds then gauged its success with a quick glance at Judy, who gave her a nod.

'Is there anybody there? Is there a spirit amongst us?' the woman called, rather too theatrically for Maggie's taste, but she suffered the performance with a roll of the eyes.

'Yes! It is coming through, the spirit is coming through!' the woman boomed, rising from her seat and waving her arms theatrically over the table. Maggie sighed irritably and leaned back again to assess the damage to her chair as the woman withdrew back into it, her eyes wide with excitement.

'Who is there?' she demanded. 'Who ventures into this house? Tell us who you are.'

There was a long silence, during which Maggie became increasingly impatient and suspected that the woman had failed as an actress but could not be silenced.

'I have Reginald here!' she announced.

'My husband!' cooed the woman to her right, dressed in a fancy purple hat.

'He sends you his love, my dear. He is a lovely man. He says he is happy and he . . . he is holding something red. Are there roses in your garden?'

'Yes.'

'He's pointing to them and he says whenever you smell the roses he will be there with you. Can you accept that dear? Can you take that from me? How lovely. Isn't that lovely?'

Judy turned quickly to check Maggie's expression.

'Oh, there is another spirit coming through – it's a lady. She's ever so small, white hair, her name begins with an M.'

The room remained silent as she peered around at them. She closed her eyes, 'Sorry, not an M, she was just making a sound to tell us how happy she is. Her name begins with a B or a D.'

Three women raised their hands.

Maggie stretched her legs under the table and blew air into her mouth so her cheeks swelled up. A nudge from Judy made her jump.

'She is a lovely woman. And she is happy. And she wants you to be happy too. She is pointing to your scarf. Was it her scarf, dear?'

'No.' the eldest of the women replied.

'Well she wants you to know that she likes it; that, or you have a serious throat problem coming.'

Maggie had lost interest. Down at the far end of the skirting board she noticed a hole. That mouse was back. Though what it was hoping for in her house she couldn't fathom; there was barely any food for herself, let alone for anyone else. Maggie felt her stomach rumble.

Her attention was drawn back to the medium, rocking about in her chair – on purpose, Maggie suspected. For a moment, as she moaned and waved her arms about, something passed the door that led to the bedrooms caught her eye. She stared at it. There it was again – a man's shadow moving, sneaking past and then back again. Alarmed, she leaned forward, but her movement sent a candle into a flicker and she realised that there was no man at all, it was just the shadow of a pot illuminated by a candle. Suddenly she thought she saw darts of light, though they were probably just her eyes adjusting . . . She looked at the medium. The woman was wide eyed, staring right at her.

'You!' she accused loudly.

Maggie stared in horror as the woman rose, confronting her, her face angry, her voice slowing down from that of a bad unemployed actress to the deep and deafening tones of a man. Maggie jumped and stood, ready to run as her chair fell backwards with deafening thud.

'Where do you think you're going? SIT DOWN!' she boomed.

'I don't like it. Stop!' Maggie mumbled, her voice filled with childlike fear.

'I don't like it!' the voice mimicked. 'I've been watching you, sitting in your room in bed at night, wondering what went wrong, wondering

31

when the man of your dreams will take you away.'

The medium turned her head to the others. 'She writes it all down in a journal. Keeps it on top of her wardrobe.' Her face turned back to Maggie, who was so white and frightened she looked close to tears. She turned to her sister, feeling so intoxicated and hot she thought she might scream.

'You don't recognise me, do you, Margaret?' the medium boomed.

Judy, too, felt herself swooning. She repositioned her sister's seat and lowered her gently into it.

'We could have married. We should have. We would have had two children if we had wed but you put paid to that with your excuses.'

'William?' Maggie was swaying, hot and nauseous.

'Then I went away and became ill. And you grew old never knowing intimacy with a man.'

Maggie swooned, tried to speak but fainted, falling back in her chair.

The medium grunted, called out and suddenly regained consciousness, and at once the room was back to normal.

'This house is filled with too many spirits,' she said uncomfortably. 'There are dozens of them, all fighting to talk at once. I'm afraid I must take my leave.' She stood, helped into her coat by her tall, gaunt husband, who had sat against the wall throughout. He bowed to them solemnly like an undertaker or bearer of tragic news and, taking payment from Gloria, he walked his wife out of the house on the heath.

❧❧❧❧❧❧❧

'I will have no part of this!' Maggie said firmly. The others had gone, and now, with the table cleared away and more candles and lamps lit than they'd ever lit before, Maggie struggled to open a heavy green bottle of brandy. 'No part of it.'

Judy remained silent.

'It is wrong. It's against nature and it is frightening. The human body and mind cannot take that kind of madness.' She poured herself a large glass and sat. 'I shan't sleep tonight. I doubt I shall sleep again. We will have to leave here. We can't go on with them watching us, reading our private thoughts. No, we shall reopen the chocolate shop and we will return to church and beg for forgiveness. The vicar was right, we all do need religious discipline – and protection! We need protection! I just hope, Judy, that we can firmly close this . . . unnatural door we have opened or we shall be cursed for the rest of our lives.'

Perhaps, Judy thought, her sister should not be a part of it. Perhaps Maggie could simply welcome the guests at the door, take their money and leave before the evening began. What Judy had witnessed, as disturbing and frightening and intoxicating as it was, was by far the most incredible experience she could have hoped for – one that she knew would turn London upside down and make this incarnation of the shop its most successful by far.

Of all the exotic travelling fairs that visited Blackheath, one particular little carriage that offered this phenomenon drew vast queues and created excitement like nothing else. She had, along with other visitors, actively sought out the little carriage that provided contact with the dead and had groaned with disappointment when the gypsy had failed to return. The Russian circuses brought wild and dangerous animals, the French tents brought dance and spectacle, but it was the Spanish fair which brought the little carriage that those in the know awaited eagerly. If she and her sister could harness this power, it would draw the whole of London to their door and they would at last become not only financially secure but perhaps, finally, able to be a little extravagant, perhaps even be able to afford some new outfits and, she dared to hope, finally be eligible for an invitation to the annual Blackheath Ball.

۵۵۵۵۵۵۵۵۵

Later, in bed, Maggie waited for her body heat to warm the sheets as she let the day sink in. The horrors that she been a party to would keep her wide awake all night, so she had brought up an extra candle. She rubbed her feet together, willing them to shake off the chill. Outside the storm was pulling at the trees and windows. A breeze raced across the pillows and her face. Yet another day had passed and she had not filled the gap between the frames with cloth.

Her mind turned uncomfortably to the vicar winning his battle against her, chipping away at her strong will, satisfied that, like it or not, as he had told her on many occasions while prowling around the village or turning up at the shop under the pretext of fancying something sweet, he would see her back in his congregation. She could hardly believe she had stepped so easily inside a church after all these years. Her mind raced back to the horror stories the women at the séance had relished telling them, each worse and more disturbing than the other. Tales of a long-dead aunt who knocked sharply at the bedroom door whenever anything untoward occurred, of the ghost in an attic who mumbled and cried on the anniversary of his death and left a puddle in the centre of the room, the story of the spirit who appeared only to women while in a state of undress whose eyes he made visible on purpose. Though she suspected this particular story to be wishful thinking on behalf of the purple-hatted lady who displayed far too much bust than was decent and had yet to secure a husband. 'His eyes devour me!' she had said, 'His groans of delight when I reveal my body piece by piece to him terrify me.' Oh there would be no sleep tonight.

Her eyes wandered nervously to the wardrobe, on top of which she did indeed keep the journal that had been discussed so freely in front of her peers. She looked around her, wondering if they were watching now, waiting for her to sleep so they could check for new entries. She winced as she considered the secret the medium had revealed about her. And then there was William, whom she should have married and the two children that she could have had, now gone forever. William had been the only man she had found herself able to tolerate as a younger woman. He had been as forthright and clear in his thinking as herself, with little time for social obligations and a firm ruling about the starching of shirts and the benefits of brisk walking. Her mother had often joked that their strolls around Greenwich Park, unlike those of Judy and her new husband George, were of so little pleasure to them and so akin to a race that perhaps they should both just close their eyes for a moment and imagine them instead. Their one shared pleasure was the taking of afternoon tea, which they did with the meticulous enthusiasm of fine young actors: he the haughty general with little time for women and a fondness of calling her derogatory names which made her laugh, she his strict but exhausted wife of noble stock and a fondness for inane gossip for which he ridiculed her. Ironically it was to be this pleasure that was at the root of her refusal of marriage when she discovered that while, for her, it was an act, for him it was not.

And although several weeks of arguments followed during which he offered to mend his ways, Maggie, as usual had pulled away, frightened of commitment, wanting her life to return to normal where decisions and effort were not expected of her. She defended this right, and to this day had convinced herself that life had been hard enough, so her remaining years should be peaceful. And now, after all this time he had returned to pester her, as a ghost! No, she would not change the shop. She would not be surrounded by these morbid people who were obsessed with spirits and death. She would not. They would reorder the chocolates and sweets, they would do it differently this time, with a new window display, perhaps, or by introducing exciting variety. She went to her dresser, poured herself a healthy glass of whisky and ginger ale and got back into bed, shivering at the breeze from the gap in the window that raced across her shoulders as she kept vigil until first light.

Chapter 4

An evening was being prepared in the dining room in the large house at the centre of the heath. With the table complete, and the meals ready, the governess, Mrs Crag, with her carefully cultivated English accent, ushered Anna out and closed the doors before sending the soft reverberations of the copper gong through the house. Dinner was never interrupted. While the count and countess ate, the staff retired to the lower floor, only venturing upstairs when the sound of the gong indicated that the room had been vacated.

During this period of safety, Anna stole silently to the upper floors, opening the doors into the countess's private apartment. She had brought with her great wardrobes of exotic gowns and garments; shimmering diamond encrusted dresses, furs and silks with delicate stitching and jewellery of such opulence that Anna could not bring herself to touch them for fear of spoiling them. She stared now at a large emerald and at the myriad of green tones within it and lit the dressing table so it dazzled beneath candlelight. She leaned in, her nose almost touching it, so captivating were the rolling lights within.

A voice from the doorway made her jump.

'You like the green one?' The accent was deep, Russian and confident.

Anna stood to attention, lowering her head, ashamed at being caught.

'It is all right, child.' The tall, elegant figure swept into the room, a black silk dress swirling around her as if it were under water.

Anna dared to look up from the woman's exquisite shoes to the long, long legs and the swirl of silk that tightened around her hips and nipped in at the waist, opening again at the cleavage, showing large, dark, barely concealed breasts. Glossy black hair tumbled down over her shoulders and thick inviting lips curled into a smile, making her dark, almost black eyes sparkle with warmth. She was beautiful. She was more beautiful than Anna had imagined possible and now, although she wanted to and should, she could not avert her eyes, making the countess blush. The woman pointed to the stone, almost too embarrassed to be looked at any longer, and lifted it from its stand. Light fell from it like a lamp as it spun on its delicate gold chain.

'Let me try it on you, just this once.'

Anna stood, swaying a little as long fingers swept up her thick mousy hair and fastened the chain, allowing the green stone to slide under her blouse and down between her small young breasts. The coolness made her shiver.

'You have goose pimples,' the countess laughed, and lifted the stone and chain a little higher.

'It is a shame,' she said unbuttoning the girl's blouse, 'that we cannot see it properly with the clothes in the way, 'Take off your blouse.'

'Pardon, madam?'

'Take it off,' she waved.

Nervously, the girl unbuttoned the faded grey work shirt, watching the countess close and lock the apartment door. She turned away, putting it down on a chair and covered her bare chest with her arms.

'That is better.'

The countess stood behind her, held her shoulders and turned her to face the mirror, watching the girl open her eyes and look away out of embarrassment, then running her hands down the girl's arms, she pulled her hands downwards away from her chest.

'Don't be frightened,' she smiled. 'We are both women.'

The girl allowed herself to look up, to see herself, pale and small and naked in front of such a beautiful, elegant and powerful woman. Her fingers wandered with nervous distraction to the glowing green stone that lay between her unimpressive milk-white breasts with their startling pink nipples stiffened and long. She looked nervously up at the woman whose beauty made her feel awe-struck and vulnerable and confused and saw her turn, saw her from the side, saw her back, and Anna's hands lifted to her lips in shock. Protruding from the woman's back was a large shape, almost pillow-like, stretching from the middle of her shoulders down to her bottom. It was not a smooth shape, but lumpy and ugly. It made no sense.

The countess turned, having allowed the girl some moments to take it in, and approached her. Anna swooned a little, frightened and confused, afraid of getting above her station, past what was courteous, Her gaze was drawn back to the countess's mesmerising dark eyes, her heart and pulse quickening, her breathing so accelerated that her lips parted and she fought for air.

'Sit,' the countess told her, and sat herself awkwardly next to her. She took her small cold fingers into her large warm hands. 'My brother and I have a sad secret, a very big secret that you must help us protect.'

In the candlelight, Judy sat at the shop counter writing furiously on her few remaining sheets of paper. She looked around, ate the last marzipan ladybird and considered the violent deranged face of the enormous chocolate gorilla that had probably scared more children away than it had enticed in to buy sweets. Putting her writing to one side, she returned to her duties, transforming the shop with black paint. With Maggie refusing to move from her bed, claiming that several days of rest were in order for a full recovery from the séance ordeal, there had presented itself the rare opportunity to move things forward before her sister could halt it . Through the entire evening and most of the night, Judy laboured with an enthusiasm she had never experienced before, blacking out the windows of the shop, darkening the walls to absorb light rather than reflect it, putting up shelves and digging little alcoves into the thick wall plaster to hold candles and lamps. It had been on Maggie's insistence that they had opened a sweetshop; now it was time to try something new, and she meant it to work. With every fibre of her being she wanted to be the owner of the Blackheath Séance Parlour.

🙠🙠🙠🙠🙠

Wednesday morning saw Maggie up early. Her mind was made up. She was determined to give the chocolate shop a whole new lease of life and hurried across the heath with a basket of cleaning utensils. She walked down the incline to the centre of the village, where, on the right, the chocolate . . . She stared, horrified. The windows were blackened, the pictures gone from them. She reached for her key, thrust it into the lock and hurled herself into the room, aghast at the sight that confronted her. Gone were the glass counters and mottled white walls, the sweets, the toys and the shelves. Instead she found herself in a dark, blackened room, with purple silks and gaudy crimson cushions on Judy's best armchairs. Thick, heavy curtains divided the room, beyond which was a large round table dressed with a dark tablecloth. There were lamps and candleholders and Judy's best sideboard on which sat a silver tray with glasses and sherry. Beyond that, the small kitchen, half filled with furniture and rubbish blocked her way.

'No!' she shouted. 'No! *No! No!*'

She walked around, aghast at the transformation, the paint still drying around her. All this had taken place against her will, despite her clearly stating that she would have nothing to do with it. She was furious that she, the older and therefore more authoritative sister had been so completely ignored.

She found Judy asleep on the floor in the empty attic and woke her with an angry slam of the door.

Judy jolted awake and was not even allowed a moment to scramble to her feet before Maggie launched into her tirade.

'How dare you come into this shop and make decisions without me? How dare you take it upon yourself to interfere?'

Judy wiped the sleep from her eyes and followed her sister down the stairs.

'This is a chocolate shop. We are going to paint the walls white again and return it to the way it was. The chocolate shop failed because we gave in. We allowed ourselves to get tired of it. We will start again, with new stock, cakes. We will get things back to normal. This,' Maggie said, waving her arms, 'is not staying.'

'Oh yes it is, Maggie,' Judy replied firmly, her mouth still dry from sleep. 'You had your shot and you demanded a sweetshop. You refused me my pie and eel shop outright, do you remember? And look how popular they turned out to be. No, you said, and you took complete control. For years we have struggled with your idea and now it's my turn.'

Maggie was stunned. She had never seen her sister so adamant and determined.

'You think the shop's failure was all my fault?'

'The shop failed, Maggie, because you would not let us change it. People got tired of everything we sold. They told us that over and over. But you refused everyone's advice. You put your foot down and latched on to your favourite word, tradition: tradition this, tradition that. Nothing changes with you. You just sit and wait with your head in the sand until it's too late. We could have been rich, we could be warm and well dressed and invited, like the other shopkeepers of Blackheath, to the ball at the Ranger's House, but no, we have to sit here not making any money because it's tradition. And here you are again, demanding that we reopen a chocolate shop when no one wants one. Well that time is gone, Maggie. I want this. You had your turn and now I want my turn. I am going to make it work. I am going to make this shop the talk of London.

We are going to be rich.'

Maggie was livid. 'I don't want it!' She threw down her basket and left the shop, slamming the door behind her.

But for once Judy did not hurry after her. She looked down at her hands and unfolded a piece of paper on which Gloria had scribbled down an address, and, turning in the opposite direction, she headed towards Lewisham.

❧❧❧❧❧❧❧❧❧

Netta Walters was, according to the ladies of the séance group, the most reliable medium in London, which was not difficult considering there were only three, and one had such a dreadful reputation for inaccuracy that she was forced to travel from suburb to suburb with her appalling reputation hot on her tail. Netta Walters was a different kettle of fish. Her séances were horribly real. She read the crystal ball and cards too. Unanimously the women had voted her the best on the circuit, despite her tendency to charge double, eat them out of house and home, and her dreadful tactlessness. Whenever asked to take into account the meagre resources of the group, she made herself perfectly clear. 'I do this for money; not for love, for money.'

Working her way along Lee High Road, Judy found the house and knocked. A few moments later, a small doddering woman inched her way to the door.

'Arthritis,' she explained, 'Come in, come in.'

She was in her late forties, much smaller than Judy, with sharp eyes and a quick voice. She edged her way across the front room with her back bent double, reaching out to a chair for support.

'I need your help,' Judy began.

'You want your fortune told? You pregnant?'

'No. I am here on business.'

'Oh,' Mrs Walters said, immediately becoming upright and flexible. 'Tea?'

'Your name was given to me by Gloria.'

'Oh yes.'

'Mrs Walters, my sister and I are about to open the Blackheath Séance Parlour.'

Mrs Walters stared, then laughed and clapped her hands.

'In Blackheath! They will hang you!'

'We are an old family there.'

'I see.'

'I would like a demonstration from you. And then I would like your help and perhaps a little pinch of deception to convince my sister that it's a good idea.'

'I see.'

𝄢𝄢𝄢𝄢𝄢

Maggie stormed furiously around her kitchen. She was not in the best of moods, and being hungry made matters worse. After her argument with Judy at the shop, a policeman – 'Who do they think they are!' she shouted, recalling the scene – had told her she was not allowed onto the heath unaccompanied and when she had told him to clear off, he had warned her that he was in authority. 'It's my bloody heath!' she shouted, opening a low cupboard yet again. Her fingers scraped around at the back, out of view, and she pulled out a rotten potato which burst in her hands and coated her fingers with stinking brown goo. She cursed again and wiped them on a rag that turned out to be her scarf, which prompted her to stand perfectly still, grit her teeth and shake her fists in a frustration bordering on hysteria. There was nothing to eat.

She threw herself down into an armchair and considered screaming.

Somehow, although both women were in financial ruin, Judy seemed to produce at the end of each day just enough food and money to see them into the night with port. She could not remember the last time that she herself had purchased anything other than alcohol. She stared at the fire, angry and starved, and was still there an hour later when her sister let herself in.

'Have you brought food?' she demanded.

Judy shook her head.

'There is nothing.'

'Maggie, we must talk.'

'If it's about your house of horrors, no.'

Judy sighed. 'Please, Maggie. I have done everything you ever wanted since we were girls, now I would like your support.'

Maggie fumed angrily. 'Judy, this frightens me.'

'Maggie,' she rested her hand on the woman's arm. 'The fear

that you felt is nothing compared to the fear we will put our customers through. You and I are going to be the most famous women in London.'

'And you think that terrifying people is good?'

'No one will forget it.'

She shook her head. 'You're right about that . . .'

'One year. If I can't make it a success in one year, you can do whatever you like with it. '

'No.' She stood, automatically moving to the empty cupboards. 'I don't want to be a part of this, Judy. It is wrong. It is unnatural. We do not know what we are bringing on ourselves or onto others. You saw what happened to me. I was ill for two days after it.'

'If we don't do this, Maggie, someone else will. And everyone will want to go. It will be a roaring success and the talk of London and we will still be here starving, staring at sweets that no one wants to buy, angry that the people who took our idea and made it a success are now eating roast beef, potatoes and ham, whatever they fancy. They will dine out and dress well and have carpets. If we don't do this, Maggie, we are fools.'

Maggie turned away stubbornly.

'I have an appointment tonight with a medium. Come with me and consider it. If you do I will buy you dinner, with the money from the sale of my armchair.'

'That's blackmail! I am starving.'

〰〰〰〰〰〰

With the courage of two stiff gins, Maggie followed her sister up the stone steps and, pretending that they had never met, Judy introduced herself to Netta. They moved past the living room to a small room made morbid with funeral décor.

'Now,' Mrs Walters said, waving them inside irritably, 'Sit down, sit down.'

Maggie moved apprehensively to a seat at the heavy dark table.

'I am sensing things about you. You are sisters. And . . . yes, it's coming clearer now.' She turned to Judy. 'You *are* a believer in the spirit world.' Crossing herself, she then turned to Maggie, her face souring. 'And you, God forgive your tarnished soul, are not ready to embrace it.'

'I just don't like it.' Maggie corrected.

'Well, I doubt the spirits are keen on you with an attitude like that, dear.' She extinguished the lamps, took a candle to a corner, throwing the room into semi-darkness, and plonked herself down unceremoniously at the table, snatching up both women's hands and giving them a squeeze before attempting a sad but understanding expression which both women misinterpreted as anger. They watched, confused.

'Now, ladies,' she said, breathing again, 'No talking and here we go!'

She let her body flop and her tongue hang out, made 'thhh' noises accompanied by a few grunts, opened one eye to see if they were watching, then jolted upright and, awake, looking accusingly at Judy.

'You have a big idea,' she said. 'The spirits are telling me that you are to be one of the most important women in London, but you,' she said to Maggie, 'you are the one they will all love. I see money. Wooo! Lots of money, and happiness too.' She shook herself awake. 'Well, this is very exciting, ladies. What is this big idea?'

Judy smiled at Maggie's impressed face.

Mrs Walters flopped back into her seat, her face grumpy and old and distracted, and lifted a finger, pointing at Maggie.

'Oh Christ! What now?'

'You, you useless piece of . . .'

Maggie stood angrily. 'I beg your pardon!'

'You heard! Sit down. Six generations, six generations!' Netta slammed her hand down on the table and stood. 'You sit there, squandering your heritage, year after year, waiting for change, never doing anything about it. Unpicking the past, our success, all our hard work down the drain. You've let that shop go to rack and ruin and you don't even care. Your great grandmother and I worked our fingers to the bone day in, day out and you just sit there, selling rubbish. Change your ways, my girl.'

She fell back into the seat exhausted, then pulled herself back up, changing her voice to a deep tone.

'I remember my little Maggie.'

'Daddy!'

Netta Walters opened an eye and shook her head. 'No, dear, it's a woman. Oh, she's gone.' She fell limp again and remained motionless.

Maggie stood.

'Could I use your . . .'

'Out the back,' Netta Walters replied without opening her eyes or lifting her head. When Maggie had gone she looked up at Judy.

'Something like that?'

Maggie was not gone long, and when she returned to the room enthusiastically, Mrs Walters had resumed her semi-coma.

'Mrs Walters,' she announced, 'we have a business proposition for you.'

Netta pulled herself together. 'Oh?'

Out in the street, Maggie turned to her sister and shook her head. 'Do you think I am stupid?'

'Thank you, Maggie.'

'Six months. If it doesn't work, we shall do something else.'

Her sister nodded.

'And I want wine with dinner.'

☙☙☙☙☙☙☙☙☙

Watching the two sisters wander away, Netta Walters moved away from the window and clapped her hands excitely. 'A proper income! After so many years!'

Although she did not often drink, she opened a sideboard in which her crystal balls and other paraphernalia were laid out like a shrine and reached to the back for a bottle. She poured herself a large brandy and put the glass down to clap excitedly once more.

Her gift had begun in the warm summer of her eighteenth year. Netta, then a young thing, betrothed to Norman Clegg, twenty-one, of Golders Green, had made the momentous decision to have her long hair, which she had grown without cutting or much interference since the age of five and was 'known for', cut – or at least reshaped. It was time for change – exciting, fashionable change. And with just weeks to her wedding, it was also time, she decided, to become a woman. She entered the salon with three words in her head: iconic, fashionable, different.

Two hours later, her eyes raw with tears, her face expressing utter shock, she made her way home with the tallest, tightest hairdo ever seen in London. It wobbled, swayed from side to side, but refused flatly to be anything other than bolt upright. Not a single inch of her hair had been cut. Once again, Netta became 'known for' her hair.

It was on this day that Norman began acting very strangely. He had assured her that it was not because of the colossal construction wobbling on top of her head, but she was convinced otherwise. Over the following week, he became ever more elusive, often going missing for entire evenings, and was seen in parts of London where he didn't usually venture. Netta was also aware that he suddenly seemed distant and distracted and when he told her that he loved her, it often sounded hollow. Netta became nervous and unable to wait any longer, she hurried to her great aunt Winnie's.

Aunt Winnie sat, turned down the lamp and unwrapped from its black cloth her crystal ball. She placed it in front of Netta and began the lesson. Netta stared into it.

'Do not blink, not once.'

Netta knew this; she had practiced for weeks in her room with candles, each night staring into the flame without blinking until her eyes watered. The exercise not only cleaned the tear ducts and strengthened every muscle of the eye but also, after much practice, allowed you to see things that the untrained eye could not.

At first all she saw in the ball was her reflection on the outer surface, her stupid tall hair wobbling like a tree trunk on top of her head. Then she turned her attention past it, to the inside of the ball. Her eyes focussed and blurred, focussed and blurred, then came the mists, grey and thin, denser and whiter, clearing and reappearing; then the stars, the variety you see if you stand up too quickly, some large and slow, some instant and bright and then, without warning, the images came: a girl, crying, pleading, in the dark, outdoors. She saw her run, turn, run again, listen, look around. Then there was a shock, a blow to the head, and Netta stared at her great aunt.

'I think I saw a murder!'

Netta's venture into the spirit world had begun.

That night, the nightmares begun: a girl, screaming, running, her heart thrashing beneath her ribs, the full intensity of fear on her face. She was being chased, caught, pulled, a hand clamped onto her face, forcing her to look away, stopping her from watching the punches come. Netta felt the stretch in the girl's neck, felt the shock of the first blow dislocate something – a bone, a muscle. The pain was searing. She felt his thumbs seek out her eyes, tried to pull away from the pressure that pushed them inward. She felt them strain, about to pop beneath his fingertips. She would be blind. If she survived this, she would be blind.

She screamed, summoning all her energy, all her womanly force, but his fist hammered into her face, stopping her, stunning her. A blow to her jaw loosened teeth. They slid over onto her tongue, clicking against each other, sliding in the metallic taste of blood.

She staggered forward, letting the blood and teeth fall from her lips, her feet trying to find safe footing, her hands reaching out, finding her attacker, holding on to him to balance herself.

'Stop! I love –'

He hit her again, slamming his knuckles into her nose, her eye, her forehead, the side of her head. She was falling, reeling, choking, her brain unable to make sense of it, her eyes blind, her nose blocked. She swallowed another gulp of blood.

'I'm sorry!' she cried, falling to the ground.

She lay there, her heart holding on, her survival left to fate, to chance intervention. He dug her grave and dragged her into it. Fifteen minutes later he was gone. She remained alive for another forty-five.

Netta woke, screaming, struggling for breath, fighting him off. Her parents, alarmed, burst into her room, her father ready to take on her attacker with the leg of a chair.

For the next three nights the same dream came at her with increasing intensity and she refused to sleep. Dark eyed and exhausted, she attended her wedding rehearsal with a cloudy mind, and when she leaned into Norman, who looked down at her and saw the adoration in her eyes, he could not resist, despite the presence of both families, to kiss her. At that moment her entire world surged into immediate chaos. The murdered girl would not leave her head, not for a moment.

In the constable's office she was forthright, demanding immediate attention. There was indeed a missing girl on the books, he admitted, and she did have dark hair and dark eyes and wore a light coat.

'I have had a psychic dream and I saw it in a crystal ball. I know that the girl was killed and I know how and I know where she is.'

She led the watchmen through Epping Forest, down along a stream, past some rocks to the girl's shallow grave, where the men unearthed her.

In court, the evidence against Netta was alarming. The deceased girl's family had pointed out Norman who, to everyone's surprise, was recognised not only by the murdered girl's parents but by her friends, relatives and even by her employer. He was forced to reveal the truth of his long-term affair with the deceased. His parents looked on in bewilderment. It was then announced that she had been expecting a child, to which he also nodded his head solemnly.

The judge pointed out that all the blows to the body had fallen precisely where Netta had told them and at the exact location she had led them.

'He didn't tell me about it,' she insisted. 'It was a psychic dream.'

'In summary,' the judge explained, 'when Miss Walters found out about her fiancé's secret love and that she was pregnant and that the cancellation of her own wedding to Norman would be necessary, it had driven her into a such an uncontrollably jealous rage that she had murdered both the woman and the child and blanked it from her mind, only to have it resurface in the form of delusional episodes of the brain.

Guilty. 'You will be taken from this place, and hanged from the neck until you are dead. Before that, you will suffer anguish; waiting, never knowing whether this will be the day that you will die. One morning, sometime in the next week, it will happen, but until it does you will live in fear.'

Netta didn't cry; she remembered how awful red eyes and a puffy face made her look with that hair.

Chapter 5

She had crouched down close to the ground, her fingers splayed in the muddy grass to steady herself. Somewhere in the dark his feet moved. Her hair in long lengths hung from his fingers. The wind tore across her face, blew away the spark from his flint, illuminating only his bony white fingers and splintered yellow nails for the briefest moment. He was close to her, listening, waiting for her to give herself away with a breath or stumble.

In the sky, the moon waited behind an idle black cloud that inched slowly north. When it passed, she realised, the stage on which they waited would be illuminated.

The disappearance of another girl could not have come at a better time, the sisters agreed as they assembled their folding chairs next to the Hare and Billet pond. The apparatus used to drain the water was precisely the thing needed to drain Cloak's Chocolates' flooded cellar. Three hours of passing heavy bucket after heavy bucket had barely lowered the water at all, but, Maggie pointed out, it had been the equivalent in perspiration alone of a drying-out clinic. All alcohol, she declared, had now left their bodies via their pores and they were therefore optimised for a rather special evening of experiment. But for the first time, Judy found herself reticent. She did not want the following day's hangover. Life was becoming too interesting and too busy. But she'd drink anyway, that was a given.

The crowd around the pond had grown steadily in size all morning, and now, with the notable presence of a tearful and apprehensive family who had reported a daughter missing, the drama of it all was tantamount to theatre. Across the pond, watching all the action, Maggie and Judy enjoyed a first-class view during which they shared a pork pie, crusty bread and pickled onions Very little happened at first; the pool water sunk a little lower, occasionally a duck would be shooed away. Then, after several hours a sudden commotion made the crowd revive. Quickly

Judy put her unfinished lunch on the grass and gave the scene her complete attention. Maggie too, putting the pickled onion she was about to sink her teeth into back on her plate, watched in anticipation.

Three of the men positioned themselves around the pool, pushing long wooden poles down beneath the water, manoeuvring something from the centre to the bank with unified precision. The spectators placed their hands over their mouths, wiped their eyes or turned away, unable to look when the cry of false alarm was raised and a rotten segment of tree trunk was hoisted out.

'Oh, for goodness sake!' Judy sighed disappointedly, loud enough for the crowds to give her reproachful glares. 'All that wait for nothing!'

Her sister agreed and returned her focus to the remaining onions.

When the draining was complete, the sisters, with a large fish wrapped in a tea towel, began the task of convincing the men that the draining of their basement was of major urgency. Using the agreed-upon tactic of (unbeknown to them, horrifyingly bad) flirting, they gained their cooperation by surrendering the fish and feeding them the last of the chocolate mice.

Handing over the fish and the mice meant parting yet again with the last of their food. Worse still, the last of the dreadful home-made port and their money. It had been over a week since the shop had closed its doors to customers and to any form of income. They still had the wine cellar, full of their not-so-favourites, but eating, from that moment on, would pose a trickier problem.

Walking back to the house, Maggie was confused. Her own provisions had been used up down to the last grain of salt, but Judy's basic supplies were obviously still sat there in the larder of her house in Camden Row. She could not make out why, given their imminent starvation, Judy had had not gone to collect them, and when she broached the subject, the topic was changed with such speed and skill that Maggie forgot what it was she had even asked Judy.

The evening was spent with rumbling stomachs and a particularly tongue-numbing nettle wine. What had promised to be a pleasant evening of baked fish and experimental alcohol slid disappointingly into an early night.

The following morning, Netta Walters was at the shop early. She knocked at the door and waited, and was still waiting twenty minutes past their appointment. She was a firm believer in punctuality and did not approve of those who had little regard for it. Giving them the benefit of the doubt, and imagining some unforeseen emergency, she crossed the road to the Blackheath bazaar, the curious emporium of worldly wonders, handmade toys, strange and rare books and all manner of other frivolous oddities. Around her, well-appointed village people carried out their daily chores. Housekeepers went from shop to shop piecing together the evening meal; businessmen hurried in all directions, politely holding open doors for the womenfolk, couples took tea with impeccable manners or peered at the rings in the jewellery shop. Blackheath, it seemed to her, would be the least suitable part of London in which to open what they had in mind.

Finally, from the direction of the heath, the two women came hurrying into view. Mrs Walters watched their troubled faces as they sought her out and hurled themselves at the door.

'I shall make this clear at once,' Netta said, stepping into the gloomy, stale-smelling shop and staring at them both until she had their full attention. 'I will not tolerate lateness. If I am to be your mentor and put my reputation on the line, you will be punctual.'

Both women nodded solemnly, but she was not satisfied.

'Say it.'

'We will be punctual,' the women said uncomfortably.

She moved to the centre of the shop, her hands on her hips, looking up and down, left and right.

'So this is it.' She sucked on her teeth, lost in thought. 'I like it. No, I do. It has atmosphere. It has . . . vibrations. It says – dead.'

'It's been dead for many years,' Judy said, for her sister's benefit.

'Of course it will have to be darker, with more wall coverings, rugs, dark curtains. What's that smell?'

'Damp.'

'Damp? Oh that's no good. No good at all. Spirits hate damp, as does my arthritis. Purgatory is damp, did you know that? Very bad.'

She turned to look at the walls on which Judy's paintings of corpses wandering the afterlife were etched onto the less than adequate paintwork, and at a skull drawn onto the back of the door. She shook her head and mumbled 'ridiculous' under her breath, but loud enough for them to hear.

'All this has to go.'

'We were wondering,' Maggie asked softly, 'and ordinarily we would not dream of ever asking, but, you see, our money has run out and until we open, we cannot afford to eat.'

'Fasting,' Netta announced, dragging two chairs and tables to the centre of the room and arranging them as if it were a school room, 'is a crucial part of nearly all ancient and modern religions. It brings the modern mind closer to its base principles – namely, survival. And while focussed on the threat of starvation, the mind closes off unnecessary distractions and focuses in on itself, therefore opening up its natural state, closer to intuition, primal thought and the spiritual. You are both to refrain from eating for two whole days, taking only sips of water when required and nothing else.'

They stared at her.

'Sit, sit. I want eyes closed until I say you can open them,' Mrs Walters instructed. 'In your minds you will think of nothing. You will simply count slowly from one to eight and then begin again. Do not expect today to be any more interesting than that. Begin.'

For the rest of the morning, while Mrs Walters took a hot soapy rag to Judy's artwork, they practiced. For the first hour it was impossible to clear their minds and keep their eyes closed, but when their eyes adjusted to the light and they came up against Mrs Walter's angry stare, they quickly closed them again. At two, Mrs Walters realised that they were both fast asleep. She slammed her hand down on the table, jolting them awake.

The afternoon session proved the most productive. With their resentment, boredom and frustration already exhausted, they did indeed manage not only to clear their minds but to feel a strange calm. They noticed they appeared to have developed hearing that picked up on smaller sounds which before had either not registered or just been so uninteresting that there was little point in acknowledging them. There was a clarity of mind, too, a new ability to focus with precision, blocking out everything except what they needed to think about. But by evening they could not escape the reality of hunger. With the door bolted and the curtains drawn, they guiltily toasted partial success with a sour but passable beetroot wine, and moved on to a bottle of white, disregarding Netta's water-only instruction entirely before retiring to bed.

By the following day, hunger had become an obsession. While they carried out the counting exercises under Netta's watchful eye they could barely hear themselves recite the numbers for stomach rumblings and the desire for cold meats, hot chicken, minted potatoes, butter, cheese.

One, two, three, four, five, six, bacon, eggs.

One, two, cheese, four, five, ham, seven, fish.

One, buttered bread, cheese, ham, eggs, bacon, chicke . . .

For Judy, there was a sudden and strange development. She felt on the edge of something. It was there just beyond her grasp, as if she was standing at the edge of a precipice and if she reached out for what was hidden there in the air in front of her, her fingertips would just fail to reach it and she would fall dangerously into something she did not understand. She was tempted to fast for another day to see it through, but when the forty-eight hours was finally over, her hunger took priority.

Hurrying, they crossed the top of the heath and scurried down Point Hill towards Greenwich. Halfway, they unlocked the gate of their allotment which they tended to, at best, sporadically. It was September: they had eaten the last of the tomatoes and beans and cauliflower, but Maggie refused to give up hope and marched past the other well-tended plots already pruned for the winter to their own ramshackle plot. It lay covered in weeds, strewn with empty pots and rusting tools. There were some sprouts, hard and woody and wild, but nothing else. Maggie was distraught, refusing to believe they had already eaten the last of the potatoes, and threw herself into digging, hurling spadefuls of earth up into the air. At the back of the plot Judy wrestled with a small marrow only partially eaten by slugs, but it turned to slime in her hands.

From other people's plots, they collected sprouts, together with several overripe tomatoes, a wilting cabbage and some mint and, light-headed with hunger, made their way home to eat.

In the silent small bedroom at the back of Maggie's house, Judy listened for the sound of her sister climbing the stairs, then, slipping from beneath the sheets, she lit a candle and moved quietly to the small table. From her bag she took out the quill and ink and sat for some minutes composing herself. The next part was meant to be written at night, when there would be no distraction, just herself and silence and those sounds that might tantalise her imagination with suspicion and fear.

Klaus Van Dayne's early experiments began with women. At first five, then a further three, and then five more each year. He impregnated each, some naturally, some artificially, but always with his own sperm. Those that did not fall pregnant were shuttled from the castle to the freezing Siberian villages that lay considerable distances away and were replaced with women more fertile. They were fed a specific diet, kept in the grounds of the remote mountain building at all times and pampered right up until the moment they gave birth.

Once born, the children were taken from them, the mothers allowed access only to breastfeed. Often, because of over-emotion, the women's hands were bound behind their backs to discourage further bonding. With the more rebellious women, a routine of breastfeeding while blindfolded would begin. It was imperative that the women realised quickly that the children were bred for experimentation, not rearing.

At four months, sooner if they were strong babies, the operations began, both on mother and child. The baby's back would be opened, muscles cut, additional muscles from the mother grafted in. The bones of a twin, usually the arms, would be attached mid rib. Yards of nerves tugged from the mother would be sewn in and carefully woven to the spinal cord through the smallest drilled holes. Recuperation and muscle training exercises began.

One by one, year after year, the children died of infections and tissue rejection. Several died on the operating table, especially during the early years; some hours later. Then one, a little girl, survived six months. His methods improved. When she died, he stormed through the castle in a rage that lasted weeks. He smashed up furniture and shouted out his fury in the secluded wings of the icy-cold fortress. The next child survived a year, the third two years and five operations. Then came the successes, two of them at once, twins that were absolute perfection.

Judy read the sheet back to herself. Sometimes she wasn't sure where her ideas came from. Often, it felt to her that she was the reader and not its creator. She yawned and considered the candle stub which no longer flickered but flapped helplessly as it surrendered the end of the wick, lighting the little room with dramatic blinking. Reluctantly, she stubbed it between her fingers and climbed between the icy sheets, shivering and rubbing her feet together for warmth.

༒༒༒༒༒༒

Although the sisters had experienced hunger before, they had always been able to stave it off, safe in the knowledge that they could generate income. A sunny day might draw a crowd, a stroll through the park with the chocolate cart would always draw attention or, failing that, they ate the chocolate itself.

Now, there was nothing. A second visit to the allotments told them what they had already known: that when things went missing, other gardeners harvested fast.

'We must open, Judy. We must open this parlour, fast. We must earn. We must eat.'

Netta Walters, with one eye on the village clock, watched the sisters appear the following morning with less than a minute to spare. She eyed them with a warning look and followed them inside.

'We'll need more tables, more chairs. Séance in the evening, crystal and tarot in the afternoon.'

She eyed Maggie.

'Don't sniff at tarot. It will be our bread and butter. I bought and fed six dogs for ten years on tarot readings. But first, that smell must go.' She dragged a sack of branches across the room and tipped it out, handing Judy the empty sack. 'Go to the heath, bring back every piece of wood you can find.' She ushered her out of the door.

Down below in the cellar, Maggie moved amongst fumes and smoke. Small fires were lit in each of the corners to which she added more branches before rushing up the steps into the shop and slamming the trapdoor behind her. She covered it with a heavy rug and fell backwards into the armchair.

'There's no time for slacking!' Netta said, hurrying her out of the shop to collect more wood.

When the sisters returned, she inspected the sacks and nodded. Then, reaching into her bag, she placed two large sandwiches on a table and pushed them in their direction.

Later that afternoon, two men on ladders arrived to take down the Cloak's Chocolates sign that many moons ago the sisters had toasted, anticipating success and riches. They watched it fall with a thud.

'Are you going to keep it?' Samuel Payne the fishmonger asked, 'for old time's sake?'

Judy shook her head, watching her sister turn away in distress. She would need cheering up after this, she realised, then, taking up her axe, began to chop it up. They needed every bit of wood they could get.

They walked home separately, Maggie first, in desperate need of a bath, while Judy waited until the fires were safely out. When she locked up the shop, she dared to think about the other thing. There was nothing in her own pantry, but in the back garden there was . . . No, she couldn't bring herself to go there, not yet. She waited until the shops had closed and then made her way around to the alleyway behind them. Pulling down her bonnet and listening carefully, she lifted the lids on the dustbins.

At seven, Maggie brought up bottles of wine from the cellar and lit the fire. Judy arrived a half hour later. She brought with her two apples, some bread and a large onion, which they ate toasted over the fire.

Outside, the never-ending gale was stirring again. The gate blew wide and closed, smashing against the post, the trees creaked and leaned dangerously low and a spiteful wind peered in, then thrust itself under the door and down the chimney, sending sparks of fire up and around the two women. They screamed, beating the embers down with tea towels, and agreed a third bottle of wine would settle them and hopefully take away the taste of onion.

'I always thought that at this age I would be with a husband I had grown tired of,' Maggie said, pulling a shawl around herself.

Judy poked the fire and added a small log. 'I was relieved when George died that I could change my surname back to Cloak and no one would call me Judy Moody ever again, and it meant I could get back to living without asking his permission for everything.'

'He was a terrible bully.'

'And a terrible snorer. I barely slept for eleven years, but I didn't realise it until he had gone. The night he died I had the best night's sleep of my life.'

'I rather like the sound of snoring. It makes me feel safe. It blocks out the sounds from outside and makes everything seem snug.'

Judy sipped. 'A month or so after George died, I woke up one night out of the blue. It was so silent I didn't know where I was. I sat there listening for sounds, to see what had woken me, until I'd convinced myself I had a burglar. I sat there in the dark cursing George for dying and leaving me to fend for myself. Then I remembered that when he was alive, it was always me that went to investigate noises with the rolling pin at night, never him.'

Maggie laughed and looked into the fire, her face warm and content in the orange glow. Judy studied her.

'In this light, sometimes you look just the same as you did when you were a girl.'

'With this baggy old face?'

'Just sometimes, just fleetingly, flickers really, and there you are, my sister from years ago, about ten or eleven.'

'To be that young again! Your whole life ahead of you. I feel so old now. Like I've missed all my chances and I just have to accept what is left. Life happens to youngsters, not old birds my age.'

'Nonsense.'

'I am so very old and boring.'

'Tomorrow is the same day for youngsters as it is for us oldies. They will spend the days to come building their futures, we will do the same. They will have tears and laughter, so will we. But, of course,' she smiled, 'they can't drink as much as us, so we could have our way with them.'

'Judy!'

'I have often wondered what it must be like to make love with a more virile man. George was so . . . placid.'

'Count your blessings you knew men at all.'

'We must change that.'

'Change what? Oh no, Judy. I'm too old now. I've passed it by. I accept it.'

'You accept far too little as your lot in life.'

'I would like to fall in love and feel the adoration you mention so often, but my body has gone. It's lost all that men look for in a woman. I would like a man that has had his fill of . . . relations and no longer requires it.'

'That man does not exist.'

She smiled. 'I want to experience the emotions of love so badly sometimes.'

Judy nodded.

'I'd like to cook dinner and wait for him to come home. I want to see what it is like to cuddle up in bed and . . . oh, I don't know, I've romanticised it too much. I want those little moments. The walks and the hand-holding and the kisses.' She looked at her sister and watched her nod, lost in memories. She changed the subject. 'I can't help wondering if we are doing the right thing still, with the shop, dabbling with dark forces and the dead as if we are an authority when we know so little, least of all what we are letting ourselves in for.'

'But there is such an interest building in it. Within a few years it will be a major activity. If we do not do this, someone else will. London is alive with superstition and questions and you and I are going to be at the forefront. If we do this properly, Maggie, we will be remembered for centuries to come. We could be the pioneers of the afterlife, you and I, Maggie and Judy Cloak.'

Maggie waggled her stockinged feet at the flames and pulled herself up. 'Time for bed,' she announced. She put the guard around the fire and tidied the plates away. Then, reaching the door, she stopped. 'Before I go up, I want to ask you about something. We have been avoiding the subject. Judy, why don't you ever go home? What is going on with your house?'

She waited for an answer, but when she looked round, Judy was apparently asleep, her head tilted, her mouth agape, her eyelids biding their time until Maggie climbed the stairs. When the floorboards above her head began to creak, she opened her eyes and hurried to the bookcase. From the top shelf she took down a box, from which she produced a crystal ball wrapped in a black cloth.

The purchase of the ball some eighteen months previously at one of the travelling fairs that passed through Blackheath had been the seed from which the idea of a séance parlour had grown. She had become obsessed with it, practicing night after night, every so often making headway, but mostly it got wrapped up and put away again with Judy cursing the enormous sum it had cost her. But now, at long last, she had a teacher who sat her down and thrashed the half-heartedness out of her.

'Impatience,' Mrs Walters had shouted at her, 'is the mind killer. You do not control time, you are passing through it, slowly, naturally – you are not driving through it in a car.'

'What's a car?'

'When you can read a crystal ball you can find out for yourself. Psychic humour, Judy, love. You'll get it one day.'

Judy dimmed the lights, reducing the reflection on the ball's surface as much as possible, and sat. Clearing her mind was significantly easier these days, she noticed, since the fasting; even when she was this drunk. She stared past the watering of her eyes, past the clouds and the sparks of light, past the prickling of her scalp until she reached the blurred and the clear, the blurred and the clear. But as soon as her vision sharpened and there, just in her peripheral vision, the images began to form, arranging themselves to be seen properly, her excitement and surprise jolted her away. She cursed herself over and over again, demanding that she concentrate, angry that her whole frame of mind now needed to be renurtured, reasoning that this was not *that* exciting. But it was. When the clouds cleared and the sharp snap of clarity came into being again and strong clear images began to form, the excitement was like nothing else. 'Soon,' she assured herself. Soon she would master it, and then she would become the best at it. Soon she would know everything about everyone.

In her room, Maggie, too, was doing a little secret study of her own, following the instructions from one of the rare parchments Netta had entrusted her with: the candle spell.

'Be careful what you wish for,' Netta had warned her, clasping her hands and staring with all seriousness into her eyes. 'And avoid asking for men. What you get through the candles is only temporary and you don't know where it comes from. Money comes and goes, food comes and goes, but men! You don't want to wake up the next day and realise you've just had it off with the devil, that's all.' The woman's coarseness and casual blasphemy never failed to make Maggie irritable.

She took the new copper-coloured candle and anointed it with her own scent by running a little saliva and perspiration along it, set it down firmly on a body-warmed coin in a still area of the room, warmed a needle with a lit spill then pushed it through the candle an inch or so from the top, piercing the wick inside the wax with it. Then, kneeling before it, she cleared her mind of everything and lit the candle.

For a moment, she watched the new wick dance and spit as the fire took hold, then she applied her mind completely. Without blinking more than once every two minutes, she concentrated with all her might on what she wanted the most, her eyes not for a second wandering from the flame, her determination unwavering. She wanted food, meat in particular, lots and lots of meat.

A full thirty minutes ticked by as the candle slowly melted down. The further it sank, the harder she concentrated; the closer to the needle, the more excited and positive her belief. And then the wax cleared and the needle was exposed. The spell was complete. Maggie wished once more, then blew out the candle and went to sleep.

Anna's parents, like everyone else in Blackheath, were curious for information on the count and countess, and after a week of noticing extreme change in their daughter, Mr and Mrs Hill refused to settle for the girl's evasions any longer. They sat her down and demanded the full story. And under pressure, the countess's secret, which Anna had been coerced into helping protect, came hurtling out.

'She is so beautiful,' Anna explained. 'So kind and wise and so trusting. You must promise not to tell anyone.'

Her parents intended nothing of the sort. Information was power, and it was rare that they were in such a powerful position. For once, the Hills had something that everyone in Blackheath wanted.

'When the count and countess were born,' Mrs Hill explained, accepting a free pound of butter and some eggs from Mr Briggs the grocer on Royal Parade, 'they were twins, you see.' She took the apples and oranges from old George Goldsmith at the fruit shop and put them in her basket, 'Though they were in fact part of a set of triplets, but there was a terrible accident.' Mr Watson the butcher on Montpelier Vale handed her some pork sausages, hanging on her every word. 'They were all joined up.'

She could never have imagined that one day she would be being bought afternoon tea by Isabella Royal, a lady and teacher of such high standing in Blackheath. When the waitress came around, Mrs Hill ordered ham sandwiches to go with her cake. 'The count and countess were on the outside and the third child was joined to them in the middle.' She watched Thomas William Smith, a hairdresser of such high reputation and unaffordable prices go to work. 'Something elaborate, fit for a proper lady,' she prompted. 'Well, there was an operation . . .' She tried on several dresses before choosing the one they would allow her to take at cost. 'And the child in the middle, died.' Elizabeth Morgan and Matilda Jewel, preening and pinning the dress on her in the window of their shop at Brunswick Place, gasped.

'Then . . .' she said, browsing the strange and exciting selection of toys from around the world at the Blackheath Bazaar. Alice Marshall leaned forward,

'Please, do chose something from this shelf.' Mrs Hill chose a board game from another shelf, aware that it was in a more expensive section and that poor Alice could not bear any further suspense. 'Then they discovered that the spines of the three children were joined together.' She was pleased with the repair and polish of her boots and walked up and down George Pugh's shop admiring them. 'So they had to cut away the third child but had to leave the spine and a lot of ribs.'

Everyone in the Sun in the Sands public house listened with bated breath as Mrs Hill waved her empty glass and Mr Hill in his new shirt gulped down his ale greedily . 'So although my daughter says they are beautiful looking and very kind, nice people, they still have big bones sticking out under the skin on their backs from the third dead child, and padding to stop the pain. When they move it can be awkward and painful. They are worried that people might call them freaks and not want them.' Edward Sibley, the landlord, topped up her glass as she slurred loudly at the crowd, 'But I say, welcome. Welcome to Blackheath. They might not like you in Russia or wherever you are from, but London welcomes you!'

Everyone cheered.

Anna watched her parents listen, their mouths open wide. She felt guilty for breaking her promise. 'Please promise you won't tell anyone.'

Her parents smiled.

'And you haven't met the count?'

'Not properly. But he is the most handsome man you will ever see, the governess keeps saying.'

It would be less than five hours before everyone, even those who rarely set foot outside their homes, knew the count and countess's most closely guarded secret – or so they thought.

Chapter 6

'*Maggie!*'

Startled and half asleep, Maggie rushed down the stairs following her sister's urgent steps, her eyes still closed. They hurried through the kitchen and out into the small paved yard at the back of the house. There in the corner, huddled together, were three large hens.

Maggie covered her mouth. 'It works!'

They chased the noisy birds indoors and locked them inside the pantry. There had to be no possibility of escape until they brought up the wire from the allotment and built a coop. Soon there would be daily eggs, scrambled and fried, omelettes, roast chicken.

The largest of the three was brought out immediately. Judy held it down, one hand pressing its head flat against the kitchen table, the other keeping its awkward body still while Maggie searched her drawers for a cleaver or butcher's knife. Eventually, the best she could come up with was a serrated bread knife. The two women winced, then, looking away, Maggie began the gruesome task of sawing the hen's head off while ignoring its screeches. Without a word, they plucked quickly and methodically, slit the bird open and emptied its insides out and, with a finger of lard, they pushed it eagerly into the oven. The feathers were stuffed into a flat cushion, the giblets into a jar with the head and feet. They would waste nothing. Sitting back, they watched the oven cook what promised to be the most exciting meal of the summer.

※※※※※※

'Tarot,' Mrs Walters began, licking chicken juice from her fingers as she marched around the shop 'the dark art born from the gypsy blood of Bologna. These mystical cards can foretell the future with startling accuracy. They reveal our problems, bring into the light the lovers we will have, the husbands, the children – or maybe not. They can tell you anything . . .' she paused for dramatic effect, 'that you want to know. Come closer.'

Reverently she placed an ancient carved wooden box on the table and opened its creaking lid. From inside she took a dark leather pouch and then, one by one, she revealed the ancient Trionfi deck with their frightening images: the devil, death, the tower, sly looking princes, spiteful queens, moons, daggers and so many other disturbing images that Maggie, and even Judy, became fearful.

'I want you to concentrate on love. Think about it now, the love that has entered your life, the love that you want to enter your life. Concentrate.' She watched the two women deep in thought, their eyes closed. Then, lifting the cards, she took Judy's hands and wrapped her fingers tightly around them. 'Think, Judy, feel the answers in your hand. Within those cards is your life. The life you have already spent, the life you breathe now and the life beginning to form for you in the future. In your hands are the answers, all the people you have met, your parents and your sister, me, all the people you have yet to meet that are coming closer to you in time. You can't change any of it. It's all set in stone. But you can see it all. It is all in the cards. All in your hands.'

Judy's hands felt the warmth of the cards, felt their rough edges, their weight. She willed herself to believe that in the images her life's story was silently being told.

'Now, cut the cards.'

Automatically, Judy cut the pile, one pile deep and thick, the other a collection of ten or so cards from the top. Netta nodded and took them.

'You are about to know everything, good and bad, about your future in regard to love. The cards might show rich, rewarding, long-lasting companionship or endless years of loneliness and heartbreak. They might reveal horrible twists or secrets of the bedroom you'd really rather have kept to yourself.'

'I'm not sure I want to know about –'

'Too late, the cards are cut. Sit. Oh, there is love coming! Passionate, all-embracing, quite energetic love.'

Judy reddened.

When Maggie took her turn and watched Mrs Walters' face with the same wide eyes as her sister, she imagined something less energetic; someone older, perhaps, who would make her feel pretty, or at least respected. She didn't want some hot-blooded smooth talker with a bedroom fixation.

'No, there is no love in sight for you.'

'None at all?'

'Nothing. You've had your lot.'

'But I haven't had any!'

'Well, it's too late now.'

Maggie sighed angrily.

'Now, ladies,' Mrs Walters said firmly, dragging a chair noisily across to the centre of the shop. 'What I propose is this. A three-way split of the profits. None of this pittance of a wage you were talking about giving me. You have the building, yes, but I have the craft, I am what they will flock to see. The dead meet the living through me. And I am teaching you everything that you will need to learn. You take all the fame, all the glory. I'm not interested in that. I remain your well-paid but secret weapon. Loyal,' she pointed out, 'but not a mug. After rent and costs, a three-way split of all profits. Deal?'

There was a pause and the sisters nodded.

'Then let's turn this place into somewhere that will really terrify London. Pass me that black paint.'

Due to the preoccupation with the murders, the closure of Cloak's Chocolates had slipped by largely unnoticed. It had sat empty, its windows blackened for several weeks now and the residents had begun to forget what had been there in the first place. But when, later that day, there was painting, and the old comfortable browns disappeared behind dark glossy black, and not just the window frames and door but the bricks, the doorstep, the chimney, so that it stood out in the row as something jarring and altogether odd, people began congregating to speculate on what such effort was leading to.

A new shop in the village was big news. A suitable addition could uplift everyone and give their lives renewed inspiration and purpose, whereas the wrong shop could lead to depression and a sense that the village was sliding into ruin. On the rare occasions that this occurred, the owners were ostracised, there was an unspoken boycott and soon, through ruin or social pressure, the shop was gone and everyone was happy again. Blackheath was a very fussy village. What was deemed acceptable teetered on a fine line, as the sisters well knew. They also knew that the reaction to what they were about to unveil would be extreme.

Graham Charles – a local artist, who, once a week for several years, as regular as clockwork, had arrived at ten o'clock on a Tuesday morning and spent the day in the shop with Maggie drinking tea, as bored and fed up of poverty as she – had been summoned. He was to add character to the shop front, weave intricate detail to the drying black with a fine brush and dark purple paint. They wanted something macabre, intricate, nightmarish – but subtle. He listened to the three women enthuse to him about how people should be made to feel uneasy, how they should see things in his patterns that others could not see or would miss.

'Wha . . . wha . . . what,' he stuttered, 'is the shop going to be?'

The women looked at each other, then shook their heads. 'We can't tell you.'

He turned to Maggie, with whom he had spent more time than any woman he had ever known, including his mother, but she shook her head apologetically. 'You will see.'

'And I can still come for tea?'

'Oh yes.'

He smiled, got down on his knees on the doorstep and began drawing great sweeping fronds uncurling and disappearing into the dark black background. Around the doorway he created the most subtle images, visible only in certain lights, and on the window, as instructed, he drew the barely visible outline of a figure that at first was difficult to see at all but, once seen, the optical illusion was terrible – a great glaring figure with hard eyes and a dangerous, snarling mouth. He painted lightly over it so it disappeared slightly into the black, and when the light changed or you looked from a different angle, it was gone entirely.

'Because of the angle,' he explained, 'it will only be visible to children or very small people.'

The women clapped their hands in delight.

'I don't like children,' Maggie confided.

'Can't abide them,' Netta agreed, leaning back and looking up at the towering black oddity. 'Well, it certainly stands out.'

⊗⊗⊗⊗⊗⊗⊗⊗⊗

The governess hurried down the corridor with a tray on which lay a mountain of raw, sliced fish. She knocked on the countess's door, and without waiting for a reply, let herself in.

'Apparently madam,' she said, setting the tray down and arranging a knife and fork, 'you have a protruding backbone, deformed from an operation which severed you from the count at the cost of a third child.'

The countess smiled, 'Is it common knowledge?'

'Oh yes.'

She motioned for the Governess to sit. 'Take coffee with me while I eat.'

The woman sat and poured.

'The charity ball . . .'

The governess nodded. 'It's the perfect occasion for yourself and the count to be introduced to Blackheath society.' She took the invitation from its envelope, adjusted her spectacles and ran her finger down the list of guests, then taking a quill, she set to work writing comments next to each of the names.

'I've underlined the most important, put a star next to the notable and interesting. The rest are run of the mill, not worth any major effort.'

'Thank you.'

The Governess sipped her coffee. 'What will you wear?'

'Judy!'

Judy looked up with a start, snatching the sheet and her quill and thrusting them quickly to one side.

Netta was furious. 'We are up against a deadline. We open in less than a week and people will be sitting opposite you, wanting quality mediumship. If you are not ready and you send them away dissatisfied, word of mouth will cost us money and reputation.'

'I just took a little break.'

'No. No little breaks. You have a very low attention span. Do you know that? Very low indeed.'

She pulled a chair up to the table then put a finger to her lips, listening to passers-by outside quiz the painter about what the shop would be.

'I don't know, ma'am,' he replied tirelessly.

'That's the twelfth in an hour. People cannot wait,' Netta wheezed excitedly. 'Now,' she took a card from the pile and held it up. 'The tower, what does that mean?'

Down below, in the cellar, fires crackled with the wood that the sisters had chopped down every night after dark for three days. It was so hot and steamy that Maggie had resorted to working in her undergarments, rushing to save dying embers, resizing heaps when the flames rose too close to the wooden ceiling. She imagined herself captive somewhere in the tropics, imprisoned by a rogue government or ferocious tribe, the leader of which, a rugged, masculine, no-nonsense type, would fall passionately in love with her, rescue her and make her his wife. And although she wanted to return to England to see her sister, she never would because he would never let her out of his sight. Despite this imprisonment, she felt safe and loved, and when there were no others around he would treat her like a queen, worshipping her, becoming soft and loving, but not for long. Soon he would be ripping her blouse open with thick dirty fingers and throwing her down in the dust between the blazing fires and . . .

Netta was standing at the top of the stairs watching her daydream.

'You only have to put logs on and come back up. You don't have to live down here.' She surveyed the crumbling plaster, sniffed the air and frowned, turning to watch Maggie pull on her clothes and follow her back up into the shop.

'We have two hours until it's dark. Ladies, if you can prove to me in that time that you have mastered the tarot, I will not only ask to see this Hare and Billet pub you try to get me into so often, but I will treat us all to something to eat and several rounds of the drinks of your choice.'

The sisters immediately set to work, barely able to contain their excitement.

While they practiced, Netta stood outside and watched the painter, up on his ladder painting the long, dark, imposing shop sign a dark purple.

'You don't think that the shop looks too sinister, too imposing?' he called down to her. 'People might be itching to take a look, but they'll probably be too frightened to step inside. They are all shocked at what we are doing. They don't like it.'

'The more imposing the better. We're not selling cake and frilly dresses.'

'What are you selling?'

'Communication with the dead.'

He stared. 'What?'

She walked back inside. 'He goes on a bit, doesn't he? Still, he might have a point.'

The sisters looked up.

'The appearance of the shop is fine for the evening, then they can look and be frightened. That's good. But in the day we should appear softer, more inviting. We need a billboard to put up to lure in the gentlewomen: "Fortunes told". "Does love lie in your future?" In the day, we don't tell them the bad bits.' She looked at the women for their opinion and found blank faces. 'Perhaps we should also sell balms for sleepless nights, a prayer for the recently departed. Tea-leaf readings for young lovers.'

'Special cushions for their heads?' Judy interrupted.

Maggie and Netta looked at her.

'Well, I was thinking. Coffin gifts. Nice things to send people to the grave with.'

The women were still staring.

'Like the Egyptians? Everyone going to a funeral can buy a coffin gift.'

Netta frowned and looked away, then reconsidered and glanced back at her with a quizzical look before shaking it off again. She held up a tarot card and sighed. 'The moon! What is its meaning? Come on!'

'Change – the end of the old, start of the new,' Maggie said.

'Love? Is it love?' Judy interrupted.

'For God's sake! *No!*' Netta dragged a chair noisily to the table at the back and made a start on the posters.

Judy picked up her quill.

When the news spread that the count and countess would not only be attending the ball but also making a generous donation, tickets, already in huge demand, began to change hands at shamelessly increased prices. Charity, it seemed, was secondary to the money that could be made by last-minute bargaining, and those lucky enough to be known by name and not by appearance, made a fortune.

Anna rushed down the corridor with the countess's freshly pressed dress. She hung it on the stand in her room, and taking a bottle of expensive perfume from the dresser, sprayed the outfit lightly. She placed the long gloves on the bed next to the fur cape, put the long black boots next to the chair and began laying out the hairclips and mirrors beside a box of long glossy human hair, which she did not want to open.

When the countess arrived back from her bath, Anna awaited full of enthusiasm but the countess sent her to bring a glass of warmed milk. When she returned, the countess was dressed and seated at the dressing table, clipping long lengths of dark hair into her own, adding more and more until the final result was imposing and breathtaking. Anna curtsied and put the milk down.

'When you come to drink alcohol, Anna,' she confided, 'you must drink warm milk first, it stops you from getting too intoxicated. Not always, just when you must not become too relaxed.'

Anna nodded and put a necklace of large bulbous rubies around the countess's neck then reached for the matching earrings. She was eager now to step into the hall, to get her first glimpse of the count, to see him in all his finery, ready to be greeted by the people of London.

The Governess passed by the door, carrying the count's pressed suit. 'The carriage will be ready in one hour ma'am.'

'Doesn't the ball begin in under ten minutes?' Anna asked.

The countess smiled and held the girls chin. 'So young.'

Chapter 9

The Ranger's House with the darkness of Greenwich Park behind it was glittering with candlelight. The grounds and the windows and the roof, pinpricked with hundreds of wavering flames was quite a spectacle. Guests in their dramatic finery and coiffured hair were greeted at the gates by the doormen who escorted them either under the head of Neptune into the house or off to the right and through into the rose garden of the park, which was bathed with the light from candles in coloured jars. Tonight, the whole of the park belonged exclusively to them. Paths were lit, the great trees hung with cascades of glimmering flames, intimate tables surrounded with rings of glowing glass jars were scattered about the lawns.

The most important people of London in the latest fashions and expensive ball gowns sipped champagne from fluted glasses, each full of their own importance, breathing in the cool night air and shrugging off the goose pimples to remember the moment forever.

Inside, the hall was fantastical with shimmering blue light, giving the impression of being underwater. Ripples of greens and blues raced across the walls and ceilings. Enormous candles the width of young trees stood in lines while tiny dancing colours in crystal ornaments sat between the whites and yellows and greens of each table's floral arrangements.

The delicate tinkling of piano keys rose to accompany the string section, lifting and falling with the rolling of drums, to add to the illusion of a rippling blue underwater room.

As the great hall clock at the bottom of the stairs struck eight, Lady Dartmouth, classical pianist, retired headmistress, twice married, twice widowed, a paragon of good manners and all round pillar of the community who was not unattractive at the outlandish age of sixty-six, swept into the room. Her blinding white lace gown was a little tight and bosomy for some, but the white hair, remarkable white teeth and soft ivory skin, allowed her not only to get away with it but positively outshine many several decades her junior. She too, it seemed, had pulled out all the stops to impress the as-yet unseen young count and his sister.

The sportsmen and landowners, judges and doctors, explorers and shipping tycoons, astronomers and notable shop-owners, each hoping to have outdone each other, began to hurry into the hall, seeking out their place cards, conscious of the seating plan, considering their rank and place within the room of peers.

Lady Beatrice Dartmouth took her place at the top table, which, ordinarily belonged to the Princess Sophia Matilda, whose house they were all enjoying. Luckily for Lady Dartmouth, she was out of the country, and yet again, as was the way in the wonderful fun-filled days before the arrival of the princess, Beatrice Dartmouth had back her role of organiser and she sat watching people take their places. Seating was her speciality. She could flatter, confuse, insult, erode friendships, influence outcomes, match-make, generate bidding wars – do almost anything simply by being given a room to organise. Tonight she had three priorities: to raise enough money to take care of the borough's orphans, to remove the windmills and quarries on the heath and turn it into a flat, pleasant park for families, and to make this year's firework display the biggest and best in London, as was tradition. But more excitingly, she would be the woman who would introduce the count and countess to London society and put an end to the already ravenous hunger to see them.

'They say he is most handsome.'

'They say he is more beautiful than she, but she is the most beautiful woman in the world.'

'An athletic build.'

'Remarkably tall'

'With impeccable manners. They say he is charming.'

'Apparently he is so beautiful that he held Paris spellbound.'

Their wealth and generosity was legendary; stories of lavish parties in Europe and New York had filled the society pages for over a year, with excitement snowballing ahead of them as they drew ever closer to England. But it was the challenge of describing their appearance which tested the journalist's vocabulary the most. 'There simply are the not words for such rare beauty,' explained one German paper.

'These are powerful people,' someone whispered to a spellbound table. 'Why are they coming to Blackheath?'

'Because Blackheath is, by far, the most beautiful part of London!' a haughty voice replied.

Everyone raised a glass.

'Such a shame about the deformity.'

'Deformity?'

'Rumour has it that they suffer with back injuries and cumbersome spines that require them to wear an elaborate structure on their backs.'

Someone else nodded eagerly. 'Apparently the pain can be quite unbearable but they don't like it mentioned.'

'Then I suggest, ladies, to make them feel welcome, that you curb the gossip about them.'

People were looking around, watching the room take order as guests were seated, aware of the two chairs that remained empty. A sense of disquiet began to grow. Having taken a sip of her wine and noticing the concern around her, Lady Dartmouth stood and tapped her glass.

'The count and countess have asked me to apologise,' she began, watching the room wait on her words with baited breath. There were audible sighs of disappointment. 'But due to unforeseen circumstances they have been delayed and will not be joining us . . .'

The outcry was audible even outside the room.

'. . . until after dinner.'

The room lifted into babbling excitement again and dinner was served.

'As well as the natural way to open up the psychic pathways within the mind,' Mrs Walters said, panting as she marched the women through the gates of All Saints cemetery in Nunhead, 'there are also shortcuts we can take, stimulants. And since you seem . . . slow in your uptake, this might speed things up a little.'

They climbed the hill, suffocating beneath thick coats and woollens, each wrestling a large bag until, finding a suitable private spot, they set out cushions and blankets and sat.

'The gates are locked at seven. We shall need to hide if the warden comes along before that,' she warned them. Then, hearing the church bell strike seven, she smiled, 'We are alone for the night.'

'For the night!' Maggie choked, climbing to her feet. 'We're not staying here until –'

'What did you think we were doing here, Margaret?'

'You told me that you wanted to put flowers on your parents' grave on the way to drop off these blankets at your aunt's.'

'Yes, well, I made that up. You're not the most cooperative of women, dear.'

'Oh no you don't! I am not staying –'

'Might I remind you, ladies, that we are not opening a sweetshop. We are offering a séance parlour. You act as though you are terrified of the dead.'

'I am!' Maggie said, clutching her chest. 'Oh no, we must get out of here.'

'We are here until seven in the morning.' Netta said, putting sugar onto a spoon and holding it above a glass. She poured onto it a large measure of green liquid, immediately gaining both women's full attention.

'What is that you are doing?' Maggie asked accusingly.

'I am taking absinthe,' she replied casually, waiting for the sugar to dissolve.

'And what is that?'

'It is a strong alcohol that opens the mind to other realities.'

'Are we safe here?'

'Perfectly safe. There is just us and the dead.'

'It's the dead I'm concerned about. Are we safe from them? They cannot harm us?'

'They cannot harm us.'

Maggie sat, then, reaching out, took the absinthe and drank it, watching the sun sink down over London. Suddenly, they were in darkness.

'When we die,' Netta said, 'we enter a place of darkness. Imagine, if you will, a large field in total darkness. On this field, thousands of spirits mill about wondering what on earth has happened. They are confused and adjusting to their new form. The feeling is said to be like being drunk while suffering from such a lack of sleep that you barely have the energy to put one foot in front of the other. They stay here for several weeks, just wandering, trying to clear their heads, trying to make sense of things. The darkness keeps them in a dreamlike state so they can adjust without panic. For most, it quickly feels normal, for others, the more alert, it can be a horrifying ordeal.'

'Oh good lord, how do you know this?' Maggie asked.

'All mediums know it. We talk to the dead. We ask questions.' She prepared another absinthe. 'Now, on this plane, there are occasional flashes of coloured lights. These are the only things visible to the dead there. Sometimes they are dull glows, sometimes bright cascades of blinding light. These lights are the living trying to contact the dead, and when they see them, the dead come rushing to them – after all, it is all they have seen of any interest for weeks. The idea of the plane is to drain away the memories of earthly life; they readjust here before moving on. Here is where they forget their jobs and keys and husbands and children. They get all the crying and shock out of their systems here. They will not move on until they have stopped missing their families, stopped being angry at the person who murdered them – until they have got all the rage and anger and revenge and hatred, all the love and the need to cling to life out of their systems. It can be a very disturbing place if you have already made your peace with dying before you go, but fortunately, in that state of mind, you don't stay there that long.'

'And the lights?'

'A dull glow there is quite an accomplishment. It is the mourning of those left behind making itself visible to the dead. It's not often seen. To generate a glow on this plane your grieving must be extreme – screaming, crying, lashing out, the total refusal to believe that the person is dead and the continual calling of their name. And when that glow appears, it reminds all those near it of what they have left behind. Their mourning often begins again. In extreme cases, when the person left behind is truly devastated and mourns for years, it can keep them there until that person joins them and they move on together. Of course, in some cases, the dead do the same to the living. Their love is so strong and their refusal to move on and forget can reach peaks where the living become aware of them. They see the ghost visiting them, and if they are both extreme characters with a very strong love, they can maintain that state, pulling the spirit back from the plane to inhabit the earthly planes.'

'So it is just love that generates a ghost?'

'Oh no. Any emotion strong enough can create a ghost – fear, anger, hatred, spite, jealousy . . .'

Around them, the last hint of light on the horizon was slipping away. A sharp evening breeze raced across the grass, tossing leaves into orderly piles at the bases of headstones. Above, the trees, enjoying the wind's combing, let go of their own dead, showering the ground with crisp browns and reds and yellows.

Netta placed another sugar lump on the spoon and dissolved it with the liquid, holding it out to Judy. 'How are you both feeling?'

'Very relaxed,' Judy admitted with surprise, 'all things considered.'

Maggie nodded, her eye on the alcohol.

'Now watch.' Netta began running her finger around the rim of the glass until a sound, not unlike a string instrument, began to build in volume. 'This sound can be heard by the dead. It draws them to us.'

Maggie choked, looking around nervously.

'On that plane, when the rim of this glass becomes hot, a small opening will appear, that they can gather around and peer through, and from inside it, they will see us.'

'Oh, good lord!'

'All of the lights that appear on that plane are windows that allow them to look back to us. The dull glow of the mourner gives the dead a vague vision of their loved one grieving, while the bright shower of light generated by mediums and psychics provides them with a dramatically clear view and sometimes a doorway. Sometimes a vivid dream or a particularly startling nightmare will let the dead see your mental state and feel your body's every move for days afterwards. They become close, in tune. They haunt.'

The sound of the glass grew loud. Maggie felt her mouth go dry and the hair stand up on her neck as the breeze hurried past her.

'Come closer,' Netta beckoned, her head rolling. 'Come closer to the sound, come closer to me.'

Judy watched, fascinated. She too began to sway.

'We mean you no harm, we would like to talk with you.'

Maggie lit the small oil lamp and looked around her at the graves emerging from the darkness. She jumped, thought she saw something, someone darting from one grave to another.

'It's too much!' she told them. 'Stop!'

'I see you, I see you all,' Netta spoke softly.

Judy screwed up her eyes in concentration, jumping suddenly as Netta's hand took hers.

'You must relax, you must let it happen, you must not try to force it. It does not require force, it calls for patience and openness.'

Maggie watched Netta sway and her sister drink and, turning her back to them, kept her eye on their surroundings, on the gravestones now eerily illuminated by the dancing flame. She reached for her glass and sipped slowly, to keep her hands occupied, for distraction.

'Make yourselves visible to us,' Netta called. 'We mean you no harm. We are from the old life, from your past. You can be reminded through us.'

Maggie was outraged. 'But you said . . .' She stopped, turning to see a dull white light hover in the distance. She took another gulp and stared at it. For a moment it just hung there, barely visible, then it darted down to a grave, then along to another. Maggie held her breath. She reached out silently for Netta, then, as her hand made contact with the medium, she felt a sudden jolt and swooned, turning to see transparent white figures, dusty and nervous, clinging to gravestones. Others moved slowly past, each step a concentrated effort, peering around, frightened. Some were hiding behind trees, watching them with sharp darting eyes, and moved jealously to ward off those getting too close to their plots. But the majority stood motionless on their graves, dressed in their white burial robes, unmoving, all facing east. Maggie scrambled backwards, climbing to her feet, crossing herself.

'We mean you no harm,' Netta explained.

'Make them go!' Maggie shouted. 'Make it end.'

Netta opened an eye, watching Maggie back away towards the path.

'They are all around us!' She was becoming hysterical.

Netta sighed and let her trance end, and as she did, the strange shapes and movements faded away.

'Maggie,' she said, pointing to a cushion on the ground. 'What do you think they are going to do to you? They are people. They are just like you and me. Now sit down, you are being silly.'

When they turned to look at Judy, she was facing away from them, nodding her head, following movements with her eyes amongst the gravestones, beckoning spirits to her.

Netta beamed. 'She's done it. She's breaking through.'

Chapter 8

Without taking off her coat, Maggie cracked two eggs into a frying pan while Judy, still heaving the sacks of blankets, struggled up the path.

'I have changed my mind. I want no part of this. It is wrong. It is unnatural.'

'It's too late now, Margaret! We need to earn. I'm not sure how many more eggs I can eat.'

'I saw things last night that I want to forget. I don't wish to know anything more.'

'I saw things last night that surprised me, too.'

'You were surprised – I was terrified.' She slammed the plate of eggs down on the table. 'Why isn't it light out? It's normally daytime by now, isn't it? This is all your doing. Look, the clock has stopped. Now we don't know what time it is.'

'It was incredible, Maggie. I actually saw the dead girl. We didn't say anything but she looked at me and I looked at her and we were both aware of each other.'

'You were drunk. You can't be sure what you saw. Oh this will alter our future beyond anything we are prepared for. It will make our lives wretched.'

'You promised me six months.'

'But that was before! I didn't know what we were getting into. Already I have seen and heard far too much.'

'Maggie,' Judy put down her fork. 'I want this. It is my turn.'

'Choose something else, anything. Please. Please, Judy. I cannot do this.'

Judy stood, leaving her eggs, and reached for her coat.

'I am going to continue training, ready for the opening of the shop.'

She was about to leave when a knock at the door alarmed them both.

Maggie's angry stare shifted upwards, to a face in the window.

'What the hell is he doing here?'

The door opened and the vicar, jovial but nervous, let himself in.

'Good morning, ladies. It looks like another storm is brewing. It seems to be one storm after another lately.'

Maggie sighed, 'What are you doing here, Henry?'

'Most parishioners refer to me as Vicar or Father Legge, Margaret.'

Maggie's eyes glazed over.

'I hope you don't mind me dropping in like this but, well, it's just that I was wondering, if . . . if it's not an inconvenience, obviously.' He looked at Maggie, who stood up, counting to eight under her breath. 'Margaret?'

'Again, what is it that you want?'

'I have a favour to ask. I know that your shop is currently empty and I was wondering if we could use it to store the costumes and scenery for the nativity. We have the poor murdered girls' funerals this Saturday and we are expecting a record turnout, so we need to make some room.'

'I'm sorry, Henry, but we are in the middle of refurbishment and –'

'It would be a great favour.'

'And the shop opens this Saturday.'

Judy looked up in surprise.

'Oh, I see.'

She smiled awkwardly.

'What sort of shop will it –'

'We're not telling anyone until the great unveiling.'

'I see.'

'What time are the funerals?'

'It's one joint funeral, at two.'

'And the procession, Father, will that be passing though the village or coming via Lee?' Judy asked.

'Through the village.'

Maggie smiled.

⬥⬥⬥⬥⬥⬥⬥⬥⬥

Up on the ladder, the artist was adding dramatic shadow beneath the word 'The'. Below, trying his patience, a small crowd had been gathered for a quarter of an hour or so.

'The' they repeated over and over as, finally, the first word was revealed to them in bold gothic lettering.

'It's a very strange "The".'

'They wouldn't use a "The" like that for a café or a dress shop.'

'No.'

'Blackheath needs a nice new café.'

'Oh yes, or a curtain shop.'

'Oh, that *would* be nice.'

'The one in Greenwich . . .'

'Dreadful, I know.'

The artist continued pencilling in and colouring a large dramatic B. The crowd raised their eyebrows.

'Why can't you just tell us?' someone called impatiently.

'He says there will be a grand unveiling,' an old woman explained.

'Well, what word is this?'

'You'll have to wait and see,' the painter called down.

The crowd moaned collectively.

'It's a very sinister looking B.'

'It's a very sinister looking shop.'

'Bookmakers?'

'Bakery?'

'Brewery?'

'Blacksmiths?'

🙟🙟🙟🙟🙟🙟

'Since you don't remember how you did it, I doubt very much you have developed a talent for it. It was probably the drink or a fluke,' Maggie told her sister when Father Legge left. 'Let it pass before it pulls you in.'

'Oh, and what is it that you have accomplished that affords you such wisdom?'

Maggie glared, pointing to their plates. 'Candle magic, the hens, these eggs.'

Judy laughed. 'Oh really? I think you'll find that the fluke. Besides, it was I who found the hens in your yard, not you.'

Maggie was outraged. 'Well, we will see. Tonight I will do it again. I will bring us . . .'

'A duck?'

Maggie glared at her, storming out of the house in a temper, knowing that the moment her back was turned Judy would be helping herself to her eggs. She stopped, turned and marched back in, catching her sister tipping the eggs onto her plate and said, staring her in the face:

'What is going on with your house? Why do you never go home?'

Judy glared, snatched up her coat and bag and slammed the door behind her.

Arguing their way across the heath, the sisters marched down past the Crown and into the village, stopping at their unfinished sign to inspect it. 'It really is too late to turn back now,' Judy told her and opened the door. Inside, Netta was heaving two enormous sacks up onto the table.

'Four days!' she cursed, just moments later. 'You expect me to have the pair of you trained and this shop up and running in four days!' She shook her head. 'It can't be done. It would take a miracle.' She turned her attention to the sacks, from which she produced horrendous portraits of the dead propped in seats or lying in their coffins.

Custom was that the deceased remained in the home until the funeral, which meant, for many who lived in small homes, sleeping in the same room or even next to the corpse in the same bed for days on end. People cloaked themselves in black to prevent being haunted by the deceased. The curtains were kept closed, clocks were stopped and mirrors were covered. Widows would mourn in black for at least two years and it became their duty to opt for expensive high-end fashion and not be seen in anything dowdy, but, most importantly of all, the dead had to be captured on canvas before burial.

Artists would race against the clock to fit in portrait sittings, sometimes having the family prop their mother or father or relative in a seat, having dressed them in readiness. Some were expensive family portraits, some were just of the deceased – sitting, lying, losing the battle against decay to hang on to their looks until the artist arrived. Often families were distraught at the wait, watching the face they wanted to capture forever become gaunt and distant, the deathly pallor washing out the colour and replacing it with transparent white, sunken eyes, thinning cheeks and blackened lips. But it was disrespectful not to have them drawn, and local artists who drew more portraits of the dead than of newly-weds, dignitaries and the living put together often found, once the paintings were completed, that the family, who could barely afford the funeral, had no money to pay them. Mrs Walters had just bought a heap of unsold portraits at cost. She held up a selection, then, choosing the most disturbing and unpleasant, hung them around the walls.

'I thought you said no pictures?' Judy said.

'No, dear. I simply pointed out that yours were dreadful.'

She produced strange gnarled figurines, ancient boxes and African gravestones brought back by the slave traders of Dartmouth Row, relics brought to England by Ambrose Crawley who had mass-produced the ankle irons and the iron collars for African slaves, many of whom his father had brought back to start new lives in London. Next there were death masks and tribal masks, great long bones from Jamaica, India and Africa brought back and left to fester in attics by the slave drivers themselves, the Innes and the Campbells, again of Dartmouth Row. From Samuel Thomas Fludyer's family at Dacre House came a monstrously large skull from the Caribbean, all bought for a song and a tarot reading. The sisters stared at her as she heaved it all out onto the table, and she paused, eyeing them. 'Too much? Too much.' She fell back into a seat. 'What does the name Mr Bodeving mean to you?'

❧❧❧❧❧❧❧❧❧

In a large rented Victorian drawing room, with its tall ceilings, beautiful carpet and expensive curtains, the sisters waited alongside an excited crowd. The room was dimly lit with two oil lamps at either door and one on the raised platform in front of the small seated audience. On this makeshift stage sat an armchair and several oddly shaped tables, draped with black cloth.

They had been seated for ten minutes or so and those who were not nervous now grew tired of waiting. Slowly the grandfather clock ticked closer to eight. A maid entered the room and closed the curtains and was gone again. The crowd fell silent. Then when the clock struck eight, the door opened and a tall caped man in a top hat entered. He closed the doors dramatically behind him then strode to the stage.

Stepping for a moment behind a screen, he took off his hat and cape, set down his cane and pulled on a strange pointed hood and sinister robe. Then, stepping forward to an audible intake of breath, he reached over to one of the sheets and whisked it up into the air, revealing a cage, inside which two tiny mechanical men shook the bars and walked from corner to corner, peering out.

'Ladies and gentlemen, these are the tiny metal people that live on the moon.'

The crowd, wide-eyed, could barely contain their shock, leaning in, horrified, at their clicking movements and small turning heads.

'Please, don't move too close. They are fascinated by you too, but they must not be approached.'

After a minute or so, he replaced the sheet and lit a pipe, leaning back into the armchair.

'Moon people can only be exposed to our atmosphere for minutes at a time. It is crucial that the special cloth be replaced as quickly as possible.' The audience was spellbound, each wanting a caged moon-man for themselves. Beneath the cloth, the ticking and whirring died. Next, he pulled a sheet from a large box to his left, revealing a tank of murky water with strands of seaweed swaying within. At its centre a lifelike small woman, but with the lower body of a fish, slept.

'Behold the mermaid,' he said, running a finger down the back of the tank. Immediately her head lifted and her eyes opened, peering out at them. 'Mermaids swim in great shoals, they surround ships until they build up such a swirl of water it becomes a whirlpool. *Never!*' he shouted, making everyone jump, 'Never look into her eyes or you will be struck down with terrible illnesses.'

The mermaid flicked her tail, staring around at the faces, which immediately looked away.

'On my travels, I have found many odd things hidden in the unexplored corners of this planet,' Mr Bodeving said, replacing the sheet. 'But what I am about to show you now are some of the most dangerous and strange things seen by mankind. We are not even sure if these things are originally from our world. Experts believe them to belong to the afterlife. The Cloak sisters sat up, watching him move to a tall thin wardrobe. 'It is believed that this box,' he said, dramatically swinging open the door to reveal nothing but an empty space, 'is a place where the dead can communicate with the living. Allow me to demonstrate.'

He closed the door and, laying his hands on it, began to mumble and chant, then, suddenly and slowly, the wardrobe began to creak and move as if something were walking inside. Mr Bodeving quickly opened the door, to the horror of the audience and the terror of the already distraught women, revealing it to be empty.

There was a sigh of relief and he sat for a moment in silence, studying his audience as they watched him expectantly. 'You are a remarkably handsome crowd,' he said, taking a sip of water. 'I could sit and watch you all night. And I am not the only one, it seems. Have you noticed there are others watching you?'

The crowd froze, at first unable to take their eyes from him for fear of seeing something unleashed into the room with them. Then their eyes wandered around the room until a sudden cry drew everyone's attention to a long wall mirror in which a dark figure moved, occasionally coming into view before moving away into darkness. The crowd lurched backwards, those closest jumping from their seats. In the mirror there was now a hand, white and skeletal, beckoning them. A few moments later, a monstrous white corpse-like figure with sunken eyes and cheeks pressed its hands against the black glass and peered out, seeking out eyes with which to lock. It was too much, the room was in panic. Mr Bodeving covered the mirror while a maid rushed to open the door.

'Thank you for coming to see my strange discoveries. I will be returning to the area after my travels to the privative Voodoo Islands in several years' time. That is, of course, if I survive. I hope to see you all again. Good evening.'

The sisters stepped out into the cold night air, exhilarated and eager to talk. 'I would like a moon-man,' Judy confided.

'None of it was real.' Maggie sniffed.

'None of it?'

She shook her head, 'But it was very convincing to the untrained eye. Let's go straight to the shop, I want to make sure Netta didn't send us here on our own so she could put up any more monstrosities.'

They made their way back through Deptford, past the workhouses and up Blackheath Hill. When they reached the top of the steep climb, the heath was dark and milling with a surprising number of people. They hitched a lift on a horse and cart, stepping off at the tea hut, where the proprietress, her gloved hands clutching warm tea, boiled more water.

'There's a lot of fuss brewing about your shop,' she gossiped, pushing them past her inside the narrow kitchen space, where they were unable to move but were relieved by the warmth. 'There are all sorts of rumours. It's going to be an opium den, it's going to be a lodging place. I don't know how many times it's been mentioned to me today and this evening. The sign reads "The Black" so that's got them even more excited. I know it's a secret, but I am hoping for an eel and pie shop. I don't see why Greenwich should have the only one, do you?'

They shook their heads.

'Lots of strangers on the heath tonight. Apparently a girl was chased screaming down towards the village but managed to get away. If you don't mind, ladies, since it's nearly ten, I will close a little early and join you. I don't fancy walking home on my own if he's got it in his head that he's in the mood to murder again.' She closed down the hatch and drew the dozens of bolts across it, then, taking their half-drunk tea cups from them, placed them in the sink, hurried them out and began the ordeal of locking the dozens of locks on the outside that had, thus far, kept it from being burgled for several years.

They cut across the grass, feeling safer as a group, but still sighed with relief when the lights of the village grew close. Here they parted ways and the sisters made their way to the shop, where Netta awaited them.

When they let themselves in, she was nowhere to be seen, but her efforts had transformed what had still had the feel of a shop into a luxurious but sinister sitting room. It looked so remarkably like an expensively furnished parlour that the sisters felt only best clothes, of which they owned very few, would need to be worn there at all times. There was a knock, then another, and the sisters looked around. Then, noticing the black mirror on the wall, they both jumped back, startled. A second later, a cold white hand appeared within it, beckoning, followed by another holding a bottle of wine and three glasses.

Chapter 9

Dinner was an opulent ten courses: bouillon, fried smelts with sauce tartare, potatoes à la maître d'hôtel, sweetbreads, plates with peas, roast turkey with cranberry sauce, Roman punch, quail with truffles and rice croquettes, Parisian salad, crackers and cheese; but it was during the dessert of Nesselrode pudding and fancy cakes that excitement reached entirely new levels. The sounds of horses and the rush of staff was accompanied by the sound of cutlery being replaced immediately on crockery. Women, almost en masse, reached for their make-up mirrors and rushed to the powder rooms, while the men, trying not to look overly enthusiastic, checked their shirts and jackets for spillages and drips before leaning back casually in their seats and nodding to each other.

Seemingly the only person unaware of the count and countess's arrival was Lady Beatrice Dartmouth, who, having just put a large forkful of pudding into her mouth, craned her neck when a member of staff whispered in her ear. She covered her mouth with her napkin and swallowed quickly, rising and leaving the room in a swish of white elegance.

Through the open front door she saw the doors of the empty carriage being closed and hurried up the stairs to the private quarters where the butler had taken the new arrivals. Then, composing herself, she let herself in.

Inside, the countess, tall and breathtakingly fashionable, in an outfit so tight and bold no Englishwoman would dare to wear it, moved across the room from portrait to portrait sipping from a glass of wine. At the fireplace, his back to the flames, facing her, stood the count, equally as fine in a suit worn in a tighter and more youthful style than those she had seen before. He looked across as she entered, his eyes warm, sparkling and dark, and almost tinged – she thought, captivated by them – with a desire for her. She blushed. His beauty, as foretold, was something remarkable. Initially she had seen just one aspect of it but within moments he seemed to shine like a prism. His mouth was strong and masculine, yet had full, almost feminine lips, or perhaps just lips that drew the eye and kept the gaze lingering. Beneath thick dark glossy hair was a strong brow, perhaps concerned or troubled or vulnerable, and then the eyes; it was the eyes that made people feel safe and loved and befriended, that scattered their thoughts and let their blood run a little quicker and made them feel that the world was, just at that moment, opening up for them, that they had found him and he had found them, and that there was, in that exchange of smiles, unexpectedly, an unbearable, all-consuming love.

'His eyes will tell you he is in love with you, and you will fall for it. And when you have fathomed them, they will only warm and change into something else to convince you all over again he is falling in love with you and you with him,' the countess had told Anna. 'You must know that this is not so. This is something he cannot help. You must spare him the ordeal of trying to be in love with him as they all do.'

The handsome young count gazed at the sixty-six year old, who felt in that moment, spellbound and dizzy and young. He bowed to her and holding out a strong hand into which she slipped her gloved fingers, introduced himself.

She could remember only that moment, despite exchanging pleasantries and talking business. She accepted their startlingly generous donation with the perfect mix of professional coolness and sincere heartfelt appreciation, taking the time to explain, as interestingly as these matters could be explained, how a donation of such significance would change many things for many people, saving not only lives but making Blackheath a safer, healthier and more attractive place to live.

The count watched her, listening contently, then with a smile, he took her hand again and kissed it, explaining that he had full trust in her and that he looked forward to seeing what she was capable of achieving with it, and perhaps in the future, working together from time to time. She became aware that her eyes had not left his for several minutes and that her mouth could well be wide open or her body slumped – though, of course it was not – and reddened again. Hoping that he had not noticed such girlish behaviour, which she had not indulged in since . . . she tried to remember. Then, aware of her silence, brought herself to her senses.

'I must announce your arrival.'

'Please,' the countess said, touching her arm. 'No announcements. We will simply mingle and introduce ourselves.'

Lady Dartmouth nodded.

'But perhaps, before I go through, you could show me the rest of this beautiful house.'

'Oh!' Lady Dartmouth said, startled, 'I would love to but it is not mine. It is home to the Princess Sophia Matilda.' She lowered her tone wickedly. 'But I suppose we could have just a little look.'

The countess took her arm and together they glided through the upper rooms with their views over the park and the heath.

'You and the princess are great friends? Do tell me about her,' the countess asked.

Lady Dartmouth smiled; nothing could be further from the truth, but she nodded. 'She is the daughter of George III's brother. She is a quiet, retiring young woman, rather plain.'

The count entered the ballroom alone. He had hoped to slip in unnoticed, perhaps take in the atmosphere for a moment or two, but all eyes were on the door and a drum roll from the orchestra and a loud announcement from the doorman left him feeling the absence of his sister, who, because the crowds favoured her brother, preferred to make her own impact a little later.

It was several long moments before anyone approached him. The crowd, like Lady Dartmouth, without realising time was passing, stood and stared until the band, tucked away in the far corner, began a light waltz and people took hold of themselves. The mood of the room had suddenly changed utterly. Several of the men became concerned at their wives' sudden doe-eyed appreciation and uncommunicativeness. Cleavages were tugged into prominence, faces seemed to find youthful form, smiles appeared far more sincere and filled with happiness than had been seen in years, but mostly, it was the eyes – the total slavish devotion of women's eyes, that barely strayed from the count's face, that no longer gave priority to a husband's warning tones and disapproval – that troubled the men most. There was something new in their wives that led them away from the tables to the dance floor, closer to him.

There, at its centre, a crowd began to form; women, oblivious to their watchful husbands, who, pretending that they were dancing or just standing having a look around, were gathering unaware of the spectacle they were creating, each wanting to get closer.

The count was taken under the wing of a portly pipe smoker, a Mr James Glaisher who had recently invented weather forecasting and was eager to tell anyone who would listen, how he, a simple man from number 20 Blackheath Hill had transformed the world forever. He walked the young count around the periphery of the dance floor, introducing him to the men and the occasional woman who was kept under stricter rule or simply did not find anyone or anything attractive, and yet even in the coldest, a little warmth and sparkle returned to their worried and tired eyes. The crowd at the centre of the room turned like the hands of a clock, following him with their eyes.

Men too, it seemed, were a little entranced by him. They could not deny he was handsome, but they were mostly impressed by his masculinity, his experience, travel and knowledge. For someone so young, he was refreshingly wise and mature. He was, after all, just past his mid-twenties but able to hold conversations with men of significantly older years on topics that left even those who boasted worldly wisdom silent. They took him aside, brought him wine and cigars, and, forming a wall with their backs that kept the women out, missed the arrival of the countess.

Her own impact on the room was somewhat different. Tall and strong with a physical confidence more common to males than females, she drew audible gasps from the women, who, taken aback at her dark narrow skirt, which lacked the bulky underskirts or hoops that were becoming all the rage, could only stare open-mouthed. When she took off her cape, she revealed a basque of such opulence, and diamonds of such circumference and sparkle that even the diamond miners themselves took sharp inward breaths. Her bare shoulders drew different eyes, and her long toned arms on which long white lace gloves displayed opulent bracelets transfixed even those with jewellery collections envied by royalty. Around her exposed neck alone hung rubies of such enormous size and clarity that if sold, Blackheath itself could be purchased. The women drew closer with fearful fascination, their minds teetering on the edge of what they understood to be fashion and what they considered tantamount to scandal.

Those uninterested in the rare stones were shocked to see the brazen way in which the tops of her dark firm breasts were exposed. Indeed, were it not for her reputation, many doubted that she would have been allowed to enter. Her enormous dark hair, tall and tumbling, would be the talk of the papers by the weekend.

The count, becoming aware of the turning of heads, came to greet her and took her hand. Both men and women's eyes followed their every move, the women breathing in his cologne, excited by his closeness, wanting him to notice them, to take them aside, to seduce them, to untie their corsets and let their soft white flesh tumble into his strong dark hands, the men spellbound by a femaleness they had never seen the like of before.

The count summoned Mr Glaisher, the weather forecaster, and taking the countess's arm, the elderly gent escorted her around the tables to repeat introductions with the powerful and the rich. With her hand in theirs, she lifted her long, long lashes and showed them her dark inviting eyes. One by one, appeared the boys each man had once been. There for her to see beyond the façade of adulthood was their shyness, their anger and ambition, their quick tempers; and beyond that, rising up to the surface, their desire and their inner quirks, the little daydreams and fantasies that no one knew. And when they saw the secrets that had passed between them glow in her eyes, they too blushed.

When she had been introduced to those that mattered and was allowed to relax, she noticed that the men around her were distracted; their ties were loosened and their consumption of wine quickened. She reached for a glass herself and, leaning back on a chair, watched them try to impress her as if she herself was the head of the pack.

One by one, unconsciously, each man of the group forgot the person he had become with age, regressing back to the ages that made them feel anything was possible and everything lay ahead. Aware again of the energy of their twenties, their late teens, embracing the long-lost enthusiasm of the men they had been on the sports field, by the excitement of the physical, of the unknown, by lust. Seated around her, she watched them talk as though filled with fresh determination, like boys ready to become men.

She surprised them with talk of sport and business and they felt, as well as desiring her with every hot breath, a camaraderie reserved strictly for male friends. It confused them; although she was voluptuous and every inch a beautiful female, she woke in them an admiration some men have for older brothers, in whom they trust to take control, with whom they can allow themselves to become weak but then the illusion became confused with lust. Rising in each grew a need to compete with each other to gain her attention.

The orchestra, moving the evening along, struck up with Henry Russell's 'There's a Good Time Coming' and the polka but to their surprise, despite these being the most popular dances of the year, no one approached the dance floor. The room was divided, each group gravitating to either the count or the countess and when, finally, Lady Dartmouth took the count's hand and led him away from the ladies whose clothing had loosened considerably, which could be excused on this occasion because of the confusion over the countess's new style, the men weighed each other up, readying themselves to be the one to ask the countess to dance. But she had considered this already, and taking the hand of a young, rather naive boy who was not yet considered an adult by many, she swept him onto the dance floor, despite his resistance, offending no one and keeping every man's hopes very much alive. Married couples, rather dishevelled and embarrassed at seeing each other again, given their blatant desire for someone else, joined them, and so began the swirling battle of who could brush up against the objects of everyone's desire.

At two o'clock in the morning, when the ball showed no sign of winding down, Lady Dartmouth ordered the cellar to send up two dozen bottles of wine and an ale barrel which was rolled through to the welcoming room, and the orchestra was paid to stay on. There were jackets and ties and shoes, waistcoats and purses left in piles on chairs and although the count and countess had moved themselves away from the crowd to more conversational tables, a visit to the dance floor had the effect of bringing the swaying room to an even more heightened state. There was kissing and touching and the loosening of corsets, buttons torn, collars removed, breasts and chests peeped past unhooked shirts, hands roamed - and often not over their own spouses. Steamy breath joined steamy breath out in the icy cold of the silent park, secret liaisons in kitchens were interrupted, carriage staff and maids saw behaviour in their superiors that evening that they dare not acknowledge.

At three, slipping as discreetly as they could out into the front courtyard, the count and countess wandered out on to the heath and home to listen, from their beds, to the sound of laughter and music continuing deep into the night.

Chapter 18

'Despite running a sweetshop all these years – ever since you were girls, you have religiously acknowledged the spirit world and you have been actively in touch with the dead since birth,' Mrs Walters told the two women. 'That's your story, stick to it.'

It was Thursday. There were just two days to go before the sign was revealed and the doors opened for business, and she was panicking. Neither of the women showed the slightest hint of ability since Judy's now highly suspicious breakthrough at the cemetery, which was beginning to appear more as a fluke, a drunken fantasy or wishful thinking, Even with the tarot they drew blanks. Disaster was in the air.

'Today, we are going to conduct an experiment,' she announced, and took Maggie down into the cellar, where a desk, chair, tarot cards, a candle and nothing else waited. She locked her in. Judith was taken up into the attic where a seat at a table and a crystal ball and nothing else waited. Once both were locked in, Mrs Walters announced in a loud voice that she would be back in six hours, locked up the shop and returned home to put her feet up.

Her plan had been to keep a low profile, to look after the séances, where, disguised by make-up, she needn't draw attention to herself. The sisters, Judy especially, seemed to crave the limelight, which Mrs Walters was more than happy to surrender to her. But despite days of training, she doubted either sister could manage a game of snap, let alone tarot. And now the shop was to open with them unprepared, with herself its only chance of its survival. She was putting herself in danger, and it frightened her. She had been through too much. There were still families who blamed her, and, after the court case, thought she had been put to death as the judge had ordered. If they discovered her alive and well . . .

She allowed herself to think of it again for the first time in decades, and it brought back immediately, and with startling clarity, first light on the eighteenth of May, 1808.

In a degrading uniform, with her hands chained behind her back, she was led through a light drizzle along the docks at Falmouth. A yell brought her to a halt. Behind her, chained to her, the other ninety-eight women were silent, shaking with fear. They looked up at the colossal *Speke-I* waiting in port for them, its mouth open, sailors climbing all over it, porters carrying stock and luggage onboard while others herded goats and pigs as wild eyed and frightened as the prisoners onboard. A shrill whistle that straightened the spine announced the arrival of a man who stirred fear even in the officers. He strode down from the ship towards them, nodding to the officers nearest Netta. They examined paperwork and counted heads. Several prisoners were pointed out during quieter discussions and the fearsome man eyed them. Then the officers signed over their lives to him – the towering Mr Hingston, master of the ship.

The women were expecting to be addressed by him, to listen to his harsh words of warning, but he said nothing, barely acknowledging their presence. They were nothing to him, just livestock under his command. Many would die; some would be thrown overboard to feed the sharks; some would remain so timid and hidden that he wouldn't even be aware of them; but they would all go through hell down there.

Netta was pulled forward, aware of her foot lifting and leaving England and the next finding footing on swaying wood. She was on the deck, the cool morning wind sweeping her face, then she stepped inside, climbing down and down, past the decks where the rich from their small but comfortable mahogany-lined cabins peered out at them or closed their doors to blank out their existence. Netta Walters stared defiantly at the faces who watched her. She would not put up with mockery or threatening behaviour. If they wanted to see a murderer, she would give them the whole show. She continued down towards the dark bowels of the ship.

In the holds, crowded together deep in the dark, the women scratched at the floors to gather up the remains of the Australian wool that had filled the space before, until finally the door slammed above them and they were alone. Netta took stock of her emotions.

'No crying,' she warned herself. 'If this is what you've got to get used to, you get used to it. You either sit here and cry or you rule the bloody roost.' She looked at the curved wooden walls, felt the chill of the water around and beneath her and listened to the screaming and pleading and crying of women who would never see their families and babies again. She was lucky to be with them. Had it not been for her aunt Winnie who had contacts and had read tarot for many of the judge's wives and had demanded time with those in power to prove her innocence, she would by now be dead. A deal had been struck, though Netta was unaware of the details, and, without warning, on the morning of the thirteenth of May, 1808, she was taken from her cell ahead of her execution, chained up and transported out of London.

There were more people down in the hold than was comfortable or sensible. The air was sour and warm. To her relief, she had managed to secure herself a space against a wall, chained to the more sane-looking criminals, or so she thought.

Long hours passed before there was movement and then, bidding goodbye to England and to her family, Netta closed her eyes and planned revenge. There were his parents; they had been as shocked as she. They knew she hadn't done it but they let her take the blame. Then there was him, Norman. She had a good mind to murder him to see how he liked being on the receiving end of it. Then there was the judge, who thought he saw everything clearly and couldn't be swayed from his initial opinion. Psychic visions, he explained, were usually the result of a womb imbalance and an over-imaginative sexual appetite, but in her case, it was plainly a confession.

The ship moved away from the land until they felt a sudden change in motion, the dip, the swell as it moved out to deeper waters. They were gone; prostitutes and thieves banished from Britain to an island filled with prisoners. Closing her eyes again, the scene came back to her, the brutal punches, the hysteria of the girl realising what the situation was, her helplessness and pleading. She shook it from her mind, meditated it away, concentrated and summoned other voices. There were lots of voices aboard that ship, too many, but she had time and she needed all the help she could get.

❧❧❧❧❧❧❧❧

At ten, Mrs Walters woke with a start in the glow of the dying fire. She hadn't meant to sleep. She was meant to be back at the shop by seven. There was still a cup of cold tea in her hand and she drank it in two gulps, hurrying to the door while pulling on her coat. She made her way up the road to Blackheath. There was a mist tonight, thick and watery, that went straight to the lungs and made them ache. In the distance, a ship's horn echoed through south London as it pulled into Greenwich. There were women rushing with bright red lipstick and revealing dresses, too late to greet the men stepping from the sea into London, but not too late to find them in the pubs, drunken and excited and generous.

Mrs Walters tutted as another group rushed past, jostling her as she began the descent into the village where a group of official-looking men stood at its heart, measuring and pointing, talking about the building of a train station.

'Where?' she asked.

'Right here,' they replied.

She nodded and hurried to the shop. Turning the key in the lock, she hurled herself at the door and lit a candle.

'It's all right. I'm back.'

She found Maggie, blinking and furious in the dark. Her candle had blown out over six hours ago and her rage was wildly out of control, but Judy, who had some light through the window from the street, was still staring into the ball and had barely noticed how much time had passed. She grinned when they entered.

'I can do it!' she told them proudly. 'I really can do it and I can do it easily. I understand it.'

Mrs Walters, overjoyed, kissed her and turned to Maggie expectantly. 'How did you do?'

Maggie stared at her furiously.

❧❧❧❧❧❧❧❧❧

They were drunk, falling from the steps of the Hare and Billet with lanterns swinging, then, bidding goodnight to Mrs Walters, the sisters made their way across the heath. Throwing caution to the wind, they dismissed the rule to walk silently and in darkness, and, laughing, told stories of how they would win at horse races. They enjoyed the fanciful talk of being rich, stepping out as ladies in society, wearing fine dresses and expensive shoes and having gentlemen acknowledge and desire them, and of maids that cleaned their homes and a carriage that collected them from the village each night.

At the centre of the heath, where the bracken was thickest and it was easy for those up to no good to hide and observe, the sound of someone running sobered them. They hurried to extinguish their lamps and changed the direction they were heading in. But the sound kept growing closer until they could hear panting. They were alarmed, clutching each other for safety, looking around, but the darkness was so complete, nothing could be seen, they could barely see each other. The footsteps sounded closer still and suddenly slowed to a walk. The women began to panic, looking at each other for direction. He was coming straight for them, getting closer, his breathing hard, recovering from exertion. They changed direction again, heading towards the house, hurrying, but they were noisy, their dresses rustled. His panting stopped.

'Where are you?' A loud, aggressive voice broke the silence and darkness with such force that both women felt weak. 'I know you are here.'

The sisters were still, holding each other.

'Come on, ladies!' he laughed, 'You know I will have you tonight.'

They turned, holding hands, creeping away, gathering speed, looking for the light, any light, there was always a light somewhere, but it was late, they could see nothing.

They were in the exact centre of the heath, Maggie realised. The point where you could see neither the lights you had left nor the lights ahead. There was not a more dangerous and vulnerable spot.

'I HEAR YOU!' he shouted again, so close that both women jumped to one side. There was silence. The women dared not move a muscle. 'I saw your lamps. I know you are hiding here. Let me see if I can hear your breathing.'

The footsteps began again, so close to them they could have reached out and touched him.

'Two little ladies. Out alone at night. All alone on the bleak heath,' he called. 'Where is my knife?' There was rustling and a laugh. 'Here it is. Now, where is my lantern?'

The sisters were shaking, waiting for the sparks of light that would show them to him. There would be a fight, endless moments of terror and fear and proper, real fighting to save their lives.

'I hear you!' the voice said suddenly, penetrating the darkness. 'I heard the rustle of a dress. Fast little breaths. I can hear that you are frightened.'

They were still, barely moving their eyes.

'I'm coming for you. Two more to add to my collection. Your house keys in my pocket,' he sang, but his voice was moving in a different direction, and when it grew fainter, the women walked, very quietly, though the darkness until there was enough distance between themselves and the stranger for them to break into a run.

In the garden, Maggie hurried with the key, thrusting it in the lock, turning it, barely daring to look over her shoulder.

'Hurry!' Judy pleaded.

They were inside, their chests heaving and hands shaking.

'We must never cross the heath in the dark again. Not until that lunatic has been caught. It's too dangerous now.'

Judy nodded, reaching for two glasses and taking a bottle of nettle wine down from a shelf as Maggie lit the lamps and started a fire.

'We must inform the police. Tell them everything.'

In bed that night, Maggie's sleep was fitful, filled with events from the day – the tarot, the darkness in the cellar, the maniac on the heath, her nervousness about the shop. She tossed and turned, moaning and mumbling, then suddenly she was awake, sitting bolt upright, staring at the door, which had come off the latch. The latch was strong with a deep well, it would not have slipped. Then suddenly there was an eye, staring right at her. She jolted, turned quickly to snatch up the lamp and the flint, and when she looked again the door had opened wider. The outline of a head was in view, the hair shaved here and there in patches as if it had been self-cut during a period of lunacy.

The moon showed only the barest features, the side of a gaunt white face, and now a mouth, sliding slowly into view, curling into a crazy grin, and that eye which refused to look away and stared deep into her own. She could not move, she wanted to scream, call her sister, hurl the lamp at it. Instead it rolled from her hand and crashed onto the floor and a cold white hand curled around the door as it creaked open a little more.

She sat, holding her breath, unable to take her eyes from the hate in the eye that watched her. The stillness of the figure that had not moved now for a minute, five minutes, six, was unbearable. Maggie felt her heart pounding, her pulse race, then suddenly the door was flung wide open and like an animal the figure sprung into the air and she screamed and screamed and woke.

Klaus Van Dayne carried his two children from the surgery, putting the young count and countess in separate incubators. He had not expected twins and they were both such fine healthy babies that he felt proud for the first time. Other children had been born so weak and fragile but this time, thanks to a strong healthy, well-bred mother, the offspring were strong and ready to stretch and grow as fast as possible. They were given sunshine and fresh air, nutritious breast milk, staff who exhausted them with mental and physical stimulation. They were happy babies.

For two months they were given four hours a day with their mother, who, happy and recovered, enjoyed the finest stimulation, alongside a strict diet of abundant raw fish served with seasoning which helped them grow strong. She too was proud of the children she had carried. Then one morning, she woke with a start; something was wrong. She was exhausted and weak, and looking down, she saw that her left arm had been amputated.

The operations had begun. She was confined, bound tightly to her bed, only leaving to exercise and wash while sedated enough not to flee. Several times a day while she sat with her head forced to look away, Van Dayne held the children to her breasts to feed and on the days where the children were tired or recovering from operations, he simply milked her into a jug.

Sleeping next to them in the laboratory and awaking to monitor them hourly, Van Dayne's vigilance with the children was obsessive. His lack of sleep led to endless headaches. To break the monotony he took endless walks around the empty building, each empty corridor making him more aware of his loneliness. The mother of his twins had been by far the most stimulating company he had enjoyed for over a year but she was no longer to be engaged with. She was now his medical subject, nothing more.

Often he would visit the other women who lived quietly in the maternity wing, each in varying states of pregnancy, happy and oblivious of what was to come and what had happened over and over to the women that had preceded them. He would spend the occasional evening there, enjoying with them the good food and comfort. The women were happy and warm, well fed and safer than they would be at home in their icy villages.

Occasionally, he would venture into these small villages for supplies and to lure the woman of his choice away with offers of money, bringing her to his rooms where they made love until he had done his utmost to get her pregnant and was given a home or if she did not catch, was discarded. All of these women that lived there with him did not question his need for children. They were happy to become pregnant and live in his strange regime enjoying the food and company of other women of the same mind. Even those outraged by his refusal of romance and marriage offered themselves to him rather than be turned out into the hard Siberian winter.

When the first muscle grafts took, and the bones he had added to the children's backs began to move upwards of their own, or rather, of the children's accord, so they could roll back more easily onto their backs, he prepared for their second operation.

Their mother woke screaming, her head falling to her left shoulder where it lay, devoid of the muscle to raise it. She moved her eyes, looked at her right arm and saw it lying thin and flat, emptied of bone and muscle. Her shock and anger were finding new forms of madness; her brain unable to comprehend his insanity or accept her trap. There she lay, tended by him twice a day, the boneless stretch of arm massaged, her hygiene and nourishment attended to with great care rigorous detail. Her head was propped up between two blocks that he had fitted to the headboard.

'Why are you doing this? What are you?' she asked over and over.

He watched her sadly. 'It is necessary. Our children will be the first.'

'Leave my children alone. Don't harm them.'

'They are loved. I will bring them to you when they are older.'

'Are you finished with me now? Is this all you need from me? Or will there be more operations like this?'

He looked at her coolly, 'There will be many more.'

She did not react. He watched her tears form and swell and tip from her eyes. He mopped them from her face.

'I want to see my parents.'

'They are healthy. I saw them just three days ago. They were chopping logs.'

'Bring them to me. I must see them one last time.'

He caressed her hair and smiled. 'No. No one can come here. It will be just you and me until you pass.'

The bones stripped from the second arm were laid next to the muscles, veins, arteries, gristle and joints. On the operating table the boy lay face downwards, his back peeled open. Van Dayne watched his breathing as the incisions brought him to the shoulder blade into which, using a hand drill, he made the first of three holes, weaving through them muscle and joint. With a close eye he sewed muscle to muscle, attached vein to vein, joined the artery to the blood supply, watching the organs fill with colour as the blood filtered through. He injected more of the boy's mother's blood into his arm, filling his expanded body with nourishment. Then attaching the bone and tendon, he tugged at the muscle and watched the new addition bend at the elbow. Finally, unfolding a sheet of skin he had taken from her now bandaged legs, he spread it wide over the wound, sewing in an excess of it, allowing the extra limbs space beneath the baggy scrotum-like flesh to writhe and jerk and learn movement.

When the boy woke, confused and in pain, his father administered what little pain relief medicine he had left until the next supplies were delivered, and sat vigilant at his bedside.

The girl took to it quicker, healing in record time, though her pain due to the lack of medicine was often intoxicating and drove her deep into troubled sleep. Exhausted, Van Dayne had little option other than to take a nurse from his official wing and bring her into his confidence. She was instructed firmly that they could not be touched, let alone moved or made comfortable. They suffered, he had said, from a highly contagious disease, transmitted by touch that could be carried on clothes. She was simply to observe them and to wake him should there be need. For an entire year the nurse never once saw beneath their heavily bandaged backs.

At the age of two, the nurse was brought back in once more to stimulate them. She was told of the deformities each were born with: the severed triplet, the exposed spine, the extra ribs; how neither she nor they must never, not ever, not even for one second, peel back the bandages to let air touch the wounds. Obeying this, the children reached the age of three with more stimulation than most six-year-olds had received in all their years. They were bright, communicative and hungry to learn. It was then, approaching the age of four, while they familiarised themselves with subjects far beyond their years, that their mother, little more than a living body that produced milk and ate well, was prepared for the final operations.

She was wheeled towards the surgery by him on a bright warm summer afternoon. As they moved down the corridors what was left of her gazed up at his face. For the first time in a year, she tried to speak but the muscles around her throat were no longer attached to anything and could not pull and contract to operate the jaw.

'Let this be the end,' she prayed. 'Let it be over.' And she surrendered to the painful incisions by opening her mind to death, calling to it, begging God to collect her.

When she woke, unable to scream, what little sanity remained died in a series of hard shocks. Her legs were gone – she knew that without looking. But there was more, something else. Death was close now, she had not imagined it would make itself known to her in such a way but it was all around her, like a new sense was opening up to her. Suddenly she was also aware that Van Dayne was sitting there with her. He was telling her that the operation had been a success. She looked at him without expression, barely able to breathe.

He had taken away her ribcage, replacing it with a sturdy metal frame that allowed the heart to lift and fall and the lung to expand. He had needed to take a kidney too. And while he hadn't needed the hip, while he was operating, a notion had occurred to him, that from it, with some experimentation, he might find a way to replicate her bone marrow with it, so he removed that too.

He could not allow himself to become emotional. He was a scientist. His work dictated her treatment. His results spoke for themselves and his latest project; his own children, would force science ahead in leaps. His children would become the envy of every living soul.

Exhausted but excited, he retired to bed, leaving the children sealed in their glass boxes under the watchful eye of their nurse. At five, he awoke in a panic. The nurse was hammering on his bedroom door.

'There are noises!' she said, hurrying with him down the corridors, 'Screaming, coming from along the corridor.'

He ordered her away, out of earshot, unlocked the door with the heavy key that he kept on him at all times and rushed in, shielding his ears from her terrible noise. Putting his tired his hand over the mother's mouth he tried to silence her but the screaming continued. Her eyes were wild and frightened, her breath heaving. He needed her alive. 'Just two more months!' he pleaded. 'Please hold on, for your children's sakes!'

But the colour drained from her face, the throbbing in the vein beneath her right eye ceased and her lips parted, becoming a lifeless grey. She took on an icy stare, her skin becoming waxy, sunken and damp. Then in an instant she lay there with the look of someone long dead. He buried his face in his hands, for the first time lost. Looking up again, he saw with confusion the colour return to her face. There was a gentle breath, for a moment the flicker of an eyelid, then they opened, the pupils distant and clouded, the sharp clear blue now a blubbery, waterlogged white, and looking at him with spite, she let go.

He cursed her, holding his tired head. Then, hurrying out of the room, he woke the nurse, ordering her to set up the surgery, to bring light and hot water and cloths and to wake the servants and send them down to the lake for ice and to keep it coming until they had plenty.

When she was gone, he dragged her body onto the trolley, surprised at how light it was, and hurried it back to the operating room. For the remainder of the night and late into the morning, he cut away, folding and preserving the skin in large sheets, draining blood into large glass bottles. He rolled lengths of veins around long spherical tubes, placed the liver and the heart and other organs into ice-baths. Then he set to work on the head. There was little he could use but he took the brain and the eyes and the workings of the inner ear. Then with just the face, skull and hair left, feeling suddenly an uncharacteristic obligation both to her and to her children, he wrapped the head in a cloth, carried it past the jumping dogs waiting for scraps in the yard, and buried it in the small plot where his parents lay. This was where he often relaxed when the weather was warm and where he planned to be buried himself.

'You see,' he told himself, 'I am not devoid of emotion.'

The final operations were frantic. The larger bones were fastened directly to the children's rib cages and collar bones, the other ends of which he connected to those already successfully grafted on and fully operational. Onto these were added another longer bone to give it the required length, and then he began on the extremities, adding from the donor's ribcage, hands and feet the smaller bones that would add width. Joints were shaved down to accommodate a new altered movement and to accommodate their small growing bodies. With the organs in ice, and Van Dayne already exhausted from many hours of dissection, he had had no option other than to operate on the children immediately. He joined veins to arteries, fed blood through them and watched it fill the new muscle, stopping them from perishing.

With the bones, muscle and ligaments in place, he unfolded and cut the sheets of skin into shape, stitching the veins, repairing severed nerves before attaching the great folds to the children's backs and securing them to the limbs so that for the first time they would be free of restriction, limbs in their own right. All the time he prayed that their little bodies were strong enough to survive.

The boy was completed, holding on with a strong heart, allowing his father to set to work on the girl. Hungry and exhausted but aware that this one day, these very hours required his fullest attention, he wiped down the operating table and strapped his daughter into the restraints. A mistake now *would undo years of work.*

His need for more blood overruled the necessity to work alone, and, cursing under his breath, he called for his nurse. She brought water, blood, ice, kept the candlelight strong, offered him food which he longed for but dare not eat for fear of the lethargy that would follow it. And then, through the blood and skin and clamps, there was a movement and then another, and something stretched up into the air, high over Van Dayne's head. The nurse stopped and stared and saw what he was doing.

Chapter 11

Maggie and Judy sat before a policeman in Greenwich police station. They had recounted their ordeal three times, each version more dramatic than the previous one, until he closed his notebook with a slap. He pointed out with regret that as they had no description, no height or hair colour or distinguishing marks, and as they had described his accent as London, they had been of little use. They smiled.

Outside, they parted ways, Maggie returning home and Judy, having concocted an excuse to get away, hurrying towards the market. Here, from her bag, she produced an odd collection of trinkets, a puppet of some strange animal, a compass and a brass bell. She took them from stall to stall, comparing the offers, until finally, settling on a sum she considered reasonable, she parted with them and began to haggle over prices to assemble the evening meal.

When she got in, Maggie watched her put the bag of groceries on the table and lifted it up, peering in.

From inside it she lifted out onions, potatoes and bread, cheese and butter, flour, pork and sausages. She turned in shock. 'Whose is this?'

'Ours.'

'Where did it come from?'

Judy froze. 'I . . . I found it.'

'But it's your bag.'

'Yes.'

'And there's a receipt, with your name on it.'

She fussed busily, ignoring her.

'Judy, where did this money come from? How did you afford –'

'I found it.'

'You found money?'

She stopped. 'Candle magic.'

'No!'

She nodded.

Maggie giggled loudly, clapping as she pulled out a large bottle of port.

She chopped up the pork and put it into the water with apples, onions and vegetables. The thought of eating proper food and not just eggs gave her energy comparable to the time she had eaten an entire box of sugar mice in one sitting. She built up a good fire, poured the port into a jug so it could breathe and set down a fresh tablecloth, then gathered her sister's novel into a tidy pile and set it on the cabinet. It was growing to quite a size.

It was the evening before the opening of their parlour. Maggie felt a little guilty celebrating their luck without Mrs Walters, but things were nice as they were, like old times, just herself and Judy and a large bottle of port. It would be an evening of gossip and drunken laughter. When the stew was ready, she called her sister from the spare room, where she had retreated for an afternoon nap, and ladled up. A minute later she called again, and when there was no reply, she realised something was wrong. Knocking, she opened the door to an empty bed.

On the heath, Judy was rushing, her dress blowing up around her and her hair flying into her eyes. She was late, she knew it, and cursed herself for not taking her leave with an excuse – a sickly neighbour, a forgotten shawl. But Maggie was so thorough, so intent on hearing everything in such detail, it was impossible to avoid scrutiny and slip-ups. It had been her surprising good fortune that Maggie had chosen to believe in candle magic, so the questions about where the money (and the chickens) really came from were not pursued further.

Lifting the latch of the gate and slipping around the back of the house, she climbed onto a crate and, taking off her shoes, struggled in through the window. Then she took off her bonnet and her layers and hurried into bed. She listened to her sister moving about and called out to her. Maggie opened the door and peered in.

'Have I been asleep long?' she asked innocently.

They ate, relishing each mouthful, toasting their good fortune with the last of their sparkling gold home-made summer cider.

'Next year,' Maggie told her sister, 'we really must invest in another apple tree to double our output.'

Judy reminded her that, by the winter of the following year, they would both probably be rich and able to afford anything that took their fancy. This sort of flighty talk both excited and worried Maggie. As a child she had had such a rich imagination. The sisters would play for hours together, embellishing games in which their dolls explored imaginary magical kingdoms. Then, one day, Maggie's imagination died and was gone forever. She marked the occasion with a very strange episode in which she downgraded an exotic palace in a land of plenty to a workhouse that her doll ruled with a fair but firm hand. And there was no looking back.

As girls, Maggie had been the apple of her father's eye and Judy the apple of no one's. While Judy would spend hours running errands for their mother, or working at her shop helping to stitch shoes, doing anything she could to get herself noticed, Maggie appeared to have it all. She spent summers at the allotment with her father, would wait for him at the end of every day at the windmill on the heath and rush to him when he appeared, dusty and grey from the slate mines. He loved her.

When he left England to work in the diamond mines in Africa, the thirteen-year-old Maggie was devastated. They had waved him off at Southampton on the big ship and he had vowed to return in exactly two years. Maggie had counted the days religiously while Judy had simply turned her attention elsewhere and forgotten him. The two years passed and he did not return then, nor did he ever. But Maggie would hear nothing said against him. Often, still, Judy would find herself pointing out that the memories of the man belonged not only to Maggie but to them both. But her older sister would have none of it and still harboured the fantasy that, despite being over seventy years old by now, he might still turn up. And if he did, even though she wanted to vent her anger at him, she wouldn't; she would fall at his feet and be once again completely happy. Judy took this slavish devotion to be the stumbling block in her sister's development.

Because of him, Maggie grew bitter and angry and lost interest in everything. For every reason to do something, she would have ten reasons not to, and most maddening of all, there grew in her a need to keep everything just so, as if her every breath anticipated his return. The *buts* and the *what-ifs* and the fear of letting go stopped her from going ahead with any plan. With this hesitancy she closed her life down around her. In her twenties there was little ambition. She stuck to a routine: each day, each season, each year was indistinguishable from the one before. She had a notion that her life might yet be saved by some outside force, but certainly not by her. Patience rather than action was all that was needed. Her father's abandonment had made her a glutton for sloth.

Judy took these thoughts to the sink, where she washed up and looked out at the darkening heath. The windmill was turning, people were returning home after working a long day burrowing deep under Kent, the watchers were gathered at the corner, discussing who would lay in wait where for the murderer. Across the heath at the Ranger's House, maids were lighting the windows with oil lamps, and, just then, a large carriage drawn by horses with the royal emblem stopped before it.

'She's back!' Judy called, stepping aside for her sister to watch with her as Princess Sophia Matilda, the new ranger of Greenwich, stepped out onto the gravel.

'Fancy another princess living in Blackheath!' Maggie said, clapping her hands. 'Though I've not heard of this one. Is she a proper princess?'

Judy shrugged.

Gossip at the tea hut had it that she was a fan of the game of golf. The sisters had stared at the proprietress blankly.

'It is the hitting of a small ball with a stick by those who enjoy gentle strolling,' she explained.

'It doesn't sound much like a sport,' Judy conjectured.

'It sounds dangerous to me,' Maggie disapproved. 'There should be restrictions.'

'Apparently we shall be known,' the tea hut owner insisted, 'as Blackheath, the home of golf.'

'Well, I hope all these people with their little balls and vicious sticks also own glaziers,' Maggie said, shaking her head. 'It was bad enough when they decided the rules of rugby on the heath.'

The women looked at her.

The princess and her entourage entered the building for an evening of unadulterated gas-lit luxury as the last rays of sunlight drifted away on the heath. Excitedly, Maggie poured out two large goblets of rich thick port.

An hour or so of conversation passed, the port and cider driving the sisters from mundane conversation to a state of babbling laughter. Drunkenness brought out the best in them; even Maggie forgot her limits and became bold and fearless, with a humour rarely seen by anyone.

'I think,' Judy said, 'that you should be introduced to possible suitors when you are drunk. You are much more pleasant and fun.'

Her sister waved her comments away.

'We should have a party, when we are rich and famous, and invite all the eligible and attractive men of our age, and no women!'

'You need not worry. According to Mrs Walters' cards, love is already seeking you.'

'I wonder who it is. The idea of it makes me worried.'

Maggie shook her head. 'Well, whoever it is, you can tell him from me that he cannot have all of you. I demand these evenings at least twice a week.

'I wouldn't change these evenings for the world, you know that.'

'Now, back to this party of yours. We'd have to let Mrs Walters come, surely.'

'Oh, she can come, but no one else. It could be an orgy! Do people really have orgies or are they imaginary? Either way, I would like to have one, before it's too late, perhaps a quieter one for older people.'

'Seated.' Maggie said, suddenly choking.

'Yes, seated, with sandwiches, and sticks with which gentlemen lean forward and lift the skirts of the ladies opposite them.'

They roared with laughter, topping up their drinks.

'And younger men, too, for the lifting.'

'When will we be rich again?' Maggie asked.

❧❧❧❧❧❧❧❧

On the heath, someone was running; a girl. She cursed herself for taking the risk. She had given the danger such little thought, convinced that nothing would ever happen to her. And now, out of breath and hysterical, she staggered, her feet negotiating potholes and slippery wet grass laced with slugs and coal and rock. There was just one thought in her head – run, keep running and do not stop. Her chest was heaving. The blood pumping in her neck made hearing impossible. She opened her mouth, choking out a gasp, and, filled with terror at the involuntary sound, she dared to stop, to take stock, to listen. Then he was close. She could hear his footsteps, hear the rustle of his clothes and his breathing.

'It seems the little girl doesn't value her life so much after all. Here she is, throwing her chances away, offering her body to me.'

She screamed, hard and violent, dragging the sound up from somewhere deep and young, where all the ages she had been converged, and thrust it out as a shield against him. She reached into her pocket, pushing her door keys between her fingers so that when she punched, if she punched, she would gouge. She would go for the eyes and she would keep going for the eyes until she got the eyes. It was impossible in her mind that she was standing here in this moment, terrified, caught up in one minute that mattered more than any other. It was her or him.

'Such a pretty smell.'

She jumped, turning around, seeking the voice in the darkness. She screamed again at him, deafening and desperate and angry, warning him, like an animal cornered into defence.

'Let's see what the noisy little lady looks like.'

And in a shocking moment, a bright spark lit both him and her and they looked at each other, saw each other's faces and angry bared teeth, the fear and lust and hunger, the wild bloody excitement in his eyes, and the determined angry defiance in hers. And they were plunged back into darkness.

'Why are you doing this? Can't you keep a woman?'

He laughed.

'Or is it that you are frightened of us?' She gripped the keys between her fingers, raised her fist, practiced a punch.

He laughed from somewhere behind her and she screamed again, in all directions, loud and angry, begging for someone to hear, but eventually the sound broke down into fear – shaking trembling fear.

'The lion is becoming a pussycat. Are you tired now? Ready to cry and give in to me?'

She screamed again with everything her aching throat could give, then she broke into a run, catching sight of house lights in the distance. She grew determined, focusing only on the lights and running hard towards them. Then he was on her, his arm around her waist, swinging her up against his side, hurling her down onto her back, the air bursting from her lungs, her back bruised on rocks. She rolled over in pain, dragged herself to her knees, pushing down on the wet grass to rise, but his hands were on her neck. She reached for the keys, falling backwards, bringing him down onto her, clinging to him, pulling him close, lifting her keys to his face and scratching them hard, drilling them into him. He yelled, fought her off, but she was holding him, throwing herself right and left, holding him tight. He fell again onto her, turning his face away from her, wise to her trick. She sliced into his neck, banging her fist and the blunt jagged keys into him. Then he growled at her and, pulling free, dragged her along by the hair, reaching for his knife, and when he had stamped the keys and her hand down into the earth so she could no longer tell what was key and what was bone, he lowered the knife and brought it up into her stomach, up behind the ribs to her heart. 'I do it,' he said, 'because it excites me. I'll dump your body in the pond, where I will wash you off me. I will change into the clothes I left there, and then, after a short walk to compose myself, I will go for a glass of wine and shiver at the deliciousness of my life.'

He wiped his bloody hands on her lifeless face, lit his flint to look at her and saw blood fall from his face onto her dress. He raised a hand, felt the gash in his cheek and cursed. His neck too was open just behind the ear. He ripped her dress and wiped his face. Then, dragging her in the direction of the pond, he waited to make sure no one was waiting there, before he slipped the rocks that he had left earlier at the side of the pond into her pockets and her undergarments and then slid her body down into the icy water.

To Anna's annoyance, the raised voices from the upper floors brought the governess hurrying through the house. She pointed the maids silently to the stairs down to the kitchen, glaring if they tilted their heads to listen. A few hours of peeling and cleaning would keep them out of earshot until whatever had wound them up subsided. But then a door slammed and the count's angry footsteps strode down the stairs and out through the front door.

The governess exchanged concerned glances with the butler. It was rare that the master left the house at all, let alone at such an early hour. In the kitchen she watched the staff busy themselves with the preparation of the evening meal demanding silence.

'Will the countess still eat if she is upset?' Anna asked.

'Our business is discretion,' the governess told her stiffly. 'Dinner will be served at seven as it always is.' And beyond her words, Anna began to detect an accent not dissimilar to the count and countess's.

She slid the sliced apples from the wood chopping board into a saucepan. Being spoken to so rudely by the governess had begun to irritate her, and, for the first time, she let her employer see her displeasure.

The governess, who was carrying pastry to the table, did a double take. 'Do not think because the countess invited you into conversation so that she could learn about her staff that you are now above your employer, my girl.' She crossed the dark kitchen and put a pinch of nutmeg into the apples. 'I am your employer. I run this house. Any further looks of that sort and I will advertise for your replacement.'

Anna remained silent, tipping a bowl of raisins into the mix.

'I had better turn down the count's room if you don't need me for anything else.'

The governess nodded, crossing the room to hand her a small pile of folded clothing. 'Put these away, and if it's not too windy, put the window on the latch to air the room.'

Anna nodded and left the room, pressing her nose into the soft fresh garments in her hands. In the count's quarters she put the black shirt on its shelf next to the others, hung the waistcoat in the wardrobe and then with a gasp of surprise, held up a vest, beneath which lay his underwear. She became flustered; she was unprepared for this, and put them quickly inside the drawer and saw to the window.

It was sunset. The last remaining bar of orange was sinking down over London as she opened the windows and stepped out onto the balcony wishing that the evening belonged to spring and not to autumn. Across the heath the windmills turned and the gates of Greenwich Park were being pulled closed. It seemed odd to her that the count had chosen the quieter heath-facing rooms and his sister the rooms facing the bustle and noise of the village. She picked up handfuls of leaves that had drifted and gathered on the balcony and freed them back into the air. Then, with a start, she saw the count, on the heath, watching her. She picked up more leaves quickly and hurled them off the balcony with exaggerated movements, then with her head lowered and one eye on him, she went back into his rooms and closed the windows.

On his desk there were several large books and some paper on which he had written. She could not work out the words because they were in Russian but she admired the strong bold handwriting, each line of which sloped down to the right until the lines beneath were forced into an desperate arc rather than a line. She lifted his cologne to her nostrils, imagining and longing for a man just like him, all the time unaware that she was being watched by the countess from the doorway. The girl lifted his comb and smelled it with a sigh, then moving to the bed she turned down the sheets, plumped up the pillow and topped up the oil in the bedside lamp. When she turned towards the door, the countess was gone.

On the heath, the count changed direction, turning towards the pond. Then noticing through the windows of the Hare and Billet that it was almost empty, he made his first visit to a British pub. In a booth tucked from view, he listened to the gossip and surveyed the affluent, moneyed locals. The same incurious barman brought him different speciality ales until, bloated, he ordered the finest brandy and realised that for some time he had been the last person in the pub. Happy, brave and drunk he paid the bill and moved on to the Crown. Here the women, turning to see who had entered, lifted themselves from tiredness into sparkling alertness, quickly becoming besotted with his emboldened eyes. For some it was his jaw line or his hair, for others it was his flawless skin and his warm, seductive smile. Some studied his hands and were hypnotised by his accent but all closed in around him, unaware of the crowd they were forming. The count stepped away, quickly turning instead to a group of men who were happy to talk. Women, though he took pleasure in their company and he desired them, often roused in their men, when he was present, a furious jealousy that he did not welcome. It began with the unwavering attention that they showed him; their dismissiveness of the men they otherwise confided all in and their new-found desire for someone else.

In Paris, this had been a major problem; wives and girlfriends, even those at the top of society, had made their feelings quite shamelessly apparent, disregarding the company around them. This attraction sometimes sent the most unlikely women hurrying to the mirrors of the grandest powder rooms in the capital to stare at their reflections and shake off their tired old looks, dramatically re-imagining their make-up and hair, returning as an alter-ego with spectacle to a surprised crowd. Necessarily he would find himself having to leave before the gentlemen whose company he had been enjoying were forced to stand up to him, guarding their wives and their own best interests.

He was not too worried about this. He had been able to look after himself from a young age. When you have battled Siberian wolves and soldiers, drunkards and even boxers, addled husbands posed no urgent threat.

However, the evening in Blackheath passed convivially, and, pleased with himself and full of drunken tales and local knowledge, he let himself into the house to wake his sister.

She waved him sleepily away, then, a few minutes later went to find him.

He was on his balcony, his coat discarded, his head back, breathing in the cold night air.

'It's time,' he said.

'It's too cold.'

'This is not cold. We know cold. It is time. We have waited long enough.'

He reached down and took off his shoes, watching her.

'We don't know the place well enough. We could be caught.'

He shook his head.

'It is dark. No one will see. No one will know.'

He pulled his shirt over his head and threw it down.

'I'm nervous.'

'You are always nervous. Undress for me.'

She sighed, hugging herself and pulling her bathrobe tighter.

'Fine! Then I will do it alone.'

Van Dayne's early experiments had concentrated on the great sea birds and eagles, assuming their size and strength would reveal the perfect muscular structure he needed. but finally, he had found the right balance, the correct angles, stronger muscles, a much wider span, an ability not just to run and become airborne, but to lift oneself effortlessly into the air.

The count undid his belt and kicked his trousers from his legs. Then, undressed, he stood facing her, watching her take off her bathrobe. He shivered as the wind tousled his hair, and stepping out onto the balcony, surveyed the land. Behind him, rising above his shoulders, were two pink, fleshy, head-like shapes, then pushing out from his sides, unwrinkling, the bulbous knots of pink reached out like arms. His head sank down and with a groan of relief two powerful fleshy pink wings opened up around him, pushing him forward, such were their strength.

The countess, as naked as he, walked towards him, her wings opening behind her, their baby pink flesh, wrinkled from disuse, finally able to stretch taut. She moved past him on the balcony, climbing up onto the ledge alongside him, and together they dove.

They hurtled through the air at astounding speeds, cupping the wind in their fleshy wings and hurling it aside. Just one swipe could send them soaring up or forward a dozen yards. They climbed slowing, stretching, flexing, fanning; the muscle beneath relieved to be free and active. It moved like thick rope beneath the skin, as thick as their mother's thigh muscle, their bones strong and hungry for nourishment, their mother growing with them, inside them as strong and natural as their own limbs.

Their flying was rusty after so long in hiding and the endless journeys in coaches and long drawn-out stays in European cities with their cramped streets and obsession with sky gazing. At last, with the long dark nights of winter and the whole of the heath at their disposal, it would not be long until their bodies were back to physical perfection.

They flew at each other, turning aside at the last perilous moment, wing skin flapping hard and fast, pale pink and wobbling and cold, whistling against the wind, then with enough speed, they held onto each other and pirouetted up, spinning and spinning, faster and faster, higher and higher into the icy sky, as had been their game since childhood. Except here there were no frenzied eagles to attack them, though the fear remained with them even though those attacks had ended when they both turned six and they were too heavy to be dragged off in claws. They both still carried scars from battles.

'One night we must follow the river up into the heart of London, to the column they have built,' the count called, turning. He rolled his shoulders downwards, his wings pulled in tight, his stomach flat and tensed, his hips light and his legs locked into a straight line. Streamlined, he plummeted downwards, opening his wings wide and swooping, flying just inches above the grass, smelling the ground and up again towards her, taking her hand and spinning upwards again with her. She laughed, clutching him tight.

The telescope was too slow. It could not make them out. At first glance she mistook them for kites or smoke billowing from chimneys. Anna too, who had remained in the house, hours after her duties had ended, was not sure what they were and finally deduced that the heath was being visited by large powerful birds. But when they came to land, as they lowered themselves onto the balcony facing the heath, stretched tall, flexing their wings wide, Princess Sophia Matilda backed away from the telescope at the Ranger's House with her hand covering her mouth.

In the house at the centre of the heath, Anna hurried into the pantry, locking it after her. She curled into a ball, and, terrified, she recited the Lord's Prayer over and over. They were demons. She was in danger.

Chapter 12

They moved respectfully past the Princess of Wales public house, thick muscle flexing beneath freshly groomed black fur, polished hooves clipping the road, majestic crests of tall black ostrich plume bouncing in unison as the beasts turned down into the village and appeared before the waiting crowds that lined the streets of Blackheath. A hush fell, hats were removed and heads bowed as the first of the glass-sided carriages bearing the first girl's coffin came into view. Behind it, the exhausted, raw, proud parents, their heads high, stern, struggling with trembling lips and swelling tears tried not to give in to emotion. But the sad smiles of acknowledgement and support from the crowds that occasionally caught their eyes made them shudder uncontrollably with gratitude and those sudden intakes of breath brought to his defiant stare and her clenched pain, tears that tipped uncontrollably down onto their cheeks. They wiped them away immediately, raising their eyes again to the wooden coffin containing their child, and they walked down the sloping road towards an empty, childless future.

After a pause, the second horse-drawn hearse came into view. Behind the coffined child, less composed parents followed. They clung to each other, supported by their remaining children who also were barely able to control their distress. Crowds of family and mourners followed at a respectful distance, joined by many of the bystanders.

Being the only parish in the whole of London not to have its own church, Blackheath relied on the neighbouring suburbs of Greenwich and Lewisham for its places of worship. Every Sunday morning, marching in one of two directions, the whole of Blackheath, washed and in their finest attire walked for miles together.

On the roof of the shop, Mrs Walters, swaying with bags full of bread, began scattering it on the tiles. It was her third day, same time, same place, she knew they were habitual. In the top windows, Judy and Maggie waited, clutching knives and the rope that held the sheet that covered the sign. Across from them the crowds stood in their dozens watching, wondering what on earth they were up to.

Mrs Walters, hands on hips, stared up and around her, cursing, 'Come on! Bloody stupid creatures.' Then, with a grin, she began showering the air with bread, watching them come.

The funeral procession drew closer but the crowds were distracted; the sky was now thick with large black rooks and the Cloak sisters, with pained, urgent expressions were hacking through the rope as if their lives depended on it. Then, in an instant, the carriages were in front of the shop, the rooks were swooping, people were being hit by bread and excrement and then, flapping loudly against the wall, the sheet fell, sliding down the wall, revealing the sign – *The Blackheath Séance Parlour.*

The crowds were aghast; to blatantly advertise themselves during such a terrible and heart-wrenching . . . and then . . . then they read the words. If the sisters had thought the crowd's reaction had been one of shock before, they had seen nothing. Now they stared in complete horror. Maggie and Judy ducked back inside, closing the windows, shaking with nerves. Mrs Walters, hidden from view, was opening another bag of bread and fighting the birds off. She shielded her eyes and looked up. The sky was turning above her, a black whirlpool of screeching birds, circling and diving. They were standing so thick on the side of the roof visible from the street that they were pushing each other off before the horrified crowds. Mrs Walters fell back flat against the roof laughing, her face and hair white with excrement.

Father Henry Legge, leading the procession, looked down from the confusion in the skies to see what the crowds were shaking the heads at. He took in the full impact of what the Cloak sisters had brought to his diocese and sighed angrily. 'This is what happens,' he told himself, 'when a village has no church of its own.' He would call a meeting that evening. He would insist that his own church – the biggest, grandest – be built on the heath itself. Blackheath would be his parish. In the meantime, he turned his head away from the shop and led the funeral procession to Lee.

When the procession had passed, the crowds gathered around the simple notice in the window announcing that the first séance would be that evening at eight o'clock and that eight places were available at an astronomical five shillings per seat, the same price as a box at the Theatre Royal on Drury Lane. People shook their heads with disgusted excitement, pressing their eyes against the black windows to see what horrors lay within.

In the intervening hours, the tension was unbearable. Maggie watched and listened to people gather outside discussing ghosts and heaven, religion and the likelihood of contact being achievable. Mrs Walters scrubbed herself clean and filled all of the vases with chrysanthemums, explaining with a shrill urgency that as there were flowers at funerals, people associated the smell of flowers with death and therefore they generated the exact same frame of mind.

'I don't think about death when I have flowers at home,' Maggie protested.

Mrs Walters ignored her.

Judy paced the room nervously behind them, her hands were shaking. Doubt and fear took hold and for the first time since the idea of the parlour had entered her head, she worried that she had made a mistake. She snatched up her handbag, pulled on a headscarf and hurried out of the front door.

The women watched her.

'She is coming back, isn't she?' Mrs Walters asked.

Maggie shrugged, then grabbing her hat hurried out after her.

Judy was walking, head down, face obscured by a scarf. She turned down into Camden Row, looked at her shaking hands and reached out for the handle of the gate to her house. Then, decisively, she turned it, stepping into her garden, now wild and overgrown. Hesitantly she walked up the narrow path, then taking out her key, she took a moment to think, pushed it inside the lock and was about to turn it but quickly changed her mind. She turned and hurried out into the street. Then taking the folded sheets of the first chapter of her novel from her bag, she walked through the village to the carriage master's office and putting them into an envelope with a brief letter, she instructed him to take it to the offices of J.J. James, Publisher on Fleet Street. Things could not return to the way they had been before. She had to do everything she could to prevent it, one way or another.

&&&&&&&&

With the place to herself, Mrs Walters went to the upstairs room and laid out her make-up and clothes. Then seating herself at the mirror, she scooped a large ball of bright white face paint and plastered her face with it. Memories flooded her mind.

On the ship, Netta had slept nearly fifteen hours a day. She ate what was assigned to her, avoided going to the toilet for fear of losing her hammock and kept herself to herself. No one knew each other's crimes in the hold; no one wanted to. It was best to keep yourself to yourself, and the darkness made that easy. Up the other end of the ship, past the oil lamp that swayed and fought to stay lit at the centre, there were arguments that sometimes went on all night and grew in volume until everyone was awake listening; two foul-mouthed women who cursed and threatened and threw their weight around until ferocious fights broke out, at which both women excelled. The other women had begun moving away from them, coming down to her side, filling every inch of space on the splintered wooden floor, crushing everyone together. There were illnesses and deaths and great swells of vomit and urine that ran the entire length of the floor soaked up by people's clothes as they sat or slept. There was seasickness and screaming and fear and thieving, but most of all there was crying.

As the weeks passed by on the swaying, creaking vessel there was little else to do other than to think; but thinking, for many, had become as real and dangerous an illness as the typhoid and scurvy. Netta used her time wisely. She focussed on her craft, honing it to such clarity that often she could imagine herself rising from her own body and spinning in the centre of the room, reaching out to the bars on the door to steady herself. Then slipping through them, she would visit the guest rooms, walk down the corridors, find herself at once transported back to the smog of London. She would venture into theatres and watch performances, eavesdrop on couples sitting in the parks or let herself into their homes to sit alongside them and see how they behaved when the world wasn't watching.

Occasionally, she visited home, watched her mother baking and her father planting or her aunt hurrying from a visit to the pub to meet her fancy man. Occasionally she would find them talking about her, shaking their heads and getting angry at the injustice of the courts and what they had a good mind to do to her fiancée who wandered about free as a lark. And herein she found her purpose, the way that she would sit through the seven years of imprisonment ahead of her. She would plot her revenge against the judge who had been so keen on dismissing every word she had had to say. She would hound her fiancée until he cracked and confessed and was hanged.

Somewhere mid-journey, the two violent women discovered her, amused by her ridiculous hair, grand ideas and her friendship with two other women: Jane Mitchell with her strange West Country accent and Elizabeth Shekel whose timidity made her an easy target. They threw themselves down next to them, imitating their voices, pulling at their clothes or leaning into their faces to provoke them. Netta did not want trouble. She let them have their fun, turning to meditation, counting from one to eight, slowly over and over again, banishing all other thought, all sounds, her racing thoughts and nervousness being allowed to gently slip away as one, two, three, four, five, six, seven, eight brought her back to one, two, three and then half asleep, she felt a punch and her eyes opened angrily.

'SALLY!' she boomed. The room fell silent. Netta's voice was unrecognisable. 'The daughter I brought up, a criminal. What did I do wrong? I should have let Mollie raise you. I might as well have turned you out into the street the good I did you. I raised a thug. My own daughter, proud of her violence. I was so besotted with you, so proud of my little Sally and you broke my heart. Showing off, throwing your weight around, robbing, selling your body to strangers. Do you remember Southend? Sitting with our feet in the sea, promising me that you could change your ways, telling me that you loved me!'

She fell back, shaking her head then turned to the even larger woman, already looking ready to pounce. Netta stared her in the eyes, her face softening, tears rolling from her eyes, her hand reaching out. 'My dear. I wish you had been there with me. I couldn't hold on. It took hold. It didn't hurt, I slept. I didn't wake. But I want you to know, despite all of the bad things and the things we've said to each other and the years of not seeing you, that I love you. I will always watch over you.'

She passed out, unconscious in the silent room that was already filling with warders who sensed trouble. Netta let out a deafening snore.

She woke in pain, a black eye throbbing, her arms bruised. She was alone, caged. The room was lit brightly. The women scrubbed the decks on their hands and knees and refused to look at her. Then there was a sudden hush and they stood, their heads bowed and somewhere out of her line of vision the loud solemn tones of a man's voice led them in prayer. A priest moved about them, blessing them, cleansing the place of evil, forcing hymns from the mouths of those who had never set foot inside a church but judging by the hearty response he elicited, the women were keen for heavenly protection. Netta tested the strength of the bars that contained her. She had become a loose cannon, a witch, unpredictable and to top that, a murderer. It was not a good combination, she realised, as she raised herself on tiptoe to watch. The priest moved theatrically towards her, his arms raised, her lips curled, spittle flying with his words.

'We will force out the evil from within you!'

Netta sighed.

On the sixteenth of November, 182 days, or over five months and three weeks later, the *Speke-I* came to a halt in New South Wales, Australia. Of the ninety-nine women who had left Britain, ninety-seven stepped out under the scorching sun. There had been just two deaths from typhoid.

'Welcome to Australia, ladies,' the wardens shouted. 'Welcome to the other side of the world.'

Her hair, after five months of towering growth, more than the terribleness of her crime, was the focus of most ridicule. When she walked from the ship the warders whooped with laughter, deciding that unlike all other inmates, her towering ragged hair should never be cut short.

෨෨෨෨෨෨෨

Thirty minutes before its official opening, Maggie and Judy left the pub and made their way down into the village, stopping to look at what had once been their sweetshop. In the dark, the building stood out like something evil and sinister. Tall and black and creepy, with its darkened windows and purple sign. In the upstairs window, candlelight and shadows made the spectacle even more eerie.

'I'm almost too frightened to go inside, and I know what's in there!' Maggie said. 'It's too much,' she said, shaking her head, 'It scares me.'

Inside the shop, pausing in the deep, red-curtained, lamp-lit reception area with its dark leather seats, corpse pictures and shelves of horrendous ornaments, they looked at each other. Then moving through the middle area to the séance parlour itself, they paused, waiting for their eyes to adjust to the darkness of the single candle. At first they didn't see

118

the corpse-like white figure seated at the head of the table, and when they did, the shock of it made them scream and swear. Mrs Walters arose smiling, which, despite now knowing it was her, was still terrifying to both women.

'For Christ's sake, Netta!' Maggie shouted angrily. 'What do you think you are doing!'

They lit the windows with candles, turned over the open sign and held their breath, awaiting the knock on the door, the arrival of their very first customers. But there was no knock on the door, nor was there at ten past the hour or twenty past. At twenty-five minutes past, Judy opened the door and looked out into the street. It was empty. Up at the Crown a couple hurried from one of the new horse-drawn buses into the warmth and up towards Lee Road a lone figure walked a dog but it seemed that to all, their grand opening was of little interest.

Mrs Walters was not perturbed. 'People need time to consider their involvement in this type of unknown phenomenon,' she explained. 'There are moral scruples and fears and superstitions to be weighed up. Contacting the dead is not a decision one makes easily. They will need to have met someone who has been here and done it and survived. Tomorrow there will be the Sunday visitors who will take news of us back to their own boroughs and soon that news will reach the ears of those who simply cannot wait to visit us.'

At nine, disheartened, they blew out the candles and locked the door.

Chapter 13

The following morning, grey with sleeplessness, Mrs Walters was not about to go down without a fight, despite the Early Closing Association who were adamant that Sunday trading should immediately cease. She sat the sisters in the back room, and over and over again rehearsed them in the fine art of tea-leaf reading; something that even someone as useless as Maggie managed to pull off. She learned the meaning of the shapes quickly, surprised Netta with her accuracy and was now thrilled that she would be the star of the show.

Picking up a large sign that promised free tea with every tea-leaf reading, Netta physically blocked women's paths and talked them into learning about their futures, their pasts, what was going on behind their backs. She wooed them with the lures of romance and children and money, pushing them inside the parlour, until Maggie, alarmed at the waiting queue, sat down to give her very first reading.

By mid-afternoon, the shop was bustling. Both Maggie and Judy, who had not stopped for a cup of tea themselves since the door had opened, continually tried to catch Mrs Walters' attention to stop her from inviting more women into the waiting area. But Netta was having none of it. At five, hurrying up the slower drinkers, Maggie could not even see past all the women inside waiting, and still Mrs Walters' voice sounded from the street, encouraging, taking their money, cramming in more.

'We,' Mrs Walters said, smiling at their furious faces as she locked the door, 'are a success.'

༻༻༻༻༻༻

Monday morning meant nannies and mothers and housewives and other women, all relieved their husbands and employers had returned to work so they could wander and drink tea and chat. It was the first Monday in over ten years that the sisters had not been nursing thunderous hangovers. Maggie, whose most promising skill was the teacup, offered readings at affordable prices, while Judy, awaiting the first customer for a crystal ball reading, played waitress, hurrying about with a teapot. They had never seen so many people.

The tea-leaf readings were cheap and fast: two questions, ten minutes, no more. Maggie watched each customer sit, waited for their questions, studied their cup and their nervous faces. Women, all looking for love. They hungered for it with wide-eyed excitement. Who would they have? When? How? Would they love each other very deeply? Was he romantic? Was he a good man? Was he healthy? Was he attractive? Where would she meet him? Even the ugliest or those with little sign of a brain and no saving graces did not doubt for a second that they would find love and settle down. It was never a question of 'Will I find love?', it was always an impatient 'When?'. They wanted dates, and information on the quality of the catch, with a glimmer of romance dolloped on top.

A spiteful part of her wanted to tell them no – there would be no man; that, like herself, not all women were guaranteed a love. But she told them the truth, that he was one year away or two months or just days away – that it would last a lifetime, five years, until he got bored and ran off with another.

Later, when she took a break, it dawned on her that she might take a peek for herself. She reasoned that if some of the lunatics she had read for were just months away from meeting the perfect man, even at this late age she herself might find a partner to see her to the grave. With a strong cup, she seated herself upstairs at the window, sipping as the world went by.

William and Catherine Church, who owned the plumber's and glazier's, were having heated words out of earshot by the Kid brook. Charles Strutt, a very aggressive man who owned the clothes shop on Montpellier Vale, and who already had one court summons for aggressive language, was on the warpath, with his poor unaware victim in his eyeline. George Goldsmith, the fruiterer, and his partner Samuel Payne, the fishmonger, who had fallen out over a woman during the summer, were overseeing the building of the wall that divided their shop, both vowing never to speak to one another again. The sisters Huggett, daughters of the coal merchant, were openly admiring Mr Charles, Maggie's friend, the artist.

Maggie studied him from the window. Perhaps it would eventually be him, Mr Graham Charles, with whom she had sat and had tea in her shop every week, year after year; perhaps it was his name that she would take. Then she remembered his inclinations, and sipped some more tea. Maybe, although he secretly attended late-night rendezvous with Mr Sterry, the bachelor from Brunswick Place, he could find in his heart a secret affection for her also. She dismissed the idea, finishing the tea and looking at the dark patches of leaves left behind. She swirled the cup three times right and once left, then set the cup down and peered inside. There would be no love. No one. Not even temporary.

❧❧❧❧❧❧❧❧❧

To the villagers, who had watched the queuing and excitement and felt their own reticence subsiding a little, a new temptation was paraded: tarot readings, more expensive than tea-leaf reading but still affordable. 'The cards offer depth and clarity,' Mrs Walters explained to the gathering crowd; 'Specifics. All your questions answered. And the first ten readings are half price.'

Judy took her seat at the tarot table with her first customer of the day, a young woman who rocked her child to sleep in her arms throughout. Judy turned over a card, bit her lip, then, looking into the woman's face, reiterated, 'You do want the truth, don't you?'

The woman nodded.

Judy copied her nod and grimaced. 'He's cheating on you, dear.'

The woman nodded.

'The cards are giving me random clues now. The next three cards will probably mean more to you than to me. They will try to help you find the answer by mentioning things you know but I don't. I cannot help but be vague with these cards.'

The woman leaned forward, watching Judy turn over card after card. 'They are telling me they have a safe place, around food, insects too, there is wood and earth, again, insects. Let's see who this woman is.' She turned over the next card and held up a queen. 'Do you recognise her?'

Maggie meanwhile, who was useless at both tarot and the crystal ball and growing bored with tea-leaf reading, was eager to turn her hand to the only other skill she seemed to do fairly well at: the technique of

122

automatic writing, in which she cleared her mind and allowed her hand to draw endless curling sprawls with a quill until words began to appear. She had been scribbling for several minutes for the woman seated opposite but had still produced nothing. Her sitter watched irritably, coveting the time another customer spent with Judy and her tarot cards. They seemed to be making enormous and exciting progress. Then, the illegible swirls began to change and Maggie's hand lifted up the quill so that it was barely being held at all and letters began to appear. M . . . o . . . n . . . e . . . y . . . a little put away. For you. Top left corner.

It subsided into squiggles again.

'Top left corner of what?'

Maggie squiggled again and again, aware of the woman's impatience. The words repeated themselves again: Money, a little put away for a rainy day, top left corner for you . . . mattress.'

The woman let out an excited squeal. 'I will go home straight away. I will let you know if it is right!' She hurried out, excited, rousing up customers who waited outside. 'She's very good. Very, very good.' Had she known how little had been sewn inside the mattress, she would perhaps have been less impressed. Indeed her follow-up visits would no longer be about contacting her husband but focussed on where people had dropped wallets, watches and other valuables.

But there was one reading that day that was to have a life-changing effect. In the crystal ball, Judy's attention was drawn away again and again from the question that the handsome man in his early thirties seated opposite her wanted answered. His mind was focussed on his fiancée, wanting to know if she was truly in love with him or just excited about being a wife with a substantial income, but in the ball a different matter kept arising and her eyes were drawn to a specific place on his body.

Across the room Mrs Walters' concentration snapped away from her ball, and she was suddenly filled with excitement. She rushed to Judy, excusing her, and pulled her through to the back room.

'That is him!' she hissed.

'Who?'

'The one you will marry. He,' she pointed, 'is him!'

Judy shook her head. He was too young, too handsome. She dismissed it as a nonsense and returned to him.

In the ball, an image of him appeared immediately, as handsome as he was in real life. But again her eyes were drawn away from his face down to his hip. With hesitation, she had the mists inside the ball remove his trousers and lift his shirt. And, blushing, she dared to look up from the ball to his honest, warm smile. She returned it, lost for a moment, then looked back into the ball to his bare legs. She felt her heart flutter and watched his shirt tails rise, revealing fashionable shorter undergarments. She held her breath, watching them fade away revealing strong muscular buttocks and a dark strong abdomen but her enjoyment ended quickly.

'You have a problem,' she said soberly, reaching out for his hand. 'There is a medical problem.'

'With her?'

'No. With you. At the top of your left leg, at your hip, there is a lump in the muscle.'

'A lump?'

'You don't know?'

He shook his head.

'You must feel for it.' She watched his hands leave the table and move to his side.

'I feel nothing.'

She reddened. 'May I?'

At his nod, Judy rose, and moving to him, allowed her fingertips to touch the hardness of his thigh, following the muscle up, to where, outside of marriage, no man should be touched and no woman should be touching. She nodded, took his finger and pressed his fingertips against it.

'You must see a surgeon. You must have it removed. If you do not hesitate, you will survive it. If you leave it, you will not.'

Troubled, the handsome young man rose. He smiled to her and took her hand, kissing it, then hurried from the shop. Mrs Walters dragged Judy outside and they stood at the doorway, watching his strong masculine frame disappear from view. Mrs Walters laughed, pressing her hand against Judy's chest. Her heart was racing.

'You and he will be married.'

'He is six or seven years my junior!'

'Bad woman!' Netta laughed, leaving her to her thoughts.

When Judy returned inside, Netta's voice was irritable. She was staring into her ball and back at the wild-haired woman who watched her from across the table, her dirty brown hands fidgeting with her ears. Her body odour was intoxicating, but oblivious to the effect she was having on everyone around her, she chewed her lips and waited eagerly.

Netta was holding her breath, turning her head to the side to breathe clean air. She stared back into the ball. 'Let's see, when will you get married and have children?' Her brow creased and she looked up uncertainly at the girl then back down. 'The ball is telling me that no man will come along until you have made changes in your life. You must show the forces beyond that you are ready to accept love.'

'How?'

'Baths. Every day.'

The woman looked angry.

'But . . .' Netta interrupted, seeing the reaction, 'Special baths. You must add mint, and lavender.'

'But lavender is for mourning!'

'Yes dear. Every morning.'

On Thursday evening, nearly a whole week in, Netta rushed out to buy a bottle of wine. She had imposed a no-drinking rule on the sisters that she now found the need to break herself. Ten minutes later, she burst through the door, shoved it at Maggie, then catching her breath, she shouted, 'We are in the newspaper!' She waved it excitedly, opening the pages and spreading it out on a table.

'Here it is, here it is.' She squinted to read it aloud.

'The funeral was marred by the scandalous opening of *The Blackheath Séance Parlour*, the owners of which saw fit to announce its arrival by revealing the sign to a horrified crowd as the body of . . . blah, blah . . . passed its doors.' She looked at the horrified sisters with an enormous grin. 'See? We did it. Now not only will the locals notice us but so will the whole of London.'

'The whole of London is shaking its head at our vulgarity.'

'The whole of London, my dear, now knows four words that it didn't until today. The Blackheath Séance Parlour. That means that we exist for a lot more people than we did this morning.'

They sat at the big séance table, excited. In the centre, the tin which contained the week's takings was overflowing. Mrs Walters tipped it into a large blue honey pot and added the day's takings to it.

'Let's divide it now,' Judy suggested eagerly.

Mrs Walters shook her head. 'Friday is payday and not a penny will leave this pot each week until then. In the meantime . . .' She carried it towards the cellar door and reached for the key.

A knock at the front door made all three jump. They froze, looking at each other. Then in a whirl of panic, Netta rushed to apply her make-up, the lamps were extinguished, candles lit, the wine was placed behind the curtain on the windowsill, and adopting a peaceful and reverent expression, Maggie opened the door.

A small pale couple looked nervously at her, their eyes tired and raw from crying. Maggie invited them in and sat them in the small curtained reception area, immediately regretting the gruesome portrait of a young girl, gaunt and long dead in her coffin, that hung behind them.

'It was our daughter's funeral on Saturday. We saw your shop,' the woman began, holding her husband's pale, shaking hand. 'She was murdered. They found her in the pond.'

Maggie nodded guiltily.

'We need to find out who did this to her.'

In the room beyond the curtain, Mrs Walters, her face painted like a doll, was backing away, shaking her head furiously as Maggie brought the couple in. 'I can't do this. No. I can't be involved. Not murder. I'm sorry. Very sorry. I have to leave.'

The mother reached out and touched her arm. 'It took all our strength to come here this evening. I don't know how much we have left. She was our little girl, our only daughter and she was a good girl. We were very close, as a family. Please, we have to know what happened to her that night. I have to know.'

Mrs Walters looked down. 'I'm sorry. I can't.'

The sisters looked at her, confused and alarmed.

'The police must help you, not me.'

'They've not told us anything.'

Mrs Walters looked at the urgent white hands clutching hers, unable to let her go, frightened to lose this chance. She sighed.

'What I tell you here cannot in any way involve me. If we discover the murderer you did not discover it through me. I will help you this once, but I will not become involved in this. Do you understand?'

The couple nodded.

'And I have your word?'

'You have our word,' the husband assured her.

'Sit.'

They took seats at the table, the parents opposite the Cloak sisters, Netta at the head of the table. Her eyes were closed and she was involved in some mental argument with herself about her involvement. Then, with a cough, she joined hands with the mother and Maggie, indicating they should form a circle, and fell silent, listening to the room.

'We shall begin with the Lord's Prayer.'

Reluctantly, Maggie allowed herself to join in, unsure what the purpose of introducing prayer was. More than likely it was just to put everyone at ease, she surmised, mumbling.

'Is there anybody there?' Mrs Walters began, her theatrical make-up suddenly losing all comedy value and assuming the guise of someone so startlingly close to death that it made the sisters realise the full extent of what they were offering to people.

'We are trying to make contact with those of you who have passed through to the next life. I feel you around me. I feel you coming near. Come closer. Come to me.'

'Oh dear!' the girl's mother exclaimed nervously.

'Don't be frightened, dear,' Mrs Walters said, opening one eye, 'I'll tell you when to be frightened.' She slipped back down, 'Come to me. The others with me cannot hear or see you but they are here to make contact. If you hear me, knock twice. Don't be afraid. I am your friend. I bring only goodwill. Knock for me. A little harder. You must knock very hard in order for the sound to be heard where we are.'

With a loud groan, the table on which they were resting lurched forward towards the parents. Mrs Walters, her eyes closed, looked right, appearing to be studying someone standing there. She lay two round stones on the table each marked with a word: 'Yes' and 'No'. Then, turning a glass onto its rim, she motioned for everyone to rest their middle finger lightly on top of it and began to push it, around and around in an uninterrupted circle, then when it had motion, she lifted her finger, barely touching it.

'We are looking for Alice. Is there an Alice there?'

The glass raced to 'No', tumbling over as the sitters pulled their hands away in shock. Mrs Walters frowned and resumed the glass's circular motion.

'She was murdered recently at Blackheath. You will see her aura. You will see a very different glow around her. Look for her. I must speak with her. I have her parents here.' She extended a hand to the girl's mother, but instead of taking her hand, found resting in her palm a small, dark-haired doll. In an instant Mrs Walters fell backwards as if struck by lightening, gasping for air, staring around her. Then clutching the doll to her chest she stood and moved out of the room, loitering in the doorway, half hidden, curious but not wanting to be seen, like a shy, naughty child. She brushed the doll's hair absent-mindedly, embarrassed as they watched.

'Why are you all looking at me?' she giggled. Then, turning her attention to the doll, said excitedly, 'It's my doll! Daddy bought it for me when I was eight from the Blackheath Bazaar. But he bought the wrong one because I wanted the blond doll but they sold out of that blond one but I like Celia too!'

The couple stared in horror as the old woman caked in thick make-up giggled. 'Daddy bit her toe off.' She slipped off the doll's stocking and held out the foot, 'See? There was a sharp bit there and he bit it off with his teeth but he bit her toe off too!' She giggled encouragingly, then she looked at her mother. Mrs Walter's face fell. She looked away uncomfortably.

'I don't want to tell you what happened, Mummy. It will upset you.'

'We need to know, sweetheart,' her father pleaded.

Netta looked down at her shoes, hugging herself, 'He hurt me.'

'Who did, darling? Who hurt you?'

'I don't want to think about him, Mummy.'

'Did you know him?'

She looked guiltily down like a naughty child and nodded. 'I have to go now.'

'Darling, please tell us his name.'

But Mrs Walters had resurfaced.

The governess, together with the gardener, were carrying a half pig up the back steps into the kitchen. Hurriedly the kitchen maid and the butler, who had come running, helped them carry endless carcasses into the cold pantry. Only Anna did not raise a finger, instead, she remained stubbornly seated and everyone noticed. The governess guessing some form of battle was about to commence, waited until she could dismiss the staff to other parts of the house and let her have her moment.

With the meat hung, the blood decanted into jars and the offal put into stone pots, the kitchen was cleared. The governess set dinner in motion; there was a schedule to observe before she became disciplinarian. She put a plate of liver next to the grinder and pulped it into a wide bowl. Next she took a long corer to several cows' leg bones and scooped out their grey contents.

'Is that what they eat?'

'Is that what who eats?'

'The demons?'

'Demons?'

She pointed upwards. 'The bat people.'

The governess didn't respond. She took a mallet to the bones, crushing them, and put them next to a pestle and mortar ready to grind, then looked up at the girls spiteful face.

'Well? Go on.'

The girl shifted unsurely, 'Go on what?'

'Well, you obviously have something that you want to say, so say it.'

'I saw them, flying. I do not want to work here any more.'

'Then leave.'

'I can't afford to leave.'

'Have you told anyone?'

'No.'

'And you want money, for your silence?'

She nodded.

'Or would you derive more pleasure from an elevated position here? Perhaps personal maid to the countess?'

She shook her head. 'How much will you pay me to keep silent?'

'And how do we know that you will not utter a word to anyone, ever?'

'Because my income will be ongoing.'

'Blackmail?'

She didn't reply.

'I mean, considering how quickly you and your family spread the news you were fed about the count and countess's non-existent third sibling, we have known for some time the level of trust that can be afforded to you.'

Anna reddened guiltily, then blurted, 'What choice do you have?'

'Oh, there are always choices.' She carried the bowl to a side table and paused with her back to her. 'I will need to talk to them. Come back at eight-thirty, talk to no one.'

Outside the count's room, the butler, carrying a request for an audience from the princess, adjusted his tie, knocked and entered the room. He was still in mid-conversation when the governess entered with too urgent an expression to be asked to wait. The count looked up at her, his eyes warming, a smile appearing on his lips. The governess waved him away, as she had grown accustomed to doing. Behind her, the countess appeared and the governess addressed the room. 'Anna . . .' she said.

Chapter 14

With the demand for cut-price tea-leaf readings out of control, Maggie found herself still at her table at five with the door closed against a seemingly endless stream of lovelorn women. Today's collection were older, egged on by their daughters and neighbours, some were even older than herself, so when she looked into their cups and saw torrid private lives and hidden lovers, she felt herself being pushed further and further from the real lives that women everywhere were experiencing. When her last customer had left, she again took her cup upstairs and sat, sipping it, concentrating on her feelings, her longing to be in the arms of a husband or lover. She closed her eyes, gulped down the tea, swirled the cup and peered in. Nothing. There was no man waiting for her, no rugged foreign lover, no set-in-his-ways widower hoping to find her. It was just her, plodding through life alone.

She was broken from her thoughts by Netta who, sticking her head around the door, announced with a barely contained excitement that they had their first proper booking for a séance. Four people, the following evening. Maggie nodded, following her towards the stairs. For the first time in weeks, she wanted more than just a drink. She wanted to be home, bored, having spent the day at the chocolate shop in a mental state that was familiar and didn't arouse in her, longings for men and adventure. She wanted to get rotten drunk, so drunk that she forgot the day. She wanted it to be just herself and Judy again, just for one night, blind drunk, laughing, telling tall tales and gossiping, making pledges to each other that they would get their acts together and earn more.

She waited until Mrs Walters squirreled the day's takings down to the blue honey pot, and took her sister's arm suggesting that they had an evening of the old sort but Judy's thoughts were elsewhere and she pulled away in a hurry. 'A drink, yes' she said, 'But not too many. I have to see someone. I will see you at the Hare and Billet.' And she hurried from the shop.

Rushing through the village, Judy caught the carriage master before he began his evening's duty of ferrying drunks from pub to pub in his new and quite magnificent horse-drawn bus.

'Did you deliver it?' she asked excitedly.

'Yes I did and he read it while I was there. He gave me this.' The stout, cherry-faced man handed her a note and moved her out of his office, locking it behind them. Judy read, almost too excited to take in the words.

'Dear Miss Cloak,' it read, 'having read your first chapter with much interest, I would like you to submit chapters two to six at your earliest convenience. J.J. James.' Judy turned to the carriage master, grinning, then gave him a hug, which he did not appreciate.

Alone, she cut across the grass where the vicar, together with a group of officials, was marking out a large square of land on the heath. She could not stop herself from laughing. Someone had read and liked her first chapter and now they wanted more! She hurried past the pond into the Hare and Billet to tell Maggie her news.

When she arrived, Maggie was out of sorts. She was knocking back whisky, eager to be drunk.

'What's wrong?' Judy asked.

The sound of her sister's voice made Maggie want to cry.

'You are going to find love again, Judy. The tea leaves tell me that it will be soon.'

Her sister listened.

'Do you know what they tell me?' Maggie continued. 'They tell me that I will be alone. And I don't want to be alone. I wish I didn't know all this. I should never have looked. But now I do. I know that no man will ever love me and I will never experience love.'

'But that was just tea leaves. Let me read the crystal ball. Tea leaves are . . .'

Maggie nodded. 'And there is that. I am stuck reading tea leaves and drawing pathetic squiggles while everyone wants the tarot and the crystal ball.'

'Maggie, that's not fair. The queues for your tea leaf reading are out of control.'

'Because it is cheap. It's the price of a cake.'

She pointed to the letter in her hand.

'What is that?'

Judy pushed it into her pocket. 'Nothing.'

CHAPTER 6

The lady in waiting rushed through the room set aside for quiet reflection, through the red room and the green silk room. She could not find the princess anywhere. Eventually she spotted her in the rose garden, and knocking at the window, motioned her inside.

'He is coming!' she announced, watching the princess in her large dress swirl and hurry through the building to the front windows.

On the heath, beyond the gates, the count was dismounting from his horse. She studied him, admiring his thick dark hair and his strong hands leading his mount. He was wearing a navy, military-style jacket that made him appear even taller than usual and cream breeches which clung to the well-defined muscle of his legs. She felt nerves rise up inside her and her heart fluttering, even though this was a meeting with a beast rather than a man.

Turning, she walked through to the back parlour in which a housemaid was already setting up a table for tea and waited. A moment later her butler knocked and introduced him. The count entered gracefully and she rose from her seat as if pleasantly surprised by his visit. Welcoming him in, she dismissed the butler and her maid and offered tea.

Her task was not easy but she would carry it out as pleasantly as possible. Once small talk and flattery were dispensed with, she went to the bureau and brought out the pledge he had given to Lady Dartmouth.

'I'm afraid there is a delicate matter we must deal with,' she told him.

His eyes moved from hers to the paper that held his signature.

'You require the money for your charity sooner? It is not a problem, I can send for –'

'No. I'm afraid, Count, I cannot accept your money at all and you must leave Blackheath.'

'I do not understand.'

She closed her eyes and summoned courage.

'Last night,' she began, 'I was stargazing. I have an interest in planetary observation.'

He nodded.

'And I . . .' she looked away. 'I saw you stepping onto your balcony.'

'You were watching my private rooms, your highness?'

'No. It was the contraption, the horizon was not as low as I had imagined and by accident . . .'

He smiled, conscious of how, since he had entered the room, she had purposely avoided his eyes.

'And you moved the telescope immediately away from myself?'

She became a little flustered and admitted, 'No, I . . .' Her face reddening, she walked a little to distract herself. 'And I saw.'

He closed his eyes, knowing he had been caught, but determined to draw her eyes to his.

'Might I ask if I was clothed, your highness?'

She reddened further. His accent thrilled her.

He allowed the silence, then after a suitable pause said, 'Then you have seen all of myself. I hope my standing before you naked does not change how exciting our friendship promises to be. Perhaps I misread, but I imagined that in many ways we have so much in common and so many experiences to discuss.'

She let his deep Russian tones seduce her for a moment, but what she had seen was too ghastly, too inhuman. She turned to look at him and he caught her eye, drawing them to his and holding them. They were as she had been warned through gossip, irresistible. They sparkled with affection and loneliness and try as she did, she could not look away. She drew her breath.

'I saw . . .'

He took off his jacket and set it down on a chair, then unbuttoning his shirt, he smiled at her.

'I know you saw,' he said, 'and I want to show you that, like you, I am flesh and blood and I am no threat. Quite the opposite. I admire you so much I will stand before you, as I would stand in front of no one else, vulnerable and subservient. I have nothing that I wish to hide from you.'

With strong hands he wrestled off his riding boots and pulled off his shirt. Then, reaching for the laces at the front of his breeches, she reached out and stopped his hand.

'Turn.'

He turned, showing her the folded wings that clung to him, wrapping themselves tightly to his body. She reached out a delicate hand, her thin pale fingers touching the soft pale flesh. The wing jolted, unused to being touched and she withdrew. Then, reaching out again, she ran her finger along the bone, felt it loosen from the count's dark body and lift away, opening as her hand slid along it, and suddenly the room was filled with the giant wingspan that stretched up to the ceiling and across to the walls. She stared in awe, terrified and sickened and intrigued. He turned to face her, his warm caring eyes meeting hers and becoming gentle and questioning, his smile fading.

'Am I so terrible?'

She came close to him, looking up, not knowing where her eyes should rest. They moved from his wings to his chest and to his strong round shoulders, then to his arms and his bare feet, to the strong legs and the hanging laces that if loosened would reveal him in his totally raw form to her. He felt her curiosity, watched her eyes study his frame and brought them up to look deep into his own. Pushing his fingers beneath the thick cream cotton, he lowered his breeches, sliding them down his legs and over his feet. He was naked, his complete self for her.

And though she felt she might scream, or faint at such confrontation she remained calm. She was royalty, decorum and control were required. She stepped back, allowing herself to look at him. Her own body reacting with quickened and hot breath, the thrill of danger making her every nerve tingle. Embarrassingly, what she felt the most, however, was naiveté - reduced to a mere girl in the presence of the body of a strong powerful man, and his eyes read it. She was lost, unsure but ready, so he stepped forward. Her eyes followed his bare feet across the carpet, felt his dark legs part the folds of her dress, his hips, strong and firm pressing against hers as his hand reached up, lifting her chin, her lips to his mouth and he kissed her.

A moment later, naked, she writhed on the carpet as his mouth, expert and hungry, moved up her legs. She giggled, reached out for breath, tried to catch it and pull it down into her lungs, but the sensations on her skin, his touches here, there, his hands moving down to her feet, his thumbs running over her instep, his fingers pushing through her toes, his body pressing down onto her, was too much and she cried out, breathing hard from somewhere unknown inside her. Her hands dared to touch him, feel the strength of his arms, slow down his hands, guide his lips to her hungry mouth. The pain was sharp but was lost in the moment, and at last she was someone else and she relished his movement, wanting it, encouraging it, taking it.

Maggie came down to the kitchen the following morning to find Judy writing frantically.

'If it's as absorbing to read as it looks to write, I'll read it,' she said, picking up the pages.

'No!' Judy snatched them back. 'It's not ready.'

'I promised once you'd written chapter six I'd read it. It says here, "Chapter Six".' She picked up the pages again.

'No!' Judy snatched them. 'They must all be rewritten first. They are my first draft. It's not good.'

'You've changed your tune!' Maggie snapped.

Folding the chapters, Judy hurried towards the village towards the post master's office.

In the evening, with the shop prepared for the séance, she welcomed the group of four in out of the blustery night and seated them in the waiting area. They were younger than the usual guests and a little drunk. She allowed them to warm themselves at the fire before taking them through to the parlour.

In the dark, candlelit room, Mrs Walters, white and corpse-like, rose at the end of the table to gasps of horror. Even Judy felt the need to take a step back but she pushed the group towards her, fearing they were about to change their minds and leave. Mrs Walters, without a word, sat down, all eyes on her. She motioned to the chairs and watched the young people take their places. Bowing her head, she remained silent and meditated for several minutes, allowing the group time to take in the situation and let their nervousness subside. Then, blowing out a candle and plunging them deeper into darkness, she instructed them to remain silent unless spoken to. Concentration, she reminded them over and over, would bring results. They began with a prayer, then, when the room was silent, Mrs Walters asked,

'Is there anybody there?'

The two males burst into laughter, quickly joined by the women, who covered their mouths, trembling. Mrs Walters stared at each of them until she sobered them with embarrassment and after several false starts, they were silent again.

'Is there anybody there?'

'Yes,' squeaked one of the men. 'It's me. I'm dead. Help!'

'If you do not intend to take this seriously, you may leave,' Mrs Walters told him, rising.

'Stop it!' the youngest girl warned him. 'I want to see.'

'Oh, she wants to see the ghosts!'

'Be quiet!'

Closing her eyes to shut out the face-pulling, Mrs Walters felt around the room for spirits. 'Come closer, come to us.'

Someone sniggered.

'I have a man here,' she said opening her eyes, confronting the rowdier of the two males. 'He says he knows you.'

'Oh! Spooky!' he laughed.

'Then I'll move on to you dear,' she said tuning to the other male. 'I have your mother here. She is quite a tall woman, with a mole just to the right of her nose. What's your name dear? Clara. She says she is with your aunt Elizabeth, the one whose carrots you used to pull up prematurely, remember? Aunt Elizabeth is a bit of a strict one, isn't she? She wants me to tell you . . . no dear. I can't say that. No . No, dear. I'll tell you why, because it's filthy! So no!'

'What is it?' the boy asked.

'It's about your bedroom activities dear. Best . . .' she motioned to the others, 'you know.'

The boy looked away embarrassed.

'Anyone could have found out his mother's name was Clara and that he had an aunt Elizabeth,' the other lad objected.

'Perhaps,' Mrs Walters said, 'but who else knows that you regularly take money from your father's business and store it all up under the floorboard in the corner of your room beneath the wardrobe? You seem to go to great lengths for that little secret not to be found out by anyone. How do I know? Your grandfather here knows all about that.' She turned to the space next to her and asked, 'What else does he keep there, dear?' She listened, cocking her head. 'It seems you have quite a little collection tucked away there, don't you? Jewellery, something belonging to her.'

She pointed to the older girl who grinned excitedly.

'It's not a ring, dear. He's not the one. Your relationship with him will be over in under a month and you'll marry his brother, but not for five years.'

She turned suddenly to the younger girl, the calmest of the four. 'There's a girl your age standing behind you. It's not a happy feeling, dear. I'm picking up . . . it's a bit muddled but it's coming clearer . . . should I elaborate?'

The girl shook her head.

'Tell us!' the group enthused.

'It seems there was a bridge,' Mrs Walters said, her eyes closed, her neck craning to see. 'The girl standing behind you was there, and another girl, and you are there too. You were a lot younger. And she . . . fell?'

The girl picked up her bag and stood, moving from her chair to the curtains.

'But dear,' Mrs Walters called, 'Wait, it's important you hear. She has a message for you.'

'I think you've upset her enough!' the other girl said angrily, rising to join her.

'No, I haven't,' Mrs Walters said firmly, reaching out her hand and motioning the girl back to the table, but she remained at the curtains, ready to leave. Mrs Walters nodded. 'She says that you've blamed yourself for it ever since and you still relive it so often in your head. My dear, you've been allowed to believe it was you . . .'

The girl listened.

'. . . by Angela.'

The girl nodded, shaking.

'Angela pushed her, dear, not you. And Angela has always known that, and she has always let you believe it was you. But it wasn't. Who is Angela?'

The girl shook violently, wiping her eyes, 'No one else knows she was there. She wouldn't let me tell. Not even my parents knew.'

The others watched her.

'My dear.' Mrs Walters reached out and took her hand. 'Your punishment is over. You are friends. You have always been friends and she is pleased that you know the truth at last. But wooo! She is waiting for Angela!'

The girl smiled.

'You can let go now. Now you must follow your heart. She also says that you are with the wrong man and that Carl, who you used to adore, is single and very much likes you too.'

She looked at the table of relationships she had just destroyed and smiled.

Chapter 15

Maggie sat on the bench up on Cade Road overlooking the afternoon smog of London. The lure of the city had never held the same appeal for her as it did for Judy. Since the arrival of the train at Greenwich, Judy travelled into the centre of London several times a year, returning with enthusiastic babble about how society was on the verge of exciting change, how fashion was reaching truly exotic peaks and how the people who mattered were adopting new phrases and greetings. 'It's so much more modern than Blackheath.'

She reached into her bag and laid out a wrapped sandwich. She did not care for travel, by train or otherwise. It seemed to her unsettling how people living in Scotland or France could all exist simultaneously and not once meet. How odd it was that people were carrying on with their household chores and their cooking and their worrying over money in Africa and America and Wales and if you travelled there, you would see them, otherwise, they simply did not exist. To exist, she considered, you must be seen. She was lost in these thoughts when her mind was again drawn back to her childhood journey to Southampton. She had abandoned all travel immediately after it.

It was in her tenth year when, as a family they had made the exhausting journey to the ship that would sever her father from her forever. Since then she had become an advocate of staying put. In her opinion these far-flung destinations seldom brought anything other than trouble or the unwelcome influence of bold new ideas and change.

The memory of the roads and the fields and the crowds came back to her. She recalled the boarding house in which the family spent their last night and she had been allowed to share the bed with her parents, snuggled tight to her father. She had not slept. She had lain on her side, her head propped on her elbow, watching him sleep fitfully. It would be two years before she saw him again, and every moment with him counted. Her favourite memory was when, temporarily unaware of his surrounds, he had opened his eyes just before daylight and saw her watching him. He had smiled, given her a kiss on the nose and turned her over, pulling her tightly to him. Then she did sleep.

When she woke, it was to the sound of shouting. They had overslept. The ship would leave within thirty minutes. He could not wait for them, so he picked up his bag, kissed each goodbye and ran with them following him at a distance. When they reached the docks, he was already on board, the anchor was rising, the bow of the ship was crammed full of men waving to their loved ones. There was a deafening blast on the ship's horn and the earth-trembling roar of the engines and the ship was moving. Maggie was pushing through the crowds, frantically scanning the hundreds of crying, cheering faces waving down towards her, terrified that the moment would pass and she would not see her father - then he would be gone. But in a shocking moment, he was there, wedged in with lots of other men, staring right at her, waving, blowing kisses, smiling at her – the saddest, most beautiful smile that told her that he loved her and that he would miss her the most. She blew a kiss back, crying loudly, wanting him back. Then the ship was gone, and all the people, including herself and her mother and Judy, turned and walked away.

When they returned to Blackheath, there was a new sense of order in the house. It seemed a more isolated place, with more rules and less time. Chores were shared, their mother took over the shop from her mother, and it seemed that almost immediately father was forgotten by everyone except by her. Every day for two years she would count down, picturing him in the diamond mines with other Londoners building his family a better future.

She unwrapped her sandwich and ate, relishing each flavour, closing her eyes against the bright autumn sun. It was rare that such a sunny day ventured so deep into the year and for a change, she sat out in it, enjoying the rays on her skin. Just over her right shoulder, activity at the Ranger's House drew her attention. The princess was receiving a visitor of some importance, perhaps her uncle George, she supposed, or was he dead? She didn't keep up with this sort of news. That was more her sister's territory. The princess was unmarried and unimportant, that was the sum total of Maggie's knowledge of her.

What had promised to be a lunch hour of pleasant indulgence was suddenly brought to a dreadful halt by the appearance of the vicar, who, pointing at her as if she were a naughty schoolgirl who he had caught hiding after being up to no good, hurried up the slope towards her. For a moment she contemplated running, then resigned herself to her fate and waited.

'Hello, Henry,' she said.

'Most people –'

'Call you father. I remember.'

'What game are you and your sister playing at, opening that abomination in Blackheath?' He sat next to her.

'It is not an abomination, Henry, it is a place of science. We are simply complementing the Church by trying to find proof that the afterlife does in fact, exist.'

He shook his head, 'So that is the defence you have decided between you?'

'Defence? Defence from what?'

'Do you think that the parish will allow such an unholy place to remain?'

'There's nothing unholy about it.' She wrapped her sandwich and put it back in her bag. 'It's 1842, Henry. We have reached an age where, finally, we can seek answers without fear. The world is embracing science.'

He shook his head. 'The world is so full of despair that there is a widespread effort to believe in something and you . . . you are falling into the trap of offering up a devilish temptation.'

'Oh for goodness sake! People want answers, not just blind herding. Society is beginning to shake off the shackles imposed by –'

'God?'

'By the people who parade their closed minds and earn far too luxurious an income in his name.'

He looked at her and she sighed.

'Henry,'

'Father!'

'Henry. We are not here to threaten you or your parish. We are here for people who miss their loved ones and want to contact them.'

'God decides what happens after we die, Miss Cloak.'

'I don't doubt that,' she lied. 'We are simply making his presence on earth more diversely appreciated. You surely can't keep God all to yourself.'

The vicar stood. He did not know how to answer, which was unusual for him. Maggie Cloak's intellect had always been a source of fascination to him. They could converse intelligently about most subjects and she would pull him up, often educate him, and sometimes he, her. In many ways they were very similar people. In that moment, Maggie looked at him and wondered; if the theory that she would never love was to turn out to be inaccurate, could Henry Legge, the vicar . . . ? Could he be the one? She came out of her stupor with a horrified no.

'Good day.'

'Good day to you.'

He marched off towards the Ranger's House and she reached for her abandoned sandwich.

∞∞∞∞∞∞∞∞

Judy was rushing through the village with purpose. All day she had had a feeling. A letter was there, burning for her to read it. She turned the door handle to the carriage master's office and burst in.

'Did the publisher send anything for me?'

The carriage master shook his head, watching her face drop.

She nodded and, dejected, made her way back to the séance parlour. He had gone off it, she convinced herself. It was too fantastical, too strange.

Inside, she found Mrs Walters in the kitchen untangling a brush that was trapped in her hair. She poured herself some tea and gulped it down.

'My hair grows too fast,' Netta complained, tugging at the long lengths and tying it back.

Judy looked at her own. 'When I get this week's pay I am going to treat myself to something nice, a dress or shoes, a hairdo perhaps.'

Mrs Walters beamed. 'Saturday. We should go into London, all three of us. Pamper ourselves.'

Judy grinned. 'Yes! Yes!' then hurried to her table, apologising and composing herself.

'I am not a customer,' the young woman said, taking a seat.

Judy looked at her.

'I have come to thank you. My fiancée came to see you and you told him he should seek medical assistance for a lump? In his leg?'

Judy's eyes at once lit up but then glazed over as she studied the handsome man's intended.

'They found the lump you saw and Christopher is recovering in hospital. He wanted me to come to tell you and thank you. I would like to thank you too.'

Judy smiled quickly and nodded. 'Perhaps you would be good enough to convey my very best wishes to . . . Christopher and tell him I do look forward to him calling so we can finish our appointment.'

The woman smiled and nodded, taking her leave.

'Very pretty,' Netta said, coming into the room, motioning after her.

'Do you think so? I thought she was rather plain. Her voice was irritating too, a little . . . slow.'

She went through to the kitchen and leaning against the door she giggled with excitement.

'Christopher,' she said aloud. 'His name is Christopher.'

Netta listened and shaking her head walked to greet her next customer. 'Now dear, you're here to find that hidden pocket watch, aren't you?'

'How did you know?'

'I was expecting you. It saves time.'

She held out her hand, took the payment and without sitting, said, 'Your youngest plans to sell it. It's hidden at the bottom of the garden in a tin amongst the blackberries. Good day.'

❦❦❦❦❦❦❦❦❦

The demand for tea-leaf reading was ebbing, Maggie noticed. All excitement now revolved around the cards and the crystal ball in which layer upon layer of information was available. Tea leaves were not that accurate, people complained. Sometimes the answers were not even relevant to the question, and when they were, the shapes did not proffer enough. The missing pocket watch for example, would have yielded the fruit or plants but little else. But, Maggie realised, if they were vague about so many things, then perhaps they too had been wrong about her never finding love. She waited until she had Netta alone and then sat opposite her.

'I want you to find something out for me. In the ball.' She said.

Mrs Walters raised her eyebrows. 'Of course.'

'I want you to tell me about love. About my future. Will there be anyone?'

Mrs Walters nodded and cupped the ball in her hands, then setting it down she peered inside.

She was preoccupied for several minutes, then looking up, shook her head. 'I don't see anyone.'

'Can that be changed?'

Mrs Walters shook her head. 'Perhaps, but I have never known the ball to be wrong.'

Maggie nodded, and rising from the table, said, 'Well, at least I shall not have to put up with snoring.'

Mrs Walters smiled.

The afternoon passed by busily. Both Judy and Netta's tables were rarely empty of customers while Maggie, who had not worked all afternoon, busied herself cleaning and welcoming people. At five, she took the crystal ball up to the attic room and sat practicing but her mind was elsewhere. There were longings that needed adjusting, the dreams of his big belly and undarned socks through which he wiggled his big toe to annoy her, of his bad cooking and his surprise flowers, of where he would sit, the cuddles in the middle of the coldest nights and the seats in the garden with tea watching the sun set. They were all gone, never to be. At least, she consoled herself, without him, she need never grieve at his funeral or suffer with the madness that accompanies losing the one you love.

~~~~~~~~~

On Friday, closing the door on their second trading week, the three women toasted their success, barely able to remember life before the day-to-day chaos. For women who barely socialised at all, they now knew more about the families in Blackheath than anyone, including the priests who heard their confessions.

With steaming cups of tea, they sat around the pot in the centre of the table and barely able to lift it up, pushed it onto its side and emptied it out onto the tablecloth. They stared at it. There was more money than the chocolate shop had made all summer long. Dividing it up, and setting aside money for bills and improvements, they shared out the remainder equally, each woman laughing as their wage grew way beyond anything they were used to.

When the lights were extinguished and the door locked after them, Maggie stole the moment and took Netta aside.

'If I were to change, drastically, could that alter the outcome you saw in the ball? I mean not just become pleasing to the eye but to change, become lighter in spirit, more sociable?'

Netta took her arm and walked.

'You want me to tell you the truth, don't you?'

Maggie nodded, 'No pretence, I need to know so I can adjust. Tell me what I must do.'

Netta should have lied, she knew it then, but something demanded that she told her friend no lies.

'Nothing can change the outcome. The ball sees the situation from the closing of your life, once everything that you will do has been done.'

'But there is a contradiction,' Maggie pointed out. 'Having this information could change the course I take. The ball can foretell that for dinner I will have fish. Knowing this, I could alter it – I could have mutton. The ball could tell me I will stay in tonight but knowing that, I could go out. I can make the ball be wrong.'

Mrs Walters shook her head. 'The little things are of no interest to it. You cannot demand love. You can immerse yourself in a room of men looking for marriage but if the ball says you will not love, you will leave the room without it.' She regretted these words, cursing herself angrily as Maggie walked on with her in silence.

'But,' she interrupted. 'Perhaps you are right, perhaps knowing . . .'

Maggie shook her head and smiled.

'There's no need. You have told me the truth.'

Netta smiled.

Van Dayne slept deeply, exhausted from hours of operating, and was snoring loudly. The young nurse listened to the racket from outside his doors. It would be hours before he could pull himself awake. She let herself inside, moving slowly and silently to his bedside, then lifting his keys, she slipped back into the corridors of the cold building and hurried down through the castle into the cellars that were off-limits to staff. She turned keys in locks, opening doors onto rooms that housed bodies, dead, alive and dying, onto rooms of pregnant women, rooms filled with the skeletons of children and adults, bones organised by size and quality. There were decaying, limbless bodies, sacks of skin that she presumed to be mothers not yet fed to the wolves. She was in shock. She had been living in the same building in which all these atrocities were being carried out and had been completely ignorant of them. The man was deranged and dangerous. She had to play a careful game, not let him suspect that she knew anything.

A month passed and when it was safe, when he retired to bed in the early hours of one morning exhausted, she let herself in the children's room to look over and examine them. Their wings were obscene, pink and wrinkled, sensitive to the touch like the male scrotum, but the children were strong and lively and always eager to see her. This made it easier, on the night that her brother brought the carriage, for her to carry them silently through the darkened rooms and corridors of the castle to freedom. She had taken week by week his gold, money, the precious stones, built up a library of his work on the children and accumulated a collection of things that they would need to survive.

They travelled for three days, along the least likely routes up into the mountains of her ancestors. Remote and abandoned, there was an ancient stone building up high that had survived even the stormiest winters of their childhoods. She relied on it still, but as they tucked the carriage out of view and climbed the stark white craggy ledges of the treacherous mountain, it appeared, from their viewpoint as if the building no longer remained. Carrying the children and the little extra that balance would allow, they stopped frequently to rebuild strength. They had hoped to arrive earlier, to have the full day, but the distance was longer than anticipated and the warm afternoon was passing quickly. Light would soon be against them. They had two, possibly three hours before there would be no light and they would need to find some form of shelter.

Finally, as they neared the top, a thick grey stone wall came into view, weather-beaten but proud and defiant. With renewed energy they pushed on and, reaching the top, they laughed with relief to find that the four walls at least had survived. It would need a roof and a door and shutters and all the comforts of a home but it was safe and strong and they would not be found here.

They laid the children down on the grass and took in the scale of work that would be needed. The trees were plentiful on the eastern slope, and there was water and wildlife, enough to sustain a meagre dependence but it would not be enough for the long term. Her brother would stay for three weeks, to help renovate the building before he returned to his family. After that, she and the children would be alone.

Busying herself, she gathered wood for a fire, made a makeshift broom and brushed out, as best she could, the inside of the building. She collected long grass to create a bed, and threw over it a sheet, attempting to inject a little of the familiar into the long abandoned interior.

As the days passed, busying herself with the making of furniture and cursing the daily trek down the mountain to carry up the collection of household items that they had brought with them, she wondered how Van Dayne was and what had happened to him. She had sent a message to the authorities and to the people who paid for his services, explaining his madness. He had to be stopped, but before that, the children had to be removed and be far away. She knew how readily they would have been destroyed. A part of her considered their survival an affront to God and to nature and that termination would probably have been the correct way to end their young lives, but she was also curious to see the outcome. In this respect, she began to think of herself almost as selfish as their creator. She appointed herself as their governess.

The three weeks of her brother's services passed quickly and when she waved him farewell, the building at last resembled a house. It had a heavy secure roof and window shutters, a door that while not hinged, could easily keep out the most determined of wolves. There were vents for fires, two large beds, warm blankets and benches which could be pulled out into the sun or be wedged against the door should she need further protection. From the vegetables and fruits they had purchased, she gathered seeds and grew them in hollowed-out tree trunks stuffed with earth, that could be pulled indoors when the snow and frosts came. There was enough work to be done to keep every day busy for a year, but it was time she had.

Three years passed. There were visits from her brother and his wife and sometimes, when the children slept, she secured them inside and took trips down into the village at the foot of the mountain and onwards a mile. This was her only contact with the outside world, and even here she rarely spoke for fear of standing out. The children became her sole focus. She taught them all she knew – reading, writing, arithmetic, poetry, science, astronomy, but as the years passed by, their animal instincts grew more prevalent. The children could not be controlled, often for periods of weeks coinciding with the changing of the seasons.

'They fly at me,' she confided to her brother as he cut her hair and they were at play, 'and they bite, drawing blood. They bring back animals to feast on, and not just rabbits and birds, larger animals – foxes and once a wolf cub. I hear them at night taunting animals, playing with them, their frightened cries wake me from my sleep.'

Through fear of them, she had built in the far corner, a room separating herself from them at night, the door of which remained closed and bolted.

'During the day they are good children, loving and attentive and eager for knowledge,' she told him, examining the length of her greying hair that fell into her lap. 'Their lessons go far beyond what is expected of their age. The boy shows great aptitude for the sciences, and his hunger for knowledge about the world and the traditions of different countries is endless. I only wish I knew more about them. Have you noticed his eyes?'

Her brother nodded. 'They have changed.'

She nodded. 'Sometimes when I am teaching him, I find myself unable to look away they are so beautiful. His sister in comparison is rather plain, her beauty will come later. She has a great love of art and drawing and is forever altering clothes on me. She will one day make a wonderful seamstress. She thinks the English language is a great game. We sometimes talk no Russian at all, for days on end. They have also developed their own language. It is basic and easily seen through for the most part but they do like to communicate secretly, usually when there is going to be activity at night. I can read everything I need to know on their faces.'

With the children out of sight, he sat opposite her and held her gaze. 'There is news,' he said.

The castle had been seized the morning after her departure. They already knew that much. For days soldiers had pillaged and stole, before turning their guns on the women and half-creatures they found locked in cells. According to his source, Van Dayne, crazy with rage, had seen them approaching, and taking to the forests, escaped them.

He knew that it was she who had betrayed him. He realised when he found the children missing. Then he found his notes on them gone. The instructions on diet and the key to the maintenance and growth of their bodies and the extra limbs. For that at least, he was grateful; even if she tried to pass them off as her own genius, if she followed his notes, they would remain alive. And if he survived, there was a chance that one day he would find them. Years in hiding had left the authorities with little choice other than to reprioritise, *relegating him to a lower importance.*

'He has resurfaced,' her brother said. 'Just recently, he has been asking people about you, mentioning your name in this town and that before disappearing again.'

'Is he close?'

He shook his head. 'He appears to be moving in the opposite direction.'

On the last day of her brother's visit, she noticed he had changed. He was eager to leave, and taking his sister aside, urged her to leave with him. 'Twice they have attacked me at night. I think perhaps you do not know them as they really are. They soften their play with you. You are their guardian. It took all my strength to fight them away in the early hours. They were brutal and vicious, snarling at me, always ready to pounce. I am a strong man three times their size but still they attacked with confidence, and at my weakest, I thought they might win.'

She listened, looked at the gashes in his arms and neck.

'They are dangerous and feral. If they turn on you, you realise that you will not stand a chance.'

She was silent.

'They should be killed.'

'I cannot.'

'Imagine what they will do to others? To other children their own age. They will tear them apart. They are inhuman.'

But she shook her head. 'I must stay. I must teach them, change them.'

Their hushed words were being listened to from the doorway and the young count and countess exchanged glances.

It was perhaps because of their intellect that she let them live. Their affection and need of her ensured her safety even when their eyes showed their most lost and distant expressions. And though in the draughty house on the silent mountain, the screaming horror of their prey filled her with terror and revulsion and often resulted in animals as large as deer crashing into the house to escape their cat-and-mouse games, she would lock herself away, cover her ears or her head with the bed sheets and pretend that nothing was happening. When that became impossible, she forced them to sit and consider the terror they struck in animals and in herself, teaching them how to kill with compassion, but her words made little sense to them.

On the stony ledges of the great cliff, the children spent summers sitting listening to the woman's lectures, watching eagles swoop down and carry *away young lambs and the great tigers tear into yaks and goats. These animals showed no compassion either, they did what was natural to them.*

On the windier days, they would sit on the small lawn of the house, next to the vegetable garden, where she told them stories, invented romances and tragedies, love poems and comedies, hoping to instil in the beautiful and sometimes refined savages, why life should be protected and admired and they nodded in agreement, but there was an exchange of the eyes between them that told her they were of a different breed. Often as she spoke she willed her brother to return - years had passed and he had not come to visit. He was fearful of them, she realised; he knew what they were capable of before and now they were bigger and stronger. She had no idea that her brother had never left the mountain at all; in fact, he had barely made it to the bottom. When he had turned into the craggy rock passageways that led past the ledges towards the final decent, he had found himself confronted with them. The icy chill in their eyes told him that this was the time and the place for his life to end. He took a moment to take in the scene, to remember it.

Ten years passed. Sometimes she could barely look at either of the children without becoming spellbound by their beauty. Then on a stormy winter's day, they came running into the house.

'Someone is coming!' they cried excitedly, pulling her to the edge of the mountain.

Below, a line of soldiers navigated the steep climb. She pulled them back, hurrying them into the house.

'You must leave now! You must fly.'

There was little time to prepare them but they were to learn in these final moments the most important lesson of all.

'If people . . . if anyone, anyone at all, sees your wings, they will kill you. Do not think they won't. They will kill you as fast as a tiger kills a goat and you will be dead, over with. They will not talk, they will just kill. All of your lives you must hide your wings. Strap them down as I have shown you when we go to the village.'

She hurried around the house filling bags with clothes, money, diamonds.

'The soldiers are coming here to kill you. They will kill me too but you must go. You must not come back for several weeks, until it is safe, and then you must not stay. If I am not here you know where we have hidden all the precious stones and the gold. You know all of the hiding places. Come back when you need those things, take them and go. They are safe and will stay

hidden for as long as you need them. Use them to set up your lives. It is plenty but it is all you have in life so spend it wisely. And if you must kill, kill silently; you must keep it a secret. You must never be seen. You are not birds, you are people. You are different. You are what they will call an abomination, a bad thing, and for that they will make you pay. You must watch how others live and copy them.'

She hurried them out of the house and across the mountain top away from the soldiers to the great cliff, pulling off their upper garments. There was no time for tears. Looking out at the stormy Chukshi Sea, she kissed them hard on the cheeks and pushed them out into the blustery winds.

Chapter 16

It was a beautiful white crisp winter Saturday, the sort of day that Blackheath often enjoyed at this time of year. Maggie looked forward to them. These were the days on which to do things. The air was clean and bracing and one could delude oneself that spring was approaching and not a deep, freezing winter. She was bringing in bed sheets that had frozen on the washing line into solid shapes taller than herself and shook her head adamantly at her sister's pestering.

'I have my day planned,' she told her. 'I am shaking out the rugs, turning over the mattresses. I mean to patch up the hole in my bedroom window at long last and turf out the culprit of the big cobwebs in the hall. I am also planning a pie, a long hot bath and to open the wine at around seven. The opening of which you are invited to, should you become bored of experimenting with your vanity.'

'Oh Maggie. Come to London. Please come! We have such a day planned! Hairdressers and dress shops and shoe shops and lunch. Come with us.'

Maggie shook her head. 'I have no interest in dress shops and the like.'

'But you must!' Judy insisted. 'It is exciting to try new fashions, to feel glamorous and fanciful and to make men turn their heads.'

But Maggie refused and Judy hurried across the heath barely able to contain her excitement. Her sister watched her from the window as she washed her hands. With Judy gone, the house was suddenly silent and Maggie found herself on a knife-edge, wondering if she should rush to catch up with Judy and throw herself into the spirit of things. But it was there again, rising up in her mind. She would never be loved.

'What is the point me looking beautiful? For who?'

She reached down and dragged the rug out into the garden, hung it over a chair and took her anger out on it with a brush. 'No man will look twice at me. That much is already established. No good at love. No good at tarot, no good at crystal balls, no good at anything; a complete waste of time.'

'Where is she?' Netta asked as they climbed aboard the train in Greenwich feeling as light-headed and giddy as schoolgirls.

'Spring cleaning,' Judy replied staring out of the window to watch the buildings go by. At Deptford, they planned their spend, agreeing that if they continued eating next to nothing the following week, today they could squeeze in a few extras. Alighting at London Bridge they took a carriage to the Strand and hurried to see the new Trafalgar Square. They joined the crowd marvelling at the unimaginably high column with its empty plinth.

'I wonder what is up there?' Netta asked, looking around to see if anyone had the answer. Her eyes fell on Judy who suddenly appeared self-conscious. She grabbed Netta's hand and, marching her away, they both agreed, to their absolute horror, that a major change had taken place in the world; that now, even their best dresses were horrifyingly out of style.

At the dress shop, they surrendered all control and were stripped to their undergarments, which raised even more horrified eyebrows, so new ones were purchased and the old added, with a look of disgust and tongs, to the parcel that would be sent on. Embarrassed, they were measured, tugged, prodded and tied into corsets so constricting that they realised their personal grooming had grown neglected to the point of sloth.

'Dresses have not had exaggerated puffy shoulders like yours since the mid-thirties. The fashion now is a thinner, more natural shoulder line. And those pleated fabric panels that wrap the bust and shoulders have been completely forgotten. They have been replaced with a triangular shape, nipping in the waist. Waists are lower and narrow these days.'

'And the sleeve . . .' the other seamstress tending Mrs Walters began, 'the detail has moved now to the cuff rather than the elbow. And of course skirts are a bell shape these days. We have done away with the conical. Have you been staying in the country? Look, see this? Now the skirts attach directly to the bodice using organ pleats so the skirt is altogether much lighter.'

Both women sighed with relief as the weight fell from them, and were so impressed they no longer noticed or cared about the women's patronising tones.

'Evening gowns are off the shoulder now with wide flounces down to the elbow, you see? Lace.'

Judy was pulled into her second dress, an evening gown, off the shoulder with wide flounces and long white opera gloves and the all-important shawl.

'Shawls are now so high fashion that a woman should own as many as possible.' The shop owner put together four must-haves, then turning to a wall display she commanded their full attention. 'And now ladies, prepare yourself for the most decadent must-have fashion accessory of the forties.' She opened a cupboard revealing a small green bag, delicately embroidered with tassels. The women stared in awe.

※※※※※※※※※

At home, with the house spotless, Maggie turned her concentration away from the crystal ball she had been staring into for the last half hour. She sighed angrily then pinched the skin on the back of her hands, smacking it flat when it refused to settle. She was getting too old. Age had happened to her one day. She could not remember when. As far as she could remember it had not come in stages, there had been one complete change, perhaps during the years when there was no mirror in her house. Now there was no escaping it. Her hip ached, there were dark bags under her eyes that she had always meant to combat with extra sleep and less alcohol but never had. Now they were past the point of recovery.

'And now it doesn't matter what I look like,' she told herself sadly.

She dragged in the tin bath from the garden and began boiling pots, shaking the thoughts aside and focusing instead on the evening ahead. Judy would be home at seven, they would get drunk and laugh and put the world to rights.

※※※※※※※※※

Outside the hairdresser, Judy was preoccupied with worry over the strange new styles and whether new hair as well as new dresses was all too much for one day. She turned to Netta who was white and trembling. She had not heard a word.

'Netta! What is wrong?'

Netta shook her head, 'I am fine. I just remembered that I am to be somewhere within the hour. I am so sorry, Judy, I must leave you.' She manoeuvred Judy in through the door. 'But you must do it. You must. 'I will see you tomorrow . . .' And pushing poor Judy, bonnet in hand, beneath the horrified glare of London's finest she rushed away.

Sinking back into a doorway Netta peered around, nervously clutching her chest, and dared to look again, covering her horrified face. She could not believe it was them. She was not sure if she should run away or hurl abuse at them. Instead she kept them at a distance and followed. They had let her take the blame, let it appear to everyone that she was capable of murder, exaggerating her temper and assuring everyone that their son was lucky to escape her. In front of her eyes, as bold as brass, they had pulled him back into their clutches and pushed her away to carry the weight of his crime. She had not seen his parents since.

Watching them laughing and chatting she could barely contain her mounting anger. They headed up the Strand, out of the centre, to an area Netta didn't know, where the larger houses gave way to smaller residential streets, and suddenly they had reached their front door.

She waited until the door slammed behind them and doubled back, peeking inside their window. She wasn't entirely sure what she was doing there. She was too numb with outrage at seeing the building that for all those years she had tried to imagine them living in while she suffered on ships and in workhouses and as the unpaid cleaner and housemaid to one Australian after the other. And although they probably thought of her from time to time, she imagined those thoughts to be easily pushed aside. They probably imagined her to be dead and they feared no retribution. All was neatly folded away and now here she was again with decades of rage and endless nights of plotted revenge rehearsed over and over again in her head. Unexpectedly the door opened and they came out into the street again. Netta jumped back into a doorway, pretending to knock. They were hurrying towards Covent Garden and she followed them again, listening to their excited chatter along street after street until they reached a pub. She waited outside a while, wondering if she should storm inside and confront them in public, but she knew she wouldn't so she made her way home confused and upset and suddenly lonely again.

⌘⌘⌘⌘⌘⌘

Judy studied her new curls in the hairdresser's mirror. She wasn't sure, it was so different and so tight that it made her head look too small. She barely recognised herself but as they pointed out, it did seem to take years off her face. Her sudden return to youth was quite startling.

On the train home, she smiled at those who studied her with inquisitive eyes, feeling light-headed. She was turning the heads of gentlemen she had never imagined would pay her attention. One man in particular made her blush so self-consciously she found herself with no other option than to alight early to escape him. She paced the station platform cursing herself for not being brave enough to simply change seat. Then her eyes caught the sign for the hospital. She smiled.

Perhaps it would seem vulgar or presumptuous, she thought, hurrying towards the door and purchasing flowers from the stall outside. It was certainly not correct for gentlemen to be visited in hospital by women they barely knew. 'This is different,' she told herself and the flower-seller, 'fate has decided he is the one.'

The cold, weather-beaten woman nodded.

She walked inside. She would make an excuse. She was there visiting a friend. She had remembered he was there. It was a quick hello.

When she entered the ward, confronted with men in various states of undress, the romance of the situation she had imagined drained away. She walked to the far end where he was sitting up in bed dressed in pyjamas and felt horrifyingly conspicuous.

'Miss Cloak?' he called in surprise. 'Is that you?'

She turned to him with feigned surprise.

'I hope you bring good news this time!'

She was flustered.

'I was visiting a friend, I thought I'd just pop by.'

'Please take a seat. I'm so very bored.'

'Of course!' She said and, without hesitation, sat herself next to the bed on a chair.

'Your fiancée tells me you are in recovery.'

'Thanks to you.'

She smiled, and not knowing what to do with the flowers, placed them on his bed and said, 'These are for you.'

'For me? Aren't they for the friend you are visiting?'

'She probably has plenty. I see you have none.'

He smiled.

'I have been thinking about your gift a great deal in here.'

She listened.

'How marvellous it must be to have such foresight. Have you always had it?'

'Even though we have run a chocolate shop for years, since we were girls, both my sister and I have rigidly believed in the spirit world and have been actively in touch with the dead since birth,' Judy recited, pulling Netta's prepared speech for such tricky occasions to mind with odd and stumbling recital.

He stared at her and laughed. 'I'm sorry,' he apologised, 'I have no idea why I laughed.'

'Are you well?'

'Fit as a fiddle.'

'I should let you rest.'

'No, no please stay. It's so frustrating sitting here day after day. Believe it or not I should be in Kenya, Africa. And here I am, no elephants or giraffes in sight.'

She laughed. 'They have those at the new zoo. Though I haven't seen them myself.'

'You must. They really are quite something. In fact, it was the zookeeper who brought your parlour to my attention.'

'Then I had better return the favour and see the zoo for myself.'

'I would offer to take you myself but I'm afraid a psychic advised me to go straight to hospital so . . .'

She smiled.

'But if you could wait, I would be pleased to escort you. Exotic animals are my field of study. In fact, I brought the rhinoceros there back from Africa myself.'

'How exciting. How on earth did you manage that?'

'It is my occupation. I study the animals of Africa and thin the herds by transporting them to various zoos. Will you let me take you someday?'

'I would like that.'

The nurses were gathering around a bed close to the door where a great deal of commotion had brought them hurrying.

'I should go. It is busy,' she said, standing.

He smiled. 'If you must, but thank you for coming.'

Judy smiled.

When she arrived home, it was past nine. Maggie was drunk and mean-tempered; she laughed at Judy's new hair and ridiculed her dress and was spoiling for an argument, so Judy made her excuses and went to bed leaving her sister angry and desperate for company. In her room she hung her dresses, unwrapped and admired her new underwear and bonnets, placed the gloves next to the satin slippers with their elegant bows and admired her small green bag, a quarter of the size she was accustomed to carrying. She sat on her bed and felt her heart racing. He was the one. She knew it now.

A sudden knock at the door made her jump. 'Show me,' Maggie slurred. 'Put on a fashion show, I want to see.' But Judy remained silent until her sister returned to the kitchen.

Pouring herself a large glass of red wine, Maggie fell back in her chair, angry at herself for spoiling Judy's day. Instead of complimenting her, she had complained about the hours she had waited, pointed out that her food was wasted, grumbled about how she did not do her share of the chores. She took another sip of wine, cursing. It was barely past ten and now she would spend the whole evening alone. She pulled herself back up from the chair and went to her sister's door, apologising and begging her drunkenly to come down for a nightcap, to keep her company but when she looked in, Judy, candle still burning, had fallen to sleep.

༽༽༽༽༽༽༽༽༽

The following morning Maggie overslept. Judy hurried about the house silently, trying not to wake her. It was not often that she had days of such happiness, and now, in her new outfit, admiring herself in the mirror, she would enjoy it all over again, without the criticisms of her sister. She left the house silently. In the village, against the passing crowds making their way to church, she kept her head low, and when the coast was clear, let herself inside the shop. It was Sunday, and the shop should not be open but she had made the appointment out of sympathy, and since Netta was more keen than anyone to accept every payment they could get it had seemed a worthwhile risk, despite the annoying vigilance of the Early Closing Association.

Inside, Mrs Walters was already in session. Judy smiled apologetically and joined the table. Mrs Walters, her head bowed, held the hands of the murdered girl's parents, angry at their return and at Judy for allowing it. Their word obviously meant nothing. Once and once only, she had insisted to them in no uncertain terms. She did not like getting involved in police business but they had to have answers, they had pleaded, before Netta had time to unlock the door. The previous week had simply scratched the surface and had made them believe in the afterlife, but now, now they needed to know who had done it. They smiled at Judy and took her hands.

Mrs Walters drifted, she saw the girl coming into the room, saw her stare defiantly at her, then turning to look at her parents, the spirit gasped, covering her mouth.

'I can see them again!'

'Talk to me, child,' Netta said, motioning towards her.

The girl stared angrily at her and hissed.

'What for? You are taking their money but not telling them what I told you. You are frightened. You are a coward.'

Mrs Walters closed her eyes.

'Tell them I don't know who the murderer is then! Tell them that! Then they can leave and not come back. If you will not tell them then stop taking their money!'

'Ask her,' her father asked, 'Ask her if it was someone that we knew.'

The girl looked spitefully at Netta, then coming close, she leaned into her ear, whispering. 'There is another girl in the pond.'

Mrs Walters did not respond. 'Do you know who murdered you?' she asked.

'Do you know who murdered you?' the girl mimicked.

Mrs Walters opened her eyes. 'She said she does not know the man. She did not see him.'

The girl stopped and stared, 'What!'

'A clue? Anything?' the mother persisted.

The girl turned her head and showed Netta a spot where a large clump of hair was missing. 'He took it. He takes it from all the girls he kills. Tell them!'

'I'm afraid she is not very communicative. She has made her peace with it and prefers to forget.'

The girl was enraged, running at Netta, beating at her. 'Tell them the truth! Stop it!'

But Netta would not.

ΩΩΩΩΩΩΩΩ

Hung-over, Maggie opted out of the day's work. Instead, she baked bread and heated the pie as a peace offering. At six, after laying the table, while she waited for Judy, she practiced with the tarot cards. There could be no art to them; since the meanings were laid out in Netta's notes, it was more a memory game. All she had to do was remember the explanations, which seemed simple enough. The trouble was that each card seemed to have five or more explanations. She tried to make sense of them, posing her own questions, turning over the cards, but time after time the readings made barely any sense at all. She tried again and again, then realising it was past seven and her sister was still not home, she put them away and put the pie back in the pantry.

Judy was probably at the pub, showing off her new look, Maggie realised, and pulling on her coat, she braved the dark heath, hurrying towards the lights of the Hare and Billet. But Judy was not there so she waited with a drink before trying the Crown, then the pub up at the pond of swans and the shop but she was nowhere to be found. After almost two hours, turning for home, she heard laughter and music and, looking up, she heard Judy bid goodnight to a small crowd in one of the rooms above the general store and listened to them object to her early departure. A few moments later she was in the street and stepping into a carriage and was gone. For the first time, Maggie felt lost. She wandered slowly homeward, confused by an emotion that almost brought her to tears. At the midway point she cheered herself up with the knowledge that although a little later than planned, soon she would have the opportunity to apologise and fetch cooled wine for them but when she arrived home, she found the house in darkness and her sister's door closed.

The following morning, an outcry tore through Blackheath, distracting Maggie from her tea-leaf readings. She made her way to the front of the shop and joined the crowds rushing in the direction of the Hare and Billet. The police were pulling a body from the centre of the pond. Maggie covered her mouth, then noticed the crowd were distracted more by her sister, who, with the most startling haircut, outlandish bright dress and looking half her age, appeared on the other side of the pond like a theatre actress.

'Look at the dress!' one of the women gasped to another. They shook her heads in shock.

Maggie was about to give them a piece of her mind for mocking her, when she realised that they weren't mocking at all.

'What happened to her? She used to look so old!'

'Oh her hair is so stylish!'

Maggie turned her gaze to her sister, for the first time seeing clearly the dramatic transition she had made. The tired, rag-wearing, worn-out woman was nowhere to be seen and in her place, a startlingly pretty and immaculately turned out woman smiled at her. Maggie studied her, returning her smile, but before Judy made it around the pond to join her, Maggie had hurried away before anyone could draw comparisons between them.

At the shop she kept her head down, reading tea leaves for those who could not afford the cards. She would take action. She would visit the hairdresser, visit a dressmaker, smarten herself up. She cursed her laziness and boiled the kettle, taking a fresh cup to the table. Her customer took a small sip, concentrating on what she wanted to know startled as a small twig rose up to the surface of the tea.

'Oh you have a visitor coming,' Maggie said, lifting it from the cup and putting it on the back of her hand. She clapped her hands together five times until the twig fell and she nodded. 'There will be a male visitor in five days.' The woman sipped with raised eyebrows. She was eavesdropping on the next table where Judy, gazing deep into the ball was telling her customer that her mother was about to have a serious accident and that to avoid it, she should not go outdoors on Wednesday. She went on to describe in detail where her husband was hiding their money, what he was spending it on and how the Sun in the Sands public house was significant. 'There is a man who drinks there,' she confided, 'who lives over at Royal Standard who will become very important to you once your husband has passed.'

Maggie coughed, drawing her customer's attention back to the tea. She finished it and swirled the cup three times clockwise, touched the saucer with the rim of the cup and asking the question she wanted answered, tipped the cup and drained it, handing the cup to Maggie.

Then, without listening to a word, she turned her attention back to Judy's reading.

'The tea leaves say you have small worries, that there is nothing to worry about and . . .' she stopped, waited and eventually lost her temper. 'Are you listening?'

'Could you do that instead, the crystal ball?'

'It is twice the price of tea le . . .'

'I'll pay.'

Maggie smiled, 'I'm afraid I don't read it.' She gathered the cup and saucer up and, refunding the woman's money, walked out to the back of the building, leaving everyone in the room surprised and uncomfortable. In the back room, Mrs Walters, looking spectacular in her new outfit, looked up from her crystal ball and rapidly concluded their session. 'So in short, unless you change your ways, your husband will leave you and there's no one else coming your way.'

The woman smiled sourly and left.

During their lunch break, while Mrs Walters shopped, Maggie took her sister aside.

'You must show me how to use the ball.'

'Let me show you tonight, I want to eat,' Judy replied, unwrapping her food.

'But I have nothing to do. I am being left behind,' her sister pleaded.

Judy did not mean to sigh but it hung between them. It had been a long morning, and the thirty-minute break was guarded jealously by all three women.

'It doesn't matter,' Maggie said, rising.

'Oh Maggie, please don't take it like that. I am just tired.'

But when Maggie was offended, she clung to it like a jealous dog savouring a bone.

'I am no longer reading tea leaves,' she said firmly on Mrs Walters' return.

Mrs Walters was confused.

'Why?'

'Because they are too vague! No one cares.'

'But for the price . . . And the money it brings in . . .'

'I don't care!' Maggie said defiantly. She pointed to a crystal ball on the shelf. 'I have to be able to do that.' She reached for it and, marching up the stairs, slammed the attic door behind her.

When her reading was over, Judy hurried up after her and knocked.

'Maggie, let me in. What is wrong?'

'Leave me!' she called.

Judy sighed, then with a flash of genius, she knocked again.

'How about a night like the old days? Me and you by the fire, port and chatter?'

There was silence.

'We could pick up some bottles on the way home and maybe a nice piece of fish?'

The silence sounded positive.

'I'll leave early, pick up the fish and the bottles, have dinner ready for you at seven, maybe a nice white wine. Well?'

'I'd prefer pork.'

'Pork it is then. Dinner will be on the table at seven.'

Rolling her eyes at Netta, she returned to her table. For the remainder of the afternoon there wasn't so much as a peep from the attic, and although they could barely keep up with the custom, Judy left at five, hurried to the butcher, then unable to resist, she popped into the carriage master's office and was greeted with the shake of his head. She sighed, turning to see one of the delivery boys come in through the door. 'Could you mention my name to him when you go past next?' she asked, 'prompt him along a little?'

The carriage master nodded, 'I'll not be seeing J.J. until Thursday but I'll have a word.'

'J.J. James?' the boy asked, putting packages down onto the counter. He rummaged through them and brought out an envelope. 'He gave me this.'

Judy took it excitedly and read her name. Tearing it open, she read the letter and looked at the official papers that accompanied it. She moved to a seat and read, engrossed. Then she realised she was reading a contract, and not only were the first six chapters accepted but there would be payment, and a further fifteen chapters were required immediately. There was talk about it being serialised in the *Illustrated London News*, then depending on its popularity, a published novel could ensue. She gasped and turned to the desk.

'You must take me there now, please. How long does it take?'

'At least one and a half hours there and back.'

She would be cutting it fine, and the pork would not be on the table at seven, but this was no ordinary day. Maggie would surely understand. She nodded and hurried out to a carriage.

J.J. James was a surprisingly jovial sort, tall and stout with a warm smile and a pipe. She had imagined someone far more austere. 'My dear woman,' he corrected her, 'with business I have no sense of humour. I govern my house and staff with a rod of iron. But there is no need to be stern with those whose enthusiasm shows so clearly as it does in you. Now, let us discuss how the serialisation of your magnificent novel will unfold.'

She signed eagerly, then signed again and again on each of the copies of the contract. She could barely contain her excitement as she hurried from the house back to the carriage. All the way back it was as if she were drunk.

The carriage tore along the roads with time against them but as they drew into Blackheath, it was already past eight. Judy hurried into the house to find that Maggie was not there. She thanked God and hastily lit the oven, unwrapped the pork and the port and the wine. Then as she hurried to light the lamps and start a fire, she saw Maggie's coat and her heart sank. She made her way up to her room and found her sitting on her bed.

'I'm so sorry, dear. I got delayed.'

Maggie was silent.

'But I'm here now, come down. The pork is on and I'll pour us some wine while it's cooking.'

'Where have you been?'

Judy couldn't help it. She knew that her sister was already jealous of her skills and her hair and clothes, so adding to those reasons this new exciting revelation was tantamount to rubbing her face in it, but it came spurting out, all of it, the excitement, the contact, the novel, the serialisation, the money.

'Please, Maggie,' she begged, 'please celebrate with me?'

Maggie nodded, allowing herself to be pulled up, and followed Judy down to the kitchen. She helped prepare the food and poured the port into a jug for it to breathe, and although the mood lightened, it was obvious that Maggie was not on form. She remained sombre and subdued, the drink appearing to pull her deeper into sadness rather than lift her mood. Finally, while it was still early, she put down her wine and looked at her sister.

'I'm going to bed,' she announced, then pausing at the door she said. 'I don't mean to appear mean or difficult, but I think the time has come for you to move back to your own home.'

Chapter 17

The governess hurried the runny-nosed boys with their dirty clothes and their wicker baskets into the kitchen. She shook her head at the state of them and watching each of the six lift their noses to take in the savoury bursts of beef stock bubbling from the pan and the warm aroma of potatoes and parsnips roasting in the oven, she shook her head with despair.

'When did you last eat?'

There was a gurgle of different answers and she sighed. 'Business first.'

She led them down into the cellar, along the hall to the door at the end. Pushing them inside quickly, she followed them and closed the door. Inside, the room was lined with owls, blinking and adjusting to the light.

'How many?' she asked.

One by one the boys untied their baskets, shaking out dazed angry tawny owls. The governess counted them, then taking the baskets from the boys, she threw them into a pile and hurried them out.

In the laundry room, she stripped them down to their underwear and, filling the big tin bath, handed each some soap and cloths with which to wash and dry themselves. Their clothes were given to the kitchen maid who cursed under her breath and held her nose as she scrubbed out the stench of sweat and urine and worse from them and hung the steaming rags before the fire.

Skinny and white, the blue-veined boys shivered into the room, crowding together in the doorway. The governess looked at their faces and marched to a clean pile of towels, giving one to each and motioned to their underwear – the state and colour of which required boiling – preferably outdoors.

The kitchen maid shook her head angrily, shielding her eyes against the bare backsides that bobbed around her and carried the stiff brown and yellow rags in a pan of hot water, rested it on top of the burning compost pile.

Inside, the governess sat them at the servants table and fed them parsnips and bread and a small ration of beef with dripping which they ate like animals. She let them enjoy the rarity of meat and heat and care without boundaries. After their meal, while their clothes dried, she sat them around the back fire, warming them through, hating to see children so hungry and lost struggle through life without parents.

'When I was younger,' she told them, 'I lived on the top of a great cliff in Russia. It felt as though it was the very end of the world. It was bitterly cold, worse than the winters here but I loved it.' Some listened, some slept, some dared to lean against her legs, their bony arms and little toes breaking her heart. If it were her house, she would take them all in, but it was not.

By the time Anna arrived, the boys, a little damp but clean and fed and with a parcel of crispy pig skin tucked into their pockets, were gone. The governess waited for her at the table, noting her determined and defiant glare as she entered.

'The count and countess are waiting for you upstairs,' she said, and waited for her to go. Anna looked at her nervously. 'Aren't you coming?'

The woman shook her head, 'I have more work to do now that you will be a lady of leisure.'

'Then they agree to my income?'

'It's not for me to say, Anna,' she said placing a large basket into the sink.

'I want you to come with me. I don't want to see them alone.'

'You are not in my employment any longer, dear, and your recent behaviour doesn't inspire my loyalty. Now if you don't mind. I have a house to run. '

Anna stood for a moment, nervous and afraid, then shaking her head, she assumed a determined face and turned, walking quickly through the house and up the stairs.

The mouth against her neck, wide and soft and sensual, threw her into giggles. She felt the winds bluster around her, lifting her skirt, running like water up one sleeve and out through the other, tugging her blouse up over her head and sending it flapping into the darkness, stretching and dancing in the racing winds. Her shoe fell from her foot, the first when he tossed her to his sister who rushed to catch her and embracing her, swirled up into the night sky, gazing into the girl's delirious and intoxicated eyes. She was not aware of the countess's feet, pushing off her remaining shoe at the heel and then it was gone. Suddenly she was falling hurtling down and laughing as she collided with the count. Her head nestled into the rough hair on his chest, her bare legs pressing against his, experiencing the intimacy of the muscle and flesh. His leg slid up between hers and pressed against the warm softness that she herself was only *just beginning to explore. He pulled off her untied corset with one tug, hurling it away, her breasts stiffening as the cold tore over them. She pulled herself against his chest, clinging tight, inhaling his smell, drawing the warmth of his neck into her nostrils.*

He turned, swooping away, letting her swing into the arms of his sister who pulled her in tight as if she were a baby. Her underwear, in his fingers, slid down her legs, over her plump calves and kicking tickling feet, tumbling down to the heath below. The gale was all over her, tearing over the soft plumpness of her belly, reaching under her, teasing at the warmth of the newly exposed flesh as her legs kicked wider into the air.

Again, their lips pressed against her neck, nibbling her, enjoying the goose pimples that raced over her, and against their tongues. She laughed, her head rolling back, her throat exposed. They listened to her gasp as their teeth bit gently down, and opening their eyes to look at each other with the briefest of acknowledgements, their teeth sunk in deep, biting together at once, knowing that she was mistaking, with naiveté, the pleasures of the flesh with the sensations that were ending her life. She gasped, breathing hard, stretching out her arms in ecstasy, then cramp ripped through her, her neck was damaged, bruised, different. She twisted, crying out, leaning into them for support, to understand, but still they fed, biting arteries that pumped her blood into their hungry mouths.

She let out a pathetic, timid cry, her eyes pleading with them to stop, to realise their mistake, to recognise her. Her hand sunk down between her legs, the other covered her breasts as her stomach contracting and pulling her tight with cramp doubled her over in his arms. Her head tilted, trying to force their mouths from her, screaming as the bites refused to let go. The wind hammered into her, pounding into her ears, blowing her mouth wide, choking her. She was falling, fast and heavy, then caught, tossed to the count who flew up with her, biting her wrists, crunching against the bones, sucking up the wet. There was a sharp pain at her navel or below, at the curve where her belly met her hips. She felt sharp little bites there and blood hot and rushing down her legs where now a mouth licked and lapped sucking, drinking, emptying her.

She was light-headed, unable to make sense of anything, drunk and spiralling, with prickling senses, embraced by his warm body, pulled tight in his strong arms while a sharp determined mouth moved around her lower body. He was kissing her, biting her lips, sucking from her. The metallic taste on his strong tongue reminded her of her panic and she fought back, kicking and punching and falling down and down and down only to be caught by arms and hugs and bites until too weak to resist, she allowed them to take her life. She was lifted higher and higher into the sky, flinching at their nibbles, intoxicated by the lack of blood and the unbelievable sensation of being thrown through the icy wind from one to another. Life left her. Her body hung from them, drained and pale.

They could not look at each other now. The lectures from their youth about sensitive and respectful killing had built inside each, a reproachful and impractical guilt, but the night was far from over. There were necessities, glands, bone marrow, sinew, liver, disposal of the remains, then the heavy mountainous sleep as their bodies processed what it had needed for months.

The blood swilled inside their stomachs, hot and filling. Their physiologies were drugged into wild excited feeding. They flew upwards, eating and reaching inside for the organs, away from where eyes and telescopes could reach them until finally they grew weak and bloated, their arms heavy from supporting her and they began the decent, gliding over the walls of Greenwich Park, over the dark flower beds and trees, coming to rest high in one of the tallest, oldest trees. They placed her body high in the branches, in such a way that despite strong winds and decay, she was held secure, out of sight in the lofty green.

They came down at the centre of the heath, lying on their sides, curling tight against the cold wet grass, their stomachs cramping, their systems in shock, too weak and vulnerable to protect themselves or lift themselves to their feet or into the air. For an hour, they slept until the count woke. Then, pulling his sister to her feet and holding her close, he carried her naked and barefoot across the heath until he reached the end of the safety of the darkness. Here in the semi-light, their movements needed to be swift and unnoticed. With all his strength he lifted himself into the air and carried her, sleeping and heavy, barely eight feet from the ground. Too low and in danger of being seen, he headed for the house.

The winter rains kept the body unnoticed, except by crows and rooks, who, enticed by the open wounds gathered at the tree in greater and greater numbers, pecking and opening and plucking out whatever they could feed on. It would be seven months before Anna's body would fall from the tree onto the spread of what would prove to be one rather distressing but memorable family picnic.

At the window of the Ranger's House, Princess Sophia was seated in her night attire and a shawl at the window, her eye pressed against the telescope. These past three months there had been no contact, no word from him. The curtains to his room which had remained open that first week, now remained tightly closed. Her requests for meetings were met with the same reply over and over, that the count and countess were elsewhere in the country on business. First Bristol, then Cardiff and that morning they were apparently heading for the great cities of the north. She turned away from the window and walked through to her bedroom.

Lying on the bed, frustrated and worried, her hands explored the growing curve of her stomach. She had told no one. Neither society nor royalty would stand for even a minor royal like herself producing a bastard. They would remove it from her or she would be ostracised. She wasn't sure which, but she was developing such affection towards the child growing inside her that she could not take the risk of announcing it. If she was careful and discreet and if her staff were as trustworthy as she believed them to be, then the child could be born and kept secret.

Maggie woke early, wanting to leave the house before her sister woke. She had barely slept a wink, turning over the words in her head and feeling as much need for her sister to stay as leave, but as light crept into her room and she pulled on her old faded, frayed skirts, she had made up her mind. It was time for her to be alone again. She closed the door behind her and crossed the heath.

There was something urgent that needed to be done this morning and, at the shop, at last, she cornered Mrs Walters and made her sit.

'I want you to contact my father,' she said simply.

Mrs Walters looked at her determined face. 'But we have to open. There are customers.'

'I don't care. I want to speak with him.'

Mrs Walters sighed and closed her eyes. When she opened them again, the murdered girl was standing in front of her, as enraged and angry as the moment Netta had turned her out.

'I am looking to talk to people who know Margaret Cloak,' she began. 'She wants to contact her father.'

The girl laughed. 'He won't come here.'

'Why not?' Netta asked.

Maggie looked up.

'He just won't, you'll see.'

The best part of twenty minutes passed, various spirits drifted by but Mrs Walters was continuously distracted by the murdered girl who sat there grinning at her.

'Why won't he come?'

'If you tell my parents what I tell you, I will make him come.'

'I don't need you to bring him to me,' Netta said out loud, 'Unless . . . unless he is not dead.'

'Oh he is dead all right,' the girl replied. 'He just doesn't want to see that one.'

Mrs Walters came out of trance.

'Nothing,' she told Maggie, rising from the table.

'Try again!'

'He is not there, Margaret,' she said rising. 'I think,' she said, 'admiring herself in the mirror. 'I think he might not be dead.'

Maggie stood, excited.

'Could you lead me to him? Find out where he is?'

'We can try,' Netta said, 'But not now. Open the door. We have a queue. Where is your sister?'

Judy was struggling with as much as she could carry across the heath. She stopped to catch her breath, furious at her sister's stubbornness. If only she had come with them to London, to experience that exciting change, she would see life through different eyes. She heaved up the bags and marched on. For several weeks she had put off returning home to face up to the inevitable, and even after having time to take in the shock of it, it made it no less traumatic. The whole notion of what was inside frightened her. But there was no escaping it any longer. The moment was on her. She reached her front door and she drew breath, turning the key in the lock, half expecting something to jump out at her. Then she went inside and closed the door behind her.

The shop was turning over a steady and growing custom. Mornings brought women who stepped from carriages from as far away as Canterbury and the market towns of Kent. They queued to secure a sitting at the parlour and filled the tea-houses or booked tables for lunch and browsed the quaint little stores. Like it or loathe it, the Cloak sister's parlour was bringing much-needed trade to Blackheath. It was benefiting everyone.

Within minutes of opening, Netta and Maggie were booked at every half-hour of the day until five, with those women whose carriages had arrived late complaining angrily at being left with the option of a tea-leaf reading having travelled such a long way.

'You must fetch your sister,' Netta demanded. 'We cannot go on like this. There is money to be made.'

But Maggie refused and, setting out her cups, sat at her table, facing another day of being second best.

The morning passed by slowly with shocked and excited cries coming from Netta's table and confused cross-examination souring the air at Maggie's. When they closed for lunch, Maggie had had enough.

'It is pointless going on,' she insisted. 'They do not want what I do. They want the ball. I cannot give them what you and Judy can.'

Netta was angry too. 'First you have a day off out of the blue, now your sister. This cannot go on. What if today I had not turned up? Where would you be then?' She washed her hands and admired her dress.

Maggie paced the room. 'I have tried and tried but it does not work for me.'

'It does not work? What is *it*? It is you that does the working, not it.' She tapped her head, 'It is all in here, not in the ball.'

'You must show me again.'

'Oh, Maggie!'

'Teach me from scratch. I will not stop until I have mastered it'

Mrs Walters sighed. 'You do not have the patience. You rush into everything. There is no unfolding with you, just the ripping off of layers to find what is inside. The art is in the unfolding.'

'I have spent entire nights looking into it, and nothing, nothing at all, none of these stars and mists and flashing images you talk about. None of it.'

Netta sighed and put the ball on the table.

'Sit,' she ordered. 'Now, you will not speak until I ask you something. You will not even think of questions to ask me later. You will simply listen. Forget the stars. Forget the mists. Forget everything. You will sit here and simply, without blinking, stare into the ball until all novelty and all expectation of ever seeing anything in it, has gone. Until the ball and everything you wanted from it is no longer of interest to you. Then, we will begin.'

She went through to the shop and turned over the sign.

'Not you!' her voice snapped at someone, 'You are banned. I'm not here to find out what the police have in their lost and found every day. Three times was funny. Now leave it.'

A mother and daughter from Hampstead were her first customers of the afternoon. News of the parlour, they told her, was sweeping through London. There was much talk of it at dinner parties. People were either outraged or fascinated but most, they enthused, were excited, and when they sat, trembling a little, staring around at the strange and eerie marvels in the morbid room about them, they appeared to Netta as if it were truly the most excited they had ever been in their lives.

'We want to know about the future,' the mother said, 'both of our futures.'

Netta peered into the ball and looked up at them, 'Oh good lord!' The women turned pale.

'Your house is haunted dears, did you know?' She tapped the ball. 'In here I am looking at a mischievous spirit running around your . . . very nice house, by the way. Whose is that portrait over the fire?'

The women stared in shock.

'It is my dear departed husband,' the mother said finally.

'I don't think you mean the word dear, though, do you?' Mrs Walters said firmly. 'The things that went on behind his back! Wooo! He knows all about that now and he's not a happy man. You could talk to him if you like, clear the air. We do séances.'

The mother smiled and shook her head.

'Now then, the ghost. A lot of things have been going missing, haven't they? Brooches, money, pictures.'

'Yes!' they both exclaimed at once.

'Attic stairs, bottom step. It lifts up. They are in there. But when you find them, you might find your little visitor gets a bit . . .' she thought of the word, '. . . nasty. Doors opening, noises in the night, the sound of crying. That sort of thing. Just ignore it. It'll be gone in a month. If it doesn't I'll pop over and have a word with it.'

'Is it my husband?'

Mrs Walters shook her head. 'No, it's a girl. Spiteful-looking little thing.'

The mother covered her mouth. 'Is it Alicia?'

Mrs Walters' brow creased.

'You'd need a séance for that sort of information, dear. I'm not doing this for the benefit of my health. Let me see.'

'Long mousy hair. Very, very ugly. I don't mean plain, I mean ugly. Face like an animal. A sort of . . . frog. Frog face.'

'It *is* Alicia!' the daughter gasped.

'Christina! Manners!' he mother snapped. 'Oh my poor Alicia!'

'She looks so lonely. I think in your case, it's necessary to put her to rest, and don't worry, I won't drag the dead husband up. You can deal with him when you pop your clogs yourselves. I'm booking you in for a séance.'

For the remainder of the day, Mrs Walters worked alone, halving the time of each sitting to deal with Judy's queue as well as her own. Maggie tried to pacify her by bringing tea but Mrs Walters snatched each cup with a look of annoyance. 'This is the last day I am left to work alone,' she said. 'No more sick days.'

Tired and emotional, Mrs Walters let in her final customer, a small timid woman who trembled and cried throughout the entire ordeal.

'We were very close, you see, Vincent and I. Very close. He was taken from me out of the blue. I had no time to prepare. We had no children, no friends, we only needed each other and now that he's gone I am on my own.' She trembled, her elbows shaking the table so that Mrs Walters leaned forward and held them still. 'I can't see in with that racket, dear, now just take a moment to calm yourself. He hasn't gone far. You just have to adjust your thinking. If you miss him terribly it means he had something valuable to offer while he was alive. All of those good things you must pick up and bring into yourself. That, my dear, is the true meaning of immortality.'

She peered into the ball in which an elderly man was peering up at her as distraught and tearful as the woman seeking him. Mrs Walters took a breath. Closing her eyes she could hear him calling out to her, crying as noisily as a distraught child, begging to be back with her. These were the worst sittings. These were the meetings that forced the emotion up into her own chest and brought tears to her eyes and kept her awake, feeling the futility of building a life only to lose it. She reached out and squeezed her hand.

'My dear,' she said. 'I see him. He was upset, very upset when he died but now he is calming. He is sending me so much love to pass on to you.' She was glad that he could not hear the nonsense she was about to invent. 'He says you are not alone.'

'But I am!'

'No. He says that you still have something very special to achieve while you are alive. He says that you must open your eyes. There is a new best friend for you, and you must find that friend. It must be your mission. That person is looking for you right now. When you meet you share some valuable good times and your grief will settle. You have nothing to fear. Your husband is waiting for you. He says he is safe and time passes quickly there so you will be with him in the blink of an eye. Time passes more slowly when we are alive but you are to be strong, to make him proud. You have to find in yourself a strength that will make him proud. When you pass over, dear, he will have everything ready for you and then you will see why it is so very important that you find this new best friend. It is crucial to you being together again in the next life.'

The woman dried her eyes.

'I don't want a best friend. I want –'

'You must do as he says. You must prove to him that you are strong. When you are strong it will help him, it will make him stronger.'

'What do I do? I don't work. I don't know anyone. How do I find this person?'

'You must take a job, dear. You must leave your house for over three hours each day. You must explore everything that is new to you without fear and as you do, you will feel how much stronger you are making him. He will be with you all along the way. You can talk to him as often as you like at home. He will hear you. But you must not ask questions. You must not expect answers. Instead, you will share with him everything that you have done in the day, that will make him happy. And you want to make him happy, don't you, dear?'

The woman nodded and reached for her purse.

Mrs Walters shook her head.

'Your payment will be your promise that you will do as he says. Will you?'

She wiped her eyes and blew her nose, shaking her head, unsure.

'I need to hear you say it, dear.'

'I will do it.'

'Good girl. Now tonight, you will make a list of ideas. And if you are frightened remember you have a secret. You are not going to the new places alone because secretly, you are taking him with you. You have something that no one else will have, you will have the confidence of two. Head high and walk forward.'

The woman smiled.

'Oh, and he says that whenever you can, you must sneak away without your mourning clothes. You must be fresh and bright and that will be your little secret. No one else need know.'

It was late, Mrs Walters was tired. She was ready to go home and climb into bed but dutifully climbed the steps to the attic where she found Maggie with wild hair and frantic eyes, cursing at the ball.

'You are too agitated,' she said walking in with firm footsteps. 'If you want to do this properly, you take a lot of deep breaths right now and you let go of whatever it is that is making you so aggressive! Can you do that?'

Maggie nodded.

'Good. Then let's start again.'

❧❧❧❧❧❧❧❧

At her home, Judy had closed it off inside the back room. She could not deal with it. For now it was better to pretend it was not there in her little house on Camden Row. Her rooms were bare, her furnishings either taken to the séance parlour or sold at the market so that she and her sister could eat, but she lit a fire and dragged what had once been her mother's favourite chair to it to warm through and she set about bringing her home back to life.

The walls were damp, there was very little firewood and the kitchen was empty so for the remainder of the day, there was plenty to do. She passed by the parlour late in the evening, surprised to see light in an upstairs window but she didn't dare enter in case it brought here face to face with her sister. She bought a bottle of wine and some wood and a pie and dawdled home, wanting to be anywhere else.

In the attic of the shop Maggie hammered her firsts angrily on the table. 'DO IT!' she shouted. 'Work!' She breathed hard, shook off what she could of her impatience and stared again. Moments later she paced the room in a rage. She lit another candle, looked out at the darkening village. She would not leave. She would not go home, nor sleep until she had won the battle. She sat again, meditating, clearing her mind, staring. Her anger foamed from her mouth as her concentration waned and her stomach rumbled but she denied herself, staring in again, seeing for a second the cloud and a spark and then she was standing, pulling at her hair, screaming to herself until again she was seated, her mind cleared, staring and seeing nothing, for a long time nothing. She was pacing again, furious and full of hate, and caught sight of her reflection in a mirror propped against the wall.

'Look at you! You are old. You are useless. You have a stupid ugly face. Look at it! Just look at it! With your nasty little eyes and your thin lips and your stupid messy hair. Horrid, horrid, stupid woman.' She stormed to the table, grabbed at the ball and, shaking with anger, sat. 'Show me!' she screamed at it. 'Show me your magic!'

An hour later she was stamping down the stairs. She opened a bottle of port, poured a glass, kicked at a chair, then sat and cried. When she felt ready, she returned to the attic and sat again at the ball, staring into it, closing her eyes and grimacing in angry frustration.

When she woke, it was light. She heard her sister down below sweeping though and cursed.

She waited. She would stay there until Judy was busy with a customer, then leave quickly and she turned her attention back to the ball, with which she had made little progress. When there was sufficient bustle down below, she gathered up the ball and her bag and moved to the top of the stairs.

Judy was surrounded by a group of women. They were admiring the second of her new dresses, a lilac and lace masterpiece that made her glow amongst them as if the sun was shining on her and no one else. They marvelled at her shoes and the shawl. 'It's so exciting that shawls are now meant to be worn in a whole new way,' one of them giggled.

Maggie swooped past quickly, avoiding her sister's stare. She stormed up through the village, the ball in her bag, her mouth sour, mimicking, 'It's so exciting that shawls are now worn differently. Oh your hair is so beautiful. Oh your gloves are so elegant. Oh you are so talented. Oh Judy, we admire you so much. Where's that useless sister of yours who is incapable of anything at all? She made a mess of the sweetshop, she gave it over to you and look how successful it is. Let her read tea leaves, she's not much use for anything else. How do you put up with her?'

In the kitchen she seated herself at the ball. Yet again she started at the beginning. She reached for a half bottle of port, gulping down a glass, then wandered through the house to the spare room where Judy had slept. The bed was neatly made, the floor was swept and the drawers emptied. It was stark and sparse with just two small bags of her things still awaiting collection at the foot of the bed. Maggie stared at them and cried, angry that she had driven her sister away. Nothing she did, it seemed, was the right thing to do.

Chapter 18

The rain had thrashed women of all ages into the waiting area of the parlour where Maggie with a tray of tea thrust her way irritably through enormous skirts.

'Who,' she demanded, 'decided that this shape skirt is appropriate for women? Who?'

The women considered her as they would a wild beast lurking in the bushes ready to pounce.

'I mean look at us! It's like we are half underwater all the time. If it wouldn't result in me being publicly flogged I'd rather walk around in my drawers.' She pulled back the curtain that divided the waiting area from the tables and moved back some chairs to make some room.

Judy looked up from her customer and grinned. Maggie was on one of her overtired rants in which she put the world to rights. 'I'll tell you who,' she said, 'homosexuals.'

The crowd gasped at the word but Maggie nodded defiantly. 'They pretend they are ordinary but when they get to work on designing clothes for women, they become more and more extravagant. They have no idea of the work a woman has to carry out because they don't live with them. And then it's free rein up here.' She tapped her head. 'I mean look at this room, twelve women in a room that could suitably house two dozen men, and no one can move. It's ridiculous.' She turned to Judy. 'And you are just encouraging them by purchasing the latest styles. If I had it my way, we should all wear trousers.'

The women objected with a chorus of headshaking and horrified disapproval but Maggie would not be deterred.

'All this preening and fussing and dressing up just to walk out of the door is ridiculous. Tomorrow I shall buy and wear trousers and that is that. Let them stare.'

The women stared in shock.

'But surely,' attempted a nervous voice from within the group, 'then people would mistake you for a man.'

'I shouldn't care one iota what people think,' she replied curtly. 'If they want to stare and think I am a man let them. At least I will be free.'

'I think it is time that you visited a dressmaker and let them show you the latest styles, my dear,' Mrs Walters said, coming through to call her next customer, 'once you are transformed I'm sure you will be much happier.'

'I shan't,' she said. 'I will not throw hard-earned money at people who force their silly whimsical designs on women while under the delusion that they are doing us a great service.'

'Oh Maggie,' she sighed.

'No, I will be firm about it. I declare fashion dead.'

Judy could not help but laugh and Maggie, turning to see who had dared mock her, caught the glint in her eyes, covered her mouth and rushed out to the back room to disguise the fact she was laughing.

Mrs Walters inked a summation of her previous sitting in the ledger and escorted the next customer to her table. She recalled her immediately. It was the small woman who was lost without her husband and whose husband was equally as lost and distraught on the other side without her.

'I have been thinking,' the woman began, 'and last night I spoke to my husband, as you said I could, and he spoke to me.'

Mrs Walters sipped her tea with raised eyebrows.

'You said that I had to find purpose, that I must find a best friend, and that the new best friend was out there looking for me.'

Mrs Walters nodded without taking the cup from her lips.

'I spoke to my husband and he confirmed what I realised. The best friend is you.'

Mrs Walters' eyes widened. 'No dear, it is not me. I am simply the first person you have spoken to since the funeral.'

'He told me. He was very firm about it. He said that I should come to work here and that you . . . you are my new best friend.'

Mrs Walters sighed. 'My dear, he did not say that.'

'He did.'

'You seem to be forgetting that I can talk to him too, dear, and I can assure you he said nothing of the sort.'

She reddened.

Mrs Walters put her cup down. 'I am a very complex and busy woman. I have my own problems and I don't need to take on any more.'

'But –'

'There are no buts. Now be quiet.' She closed her eyes, not even attempting to reach into the afterlife. More than anything it was a relief to simply close her eyes. She had been up all night reliving the nightmare of seeing her ex-fiancé's parents and masterminding disturbing acts of revenge. She was silent, simply enjoying the relaxation and could quite happily have fallen asleep were it not for Maggie's annoyed cough.

'He has told me what it is you are meant to do,' she said finally, opening her eyes. 'You are to learn to play the trumpet.'

'The trumpet?'

'Yes. You are to join a marching band.'

'But I –'

'I told you once dear, no buts. You are to purchase a simple trumpet and take lessons and you are to force yourself into the realms of marching bands. It is your destiny.' She leaned to one side and creased her brow in concentration, 'What's that, dear?' She nodded and looked back at the woman with a troubled face. 'He says if you don't you will alter the path back to him. You must master it and excel. He will be listening and he wants to see you in that parade.'

Shocked and disconcerted, the woman paid and left. Her husband had always detested music.

In the back room, Maggie was peeling off her underskirts and hurling them aside, almost falling over while she half-listened for signs of anyone approaching. She struggled to put on her overskirt again and walking to the mirror with the excess of material now trailing behind her, considered her more svelte frame. It looked odd and she felt rather naked but she would try it. She would walk out to all the women in the waiting area and confront them with it, gauge their reactions, then she would make up her mind.

But as she walked back into the crowded room, all eyes were turned to the door, where a handsome young man stood with flowers.

'I apologise,' he said, embarrassed.

Judy was blushing and Maggie, whose eyes moved from one to the other, realised the situation was her worse nightmare.

'I thought,' he said nervously, stepping forward into the midst of the women, 'I would bring you these as a thank you for saving my life.'

Judy beamed. 'You are well?'

He nodded

'And your fiancée? How is she?'

He smiled uneasily. 'I'm afraid that is the drawback to my recovery. You see, ordinarily I am a rather busy man, prone to making good business decisions but ill-prepared personal ones, but hospital afforded me the time to consider things properly. I'm afraid my engagement has ended.'

'Oh that's a shame.'

Mrs Walters head reappeared through the doorway with a big grin, she took the flowers from him and plopped them into a vase.

'She was a little young and light-headed for me. I'm afraid when it comes down to it, I cannot resist a woman with a more industrious nature.'

For the briefest of moments they looked at each other and something noticeable to all passed between them.

'Well,' Judy said at last, uncomfortable under the scrutiny of the room, 'you must visit me again.'

He nodded. And looking at each other with a fresh curiosity, they said their goodbyes. When he had gone all eyes turned back to Judy whose blushes had turned her a beetroot red.

'MAGGIE!' Mrs Walters shouted.

All eyes turned to the limp sack she wore around her waist.

'What do you think you look like! Get back in there and get dressed!'

❧❧❧❧❧❧❧❧

There were various sightings of the young gentleman in Blackheath all afternoon. He took lunch in the Crown Tavern, seemingly lost and in a world of his own. He strolled along the shops as if wishing time would pass quicker. He sat next to the horse trough watching the world go by, all the time wishing that Judy would appear and notice him but she did not.

Instead, she gazed into nothing, pulled from her daydreams only when necessary or to concentrate on customers. Maggie watched her from her tea-leaf reading with concern. It was beginning. Soon her sister would be someone else, gone from her again.

'Who will I marry?' her customer asked. 'I have two possible suitors, you see, and I cannot make up my mind. Mark is such a loving man but rather dull but Simon is carefree and exciting and –'

Maggie had had enough. 'Neither,' she said, 'You have been rather a slut. And for that you must give up both or someone close to you will die before the month is out.'

Mrs Walters looked up from her table.

'Love is not something one can take for granted. It can be taken away from you for good and forever and by seeing two men at the same time, you are souring your heart and making one of them broken-hearted. That has consequences.'

The customer was outraged.

'Greed,' Maggie said angrily, 'has made your heart fickle. Any more of it and what you consider to be love will not be love at all.'

She stood and left the room, leaving the customer and both Judy and Netta speechless.

In the upstairs room, Maggie sat in silence. She had expected to cry or work herself into a temper but she was strangely calm. When Judy entered, treading softly, she turned away. 'I do not want to talk,' she said, listening to her sister leave without a word. Her mind was empty, which was disconcerting for a mind that was usually preoccupied with several dozen things of varying importance at any given time.

Netta entered some time later with a more resolute tread.

'And I suppose you have come to tell me I need to buy a trumpet?'

'No dear,' she said, setting something down beside her, 'I've already bought you one.'

Maggie turned angrily to look but saw only tea. She turned her head away, almost giving in to a laugh.

When she came down the stairs at the end of the day, she found her sister in intimate conversation with the young man who had returned and stepped back into the shadows to watch.

'It dawned on me,' he said, shifting his feet uncomfortably before her, 'that in my hurry to see a surgeon, I managed to escape without paying. I'm afraid my manners escaped me.'

Judy smiled, happy to play along with the excuse.

He was unsure of how to move conversation forward and blushed, Maggie observed, almost as crimson as her sister had.

'When you came to see me in hospital, I think I recovered in double time.'

Maggie rolled her eyes, waving an urgent hand to stop Mrs Walters from barging in from the back room.

'What I didn't tell you this morning was that while I lay on my hospital bed recovering, you rarely left my thoughts for a moment.'

Judy was bright, bright red.

'And I wondered, if I might be so bold . . .'

He was at least ten years younger than Judy, not a boy by any means but younger. In her mind, Judy reprimanded herself for allowing such hopes.

'. . . as to ask you to dinner.'

She was lost in her thoughts, frozen, staring up at him, watching the eagerness in his face and the something more than a desire for friendship lurking behind his eyes. He waited for her response but Judy was not sure what was expected of her, or even if she had heard him correctly.

It was a look that Maggie had not seen on her sister's face before, not even with her first husband. Judy was blushing, lowering her eyes, then she looked up at him with an expression almost too innocent and pure and full of hope for a woman of her years. It told Maggie everything that she needed to know.

Netta looked at Maggie, looked at Judy, looked back at the handsome stranger, wondering if somehow, time had become frozen until Maggie coughed, bringing her sister to her senses.

'I beg your pardon, what did you say?' she asked.

He looked a little nervous, realising they were not alone. 'I was asking if it would be too bold of me to invite you to dinner.'

'Dinner? Dinner, yes, how nice. When?'

'Friday evening?'

'Friday? Yes, that would be lovely.' Lovely! She cursed herself; lovely sounded wrong. Lovely sounded like something an aunt would say to a child bringing her a dreadful arrangement of wildflowers.

In that moment, Judy was changed, Maggie knew it. All semblance of what had been before this day was gone. The familiar poverty-stricken existence and drunken closeness would be no more, and all because of the closing of one shop and the opening of another. The rug had been pulled out from under Maggie and she still had yet to climb to her feet. Now there would be no return to the life she missed so much. The man smiled and walked out of the shop, leaving the room and everyone in it spellbound, looking from one to another in silence.

✄✄✄✄✄✄✄✄

At a table in the Gypsy Moth public house in Greenwich, Maggie was drunk. She watched girls flirt with sailors and the older women use the same technique on the local men of the borough. They batted their eyelids, looked away coyly, gave the men a glimpse of leg, giggled at their every pearl of wisdom. Maggie ordered something stronger and adjusted her bonnet.

In her mind she was fresh off the boat in a foreign land, suitcase at her side, starting anew, the sea dividing her from her past. She must find a fresh life now, become someone new. The sailors flirted with the young women, the older men chugged on cigars and pipes and laughed jovially and she looked around the old tavern for the man who would take her away from herself, in whom she would find love and passion and stability. Her eyes fell on a rather portly gent, who, distracted from conversation by her rather over-the-top suggestive looks was unsure if the woman was a little mad or suffered from some sort of nervous tic. He manoeuvred himself in the group so his back was to her. This, it turned out, presented to her a new and much better looking man who, for a moment studied her with some interest. She batted her eyelids until it felt ridiculous, and growing considerably drunker, dared to lift her skirts a little, revealing the shapely curve and poise of her ankle in horrendously unfashionable shoes battered with age. He looked away, daring occasionally to look back at her with concern.

She called to mind the evening with her sister during which she had considered herself too old and set in her ways to take on the burden of a husband. Indeed until that night, love had rarely entered her head, except as a fleeting fancy. Now it was all she thought about. Her lack of it had placed her somewhere unsettling, somewhere forgotten that she needed to escape from. Perhaps, she considered, if she forced her mind backwards, she could live happily convincing herself that life was better alone. But she doubted it. The look in her sister's eyes that afternoon had made her see it for what it was. It was all-consuming, magical, something that lifted you to unexpected happiness and she wanted it too, now more than ever.

185

At the bar an older man, strong and impatient, looked her way but uninterested, turned his eye to another woman of significantly older years. Maggie felt conspicuous, vulgar almost, but she brushed her feelings aside. She had always been too keen to listen to herself, that had been her problem. Too careful, too worried, too ready to bring things to a halt. A man, sitting close to the door, caught her eye and nodded good evening to her. She smiled back. He was a rather passive sort, a book-keeper perhaps or someone worn down by a stronger wife. He stood and passed her, ordering another ale before turning and plucking up his nerve to offer her a drink. She accepted port, the thrill and terror of the situation scorching her cheeks. She invited him to join her.

His name was Benjamin Ferrey. He was an architect, working on the new church at Blackheath, staying in lodgings at the Clarendon Hotel. She did not listen, her smile was frozen, her mind full of nerves. She was awkward, her words spilling out in confused panic, saying either too much or too little.

'Blackheath is such a beautiful part of London,' he said, attempting to pull her from her thoughts. 'I am tempted to set up home there.'

'Oh I shouldn't,' she told him, unsure what was coming out of her mouth, so wild was her panic. 'There are so many murders of late, and they are building some dreadful large building on the heath and with the train coming, Blackheath will soon be unrecognisable.'

He smiled.

When she returned from the powder room, the table was empty. She had expected it, had willed an end to it and had assumed that she would feel relieved by his departure. Instead, there was simply a fresh emptiness and she felt the hurt of his rejection even though he mattered little to her. She hurried to the door, cursing herself for making such a display.

Along Greenwich South Street she acknowledged no one, her head down, her eyes holding back tears. She wanted to be home with the door locked and everything else outside banished. Even the steep climb up Point Hill went unnoticed in her hurry to be away from it all. The heath was blustery and wet, in the distance men were shouting, there was running, another lone walker mistaken for the murderer, she suspected, and turned into her garden.

Drunk and tearful, she let herself into the kitchen, wishing Judy was there, wishing she had never given in to the stupid whim to put to the test her attractiveness to men. She brought up the last of the home-made potato wine from the cellar and opened it. It was sharp and tart and left a taste of rust and lemons on the tongue but she would grow used to it. She sneered at the thought. 'You get used to everything. Settle for anything.'

'You will banish the idea of love from your mind. You will turn things back to normal!' she shouted at the fire that refused to light. Again it felt as if everything in life was made to punish or push her to her limits, even the cold and damp wood that refused her lit spill.

'Oh but men flock around her now!' she told the logs. 'She who has already buried one husband and had more than her fair share of men in between and is again ready to flaunt a new love in my face knowing I will never . . . This is what happens! This is what happens when I let control of things leave my hands. I should never have listened. She's taken it all from me. And look at me! Look! I have nothing.'

She lifted her glass and drank, reliving the embarrassment of the evening, remembering he was an architect, remembering her dismissiveness of the space being cleared on the heath, recognising her mistake. Her breath was hot, she was angry and stupid and thoughtless and – she was Maggie Cloak. Maggie the useless, hopeless, thoughtless . . . No wonder no man would ever love her. No wonder at all.

She reached for the crystal ball and sat down.

Two days had passed since the count's supposed return and as he showed no sign of visiting her, the princess sent her lady-in-waiting to demand an urgent meeting that evening without fail but her letter went unanswered.

As evening fell, freshly bathed and dressed, she waited at the window to watch his approach, but he did not come, nor did he send word. Stooping to the telescope, she watched him in his room hurrying to dress and when he left the house and turned in the wrong direction, she summoned her own carriage and followed.

He came to a stop at the home of Lady Dartmouth, the society widow that had introduced him at the ball. A woman with whom the princess had, on several occasions, found herself in competition at royal galas and charity events. Despite the difference in their age, she being young and virginal and royal and the Dartmouth woman being old but incredibly well preserved and startlingly attractive, it infuriated her how she could be so easily upstaged.

She need not have ordered the carriage, for the walk was short and she felt foolish at dismounting a mere hundred yards from her home. She dismissed the carriage immediately and waited for it to return inside the gates of the Ranger's House before taking it upon herself to venture into the grounds of Dartmouth House. Walking its perimeter, she sneaked angry glances into each of the windows.

Lady Dartmouth found herself surprisingly at ease with the man that she had sought, since his arrival, to spend an evening's conversation and dinner with. They reclined informally in armchairs with wine while the kitchen prepared a lavish dinner and he regaled her with tales of foreign cities and the primitive villages that dotted the lands between them. She was besotted, unable to take her eyes away from his, her heart forcing more blood than was needed to her cheeks and lips and chest. He chose not to notice this, or at least not show her that he had.

As she spoke about her own journeys to France and to Wales and to Bournemouth, he watched her with growing interest. Older women had always been more of a challenge, more interesting. What they lacked in firmness of body they made up for with inventiveness and craft, the beauty of embarrassment and the tenderness of shame. She was unaware of his thoughts as she spoke and at the sound of the bell they made their way through to the dining room.

They ate honey-blackened duck and poached bream with eggs. Afterwards they drank a fine champagne before retiring to the privacy of her private rooms. Here they took brandies at her piano, which she insisted he played. He did not hesitate; piano had become his passion. In America, where he was taught each evening by a man he had considered father-like until it became necessary to eat him, he had received much praise for his concertos. The blood of the old tasted different to that of the young. Although less rich and metallic, often it was impossible to drink as much for fear of becoming tired of it. It was not so much an acquired taste as something so special that it should only be taken on special occasions, or when one needed much more than the ripening flow of a silly little girl or a fiery drunken male. He was still considering the taste of her very well-preserved and attractive body when he noticed she had caught him out.

'I do believe, count,' she grinned, 'that you are flirting with me.'

He smiled and took a sip from his brandy. Something should be said, he realised, only boys remained coy at moments like this. 'I was observing,' he said, 'how much more beautiful you are than many half your age. How old are you?'

It was a question that no one should dare ask, he realised, but he knew from the glint in her eye that she would enjoy the game.

She was surprised, but without hesitation looked him in the eyes and replied, 'I am sixty-six.'

He sipped and let a playful sparkle rise into his eyes. 'And do you look as beautiful as you do now without your clothes?'

Her eyes lit, marvelling at his nerve.

'I am old enough to be your mother.'

'I had no mother, she died when I was a child so I am afraid I lack those boundaries. Not that I consider them to hold any value.'

She smiled, considering her next move.

'And has this lack of boundaries brought you to the doors of many older women?'

'Only to the ones that were worth pursuing.'

His eyes were dark and probing. She felt herself being seduced by them but looked away, drawing on her experience not to rush into such situations. He raised his eyebrows and took a sip, impressed; eyes rarely looked away when he commanded their attention and it was only ever the older women that attempted it but even they eventually succumbed as would Lady Dartmouth, though not without a fight, he hoped.

An interruption brought her to her feet as the butler entered. 'Princess Sophia Matilda is in the hall, madam. She would like to speak with the count.'

Her face fell, watching the man rise and the game end.

'It is getting late,' she said with a well-hidden fury at the silly little princess who yet again encroached on her territory. 'Perhaps we could continue this conversation another night?'

'I will look forward to it.'

When he entered the hall, he acknowledged the princess's smile with a nod and they stepped out into the night.

'I left instructions for you to visit me this evening,' she said, marshalling her agitation.

'It has been a very busy day. I planned to call on you tomorrow.' He studied her. 'Something is different about you.'

'You've been away for quite some time.' Her words were sharp and she turned away from him, stepping out onto the long grass of the heath. 'Did you not think to mention you planned such a long journey?'

'There is something ...' He rested a hand on her stomach, surprised as she pulled back outraged. 'You cannot just touch me at your will.'

'You are pregnant.'

She looked around nervously.

'It is mine?'

'Of course it is yours. There has been no one else.'

'We must go to your house at once. I must see you out of your clothes.'

She stared at him.

She had expected him to break bad news to her, to confirm the panic that had absorbed her every thought since she had discovered her fullness, he would tell her that she must not have it, that because of his altered body, it was unwise and dangerous to keep it inside her. Instead, pushing her inside her rooms, he pulled her to him and caressed her stomach gently. Then pulling his shirt over his head and forcing off his shoes, he picked her up off her feet as if she were as light as a feather and carried her to the bed. She was unsure, considerate of the baby, worried, but her concerns began to fade as the first sigh broke her lips and she felt her breasts covered with his fingers. She trembled and arched her back and ran her hands across his shoulders driving her nails down against his chest as he forced his mouth hungrily against hers and ever so discreetly, he bit her lip. She jumped but he kissed her again, more aggressively and ran his tongue over the wound, tasting her.

Chapter 19

The ladies of the spiritualist circuit arrived for their usual afternoon séance in the upstairs room. Now that there was a suitable venue, they had given up taking it in turns to meet at each other's houses. Here, free from the scrutiny of husbands and children, they enjoyed the comparative freedom of a room at reasonable rent. Netta took up a tray of tea.

Their séances, she had found, were often rather limp affairs, dependant on a visiting medium, few of whom were genuine. She had sat in on the last, barely able to restrain herself from ordering him off the premises. The women, whom she had been led to believe were seasoned experts, accepted anything that the man told them and he told them very little. Netta had watched the spirits move around the room, ignoring him, saw him pretending to talk to a spirit who was not really there and before he left, gave him a piece of her mind.

Today they had a very special guest. Netta had turned over the closed sign for ten minutes to see what all the fuss was about and sat ready to be thrilled by 'psychic art' in which a tall, rather manly woman with a large nose, an easel and a selection of charcoals, changed the face on her parchment several times until someone sitting in her audience recognised it. It had been transformed from an old woman to old man, then to a middle-aged man to something barely human at all and finally to a boy that at last one of the women claimed to be of an 'uncanny likeness' of someone or other. It was available to buy at a not-so-reasonable price.

It was a creative approach, Netta reasoned, but since yet again, she had not seen the medium acknowledge any of the spirits in the room, it was fairly obvious that the woman's talents lay in her hands, guesswork and the audience's wishful thinking rather than communication with the dead.

She slipped away, dreading the following week's guest and his 'psychic singing'.

Downstairs, the sudden appearance of an expensively dressed woman stopped her in her tracks. The woman, aware of the spectacle she was creating in the room, motioned Netta aside, indicating that she would like privacy. Nervously Netta lead her through to the back room under the eager gaze of both Maggie and Judy.

'Oh good lord!' Judy whispered to Maggie. 'Do you know who that is?'

The customers whispered with excitement.

When she left, Netta ushered the sisters into the back room, much to their customers' annoyance.

'That was the lady-in-waiting to Princess Sophia Matilda! The princess is keen to have a reading!'

Judy laughed excitedly.

'You must do it,' Netta said sternly to her.

'No I couldn't.'

'She asked for you,' Netta lied.

Both Maggie and Judy's faces fell.

'I want to go too!' Maggie said. 'I want to see.'

'No,' Netta said firmly. 'She wants only one and it will have to be Judy.'

'It's my novel!' Judy panicked. 'She has found out about the novel and that she has been written about in such a scandalous and ungodly way. That's why she's asking for me!'

'What are you talking about?' Netta snapped nervously.

'I can't go!'

'Of course you will. You must be there in one hour.'

'I will go with her,' Maggie said firmly.

'No you won't. She wants someone who can read the crystal ball. She won't tolerate someone who is there simply to see. She made that quite clear.'

Maggie turned away angrily.

∞∞∞∞∞∞∞∞

Walking in through the door, under the head of Neptune, just as the guests to the ball had in her book, Judy stepped into the princess's world. She was taken aside, instructed on how to bow and how to address the princess and how to behave in her presence. Judy barely listened to a word, fascinated with the large high-ceilinged room and the elegant furniture within it. But this was nothing compared to the rooms she would pass through before meeting the princess. The great ballroom which Judy had longed to see,

Sophia Matilda was having made smaller, dividing the great expanse into three, which Judy thought to be a shame and a mistake. In her novel the room had looked much bigger and more beautiful.

The princess met her at a small table at the rear of the house overlooking Greenwich Park. From here Judy saw the spot where she and her sister often stood looking up at the house and she wondered how it must be to have the freedom of the park at night, locked and private and safe; to have the observatory at your disposal and be able to look up into the night sky and see planets so far away in such detail. Judy smiled, curtsied and was seated. She took out her crystal ball and placed it on the table, asking for the curtains to be drawn.

The princess dismissed her maid and drew them herself. How similar she was to the woman Judy had portrayed in her book, Judy marvelled and watched her sit and wait as she nervously tried to compose herself.

'I would like to know about my future,' the princess said softly. 'Although it would rather depress me to learn that my own contribution to life amounted to something so small that it was barely as if I had existed at all. I live such a small life here, you see. It's all rather uneventful. I will be the one member of the royal family that people will know very little about, I'm afraid. Those who seek the glamour and excitement of royalty are always rather disappointed with me.' The cherub-faced princess smiled. 'But I am so excited about this. Do continue.'

Judy looked into the ball. What the princess had said was right, she had contributed very little to life to the point where Judy found herself scraping around for anything, any flicker of interest but it seemed that her funeral was the most exciting thing about her and that wasn't too far off. Then it came into sight and before she could hide it, the princess had seen it on her face. 'There it is!' she said. 'Tell me, tell me what that was.'

Judy swallowed. She felt as if she were drunk or hallucinating and that her worlds were colliding, merging confusingly together. The princess in her novel had, in this moment, stepped off the page into real life and was sitting right there with her, confiding in the most unlikely way with her; as if they were great friends. It was already intoxicating to be inside the Ranger's House, whose balls she had dreamed of attending over and over year after year but now, seated, drinking tea from fine china . . .

'Do tell me,' she persisted.

Judy swallowed. 'It's a delicate matter.'

'Be frank.'

'There has been a meeting, with a man. A strong man, quite bold and charismatic.'

The princess nodded, looking around her to see the doors were locked. She reached for her fan nervously.

'There will be a child, a child that will need to be hidden or denied.'

The princess appeared embarrassed. She stood. 'I must lie down. This excitement has quite drained me. Miss Cloak, I will ask that everything we have spoken of remains secret between ourselves and be told to no other person. Do you agree?'

'Of course,' Judy assured her. 'I shall take it to the grave.' Which, if J.J. James the publisher had not removed the princess's name as requested by her, might prove to be sooner rather than later.

Judy stepped out of the large house and walked to the heath. She was exhilarated. If only her mother had been alive, she would have been so proud. She was broken from her thoughts by the proprietress at the tea hut, who beckoned furiously.

'Have you heard?'

Judy shook her head.

'The police have received a note, from the murderer!'

'No!'

She nodded. 'I was talking this morning to . . . someone I shall not name but is very high up in the police.'

'Was it Sergeant Graham?' Judy asked sipping the hot tea.

'It was, yes. And he said that the note said, let me remember. Yes, something along the lines of, "Help me. I can't stop myself. I am compelled to do it. You do not notice my clues."'

'Oh, good heavens.'

'They are going to exhume the bodies of the girls!'

'No!'

'Yes!'

'Oh that's dreadful. The poor parents . . .'

The proprietress had suddenly leaned out of the serving hatch and was staring with a look of murderous defiance as an official-looking man passed in a carriage. Upon noticing her, he looked sheepishly away.

'They are trying to close us down again. It's always the same people. They said because we are a wooden building and every so many decades we need to rebuild, that each time we should apply as if we are a brand new business. It is so they can say no to us. This is, and always has been, our part of the heath. But every time they refuse to acknowledge the previous hut so they shorten our history. Well we've built it strong this time. This hut will be here well into the 1920s. Let them stick that in their pipes. They say that we attract the wrong sort but everyone knows it is because we draw the crowds that refuse to pay the scandalous prices of the tea room in the park.'

As Judy wandered back towards the village, looking longingly in the direction of Maggie's house, she wished again that her mother was with them. That for once in her life, she could tell the woman something that would make her proud of her. She imagined her mother hurrying her to the table, pouring her tea, wringing out of her daughter every detail, from descriptions of the great ballroom and the attire of the staff to the condition of the skin on the princess's hands. But she was gone.

Death was such an ill-conceived ending to life, she considered yet again. It seemed an outrageous trick, something spiteful put in place by someone with little patience. To simply live and die and not amount to anything other than someone who starts the cycle all over again with children seemed little more than a game. For a moment, she found herself in tune with her sister, who saw no reason to celebrate a god who took away the people you loved as a matter of course.

'If we all lived forever,' a priest had said, contradicting Maggie confidently and with loud condescension for the benefit of others, 'don't you think you would become incredibly bored? It would be an awful thing. No it is best that we die.'

Maggie's profane response had earned her the hardest slap across the face from her mother that either of them had ever witnessed.

The worst part of death was that Judy still wanted to fill her mother in on everything from the important to the trivial. Why, she often considered angrily, spend a whole lifetime learning, mastering your craft, becoming knowledgeable and respected only then to die?

Suddenly startled at reaching her front door, her heart sank as she considered what lay within. Perhaps it was time, she thought. Perhaps today was the day it should be faced up to and put to rest.

Inside, she lit the fire and poured herself a whisky, considering the matter more carefully. What she was about to do would change everything, forever. Nothing could be the same once she had looked but it could be put off no more.

'It is the right time,' she said and opened the door to the room where it was kept.

Chapter 20

'*Racing up the old Dover road from the coast two large black carriages pulled by four muscular black horses attempted to outrun the storm that had kept pace with them since their arrival into the country.*' Netta read aloud from the pages of the *London Illustrated News* to the hastily assembled room of excited women who hung on her every word. '*Finally Blackheath opened up to them, the storm a dramatic black sea above it . . .*'

'Oooh!' they all exclaimed with excitement.

Netta shot them a stare and continued with dramatic emphasis, '*The carriages veered and swayed as their wheels hit verge and pothole, turning the corners too fast and at alarming speeds. They threatened to topple as they approached the Princess of Wales public . . .*'

She clapped her hands. 'Isn't it exciting? Who knew we had our very own novelist sitting right here all this time!'

When Judy opened the door, she was met with a round of applause. She stared.

'You are published!' Mrs Walters cried, waving the newspaper. 'Chapter one, the count and countess have arrived at Blackheath!'

Judy took it excitedly, looking at the illustration, the words, – her words. 'We've all read it,' enthused Ann Thies from the milliner's shop, who rarely got enthusiastic about anything. 'I can barely wait for next week's second chapter. You must tell us what happens, you must. Who are they? Why are they here in Blackheath?'

Judy reddened with excitement. 'You must all wait for chapter two to find out.'

From the doorway, Maggie watched with a sour face. She turned away and walked to the centre of the heath, sitting on the bench with the hillock behind her. First the success of the shop, then the clothes and the popularity, then love and infatuation, and now even more success and fame too. Judy was gone. Maggie was alone. All semblance of her cosy past wiped away, destroyed. Yes she had food and money, but what use

197

were they? Part of the excitement of day-to-day living was figuring out how to make ends meet. It was what she was used to. Now she had a full larder, more money than she knew what to do with and an empty life devoid of purpose. Her sister had announced a contest and had won and Maggie had lost, lost her shop, lost her purpose, lost her sister.

'You are looking a little down in the dumps,' a voice said.

Maggie turned, her face falling.

'How do you do it?' she asked as Father Legge sat next to her with a sigh. 'How do you find me when I least want to speak to anyone, least of all you?'

'It's a gift.'

'From God, I suppose.'

'Of course.'

'Well his gifts aren't up to much.'

'That is blasphemy, Margaret.'

'What do you want Henry?'

'You looked troubled, I thought I might be of some help. I've noticed you've not been yourself recently. Looking rather lost, like someone who has lost their inner peace.'

She sighed.

'You know we could do with a woman like you at church to –'

'No thank you.'

He rose to his feet, 'Well the offer is there if you need someone to turn to. If you need to rectify your mistakes and ask for forgiveness.'

She didn't respond, her head turned away, her eyes lost on a blurry horizon.

✿✿✿✿✿✿✿✿

An hour later Maggie opened the port, closing the kitchen curtains on the dark room. She lit a spill and took it to the wick of a candle, placing it next to the crystal ball and sat. She would not be beaten. Anything her sister could do, she could do, and better. She peered inside and cleared her mind. There would be clouds and sparks; she must not react, she must not blink, she must be patient. That was all she needed to know. No other thoughts must enter her head, not until she had succeeded.

The house creaked around her, daylight faded through the curtains. She lit the fire and poured another glass and returned to the ball. Across

198

the room the dancing light of the flames painted the walls, dragging shapes out from the shadows, stretching her shadow up over the picture her mother had drawn of the room itself, barely changed. A creak from upstairs drew her attention but she shook it away, her eyes looking through the imperfections in the crystal to the secret space within it, to the place where the magic happened.

Some time passed; she was not sure how much but something seemed altered. She looked around the room suspiciously, noticed that the light had changed; the colours drained. Judy was there, young and frightened and moving furniture to the door, pressing her hands against her ears, mouthing something urgent to her. Something was outside. Maggie rose from the seat, turning to the room as if it were spinning around her and reached out for support. Judy was emptying a tea tray, pressing it against the curtains, lifting the fireguard up and pushing it hard against the window. She turned to Maggie, begging her for help and Maggie shuddered. She knew this moment, she hated this moment. She turned, listening to the creaks above her head, hearing outside the distorted sound of howling and barking and seeing her sister's horrified face turn to the stairs. Maggie turned her head, saw the small feet appear at the top of them, watched each step move downwards towards her. She saw her mother's frailty coming into view, the cold blue legs, the hem of her nightdress, the quivering blackened hand reaching for the handrail. She shook herself, wanting it to be gone; wanting to be awake, to leave the house, not to be here again in this moment but her mother kept coming, step by step until suddenly she was in the room, dead and distant, hypnotised by something that drew her towards the door. She moved unsurely, taking small steps, her tiny voice saying over and over, 'I'm coming, I'm coming,' to the dogs that howled, drawing her to them.

Maggie jumped, seeing a figure move past her, herself but younger, going to the woman, reaching out, softly taking her by the shoulders, reassuring her, turning her back towards the stairs, but the old woman refused and resisted, trying to push her aside with the little strength she had left in her arms. She was fixated by the door, so weak and so close to death that both girls feared their actions might be too much for her. Maggie turned her, catching her as she slipped down against her to the floor, screaming.

'Why do you hate me? Why do you hold me back?'

Judy was crying, her hands clenched before her mouth as timid as a mouse. 'Mother . . .' she mouthed, her eyes turning to Maggie to take control, to stop it all.

Maggie lifted her, stroked her hair, pressed her screaming objecting mouth against her chest and rocked her gently. 'You must return to bed.'

'I am dead.'

'You are not dead, Mother. Not yet.'

'I am dead!'

Maggie turned to the stairs and carried the woman upwards with Judy following. Both were in shock. Both had thought her already passed away.

She would not lie still, climbing at every opportunity to her feet, pushing their hands away, screaming at them to leave her, to get out of her room. But they stayed, watching her, soothing her, protecting her and confining her to her bed until, still fighting them, something inside failed and life was gone from her, her face agitated and confused.

The sisters closed the door again and sat in the room below crying at the horror of what had happened.

Maggie was alone again, standing in the kitchen, the crystal ball next to her hand on the table. She was shaken and upset. The memory always came to her when she least expected it and when she could least cope with it. Usually she would pull on her coat and hurry across the heath to Judy's, waking her in the middle of the night with two words, 'You know,' and Judy would make her hot milk and turn down the spare bed for her. Now she was alone, but for the first time she did not need to escape. Instead, she turned her eyes back to the ball and stared inside, unsurprised as images began to appear inside it.

It was a blustery night outside. The wind screeched through the holes in the window frames. The smell of tomato soup rose from the stove, the empty port bottle sat in the sink ready to be washed and refilled and the logs spat furiously in the hearth. Maggie sat entranced as the homes of her neighbours opened up to her inside the ball and their secrets were revealed.

'Show me again! Clouds and stars and mists!' she laughed, 'What a lot of nonsense. No wonder I was getting nowhere.' She clicked her fingers. 'Show me my sister.' She peered in, seeing her sister asleep in her bed. 'Boring, boring woman.'

She poured some soup into a bowl and pulled on a cardigan, her mind alight with possibility.

'Will I ever find love?' she asked, but the ball remained empty.

'Correct, but of course we already knew the answer to that one.'

She stopped as if something miraculous had been revealed.

'Show me my father.'

But the ball remained empty.

ꙮꙮꙮꙮꙮꙮ

When Netta heard a key letting someone in through the shop door the following morning she called out quietly.

'Judy? Are you alone? The police want me to attend the exhumation. I won't go. I won't be involved. If they come . . . tell them I'm caring for your mad sister. Tell them she is very ill.'

'I am not mad,' Maggie's voice shouted from the doorway.

Netta turned, startled to see her. 'You are drunk!'

'Yes I am. And I need to talk to you.' She pointed to a seat. 'Sit down.'

'I don't care for the way you are talking to me!'

Maggie staggered forward and sat, waving away her words. 'I need to ask you something.'

Netta listened.

'How do you do it? How do you talk to the dead? How? I need you to show me.'

Mrs Walters looked at her. 'What about the ball?'

'I can do that. That's easy. I want to know how to see the dead. Show me how.'

Mrs Walters sighed.

If you can read the ball you can start working here every day as you promised. We cannot cope alone.'

'All in good time. Tell me how you contact the dead.'

Mrs Walters sighed, plumping her hair in the mirror and adjusting her dress. 'It's the same technique as seeing into the ball, except, this time you are looking into the room. You will see the same – clouds, stars.'

'I don't need any of that, that is unnecessary.'

'You can read the ball without them?'

'Of course.'

Mrs Walters was impressed and for a second, catching the look,

201

Maggie felt proud but she pressed on. 'Show me.'

'I can't just show you, just like that!'

'Well try.'

'It's better to begin in a darkened room, but look around you. What do you see?'

'Nothing.'

'Watch.'

Mrs Walters held her hand against the blackness of her skirt. 'Look at my fingers, then at my fingertips, do you see they are encased in light – dull white light?' She held them against the window. 'And now, do you see vapours moving around them, like heat rising from the grass when it has rained on a warm day?'

Maggie stared. 'I'm not sure.'

Mrs Walters nodded and reached for Maggie's hands which she snatched back, but Netta took them again and shook the tension from them. 'Trust me, Maggie. I am your friend, not your enemy.'

The woman relaxed a little, watching Mrs Walters' hands warm her cold bony fingers. She pressed the fingertips of both index fingers together, lifting the blackness of her dress behind them. Maggie stared without blinking until she saw that they were clouded with white light, then moving her finger tips apart she raised her eyebrows.

'There is a light,' Maggie said, 'It's joining both fingers together.' She moved her fingers away from each other and back together, raising one higher than the other, following the white blue line until it grew so clear that Maggie could not help but laugh.

'It's like I am wearing huge gloves! The colours!'

'Are we all surrounded with this, always?'

'Always.' Mrs Walters said, taking her hands again, hoping to comfort her. Maggie looked so manic and nervy that she appeared lost. It wasn't until she looked down and saw her hands were being held that she shook Mrs Walters off. Netta rose and made them tea.

'That is the aura,' she explained, reaching for the camomile. 'Spirits . . . well spirits are similar, but harder to see. It will take patience. But now that you see auras quite easily, if you sit quietly and watch the room, from time to time you will pick up on flickers, some will be tricks of the eye, others won't.' She paused and dared to change the subject. 'Maggie, when did you last sleep? You look unwell.'

'That's my business,' the woman snapped. 'So that's it? That's all I have to do, watch the room and look for auras?'

Mrs Walters nodded and was about to hand her the tea when Maggie pulled herself up and left the shop. Netta didn't attempt to order her back, the fumes she left in the room would take enough clearing out as it was.

The day was filled with oddballs, men who wanted to win at business by learning what their rivals were plotting, women who wanted peace of mind, youngsters who wanted to be thrilled, young couples wanting to know if their love would last. The occasional person edged in suspiciously from time to time, not wanting to be seen, asking about the availability and procedure of attending a proper séance only to find themselves coerced into putting down a deposit and settling on a date by Mrs Walters who refused to let them leave disappointed now they had plucked up the courage to come this far.

'They are increasing, you know,' she told Judy as she jotted down the events of the day in the ledger. 'People are becoming less frightened of séances at last. They are relaxing with the whole concept of what we do here. Soon we will be able to stop the tarot and the tea leaves and make some real money.'

'We don't do too badly now.'

Mrs Walters sniffed. 'Séances are where the big money is, you mark my words. Once we're doing three of those a day, this will seem like peanuts. What are you doing tonight?'

'Nothing, as usual.'

'Then you will let me buy you supper at the Trafalgar to celebrate your first published chapter. I don't want to be at home.'

'Why not?'

'Because that murdered girl's family have been knocking for two days insisting I attend the exhumations and I want nothing to do with it.'

'I don't understand. I thought it would interest you. You might make stronger contact with her, solve the crime.'

Netta shook her head, 'I want nothing to do with it.'

⁂

The women took their seats at a table overlooking the Thames and rubbed their hands as two mounds of whitebait were placed before them.

'Your sister has gone quite mad, you know,' Netta told her.

Judy nodded.

'She can use the ball now and she's already lost interest in it and wants to contact the dead. I imagine your poor father will have no rest once she breaks through. She asks me to contact him at least twice a day.'

'And nothing each time?'

'Nothing at all.'

'They were very close. Our father has been her whole life, even though he hasn't been there for most of it. She still thinks he will return.'

Netta sighed. 'What is to be done about her?'

'I think she would benefit from a trip to London, some new clothes, like us.'

'I should have lied. I should never have told her there would be no love in her life. If I could take that back.'

'Perhaps you could lie, tell her you made a mistake.'

'Not now she can read the ball for herself. She will know everything she wants to soon.

I hope she doesn't look too persistently for our father. Some things should just be left alone.'

Mrs Walters studied her worried face. 'Sometimes spirits do not want to be found,' she said, forking the silver fish into her mouth and looking at the other customers who lounged around the long wood-panelled rooms. 'Sometimes when they have done things so bad, they hide or move on quickly. If he does not want her to find him then she will not.'

'And if he does?'

'If he does, we have one very unpredictable or happy woman on our hands.'

'She won't be happy,' Judy muttered.

Netta turned to see a man and woman standing at the end of their table and groaned inwardly. It was the parents of the murdered girl.

'We saw you come in,' the mother said. 'We have been calling at the shop and your home but we seem to miss you. We would like to ask you both if you would accompany us this evening.'

Netta Walter sighed angrily.

The exhumations took place, as was usual, at night, when most people were off the streets and relative privacy could be ensured. Both sets of parents, together with the undertakers, Judy and a furious Netta, a doctor, a priest and a bobby waited in a respectful silence as the gravediggers lowered themselves into the holes and removed the last of the earth. They heaved the first bloated wet coffin from the suction of the wet ground beneath and lifted the head of the box up to the men who grappled to maintain a hold. Their fingers slid as each grabbed to stop it from sliding back but the wood was caked in thick red earth and inside the box, the body had begun to slump downward; gravity was against them.

The screws holding the coffin together were beginning to come loose. The girl's parents looked away in horror. Netta recited the lyrics to favourite songs in her head, distracting herself, stopping the spirits from breaking through. Judy watched fascinated. The gravediggers lifted carefully, waiting until the men above had a firm grip before letting go and suddenly, the first was up, lying safely on the grass, being lifted by the undertakers onto the cart that would take it to the police station for examination.

The second coffin, of a cheaper wood, was already buckling as they lifted it. The bottom sagged, the lid was loose, the knees of the body inside were lifting it away from the container as the body slid down. They raised it slowly, tilting the head of the casket upwards into the hands of their co-workers, who, sliding in the mud, pulled it in sharp jerks away from the men beneath it and then yelling they fell, backwards, towards the crowd, the coffin with them, the bottom bursting open, the body sliding out onto the mud, towards the edge of the grave and back down onto the men beneath. The parents screamed and were hurried away by the policeman. Below, the gravediggers, retching and crying out in disgust, stood the body up between them, the slippery rotting flesh sliding between their fingers as they lifted the corpse up once more. Its blackened face rose up into view before the distraught crowd above. The policeman took an arm and felt the flesh of it come away in his hand and the body slip backwards and down yet again. Judy was transfixed. Finally, wrapped in a sheet, the girl was lifted up and placed coffinless on to the cart that hurried through south London.

Mrs Walters held her head, she was staring past the grave, looking directly at the murdered girls watching. The girl with whom she had conversed regularly was staring with a fury at her. 'Tell them!' she screamed.

Mrs Walters stumbled over her words. 'The hair,' she said, 'I feel there is something amiss with their hair.'

Chapter 21

'Shhh now, little one.'

The governess stroked the head of the small owl in her hand. She held it up and stared into its eyes. From looking at it, one would deduce that its skeleton was that of a short fat thing, but it was no more remarkable than that of any bird. She reached for the pruning scissors and placed the blades around its neck, holding it over the sink.

'I'm sorry, little thing. I know, I know, it hurts. Shhh now.'

With a skill mastered over decades, she scooped out the eyes, added them to the collection in a small glass bowl and took them to a brighter spot where she sat with a scalpel and tweezers. She removed the macula and the fovea, then squeezed the gel-like vitreous humour into a cup. The pecten oculi was the key, the organ that increased the nutrients to the eye. In it were invaluable substances that gave the eye protection at great speeds while flying, that gave the pupil such clarity of vision and made the eyes so very beautiful. She spooned the fluid into small syringes and took them upstairs.

Maggie read the first instalment of her sister's novel in the newspaper and grunted. She threw it aside, next to the empty bottles and plates strewn everywhere and closed the curtains. Then turning to face the darkened room, she sat and said aloud. 'Is there anybody there?'

She saw flickers here and there but dismissed them as tricks of the light or the eye. She looked at her hand, saw the glow around it, held it up to the room and played with the light. 'More than likely just heat,' she told herself and dismissed it. 'Come on!' she ordered. 'Show yourselves. It won't be long until I can see you so you might as well show yourselves now.'

Another long evening passed with an excess of alcohol and violent rages. There were glimmers and shadows and at one point she saw something move but by midnight nothing of any significance had occurred. She ate spoons of sugar, poured sweet wine, roused herself.

There would be no sleep until she had brought that which eluded her under her control. But suddenly things had altered again and two small white feet stood at the top of the stairs. Judy was at the door, checking the lock, pushing an armchair against it. Maggie covered her ears and closed her eyes. The strength of the memory and the guilt of seeing her mother confused, her last wish refused, forced down into her death bed and held there by her was too much. She closed her eyes but even beneath the lids she could see those angry eyes looking into her own. A wave of sickening guilt washed over her, remembering that all the time she and Judy had been drinking and talking beneath her, assuming she was dead when she had been alive and listening.

And suddenly the room was back to normal. Maggie leaned back into an armchair. Her eyes were red and framed with drooping black bags. She was exhausted, and for a moment considered allowing herself a short sleep, but she was too close now. Judy might be able to tell fortunes and Mrs Walters might be able to push a glass around a table and have conversations with those who had passed on, she herself might have lost the shop and her sister and all semblances of her old comfortable life, but not for long. If Maggie Cloak had one thing left, it was determination, and she knew that when she put her mind to something, she would have it. And there was something she wanted more than anything else – she wanted to be better than them, she wanted to leave the pair of them pathetic in her wake.

She forced open her eyes and shouted 'Again!' But nothing came.

Screaming with rage, Maggie stared at herself in the mirror, her eyes dark, her skin old, anger foaming from her lips. She contorted her face, making herself look uglier and more extreme, hating herself more and more. Then reaching for a knife she hacked violently at long lengths of her hair, her hands shaking as she hurled abuse at herself. 'You will change, Margaret. You will stop being you. Stop it! And now look at you, crying because you are cutting away your hair! Crying because you have stopped passing monthly blood. What does cutting your hair matter? It doesn't matter. You are ugly. You are left behind. No man will ever love you. Why would they? Not even Judy cares now. You finished her off. She has her new clothes and her new hair and her bags and her stupid writing and being good at everything. Every single thing!' She screamed out her fury again, cutting more hair. 'Look at you. Just look at you! This is your punishment for being so lazy and useless and ugly. So very, very ugly.'

She threw herself down into the armchair, scratching it with her fingernails, punching it, screaming and swearing and crying.

In the mirror she stared at herself again.

Her hair was ruined. It was long in places and short in others with clumps cut away so close to the scalp she looked crazed. Then turning again to the room she shouted at the top of her voice.

'SHOW YOURSELVES TO ME!'

〽〽〽〽〽〽〽〽

'This cannot go on,' Mrs Walters hissed across to Judy as they struggled with queues the next morning. 'If she can read the ball then she should be here. I will not give up any of this week's wage for her. She has not put in a single day.'

'Oh don't agitate her even more, Netta.'

'No, I mean it. She will not be paid. It is not fair. Who does she think that she is? I've a good mind to go over there now and drag her back here shouting and kicking.'

'Please don't!'

The proprietress of the tea hut burst through the door, barely able to contain her news.

'You will not believe the story I have heard!' She took off her coat and gloves and threw them down, taking Judy's tea from Mrs Walters' hand. 'Lovely.' The women watched her expectantly.

'The exhumations – of the girls, last night.'

'We were there,' Judy said.

The woman shook her head.

'It turns out, before they exhumed those graves, they accidentally dug up the wrong grave. The lid was loose and they found a man contorted, all his nails broken and scratch marks on the inside of the coffin lid. He'd nearly dug a hole through.' She stared at their confused expressions and blew steam from her tea. 'Buried alive!'

They shook their heads in horror.

'And that's not all. They suspected the doctor of foul play so this morning they dug up another of his patients – same thing, scratching, broken nails, face frozen into a scream, buried alive. Tonight they are digging up more of them. She sipped her tea quickly. It was too hot, she blew, looking at the women hanging on her every word.

'Why?'

'I imagine that he drugged people close to death and let them be buried so he could lie awake at night and judge by his clock the approximate time they would wake. I think he liked to imagine their panic and their fear and know that right then he had done it.'

'Oh good lord!' Judy said, shaking her head.

'But there is bigger news!' She grinned.

The women could barely breathe, watching her fish something out of her bag. She waved a newspaper. 'I see someone has been published!'

The women sighed, relieved that was all.

'The count and countess! So exciting!'

Mrs Walters suddenly sprung from her chair. 'Oh good lord! The time is perfect!' she laughed. 'My invention!'

She reached for some paper and dark chalk and drew. 'It's a pole that attaches to the coffin. When you bury the coffin, the pole sticks just an inch or two above the soil. Inside it, a flag, attached to a cord. If the deceased is not dead, he pulls on the string, the flag pops up and rescue is on its way.'

'You are going to make and sell these?'

'I've made them. I made them ten years ago. Didn't take off. Now they might. I will take out an advertisement next to the story in the paper. This will make me rich, you mark my words.' She gathered up her things and hurried to the door. 'I will see you both later!'

The afternoon's trade was relentless and by the time Mrs Walters returned from her trip to the newspaper, a queue awaited her.

'We will give your sister today,' she told Judy. 'If she does not show tomorrow, we must employ someone else. This cannot go on.'

Maggie showed up at four. She looked ill, her eyes sunken, her face grey, her scalp itching against the tightness of her bonnet. She did not want to talk, just collect her wages.

'You have not earned any!' Mrs Walters replied incredulously. 'You have not worked. Are you asking us to pay for you?'

Maggie slammed her hand down on the table.

'This is my shop!'

'This is *our* shop!' Judy interrupted.

Mrs Walters left, leaving the sisters facing each other in uncomfortable silence.

'Maggie, please stop this. I don't understand why –'

'You don't understand!' Maggie shouted. 'You made us close down the sweetshop, you made us open this parlour. And now that you have it you have forgotten me. In your new dresses with your new hair and your ability to read the ball. While I struggled, you just ignored me. You let me sit there useless and hopeless while you took all the glory. You left me behind even though I asked for your help. We used to enjoy each other's company. Now you barely have time for me at all. You're so obsessed with all the money you are making and how popular you are and how much people admire you because of your writing and your talent with the ball and your looks and your hair and your clothes, and look what it has brought us.'

Judy stepped back frightened as Maggie leaned in, jabbing at her with her finger.

'I know things about myself now that no woman should ever know. I know that no man will ever want me. That I cannot be loved. That I am repulsive to men. That I am not worthy of love. Something in me has broken. I am altered. Before I could have pretended and even if love didn't come I would have still been allowed hope and the dreams but now I know. I know I am alone. And still you take away even more from me. You abandoned me! Well just you watch what I bring, Judy. Just you wait.'

She snatched a handful of money and stormed out past the customers who jumped from her path, staring after her.

∞∞∞∞∞∞∞

In her kitchen Maggie moved around the overturned chairs and kicked empty bottles aside to create a path. She took several large bottles from her bag, plucked a greasy glass from the sink and filled it with port. She swallowed it in three gulps and poured another, turning to the one remaining armchair that faced into the room. She sat, closed her eyes and took a deep breath.

'Come to me!'

When she opened her eyes Judy was running towards the windows with the fireguard, pressing her hands against her ears, blocking out the death call of howling dogs. Maggie sighed, turning to the stairs where the little white feet began their decent.

'NO!' she shouted and closed her eyes. 'NO!'

When she opened them again, the room was still. She drew breath, relieved, and looked around her. There were no dog howls, no younger version of Judy, no boarded-up windows. She turned her eyes to the stairs and jumped. There at the top, perfectly still were a pair of small white feet; not descending, not moving, but perfectly still. Maggie was frozen. Something to her right caught her eye and she turned to see a shadow moving about the room. Beyond that, another human shape, barely visible, lowered itself onto some invisible seat and sat.

When she looked again at the stairs, the feet were still there, still and cold and white. Maggie stood, moving nervously to the bottom of the stairs, jumping back as they began to descend. She turned, looking for Judy, looking for the confusing blur of the memory to be there – the old smells, the flowers, the way the room was – but all was in chaos as it had been on her return.

The feet moved lower, hips coming into view, the nightdress moving, lifted by each knee, the blackened hands reaching for the handrail, the collar, her neck. Maggie moved back, unsure what was about to happen, ready to flee. And suddenly her mother was in the room, looking around it, looking at the overturned furniture, looking at the long-dead flowers in the vases and finally lifting up her head to look at Maggie. Maggie was frozen, terrified. Her mother tilted her head, waved something away from in front of her as if whatever was there was obscuring her vision and then she locked eyes with her daughter.

'Mummy?' Maggie said.

The woman turned her head to listen, her face confused.

'It's me. Maggie.'

The woman had turned away, was looking at the chaos of the room, looking up at the picture she had drawn. Then she turned back to Maggie, mouthing something.

'I can't hear you,' Maggie said.

The woman spoke again but Maggie could not make out the words and suddenly everything faded and she was alone.

 තතතතතතත

'I can't hear them!' Maggie screamed, letting herself into the shop. She knocked over a vase, took Mrs Walters arm without stopping and pulled her from the table and away from her client into the back room. 'I cannot hear them!'

Mrs Walters was furious but her words were drowned out beneath Maggie's drunken shouting. She turned away, again finding herself in Maggie's grip and slapped her hands away furiously.

'This cannot go on!' she shouted angrily. 'You are drunk. You are deranged. You do not grab at me. You never grab at me.'

'I cannot hear the –'

'I don't care!' Mrs Walters screamed back, pushing her away angrily. She stood her ground. 'I don't care what you can and can't do. I am fed up of you. You are a selfish, demanding, uncaring woman.'

She turned away, leaving Maggie furious.

'I can see them.'

'Well let's put out the flags.'

'I'm sorry.'

'You are not sorry. All you want, Margaret, is me calmed so you can get what you want from me and then you'll storm off again. We are working ourselves to the bone here and you are taking advantage. You barely show up except to take your wages from the money we earn. And by the state of you, you intend to do the same for as long as you want to. Well there will be no wages, because you have not earned any. And there will be no answers because I do not want to give them to you.'

She marched through the shop apologising to Judy and let herself out into the street.

Chapter 22

Netta's anger had shifted focus by the time she stepped from the carriage and hurried up past Covent Garden. She had discovered, over the past week, that her ex-fiancé's parents were not the type to stay at home. Mostly they visited the same public house where they enjoyed a modest popularity amongst the locals who encouraged sing-alongs at which they excelled.

Her mind returned to the arrangements for her marriage, to their tactics of luring her into public places to discuss things calmly, to being seated with them in a pub and told that her friends would not be invited and that the number of her family guests would have to be reduced, that they too had a big family, none of which could be excluded. She was marrying above her station, they would be paying, her parents contribution amounted to very little and no, she could not have the smaller, cheaper wedding that she demanded because their own family celebrated weddings in a way that was expected of them. Their son sat torn between both parties.

Tonight, however, the couple took a different direction up towards Holborn. It was the first time they had ventured anywhere else in two weeks. They turned off the busier streets into smaller, quieter lanes where Netta was not so easily concealed, but she kept her distance and on the rare occasions they turned to look behind them, she managed to jump into doorways or change direction in time, avoiding raising suspicion. Eventually, they stopped outside a tall townhouse and knocked. Netta slowed her pace, frightened that all too soon she would be upon them, and was relieved to hear the door open and a happy squealing woman welcome them, followed by cheery male tones that she recognised immediately. She had found him.

※※※※※※

Maggie was alone. She paced and shouted, demanding that the spirits

213

come to her. And when she saw one, she rushed toward it, wanting to corner it and exhaust it until at last, she could hear them. But the shapes faded or moved through the walls or ignored her. A knock at the door gave her a start and she swung it open, hoping that Netta had come to her senses and was here to unlock whatever was stopping her progress. She let out a groan when she was confronted with Father Legge.

'Some of the villagers are concerned about you,' he said, 'Apparently you are putting on some wild displays in public and they asked me to have a word. Is everything all right, Margaret? You seem a little stressed of late. Not your usual self.'

'Everything is perfect,' she replied, waiting for him to say his piece and leave.

'You have the look of someone who has bitten off more than she can chew.'

'Keep it for your sermons, Henry. I am very busy. What is it you want?'

He looked inside, at the overturned furniture, the strewn bottles, the clothes tossed across the floor. She sighed impatiently.

'Margaret, you and I go back a long way, religion aside. I have come here to help you.'

'Father Legge, I do not need your help, now please . . .'

'You called me Father,' he smiled. 'Small changes, little steps forward, we'll get you there.'

She glared.

'Well you little ladies, be careful. You don't want this sideshow leading you past anything the Church can't pull you back from.'

Maggie slammed the door in a rage, the vicar's words repeating themselves over and over in her head. 'Little ladies, sideshow, you called me Father, little steps,' she screamed out in frustration. He always brought out the worst in her. She recalled the day he had refused her mother the right to marry again despite her father not having returned from Africa for over ten years. Young and green, he had stepped into the role of vicar of Lewisham.

'Until his body is found, you are still married in the eyes of the Lord,' he had told her in front of her daughters. Their mother was distraught and her husband to be, so eager to be married, allowed his love to temper and his eye to wander and her mother, alone again, cursed the day she had met the girl's father, only to be scolded by Maggie, who would not have a word said against him.

Maggie poured herself a whisky, studied her face in the mirror, pulled off her cap and looked at the scalped hair, shaking her head. She threw herself down before the fire and turned her seat to face the room. 'Well?' she shouted, 'show yourselves!' She studied the room, nodding as more and more dark shapes and outlines appeared to her. 'If he wants a sideshow, I'll give him one he won't forget in a hurry.' She took a large swig and took a deep breath, closing her eyes. She had all night. Whatever patience she needed, whatever discipline it took, she would find it and she would use up every night until she was not only good at it, but she was the best.

※※※※※※※

'Oh good lord!'

'Good heavens!'

'She can't write that, can she?'

'She has written it! Listen to this, where is it? Here:

'*. . . swept up her thick mousy hair and fastened the chain, allowing the green stone to slide under her blouse and down between her small, young breasts. The coolness made her shiver.*

'*You have goose pimples,' the countess laughed, and lifted the stone and chain a little higher.*

'*It is a shame,' she said unbuttoning the girl's blouse, 'that we cannot see it properly with the clothes in the way, 'Take off your blouse.'*

'Oh good lord!'

'Are we actually allowed to say breasts, then?'

'Apparently!'

The gathering of women shook their heads as Mrs Walters handed out tea. 'Go on.'

'I must skip to this part – it is marvellously obscene – in which the count undresses at the Ranger's House . . .'

'No!'

'In front of the Princess Sophia Matilda . . .'

The women were shocked.

'And then he impregnates her, with his wings all over her!'

They burst into raucous laughter.

'It really is terribly bad, but in a good way.'

Judy hurried into the room and snatched the paper from them. 'Oh Good lord! Oh heavens, no! Please tell me they did not leave the princess in. I left strict instruc . . . Oh No! Oh this is bad!'

ΩΩΩΩΩΩΩΩ

Tightening her bonnet to hide the patches of scalp, Maggie made her way to work. It would be awkward, she didn't doubt that, but life had to regain some level of normality. She would work in the room upstairs, away from the others.

Her breath smelled slightly of whisky but she had stuffed her pockets with mint and parsley and chewed ferociously as she crossed the heath. In the village, people noticed her, congregating in small groups to stare and gossip. She grunted and rolled another ball of mint in her hands.

Her appearance cleared the room, leaving Netta and Judy to face her alone.

'If you are here for money . . .' Netta began.

She took off her coat and threw it down. 'I am here to work. I am back,' she said angrily.

Judy's heart sank. The days were simpler without her. There was less tension, it was easier to read from the ball and the customers were not frightened.

'I can see them now,' she announced. She lifted a table and took it to the bottom of the stairs. Her breathing was laboured, her face tired. 'I can see them clearly. Oh you would have laughed at the mistakes I made. You would have chuckled at the way the dead treated me, refusing to acknowledge me, refusing to talk, but I found a way. 'She turned to the room and shouted, 'DIDN'T I?' She laughed. 'I found a way all right. They know me now.'

'Maggie, you are in a state. Look at you.'

'Oh I know! All this?' she pointed to her dress. 'None of it matters, I can clean all that up. I am different now. I have the gift. That's what is important. I have the gift. And soon,' she jabbed her finger in the direction of her sister, 'you will no longer work here.'

Judy looked away, ignoring her. Outside the window she saw two policemen approaching and she let out a cry, clutching at a chair as the

216

men entered.

'I am so sorry,' she began. 'I will retract it. It should never have been published in the first place.'

'Be quiet, Judy!' Maggie snapped, pushing through them. 'They're probably here for her!' she said, pointing to Mrs Walters who did a double take. 'I know some things about you now, lady.'

The policemen stared at Mrs Walters. In an instant, the horror of her arrest flooded back with sickening clarity. The procedures, her rights taken from her, her words no longer worth anything, the drained feeling of helplessness. The tray of cups was shaking in her hands and she put it down hurriedly.

'Mrs Walters?' one of the officers asked.

She nodded, almost swooning. Norman must have seen her, knew she had followed his parents to his door, had called the police to keep her away, to stop her from rehashing the murder and telling how it really had been. His parents were protecting their son again, probably calling in favours, stopping her before she put their son behind bars. She considered her options, to flee, to leave London if she found even the slightest window of opportunity.

Behind the police, the parents of the murdered girl came into view.

'We are sorry,' the father pleaded. 'We know we said we wouldn't involve you, but we feel that you are getting so close to finding our daughter's murderer.'

Mrs Walters stared.

'You were correct about the hair, madam, portions of hair had been removed from all the girls, so we would like you to assist our enquiries further,' said the tallest of the officers, 'though I don't believe in any of it myself.'

'We would like you to conduct a séance in our presence to see if you can unearth anything more,' the shorter and more formal of the two said firmly.

Mrs Walters shook her head, 'No, I'm sorry. I've heard of this leading to the arrest of the medium. It's too easy for the medium to be framed.'

'Madam, we know the murderer was a man. He has told us so much in his letters. We really must insist on asking you to cooperate.'

Her eyes darted shiftily from one face to another.

'Come back this evening.' Maggie said irritably. 'Séances are in the evening. No exceptions.' She handed them the newspaper, open at her sister's story. 'You might want to have a look through this in the meantime.'

Netta moved back into the kitchen and sat, gathering her thoughts. She had to leave, get away from London. She could not go through it all again. Her face was still ashen when Judy came through.

'What's wrong with you?'

Netta stared at her. 'You must do it. I don't want to be involved, not with murder.'

'But I can only read the ball!'

Mrs Walters shook her head. 'Make it up. Tell them anything. Tell them I was called away on urgent business.'

'Of course,' she replied concerned. 'Are you . . .'

A stamping of footsteps hammering down the stairs drew their attention. A woman was shouting, pleading with Maggie to stop. Judy and Netta rushed out to the shop in concern.

'She is a madwoman!' the woman shouted, struggling with her coat. 'Mad in the head. She told me everything. When I would die. How I would die. How much it would hurt. How no one would come to my funeral. She is crazy.'

'Oh get out!' Maggie bellowed down after her.

Netta and Judy exchanged pensive looks.

৯৯৯৯৯৯৯৯৯

At five, Mrs Walters pre-empted the murdered girl's parents' early arrival, as was their customary tactic, and hurried to fetch her coat. She was too late; as she slipped her arm into the sleeve, they stepped inside, She swore, furious at herself for not escaping earlier. And then she saw the police, blocking the doorway, aware of her continual reluctance to deal with them.

She turned back into the kitchen and took off her coat.

'We are so sorry to do this to you. We tried to make appointments but you wouldn't see us,' the mother explained.

'And so you call the police to get your own way?'

They looked uncomfortable.

'Our daughter was brutally –'

'It is nothing to do with me!'

'But you knew about the hair, the doll, you can reach her.'

'We would appreciate your cooperation, Mrs Walters,' the policeman said authoritatively.

'Bloody policemen,' she muttered to herself. Whoever had thought up the newfangled idea of creating bobbies to rule the streets needed hanging. 'Judy will be reading the ball for you,' she called back.

'No, it has to be you. She has spoken to you. She knows you!' The mother objected. 'It has to be you.'

Netta sat down out of view. She felt sick. Policemen always made her feel ill. She felt her heart racing and tried to reason with herself. The police were not after her. There was no need for her to panic. Perhaps she should do it. Exorcise her demons or even lead them astray, make it all up. If everything she told them turned out to be far from the truth they couldn't frame her. She felt sick. It could happen again. She felt it building up around her. She could sense the danger she was in. And suddenly Maggie appeared, ushering everyone through irritably, moving them along as if their presence was a great inconvenience to her too.

Mrs Walters stood, alarmed at their number. 'Who are these others?' she asked, pointing to a group of assorted men and women who took positions away from the table.

'They are here to record the proceedings.'

She closed her eyes. This was it. This time they would pin it on her and she would hang. She took her place reluctantly at the head of the table and closed her eyes, waiting for the room to settle and concocting the nonsense she would tell them. She would not draw the spirits to her; instead, she would draw blanks, misguide them, deflate their excitement, end it, once and for all.

The doors were closed and the room darkened to the glow of a solitary candle. There was silence and the expectant nervous breathing of those around her. When she was ready and her nerves had been mastered, she let out a deep breath and allowed her head to fall forward. The worst scenario now was that she would go into a trance without knowing it, but she would not allow that to happen. Too much depended on it. She felt the atmosphere begin to change around her, felt the spirit world aligning with her, recognised the breezes and whispers around her ears of people trying to communicate. Her attention was pulled back to the room by Maggie, who, dragging a chair noisily across the floor, moved everyone along to make room for her.

She sighed angrily and closed her eyes.

Almost immediately the girl came through, as if she had been there waiting. Mrs Walters ignored her.

'Is there anybody there?'

'You know I am here, you can see me,' the girl replied.

'Is there anybody there?'

She opened her eyes. 'I'm not getting through.'

'Please keep trying!' the mother begged.

Maggie stared at her, confused.

'Come forward, come to me,' Netta offered.

'I am here!' the girl screamed at her.

Mrs Walters flinched, recoiling in her seat, causing everyone to jump.

Maggie shook her head, annoyed.

'Is there anybody there?' Netta asked. 'We need the name of the murderer. Can you help us?'

The crowd watched, transfixed, their eyes unable to pull away from Netta's eerie performance, in the midst of which Maggie opened her mouth and let out such a monstrous scream that even the men screamed back at her. The note wavered in depth and volume until it turned dramatically into choking and fast breathing. Maggie felt the breath pouring from her lungs, tasted the fumes of two-day-old whisky at the back of her throat. She turned to the girl's mother and in the most unnatural tones for a woman her age, screamed hard.

The woman jumped back in shock, steadied by the policemen who were already on their feet and white with fear. Netta and Judy stared. Maggie was on her feet, waving her arms in front of her, fighting something off. She screamed hard and blurted, 'No! Stop! Stop it. You're hurting me, you're . . .' She was clawing away invisible hands from her throat, stretching her head away, gasping for breath. Her voice was thin and hoarse. 'Get away from me. Get off me!'

The mother cried out, shaking her head, 'That's her voice! That is her!'

The father leaned forward in shock, unable to do anything but listen.

Maggie stopped, her eyes snapping open, staring at each of them in turn.

She, swooned, falling forward at the hips, her head banging loudly down onto the table, then the muscles of her neck snapped her head backwards and up into the air. She was rigid, standing tall, pulling at something from around her throat, letting out horrible gasps for air as one hand fought something away at her hips and grabbed at her shirt, pulling it down over her.

The parents looked away, comforting each other. Maggie's legs were open, her head was turned away, she was grunting, fighting, pushing away a weight that forced itself onto her body. Her head fell limp. She stood motionless, her head hanging to one side, her eyes open and lifeless. For several minutes she did not move and no one dared to make a sound.

The sight was so awful that not even the policemen dared to look for long. Then Netta rose from her seat, taking Maggie's shoulders into her hands and lowered her into her seat.

'Maggie,' she said softly, 'Maggie wake up now.'

Maggie was lifeless.

'Come on now.'

'MAGGIE!' Judy cried.

Maggie's head rolled forward. She grunted. Then she spoke again in a voice neither Netta or Judy recognised.

'He is still there,' a girl's voice whimpered. 'He wants more. I wasn't enough. It was never about me. I didn't matter. I was just one.' The unnatural voice subsided and Maggie dribbled great strands of saliva down her dress.

'Tell us his name, sweetheart,' her father demanded softly, but Maggie was back, looking violent and psychotic and confused. She stared around the room madly.

'I'm not doing that again,' she announced. 'Fetch me a drink.'

Judy rushed to the kettle.

'Not tea, you stupid cow!' and suddenly she was swaying again, her eyes closed, her shoulders rocking.

'He is going to kill again,' she said, her eyes watery, pulling lengths of saliva from her mouth that clung to her hands and kept coming until she reached the point of irritable annoyance. 'Oh for God's sake! 'Is anyone going to get me a bloody handkerchief or what?' She wiped her hands on her dress. Not tonight. He will be drinking tonight, in the

Princess of Wales public house.' She pulled a thick length of sticky saliva free, wiping it on herself. 'He sits at the bar at the front over to the left. Most often in a chair in the corner, in front of the fire, where he criticises in silence and watches, always watching.'

She swooned, her forehead resting for a moment on the table, where she threw out hot breath and tried to inhale the cool. She felt sick, her mouth watering, her throat tight. She shook it away, controlled it. 'There is a lust in him, an excitement.' She said pulling herself up, breathing out the heat, swaying. 'He loves it, he is compelled to hunt out that moment when they are broken and begging and he is strong again. That is the moment he likes. That makes it all worth it.'

'The name of the murderer?' the policeman asked.

Maggie turned to him irritably, her eyes glazed, as if she could not see him. 'John Druitt. Number 9, Elliot Place. He is just about to leave. The hair is laid out in a drawer, pride of place. He will go to the Princess of Wales pub. The note he'll leave on the next body is inside the lining of his jacket, with the knife, just in case he gets brave and decides tonight is the night after all, but it won't be.'

Chapter 23

The early edition of the weekly London magazine which contained longer instalments of Judy's novel than the newspaper brought a bustling cluck of women into the shop.

Netta cleared her throat. '*The count visited Lady Dartmouth late, charming as always, but tonight, eager to push quickly past the formality of food and polite conversation. She opened the door to her private rooms in her bathrobe, surprised and unprepared for the late visit.*'

The women listened without a sound.

Tonight, the count's eyes were more dazzling than ever. There was a freshness to them, as if filled with new ideas. He smelt of cologne and new leather and there was a deepness to his voice that made her a little more receptive to him. Taking off his jacket he moved to the fire, placing his brandy on the mantelpiece. Hardly a word had been spoken but they both knew why he was there. He looked down at her, his lips parting, her eyes drawn to them. She turned away. The front that she showed him was being challenged. With words she could win and manipulate and flirt but now her body was required and her lack of confidence showed through her façade with the most fragile and vulnerable expressions.

'You are a young man. I am an old woman.'

He nodded. 'You are old and I am young. That is a fact. For me, it is perfect.'

She stared at him, wondering what game he was playing with her.

'You have ownership of your body whereas young girls' minds are confused with the newness of their own. They have yet to feel the purpose of it, smooth and vain and silly and beautiful as they are. I enjoy them but in my eyes, a woman's attractiveness begins when all that naiveté has long gone, so long gone that even the mourning of it has passed.'

She listened.

'In the later years, the real woman emerges. It is then, to me, that a woman

is attractive, depending, of course, on what she now brings out from within to show.' His eyes caught hers. 'You are very attractive. You know that.' He took a sip of his brandy. His eyes were now so magnificent and captivating that she wanted to believe him. He took three steps towards her, put a finger to her chin and lifted her lips to his. Hers were soft, thin, unsure. His mouth was bigger, stronger, his lips fuller and although her kisses were dainty and frightened, he teased her mouth a little wider and felt her tongue reach out timidly. His pressed against it and he felt her exhale, sensed her pleasure.

His hands rested on her shoulders, caressed her earlobes and neck and then moved downwards, sliding the robe free, feeling her tense and pull away.

'I am not ready.'

He smiled. 'A period of thinking will not prepare you any better.'

'It's been so long. It's been nearly fifteen years.'

'Are you naked under your robe?'

She nodded.

'Take it off.'

He sat.

'Show me the body that no man has touched for so long.'

She was unable to; her breasts were emptied, flattened, stretched with age. Her stomach was white and wrinkled, the tops of her legs shapeless and bony. She could not bear to think about her rear, and there were other areas that were also less firm. She could foresee him recoiling at the sight of her, as she imagined all men would if they were to see her naked.

He stood and pressed gently against her, kissing her again on the lips, opening her mouth a little wider, pushing her to be braver, to relax, to want him. He undid his shirt, took her hand, placed it on his chest and loosened her robe, feeling her nervous hands give in and allow it to fall open. She shivered, pressing quickly against him to hide herself, wanting to turn out the lights or think of an excuse to bolt to the door but his hands were already moving down her back, strong and curious, feeling her ribs, her spine, her hips and with a lingering kiss, he stepped back and looked at her.

She froze, covering herself, blushing, reaching for the robe but he shook his head and put a finger to his lips. 'Shhh. Let me see you.'

Nervously, she moved her trembling arm away from her chest, revealing the breasts of a woman long past her prime. She let the hand in front of her crotch fall to her side revealing an overhang of stomach. She watched him looking at her and saw that he was not repulsed. He was pulling off his boots.

A new nervousness filled her, the panic that this was actually going to happen.

Tightening the muscles of his back into the knots that they were used to forming to conceal at all costs his secret, he undressed without ceremony, the eagerness and confidence of youth giving him no reason to be shy, and she found herself looking at what was forbidden, the body of a younger man, strong and forceful and limber, able to run at speed, wrestle, fight, climb, punch, carry things, all of the abilities that her body had now lost. She felt a curious braveness rise in her and allowed her eyes to look where she liked and then he came to her.

'Please,' he whispered into her ear, 'do not touch my back.'

She nodded, closing her eyes as his hands touched her breasts, alarmed to find that despite years of neglect and indifference, they were sensitive to his touch, alarmingly so. Her stomach too, was alive with the firing of nerves as his hands explored her. She tensed but he soothed it away.

'There is no need to worry,' he told her, opening her arms away from her.

There was a rare eroticism in moments such as these that the count enjoyed more than anything else. It happened in just a few moments, sometimes in a single expression but more often in a gradual shift. It was the abandonment of a frightened and preoccupied mind. He loved to watch it and anticipated it hungrily now. She would change, a sigh, a long breath, the lifting of worry and a look of embracing the moment, being there, naked and brave. Everything else abandoned from a mind that was usually aflame with misconceptions and blind panic. Even the ugliest and fattest of women became beautiful when they reached that moment. It was a look of the carefree, of trust and bravery and of daring, all brought together to switch off the mind. She was ticklish and breathy as she got used to the sensation of being touched again, feeling how reassuring and pacifying and natural the feeling of hands on her body, even at this age, was. It was important. She had forgotten that.

She was lying on her back. He was on his side, nibbling her ear, taking his time, playing with the parts of her that made her giggle or feel ticklish. There was no hurry, he liked to watch the pleasure. He looked forward to the moment when the face let go of the tension and the eyes became free and the embarrassment left. The transformation of the face, for the count, was the most erotic part, and, as his fingers dared to creep to the warmth she feared his reaction to the most, the nervousness reappeared on her face again. His slow delicate reassurance brought down her nervous breaths and her whole body relaxed. Finally she lost the expression of concern that age brings and she allowed herself to forget how she must look. Her face had shaken away all concern and worry and sensing it was time, he moved gently on top of her.

The women stared at each other, red-faced and silent.

In the village a group was crowded around the newspaper seller, thrilled by the front page. Shrieks of excitement drew the attention of everyone in the street, including Maggie, who pushed through, taking one with a dry smile. She didn't pay.

Walking into the shop where the ladies were discussing the count and, more importantly, Lady Dartmouth who they all knew personally, Maggie sighed at them indifferently and threw the paper down in front of them. She walked upstairs. Now it was her turn for fame and glory and she intended never to give it back. By the time she reached the top stair, the women were screaming.

On the front page was a drawing of the séance parlour with the headline MEDIUM CATCHES MURDERER. He was caught, she had been right. He had admitted it all. He had even been found in the exact seat in the exact pub at the exact time that she had told them he would be. The paper and the police heralded Margaret Cloak as London's miracle. A little dramatic for Maggie's taste in public, but in private she experienced rapture. Beyond the front page, a gripping editorial by the owner of the newspaper who had arrived at the séance a sceptic and left convinced, thrilled readers with details. He could not recommend Maggie enough.

'It was proven beyond all doubt that Miss Margaret Cloak was in fact communicating with the dead and is the possessor of a rare and magnificent gift,' it read. 'She provided the police with the name, address and thoughts of the murderer, which led them directly from the séance to the seat in the public house in which he was indeed sitting, with the knife and a note intended for the police with further clues in the lining of his jacket as pinpointed with magnificent clarity by Miss Cloak. A more shocking phenomenon occurred when Miss Cloak reunited both parents with the voice of their murdered daughter which they verified the authenticity of without a shadow of a doubt. The voice, obviously not that of Miss Cloak herself, reached all of our ears from beyond the grave. A rare opportunity that surely all of us would like again with our departed loved ones. The Blackheath Séance Parlour has this newspaper's unequivocal endorsement. It is a phenomenon the like of which has never before been seen in the world and perhaps never will again. I urge you to experience Miss Margaret Cloak for yourselves.'

Mrs Walters ushered everyone out, took a damp rag to the price list and locked the door.

'We'd better brace ourselves!' she said, hurrying Maggie through to the kitchen. 'We're about to get very, very busy.' She put the board down on the table, pressed the chalk against her chin, then nodding, wrote, 'Miss Maggie Cloak, the world's only Voice Medium appearing here today. Hear the voices you thought you'd never hear again. Tickets available at scandalous prices. All other readings cancelled.'

By the time she took the board back to the front of the shop, the crowd was ten deep, with Judy fighting her way through the middle. She fell into the shop with alarm.

'What is going on?'

'Well it's not your little story, I can tell you that,' Maggie said. 'No one's interested in that any more.'

Netta frowned, a quill and parchment in her hand.

'One at a time! I will try to get to you all.'

Each voice roared desperately to ensure a sitting.

Maggie smiled.

'There is just one other thing,' she said with a look of spite. 'I will only work here if Judy never sets foot inside again.'

Judy stared at her and turned to Netta, who looked down at the floor. Turning, Judy marched from the parlour out into the crowd.

Maggie took her place at the table, nodding for Netta to bring through the first group of customers that insisted on seeing only her. Some were news reporters, Maggie knew that, here to get their scoop and rather naively thinking that she wouldn't see past their disguises of a highly jewelled housewife and a musician who had even gone to the lengths of bringing with him his flute. Accompanying them at the session was a ship's captain from Dartmouth Row and various others undeterred by the quadrupled prices.

When they were seated, she walked, snuffing out the candles between her thumb and finger.

'I would like to do things a little differently,' she told them, leaving just one spluttering candle fighting for survival. She moved around them, touching their hair and shoulders, for her own amusement and to put them ill at ease rather than for any other reason. Then turning so sharply to the housewife that she nearly fell off her chair, Maggie let out a deep howling noise. Looking at her with devilish eyes she said, 'Ci-i-indy, oh Cindy!'

The woman was panicking.

'Such a loving dog, so trusting but so stupid. It still hurts you, doesn't it? You still wake up with a jolt, your whole body leaving the bed. You still see her as clear as day, chasing that stick you threw for her over the cliff in Westbourne. You still see her running towards the edge, eyes on the stick, barking excited at it and seeing the edge but oh so excited it took the leap. Bones like powder.' She shook her head.

The woman was horrified.

'Is she there? Do you see her?'

'I've never seen animals. No, your brother is here. He told me. He's a funny little thing. Died young, out of the blue.'

Maggie's eyes were now fixed angrily on the ship's captain. She shook her head and coughed hard, pacing the room, her steps wide and exaggerated, then she looked back at him and with a loud booming man's voice shouted 'I should forgive you, William, I know I should. I should let it go. They all tell me to but it goes through me. You knew about the will. You knew what was agreed but still you tried and tried to take it all for yourself; you and your accountant. I watched it, watched it all and I didn't like what I saw in you. You would have left Liz and Norma penniless. But I knew you would do it. That's why I put the trap in place. You were no friend. Is that why you are here? To see how the land lies? You are even too greedy to be ashamed of it.'

The man looked towards the door, his face hot, his eyes worried and his chubby hands fidgeting. He wanted to leave, to escape the stifling attention now focused on him, but much as he willed it, his body would not respond and he sat, trapped, with little else to consider other than his place in the great scheme of things was not as grand as he had imagined after all.

Maggie eyed him irritably and leaned on the table, turning to the musician. She stared hard into his eyes and kept staring until he grew so uncomfortable that he had to look away, glancing for support to the others who were as unnerved by it as he. When he looked back at her, her eyes were still staring, drilling into him, and before him, on the table, the flute began to vibrate and shake. It turned a little on the table and then, shocking even Maggie awake, it began to play feeble, eerie notes.

Maggie staggered back, her feet giving way, her back crashing to the wall, and she slid down, flopping like a doll, then as the sitters hurried to help her, her head turned to them angrily and her arms waved them away. She pulled herself up onto her seat, retching hard. Her eyes rolled back into her head as her jaw fell wide open, opening and closing with the loud click of her teeth until she appeared to foam at the mouth. Netta rushed across the room to her, stopping in horror as a large white egg appeared at her lips. She stared.

Maggie retched again and the egg tumbled from her mouth embedded inside what appeared to be a thick white dough that dangled from her lips. The egg shape grew bigger, becoming heavier, pulling more of the white dough from her mouth. It settled in her lap against her stomach, filling as more and more spilled from her lips.

'What is it?' someone asked.

Mrs Walters stared at it and shook her head. 'I don't know.'

'We should fetch a doctor!'

Then, when it had appeared to have stopped growing, it gave the impression that it was moving independently in her lap.

The room was silent, no one daring to make a sound. The bulbous end seemed to be bubbling and rising, strange stalks grew from it, testing the air around it, touching and recoiling like the eyestalks of a snail. It was taking form, becoming long and slim. At its base, it began to bend, swaying out like an arm from an elbow and then a fist appeared to form, with knuckles and a wrist. Horrible wet worm-like shapes reached out, filling into fingers, a thumb uncurled, folds of lose skin appeared at the finger joints and from Maggie's lap, a perfect white arm lifted, the hand flexing. At the fingertips, nails formed. It pointed to the ship's captain and, around the wrist, a heavy round cuff began to form.

The man nodded, bowing his head, he seemed to understand the message. He turned away from it, refusing to look. No one else dared move. They were all watching the arm relax back into shapelessness, as it pulled itself up towards Maggie's face and began cramming itself in her mouth, overfilling it, causing her to choke and gasp for breath. She woke, panicking, gasping for air, clawing at the thing in her mouth, pulling at it.

'No!' Netta screamed. 'Let it go back in. Hold your breath!'

She hurried to the kitchen and brought back a tablespoon to press it flat against her tongue.

Maggie was red, the blood filling her face as she battled to breathe. And suddenly it was over. She was safe. Without a word, she left the room, climbed the stairs and fell asleep in the attic.

Netta Walters scanned the troubled faces and ushered them irritably out into the street. When they were gone she rested her hands on the table and stared at the open ledger in which all daily events were recorded. Her trembling hand lifted the quill but it trailed off at the first word. She had heard of it happening before but had always written it off as a hoax. 'Ectoplasm.' She re-read the odd word before allowing herself to flop down into an armchair. For a moment she felt little other than fear. Then with a smile, she realised what she had on her hands.

Chapter 24

Judy was hurrying across the heath, the frozen white grass cracking under her boots. It was the night of her big date. She had expected to be more nervous but all she felt was excitement. In the distance, the Clarendon Hotel illuminated the entire row of houses. It was being turned from shipbuilders' lodgings to what its owner boasted would be the finest hotel in all of England. She had not been there before but whereas once she would have entered rather timidly, these days she had her confidence about her. She stopped to compose herself at the entrance and, allowing her quickness of breath to soften, smiled at the owner, Mr O'Donell who opened the door for her and stepped into the bright warmth.

In the dining room, her entrance turned heads. In one respect or another, people had a lot to say about Judy Cloak these days. Those who were not interested in her serialisation marvelled at the séance parlour and hoped to hear stories that would make their hair stand on end, and those who dismissed that were in awe of her incredible transformation and style.

When she saw him her boldness vanished and her eyes swept down shyly. He was smiling and stood, pulling back her seat for her. Sitting, she took in the dining room. It was lit with a soft orange glow and busy; six or so tables chattered politely, basking in the rich tantalising aromas of steaks and puddings.

The shyness faded away immediately, surprising her. It felt quickly as if they were old friends, comfortable and excited with each other's company and eager to catch up on each other's lives. They shared Whitstable oysters and French champagne, needing to look at each other but not wanting to be seen looking. When they caught each other's glances they smiled and giggled like children. It was as if the rest of the room had vanished around them. Only the waiter's interruptions brought them back to clarity.

231

Christopher was an accomplished diner, she realised, knowing what to order and being specific about how he liked his food cooked. She was surprised to find such requests met with approval rather than rebuff and took the time to study him. He had a kind face, boyishly mature. His clothes were expensive and crisply pressed. She imagined he liked order at home too; perhaps he was a fussy person but she doubted it. As he questioned the waiter he felt her eyes on him and turned to look at her. She blushed and watched him try to suppress his smile as he turned away again. When the waiter left they looked at each other, silently studying each other's faces. It was a strange moment in which neither spoke but both needed unspoken answers. His eyes sparkled, his mouth formed a smile and she felt her cheeks begin to ache from the wideness of her own smile. Then reaching across the table, he took her hand and squeezed it. She thought she might collapse.

The evening disappeared, over with before they felt it had begun. There was so much still to say, so much they wanted to know and tell, both knew they had barely scratched the surface.

They were the last two at the bar, aware of the barman's impatience but willing it to remain open all night so they could sip brandies and remain together.

'I will be away for four weeks, I'm afraid,' he told her as the evening drew closer to its end. 'In the morning I go to Southampton on business. I am awaiting the delivery of various animals including two aggressive brown bears for London Zoo.' He could see her disappointment. He felt it himself. 'But I will hurry back.'

She nodded, aware suddenly of the inappropriateness of holding his hand and yet it had been there for minutes and she could not, did not, want to take it back.

When they left the hotel and she watched him head towards Greenwich in his carriage and she found herself close to tears, already missing him.

That night, feeling girlish with her heart aflutter, she slept restlessly, wishing that they could meet again the next day and the next and that his trip to Southampton could be postponed. She dreamed about him pacing bravely around caged bears and lions, all the time wanting to get back to her. It would be too presumptuous for her to visit him there; instead she prayed that the trip would be shortened or he would send for her. The excitement she felt now made four weeks seem like a lifetime. Finally, happily, she slept.

The following morning's newspaper reviews of Maggie's latest phenomenon had brought Blackheath to a standstill. Judy read the events with horror as she made her way down into the village only to be confronted with crowds surrounding the parlour. Netta had told her that every day within minutes of opening, the day's appointments were sold out and she was having to close the doors against the crowds and still they gathered and knocked but Judy had not expected such a scene as she now stood to helplessly witness. It seemed that she had created not one monster but two.

Not even Mrs Walters' insanely steep prices which, in most cases, were the equivalent of a week's wage for a mere ten-minute sitting, had deterred people. Maggie worked through them all, never once showing any sign of tiredness. With each new spirit she appeared to become more transfixed, more in tune and more in control. She was now pulling voices from the beyond that were so horrifyingly out of place for a woman of her age that Mrs Walters could no longer remain in the room. There were accents she had never heard, bad language and anger of such ferocity that on one occasion both Netta and the customer wondered if the spirit had taken her over entirely. But Maggie was magnificently stronger. When she wanted to shake the spirit off, she did so at the click of her fingers.

There were six sittings a day, Netta told her some days later, but at the midway mark, Maggie would need to retire upstairs. Exhausted, she slept deeply for one hour and then reappeared, eager to move on to her next. Netta was enthralled by what she was seeing, as enthralled as everyone else watching her. All thoughts of leaving London had been abandoned. And Maggie's exhaustion and the toll the sittings were taking on her was easily brushed aside as the money came pouring in.

Musicians, actors, gentry, minor royalty, property tycoons, hoteliers, foreign visitors fought for places in the queue to see her, often outbidding those higher in the queue than themselves to secure a sitting. And as they thrilled audiences at dinner parties and social gatherings with their shocking accounts, each eager to prove Maggie's unquestionable talent with examples of things she could not have possibly known, the queues grew longer and more insistent,

Judy turned away from the village and spent the long empty afternoon at the Trafalgar Tavern and, seated next to the window, with quill and paper she was relieved that she at least had the company of her writing. She gazed around the large wooden interior and added it to the page.

The princess was dining in the private rooms of the Trafalgar Tavern along the river. She gazed out at the uninspiring view of the Thames, rehearsing what it was she would say when Lady Dartmouth joined her. It would be an uncomfortable lunch but only the princess would be expecting it. She had seen him visiting her, watched him leave, seen the change in his demeanour, the lightness in his step.

When she arrived, she ordered wine that Lady Dartmouth had not heard of – yellow, rich, young and tart – but her enemy sipped it without complaint.

'The count . . .,' Sophia said.

Lady Dartmouth nodded.

'. . . is mine.' Young and innocent, but wielding the power of monarchy, she asserted the rule that royalty could, ending her rival's rights at a whim. She squeezed lemon onto the crisp, little fish that awaited her fork then lifted her head and smiled. 'You were close?'

'Yes,' the older and much wiser woman replied calmly, 'we are close.'

'The count and I are also very close,' the princess said, curious to see which expression her words would provoke.

Lady Dartmouth, recently awoken in all ways, was not about to surrender graciously. Her body was changed, thrilled with itself, every synapse was fighting fit, her confidence renewing her. 'The count, your majesty, is mine.' She smiled.

The princess cocked her head graciously, beckoning her forward, to share a whisper and with the briefest of smiles said. 'Then why is it that the count and I are to be married?'

Lady Dartmouth shook her head. 'No. You really are not. The count does not love you.'

The princess took a sip of wine, remained silent for an unnatural time, then looking the woman in the eye, she threatened, 'If you think you can take him from me, I will expose him.'

'Expose him as what?'

'As a demon.'

Lady Dartmouth laughed. 'Oh dear child!'

The princess glared at her. 'Do not think of using that tone with me. Remember your station!'

'A demon!' she laughed.

'I take it you have not seen the count undressed.'

'On many occasions,' she replied defiantly.

The princess closed her eyes, overcome with jealousy that fizzed in her throat and reddened her face. She was outraged that he could show and share his body to other women so freely when she was offering him her heart. She reached for her gloves, pushing aside her meal, aware of the waiter watching them. 'If there is another opportunity,' she whispered, 'though I doubt it, you will find what makes him a demon on his back.'

Lady Dartmouth pushed the wine away and called over the waiter, 'Bring me a glass of something less vulgar'. And my dear,' she called after the princess. 'You might consider a diet.'

The princess ignored the remark and left in a fury.

Lady Dartmouth, aware of the count's thoughts on silly little girls, was herself full of girlish excitement. She sipped her wine and looked out at the view, feeling as though life had just begun all over again.

⩔⩔⩔⩔⩔⩔⩔⩔

Lonely and dejected after spending days without company, Judy took off her coat, filled the kettle at her kitchen sink and looked out at the night. Wind was battering the garden, throwing about the branches in all directions. She was distraught. In her mind she played over and over again the expression on her sister's face. Maggie had relished rejecting her and had refused even to speak until Judy had left the parlour, but it was not this that worried her, it was that Maggie did not know that she was out of control, nor would she. As a girl either she or her mother or her father had been there to slow her down when her obsessions became all-absorbing. There was the incident in which she had insisted on working in the mines alongside her father and had to be dragged from there screaming and fighting, when at thirteen she had not yet developed breasts and tugged at her chest until the bruising was mistaken for serious illness. There were other examples: her obsession with carpet-beating, the months of introverted shyness during which she spoke to no one but Judy. She would damage herself. This, like all her other obsessions, would end badly.

She stirred honey into her tea and stood looking past the rivulets of rain twisting down the window, then she noticed a letter addressed to her beneath her front door. She had walked right over it. It was from Christopher and simply said, 'Good morning, I will miss you. Please be patient.' She wished he would hurry back. Barely a week had passed but she could hardly contain her need to see him again.

This time alone now made her worry about him too. Was she really ready for another man, a complete life change? Was she ready to share, night after night, her bed, her secrets and whatever life remained for her? She thought of him, lying in a strange bed, perhaps having the same thoughts as she. For a moment she went to reach for the crystal ball, to peer in and see him, but it was too invasive. Instead, she recalled walking into the restaurant, seeing his face and immediately she had the answers to all of her doubts. The decision was out of her hands. She could not wait for his return.

In her cup, even the leaves were offering to show him to her but she would wait. It would unfold as it was meant to, without warnings or the advantages of her abilities. Her mind wandered to Maggie, hurt that she would not find love and grow older happy and contented with someone. Poor Maggie, she had never been an easy puzzle to solve. Men had tried but backed away, shut out by her moods and her need for isolation. Once, in her twenties, there had been a promising period during which she was smitten with one of the ranger's men who herded the county's boars and deer but when he showed romantic interest, she closed down, avoided him, became introverted and barely left her room. Judy had tried to get to the bottom of that episode time and time again throughout the years but Maggie was never forthcoming with answers.

'And now,' she said aloud, 'there is a whole new Maggie to contend with. A furious, vengeful, jealous Maggie.' She shook her head. She was used to Maggie's foul temper and stubbornness but this was new. Now, furiously competitive and hell-bent on belittling her, it seemed that Maggie was stamping a new path that not even Judy recognised.

But all thoughts of Maggie were swept away as her mind returned to Christopher, to his eyes, at the wonder of having so much to talk about and how raw the feeling of needing to see him again felt. For a moment, unable to stop herself, she reached for the ball, gazing into it, willing him to appear, and in no time at all, there he was, sitting upright on a bed at a hotel, alone, reading, his mind wandering, perhaps to her, for there were long periods where he simply gazed into space lost in his thoughts and she became lost in hers, watching him.

Lady Dartmouth watched the count take off his shirt in his private rooms. He was nervous, an expression she had not seen on his face until now, and it beguiled her.

'It is not something that you will find easy to come to terms with,' he told her.

She nodded, unprepared for what she was about to see. It was beyond her imagination, ridiculous, and as she relaxed back into the armchair, she studied his face, his strong jaw as powerful as the muscles of his neck and shoulders. He was magnificent. Physically, no other man she had ever seen or imagined could compete with what stood now before her. He pushed down his dark grey flannel trousers and, in his undergarments, took her hand and kissed it. She looked into his eyes.

'I do not want you to be frightened. I do not want you to panic and think I am something I am not.'

She was silent and nodded, watching him turn.

At first all she saw was a great deal of excess skin, ugly and wrinkled and bunched up, then the whole mess lifted, bones tugged within it, lifting it above his shoulders, arms or an arm-like structure seemed to come to its surface, spreading out, stretching it wide, so wide that there was insufficient space in the room. She was beyond shock, covering her mouth, horrified. He turned, the wings brushing the ceilings and walls and stood for her to see. She shook her head. 'Are you a demon?'

He shook his head, embarrassed, with a look of child-like innocence, and held out a hand for reassurance, but she shook her head and moved away.

'You are a demon.'

The wings folded away and he stood again, beautiful and strong but his eyes were filled with sadness. It made her ashamed of her reaction and she stepped forward, feeling the maternal rise within her to caress his face. 'You poor, poor child. Were you born this way?'

He chose not to tell her the whole truth and nodded.

She was hesitant but allowed his arms to pull her to him and she nestled against his chest, struggling with her morality and her fear. Then he lifted her chin and placed his lips on hers.

Princess Sophia, through her telescope, watched Lady Dartmouth move to him inside his rooms and in due course, the curtains close them inside. There would be relations, right there and now, with total disregard of her and it stung. She felt her heart break. It was not so much that her rival was looking adoringly up into his eyes; he, the father of her child, that she found so intolerable, but that he had looked lovingly – at her weak and desperate for her acceptance.

'She is an old woman!' the princess screamed, hurrying through the building and across the heath.

She would give him one last chance. Perhaps she was mistaken, perhaps he felt only sympathy for the old maid. She strode into the grounds, pushing past the butler, into the house and climbed the stairs to his rooms. She found him dressing and surprised to see her.

The princess looked around, astounded to find the room empty.

'You will marry me,' she said. 'I forbid you to see Lady Dartmouth again.'

He watched her performance as she strutted about the room, stamping her feet, banging her hand petulantly against the desk. 'You will marry me!'

'I cannot marry you,' he said, taking her hand gently.

'Why? Are you married already?'

He shook his head. 'I do not love you.'

The horror of his words stopped her. She stared at him, comprehending the finality of it. She could think of nothing to say, then turning, she marched to the door and through it, the click of her heels echoing loudly behind her.

Downstairs, at the drawing room window, Lady Dartmouth watched her struggle with the gate and run distraught onto the heath.

𝕍 𝕍 𝕍 𝕍 𝕍 𝕍 𝕍 𝕍 𝕍

As the months of her pregnancy filled her and, with the guise of several invented illnesses, Sophia withdrew from royal obligations. She grew more and more isolated, talking only with her lady-in-waiting who brought home news and conversation from the village. Then in the eighth month of her pregnancy, a visitor arrived under the false pretext of delivering a letter.

The princess received her privately in her rooms and offered tea. The governess smiled.

'My dear,' she began, 'word has reached me, through the concern of a dear friend, that you are hiding a child.'

The princess stared at her.

'Your source being the count?'

She nodded. 'And because of your standing, you intend to deliver the child here, without a midwife or doctor.'

The princess looked away.

'Before my arrival here I studied medicine. I am old now but in my prime I delivered many, many children. If you wish, you can summon me privately when you are ready.'

Sophia was outraged at the discussion of such intimacies with a total stranger but the woman persisted. 'The birth of the count and countess was complicated.'

'He sent you?'

She shook her head. 'I came out of concern that you will attempt to give birth alone.'

'I will not be alone. My lady-in-waiting will be here with me.'

The governess nodded and stood. 'That is good. I just wanted to be sure that you will be in safe hands.'

The princess nodded and felt the need to ask rising up in her. She tried to suppress it, then blurted it out.

'And the count? Is he well?'

The governess shook her head. 'I despair of him. He has taken up the hobby of kites.'

'I see them on the heath often.'

'Surely it is the pastime of boys, not men.'

The princess topped up her cup.

'And Lady Dartmouth, is she still visiting?'

'Oh that woman!' the governess said angrily, resuming her seat.

Judy made her way across the heath. The night had brought with it several feet of snow. Whatever the weather, Blackheath seemed to encounter it first. Her face was red with cold and her fingertips already frozen but she did not care. In her hand was an unopened letter from Christopher and she was filled with excitement. She passed a group of children throwing snowballs at each other, and in light spirits, scooped up a handful and hurled a ball at the tallest. The group stopped, watching her, unsure what her game was, then seeing her scoop up another, they declared war and pelted her again and again until she was white. Laughing and catching her breath she suddenly sunk down into it high above her boots, where she tottered for several minutes, struggling to pull out her feet until she was flat on her back, bootless and shrieking and calling them to help. The boys pulled her up and rescued her boots, lowering her back down into them and freed, she hurried on and began the decent into Greenwich.

At the market, she ordered a lunch of steaming lamb and potato and hid herself away in a corner seat where she wouldn't be disturbed. Then with a deep excited breath, she tore open the letter.

'My dearest Judith,' it began. 'I cannot be without you any longer so I am beginning my journey home early in order to discover more about you from your drunken ramblings. You will be pleased to learn that my retelling of the story of the biting pig at your tenth birthday party has entertained several crowds along the way and in one instance caused an unfortunately large man a laughing fit of such magnitude it brought him worryingly close to death.

'I consider myself to have been rather lucky to be besotted with a woman of literary importance. Here in Southampton, where they have not heard of Blackheath, they gossip about your characters as if they knew them personally. There was a huge fuss over the chapter in which the maid saw the count's bare legs that went on for days but that was put swiftly to one side when new scenes proved to be so provocative that people seem only to be able to talk in alarmed whispers. When I notice people in cafés whispering, you are more often than not the cause of it. And herein lies my problem: unfortunately your writing has me troubled. Judith, I am not sure if I can compete with this count character whose prowess, handsomeness and charisma far outshines anything I have to offer. I'm afraid I find him rather intimidating.

'Might I also suggest at our next meeting that perhaps we begin consuming our wine earlier. The disappointingly early closing hours of the venue we chose, or rather I chose, cannot be allowed to get in the way again. In fact, I am, herewith, vetoing all venues in favour of somewhere a little more special.

'Please meet me at seven on Thursday evening at the gates of Greenwich Park. Should you arrive before me, simply mention your name to the guard and he will escort you to my hidden lair.

'Yours in great anticipation

'Christopher.'

She read it over and over. Her heart thumping noisily, then picking up her bag, she raced home to squeal with excitement where she would not be heard.

Deep into the night, a junior member of the Ranger's House sent the echo of knocking through the large house in the centre of the heath. The governess hurried, her case swinging as she huffed across the heath. She was inside, racing though the rooms, aware that now, barely any staff remained. The house was dark and cold with many rooms locked.

She rushed to the princess's chambers and found her brightly lit in the golden orange glow of the fire.

'It is time!' she breathed.

Water was brought, sheets were laid, knives and needles, thread and large metal spoons were lined up.

The lady-in-waiting watched anxiously while Princess Sophia stared at the spiralling flames in the fireplace, preparing herself for the pain.

More and more she became aware that there was the sound of another in the house and she turned her head, listening, tightening herself against the dull pain that pushed between her legs, attempting to delay it. There were shadows across the room that sank back quickly under her gaze but the pain at her hips, at her core, threw her mind into a scream.

The heavy thing desperate for release was moving about inside her, inching down, the pain of it intoxicating her with unbearable spasms. She hated it, despised that something was in control inside of her, dictating her pain by each movement. It edged down inside a fraction more and she felt a new part of her stretch. Her head fell back, her mouth wide, pushing out growls of hot angry breath. It pushed again. Her legs wanting to close, to hurt it, to crush it and stop it but hands pulled them wide, too wide, making the joints ache. And suddenly the movement was relentless; she screamed, feeling it claw and kick, feeling the smallness of her opening stretching beyond what was possible, feeling the snip of a blade and the warm rush of hot blood and the insanity of the force with which the child inside her would get what it wanted and then it was there, right there. She could feel it: huge, ripping her, turning and writhing as if to torture her further. It stopped, took a break, then again it was happening, it was being pulled, it was as if she were being emptied of everything. She clamped her legs closed to stop it, worried that more was being delivered than was necessary. And there, in the shadows, she saw him watching, careless now in his disguise.

'It is a boy,' the governess announced, and turned it over in her hands, running her fingers down its spine. Feeling the ribs, she felt a little something tucked there, not wings but odd growths of bone, barely noticeable. She nodded, then turning it over she gazed at the little thing opening its eyes. She was spellbound.

For several days, the princess was besotted with the baby but the teeth came quickly and her breasts could not take the savaging. The governess took him from her to a seat at the window, rocking the hungry cries from him in the sunny afternoon breeze. It was summer, the roses were flowering again. She would bring some seeds from the wild rose bushes of her mountain to the gardeners. Perhaps, she mused, they might name it after her. Then as the princess slept and the room was hers, she rolled up her sleeve and pricked her arm with a sewing needle, then pressed the little cuts against the child's mouth, letting him bite and drink.

Across the park beneath the tallest of the trees a family had gathered. They were laughing and laying out a large tartan blanket on which they assembled an impressive picnic with cakes and jams. The governess smiled and, turning from the window, was not witness to the body hurtling down from the tree above and crashing onto their spread.

Chapter 25

It was during the second week of Maggie's reign, standing before the never-ending queue, that Mrs Walters had a brilliant idea. She locked the door and abandoned the crowd, hurrying away unable to control her excitement. An hour later, she returned, bursting into the shop, red faced, out of breath and unable to control her breathing. She ushered Maggie into the kitchen.

'We can't go on like this,' she told her. 'You are becoming too big – it's just too much.'

Maggie agreed.

'There is simply not enough of you to go around. So,' she paused, 'I have hired,' she looked at her, ready to burst, 'the great hall!'

Maggie was stunned. 'That's . . . that's two hundred seats!' she said, shaking her head.

'My dear,' Netta replied, 'It is four hundred seats, and unless you have had your head buried in the sand these past days, you would realise that I could have those seats sold within the hour. You are the talk of London. The whole of Britain wants to hear a ghost talk aloud. I do not even need to waste money advertising it. Those seats will be sold by tomorrow evening and at the same price per ticket as we charge now. My dear, we are going to be beyond rich.'

She reached into her pocket and dangled the key in front of her. 'Let's go take a look.'

⨯⨯⨯⨯⨯⨯⨯⨯⨯

At the end of the day, with the shop closed behind them, Maggie and Netta hurried to the hall, slipping the big key into the lock and stepping into the deserted foyer. It was grand, there was no doubting that, and big. For the first time since it had entered her head, Netta wondered if she had made a mistake.

She watched Maggie push the door into the great seated hall and found the envelope the owner promised to leave her. Four hundred tickets, a solid block as heavy as a young hen. They did not mention Maggie or the event, they simply stated the date, the seat number and at the top, the words: 'The Great Hall, Blackheath. Admits one.' Netta sat down at the counter, daring again to imagine the riches that were coming her way. In one night alone, she would make more money than the séance parlour had taken since its opening. The big time, as she had always promised herself, would happen to her.

The hall itself was empty and dark. The skylights sent pillars of grey light reaching down into the aisles, great pillars swirling with dust. It smelled musty, like decaying old books or damp cupboards but Maggie enjoyed that smell, there was something mysterious and private about it. At first the hall appeared small to her and although she had never stood before an audience of more than ten, she felt disheartened, but as she climbed the stairs to the stage and looked out, the scene filled her with apprehension; it was vast.

She imagined the applause and walked to the middle of the platform, picturing people in the rows of red seats watching her eagerly, and she breathed in the dust and damp with a quickened heart. There was silence. Pulling a chair across from the wings, she placed it facing the auditorium and sat. It was rickety, and the squeaks jarred against the quiet around her. She closed her eyes, lifted her head and called out.

'Father?'

The word echoed around the huge space. She had called his name out into the darkness a hundred times, and each time it had been met with silence.

'Sometimes spirits move on quickly,' Mrs Walters had told her. 'Sometimes they find themselves at peace with their death and if they are not waiting for anyone still alive, they are swept onward.'

'But I need to speak with him!'

'Father!' she shouted again angrily at the room.

'And sometimes they hide. Sometimes they do not want to remember the life they left behind'

'I know you are there! I sense you. It's me, your Maggie, please talk to me. 'FATHER!'

In the foyer, Mrs Walters listened. Her own father had passed during her incarceration in Australia. They had not told her but he had found

244

her, woken her from a deep exhausted sleep. At first she thought that the owner of the house had come to the servant quarters to force himself on her but when she pulled herself up onto her elbows and looked around the room, there was a thin, wispish light, the outline of a spirit standing in the corner. The more she studied it, the more she began to recognise him, and when his face came into focus, her hand reached to her mouth and she cried. There were no words, no reaching out to each other, it was simply an acknowledgement, and then her father faded away. Every night for the following week she tried to contact him and sometimes, there at the peripheries, he came into view, but never strong enough, never close enough, not once acknowledging her. He simply walked, slowly and tiredly. He was not close to the earthly world, he was making the long walk in the afterlife, around and around the empty planes, waiting with the others for whatever happened next to unfold. She shook herself from her thoughts, called out to Maggie that she was leaving and to lock up after her and left.

Hours ticked by without Maggie noticing. The skies had darkened and the early hours of the next day had arrived. She remained alone, on the simple seat on the stage in the dark auditorium calling out for her father in complete darkness. Whereas before she had lacked the patience, now patience had become her weapon; with it, she could endure and achieve anything.

After a while, she felt along the back of the stage to a cupboard and took out the lantern she had noticed earlier. Her shaking fingers moved a lighted spill inside and pressed it against the wick. Now the room was opening up around her, a brown and orange glow bringing the front rows into focus, catching the glass on the doors at the end of the long wooden aisles, sending a ring of golden light up onto the ceiling.

'Father!' she demanded.

From the crystal ball she had pulled memories, but only her own, resurrecting the mind of the little girl, distraught and angry. It had been hard work and refreshed the rawness of her panic and loss but suddenly there he was, lying next to her, in the hotel room close to the docks, on the morning of his great journey. His arm was around her, pulling her close. She was nestled into his chest, never wanting to let him go, terrified of being without him for one whole day let alone two years. Then suddenly they were awake. There was panic. He was dressing, kissing everyone goodbye. Judy was there. She was trying to get his attention but he was preoccupied with Maggie, and Maggie was furious that her sister was even attempting to pull him away from her. She shoved her sister back and hugged him. Then Judy was pushing in again, taking her father's hand, pressing something into his palm, closing his fingers around it. And with a last look at his family, he had gone from the room.

The two girls and their mother were racing down unfamiliar streets. Maggie's heart was in her mouth, she was panicking, wanting to scream at the people in her way, wanting to cry. Then the ship appeared before them and then it was gone and Maggie turned to her sister, taking her aside roughly.

'What did you give to him? I saw you!'

But Judy shook her head stubbornly.

Maggie felt outraged and slapped her sister hard but Judy stared defiantly back and refused to cry, turning to her mother for protection. With a horrible mix of emotion they returned to London.

Years later Judy still relived this scene but not with the suspicion her sister did. Maggie had maintained that Judy had done something spiteful behind her back but Judy still refused to tell her what it was. It was her own private moment and although she had been too young to read or write, the simple kiss drawn onto the crumpled paper was meant to mean, 'I love you too. As much as Maggie.' But she had suspected, even at that young age, that as he read it, and as he waved to them, in fact, he cared for them both very little and when they returned to London, Judy tried to forget him entirely.

Maggie moved the lantern closer, took the ball from her pocket and stared into it, at the paper passed to him, at his expression when he curled his fingers around it and smiled at Judy. Maggie forced the fingers open in the ball, uncurled the paper, tried to see what was written on it but it was blurred and, as hard as she tried, it would not reveal itself. She lifted her head and shouted her father's name.

The first light of morning filled the hall with its depressing wintry grey. Maggie had gone past tired. Lately she had taken to sleeping in a chair, taking naps here and there and existing on what little energy they provided. She stood, took the chair back to the side of the stage and caught sight of herself in a mirror. Standing before it she studied what everyone would see when she stepped onto the stage before them. It wasn't even close to how she wanted to appear to them.

A carriage took her to a snowy Bond Street where she marched dismissively through boutique after boutique, until finding, along the Strand, a shop filled with strange and questionable fashions which appealed to her. She opened the door to face the questioning eyes of the shop owner and her assistants who studied her dress with an open disgust. Maggie watched her angrily, summoned her with a click of her fingers and stepped before the mirror to look at herself, amused at the shop owner's anger at being so rudely addressed. Maggie pulled off her bonnet, revealing madly scalped hair.

'I've had a bit of an incident,' she began, 'and I am here for you to transform me. I will be needing an entire new wardrobe. Nothing flowery.' She pulled a handful of bank notes from her purse and slammed them onto the counter.

The woman smiled and locked the door.

Maggie was undressed, fitted into new undergarments, corsets, underskirts. Her make-up was washed off, her face pampered and rubbed with lotions, repainted. She was shown a mirror, at which she shook her head impatiently. 'Entirely wrong,' she said, wiping away the mask. She took off the dress, walked boldly around the shop in a state of horrifying near-nakedness. 'This,' she said, pulling out a black dress, 'is a move in the right direction.'

'But that is mourning attire.'

'Perfect, I want to see them all, in all the styles they come in, and I'll need them modified into something more . . . extreme.' She stepped into the dress, holding her breath as the corsets were tightened. 'Make it tighter.' The shop girl tightened the dress with pins. 'No! Tighter! Much, much tighter.' She studied her face as the shopkeeper tried out the latest make-up on her. 'You're making me look younger. I don't want to look younger. Use lots. I don't want to recognise myself.'

⋙⋙⋙⋙

Judy hurried to her bedroom, unwrapping a large brown package. Inside was a new dress in the latest fashion in a bluebottle navy. It shimmered and shone in the waning daylight. She brushed it down and admired it, her bare feet hurrying across the creaky wooden floorboards to the cupboard in which she kept her new shoes. She took out a pair in matching navy and wiped the heels with the dresses she had worn for years and now used as rags.

Downstairs she poured the last saucepans of water into the tin bath, added some rosewater and hyacinth, and stepped in, relaxing against the roar of flames in the fireplace, imagining how it would be to see him again. She anticipated that she would be filled with nerves, not know what to say, but as she dried and hurried up the stairs, she wondered more if she would be able to say goodnight to him and walk away.

She dried herself, stepped into clean scented underwear, tightened her corset, slipped into the new dress and lifted her hair. Before she had any time to think, a glance at the clock set her into a panic. Time was against her and, snatching up her bag, she hurried across the heath. Across the way on Shooter's Hill Road, workmen were erecting a new invention, street lights, whose glow opened up the heath miraculously. The proprietress of the tea hut stood with them, shaking her head, pointing them closer to the hut and dutifully, they moved the great toppling structure to where she wanted it.

Judy grinned and crossed the road to the park. Waiting for her at the gates, a guard stood with dogs holding up a lantern to light her path. He wasn't a man of words; once her name was established, he escorted her silently through the darkness to the great observatory and with a nod, he opened the door and let her in, closing it again behind her.

She stood alone in the great domed room, dwarfed by its size and importance. To the left, a table was set up with wine and brandy and covered plates. Little candles danced at its centre and, feeling incredibly privileged, she clapped her hands with delight. Then turning to see the great telescopes, she wondered, if she looked hard enough, if she might after all, see the movement of the little metal men who lived on the moon. Then she saw him, tucked away in the shadows, observing her, and her face reddened. She felt self-conscious and shy, happy and nervous; lots of things all at once. He laughed, beaming at her and stepped out into the room, moving to her and lifting her chin to look into her eyes.

'I have been waiting for this moment for far too long.'

He kissed her and she pressed against him, opening her eyes, watching the concentration on his brow, the tightness of his closed eyelids, felt his fingers slip between hers and his free hand pull her closer. She closed her eyes, lost in the moment and so comfortable with his affection that she thought she might cry.

'I thought it might be awkward,' she said softly, her eyes not leaving his face, 'us meeting again after so long but it feels right. I have missed you very much.'

He smiled, kissing her gently on the lips.

'Ordinarily I am a straightforward man,' he said with a glint in his eye, 'but you have made me rather lost. I'm not sure what I am to do with all these feelings.'

Later, a little drunk, he guided her eye to the telescope, focussed on the moon, showing her the craters and seas.

'The sky makes some people feel all alone in the world,' he said. 'For me it has always made me feel rather adventurous.' He moved the telescope lower, pulling into focus a smaller red dot. 'The red planet, Mars,' he told her. She was in awe, pressing back into his chest, feeling his warm arms wrap around her, squeezing her close.

The candles burned down. More candles were lit. Dinner remained untouched; it did not matter, she was lost. There was so much to be said, so much to discover. She reached for his hand, her fingers exploring the bones of his fingers, the skin, his wrists, his arms, wanting to know everything. It felt as if she was writing her best scene and the writing was spilling from her, too fast, too eager.

He laughed, taken aback by her expression and kissed her again, beguiled and besotted, feeling as if by uncommon fluke, he had at last found the one. Then she noticed a worry in his eyes, sensed something urgent was on his mind and watched him as he took a moment to compose himself. He moved slightly away. 'We must talk,' he said soberly.

※※※※※※※※

The following morning, Judy stared at the book-shaped package in the carriage master's hands and gasped, covering her mouth with excited fingers. She tore open the paper, pulled out a green clothbound book on which the word BLACKHEATH was emblazoned in gold. She squealed, marvelling at it. There it was! In her hands, the finished object! She opened it, saw her words, her name, read the paragraph in which the housemaid was being eaten midair, flicked through to the count and Lady Dartmouth having liaisons. Again they had not changed the names. She prayed the real Lady Dartmouth would never read it. She opened it again, saw the chapter in which Van Dayne was led out before the firing squad and closed it again with a cry.

Pulling on her coat, she rushed into the village, stopping in surprise to see her book in the window of the bookshop with posters! She hurried inside, saw the shelf with its dozens of copies and cried out in surprise, alarming the seller.

'You must sign them!' he said, taking her arm and walking her to a table, 'Please, sit!'

She opened cover after cover, saw the bookseller out in the street, waving the book to passers-by, enticing them in, and they came in their droves.

After an hour had passed and only her very own copy remained, she hurried down into the village to show Netta but as the shop came into view, her footsteps slowed and she raised her hand to her mouth, a wave of nausea engulfing her. There stood an official carriage with the royal emblem, its door open. Guards securing the area around it stood before the shop. The guards stopped her, ordering her back, informing her that the area was being used for royal business. Judy's heart leapt. It was her book! The princess! She closed her eyes. There was the pregnancy, the secrets, the treason against the crown, the scandal! They had discovered it. The game was over.

Her heart hammered, then her sister was being walked from the shop. Judy panicked, pushing past the guards. 'It is my shop!' she shouted at them. 'It's not her you want. It's me!'

'How dare you!' Maggie spat. 'How dare you!'

Judy was confused.

'Queen Victoria has asked to see me, not you. How dare you try to steal my thunder.'

Judy stared, felt the relief.

'I thought it was about something else.'

'Of course you did!' She stepped onto the first rung of the carriage and turned, 'And as we discussed, it is not your shop, nor anything to do with you.'

She stepped into the royal carriage and closed the door.

When the carriage pulled away, Judy squeezed inside the shop, turning over the closed sign and pushed Netta through to the kitchen to make tea. When they were seated, she took out her book and placed it facing her on the table.

Netta was distracted, 'Queen Victoria!' she said, 'The queen knowing all about us. Can you imagine?'

Judy nodded. 'Look!' she pointed to her book.

'Oh, is this it?'

Judy nodded watching her flick through it half-heartedly.

'We should move, leave Blackheath, move to central London, get bigger premises, forget the crystal balls and the cards, concentrate on the dead, séances.' Netta put the book down. 'She talks to them all the time, you know. When she is at home she wanders about arguing with them. I've never known a woman to enjoy arguing so much. It's like she's finally found a profession she's good at. When she conjures them, she doesn't know who is coming. It could be a man, a woman. It really is a gift.'

Judy nodded, pushing her book to one side.

'And she is obsessed with your father – all day, every day, contact him, contact him.'

'He has asked me to marry him.'

Netta stopped and looked at her.

'He wants me to move with him to Kenya.'

'Kenya? Where is that? Up North?'

'Africa.'

'Oh good lord. And what did you say?'

'I said I would need to think about it.'

Mrs Walters reached out and took her hands. 'I'm sorry, dear. I've been so preoccupied with your sister. I have barely had time to catch up with you. Maggie is such hard work. She has gone totally insane. Have you seen her new look? She looks like Satan. People in the street are frightened of her. She terrifies children – you see them screaming and hiding behind their mother's dresses trying to drag them across the road away from her.'

Judy smiled, then finishing her tea, squeezed her hand.

'Will you tell her?' she asked, 'That I am considering taking his hand?'

'And moving? Should I tell her that too?'

Judy nodded uncertainly and stood up. Leaving the book on the table she left the parlour. Netta watched her fondly and sighed, then reaching across the table, picked up the book and flicked through it. Her eyes caught the part about the princess and the birth and with excited eyes and pursed lips she thumbed urgently past it to where the newspaper serialisation had ended, mumbling and tutting until she found her place, then raising her eyebrows even higher, she leaned back in her seat to devour it.

More and more the princess refused to feed her offspring; it became obvious that the child was malnourished but still the woman refused, making it clear that she did not care.

'It is not human,' she confided in the governess. 'I feel no affinity to it.'

The governess nodded and, wrapping the little pink thing in a blanket, the boy left the Ranger's House for good. Reappointing staff, the house was modernised, and the princess set her mind to the planning of the summer ball. She refused to think of the child again but now there was something else, something not healthy inside of her, she felt it and knew it and as the summer passed, it weakened her and drove her to her bed, where, with a quill and parchment, she set about the destruction of that which had destroyed her.

It was not long before the comfortable pillows and the soft cotton sheets were changed to a more formal arrangement and she was placed, dramatic and distraught, into her deathbed.

In the bleak hours before her passing, those in the room felt compelled for their own sanity to cover their ears against her screaming and close their eyes to avoid acknowledging her outstretched hands but the horror of the room drew back those with a morbid curiosity to witness her final moments.

Then it was upon her, engulfing her, her life's end, the terrifying and unimaginable reality of her final moments and she concentrated on the experience, wanting to see every minute truth of it. Her screaming stopped, her breathing became laboured and her arms failed, falling to her sides as her neck stiffened

And in that closing moment as she let go, she turned to look at those still watching and opened her hand revealing a parchment that led them to her journal.

Lady Dartmouth hurried across the heath, knocking urgently at the door of the house at the centre of the heath. When the door opened she burst in, taking the governess by the arm and forcing her away from the staff into a small side room.

When the door opened again, the governess summoned the whole staff.

'You must pack,' she commanded them. 'Everything.'

She hurried up the stairs calling the count and countess with urgency.

'You must leave now. Take the child, return for a while to Russia – to the house on the mountain, if it is still there. The child can grow safely there. I will organise the sale of the house and the passage of your things. We have been found out.'

'And if the house is no longer there?' the countess asked, trembling.

'I will find you in the usual way.'

She smiled and squeezed the countess's hand. 'Go!'

A knock at the front door and the sound of men's voices brought the house to a sudden halt. The governess closed her eyes and moved to the stairs to block their path but they were many and their force was such that she found herself easily pushed aside. In his rooms, the count was pulling off his jacket, opening the windows. He turned to see the men crowding the hall outside.

His sister closed the door on them, snatching at the lock, but the door was being heaved towards her, crushing her back against the wall, and suddenly she was pulled forward to their centre, held fast.

'Let my sister go. NOW!' the count ordered angrily.

The men shoved her forward two steps, then tugging ferociously at her dress, tore it from her.

She screamed, pushing them back, away from her, but there were too many hands on her, ripping and pulling.

The governess hurried down the stairs, pulling the kitchen maid into the pantry.

'You must take the child and keep it safe until I light candles in all of the windows. Then it will be safe to bring him back.'

The maid nodded, picked up a basket and hurried through the house.

Upstairs, the countess's screams were frantic. The guards were cutting away her underskirts, others moving forward to restrain the count.

Her eyes sparkled and she looked around at the men who had once longed to embrace her but who now treated her like an animal...

'Do not look at the eyes,' a strong voice commanded. 'The eyes will bewitch you.'

They cut, tore, hacked at the skirts, exposing her legs, pulling off her underwear until, naked, her secret exposed, she felt true panic for the first time in her fearless life. She lowered her head as they took hold of her wings and pulled them wide.

The men were shocked but most of all in this moment of horror, they were afraid.

The count pulled away and stood ripping off his shirt and pulling off his boots until disoriented by being in the presence of two naked people, the men looked at each other questioningly. In a moment his wings filled the room and he gazed into his sister's eyes. They knew what had to be done. At the doorway the governess recognised the look, the same look they had given each other as children when her presence meant unspoken plans had to be made. She knew what to do. Bursting into the room, she screamed, threw herself at the guards who held the countess, knocking them backwards. The countess lurched forward, stretching her wings to fullness and blocking out all light. Together they fought with everything, plunging the room into chaos.

The governess moved to the window, throwing it open wide, filling the room with blustering wind. The countess ran, her wings folding downwards, dragging heavily on the floor. Her feet racing across the carpet, out onto balcony and onto the low wall, she hurled herself out and was airborne. The count followed, pushing away the last hands and throwing himself out in a ball into the air.

The sound of bullets echoed around them. It seemed that the whole of London had been given free rein to bring them down. The count swooped downwards, trying to get within a safe distance of his sister who was panicking and unfocussed and far too low.

'You must get higher!' he shouted.

The countess was crying. She nodded, clawing her way higher into the afternoon heat, the sun beating down on wings that had been hidden from it since childhood. Something punched her, she felt herself being thrown forward. A burning heat seared through her shoulder. Her brother turned, swooping down, reaching for her hand, dragging her upwards, feeling the jolts of bullets batter her body. She began to falter, her wings slowing, one working harder than the other. His grip tightened on her wrist, tugging her upwards, feeling her body becoming limp and heavy and her wings begin to fold.

Up where the bullets could not reach, his ear pressed against her chest told him that there was little hope and he pulled her tight, swooping down over Greenwich Park to the river, confused and unsure of direction. He must head *for the coast, board a ship, or follow the path of one so that he might land at night and rest. Shocking gunfire started up again beneath them and he looked down to see men lining the river, climbing to the decks of ships, raising rifles, aiming at them. Further down the river, more boats were being boarded and telescopes flashed in their direction.*

A shot turned him inland, several more moved him closer to London. He spiralled upwards, trying to turn back to the coast but it was too dangerous and so he fled up the Thames, darting around the bullets, peering down at the increased numbers of police and guards and mobs. They were forcing him into a trap. Of course they wanted him inside London where police numbers were significantly higher. It had all been a trap, well planned, not spontaneous as it had been made to appear. Steps had been taken, strategies put in place.

He hung in the air, looking down at his sister whose head fell backward, devoid of life and screamed out, shaking his head, pulling her to him, crying into her face. He called her name, shook her, but there was nothing. Lifting her higher into the sky, he now had only one thought. They must not have her. They would not take her to their hospitals to take her apart. Her body would not be exposed to the eyes of the curious. He felt his shoulders ache. She was heavy in his arms, pulling him downwards, requiring double the effort from his wings. He must hide her, he realised, somewhere high-up, somewhere they could not reach her until he could reclaim her and take her out to sea.

Something whistled past, clipped his wing, stung. He turned, thrashing against the wind, opening his span to its fullest, scooping up and hurling away the air around him. He was fast now, moving above the men that lined the river, veering right, over the Tower of London, aware that their combined weight was pulling them closer to the ground.

Beneath, the crowds were screaming and running, pointing up at him. His eyes locked onto the dome of St Paul's Cathedral and he hurled himself through the blustering wind to its pinnacle, landing heavily, clawing himself against the curve to cling to safety. He breathed hard, studying his sister's cold, lifeless face. There was no heartbeat, no breath. She was slack, her life taken from her. He bit the back of his hand and screamed into it, his eyes terrified and enraged. He was out of breath and exhausted.

From this vantage point, he could see men gathering on the rooftops below, hear them climbing up inside the dome beneath him and saw a door to the roof slowly opening. He pulled her upwards, onto her sagging lifeless legs, and clasped her to his chest, lifting them both off the rooftop but falling outwards and down, swooping lower pulled by the weight to where the gunmen on the rooftops gathered. He swooped down lower, above the heads of people on the street, where the police dare not fire. People fell, pushed down by his speed and the force of his wings against the air around them and he rose again up over Southwark Cathedral, turning this way and that to avoid the flying bullets. He clung to the spire, trying to catch his breath. She was cold, heavy, gone, but he could not let them have her. Below in the churchyard, they were massing, taking aim, but he could not move, struggling to regain strength, grabbing at the moments to rest his wings which ached and bled.

Again he was airborne. He could not turn right or left, his only option was to be where they did not fire, an empty stretch that was designed to contain him and guide him up to Trafalgar Square. He swept upwards and raced over the Houses of Parliament, past the construction of the great clock that was nearly completed. Here the bullets were more dense and every ounce of his energy was spent escaping them.

They knew how to bring him down. They would keep him airborne, exhaust him until he fell from the sky. Again he soared away, turning and spinning and clutching her tight, shielding her as he soared up to Trafalgar Square where he clung to the rafters of St Martin-in-the-Fields. He was where they wanted him, where they had hoped to drive him. The rooftops were lined with men, the streets were cleared. He was exhausted, panting, his lungs gasping to be filled.

In a last bid for escape, he pulled his sister up, threw himself into the air and struggled through the bullets to the empty plinth on top of the great column.

He laid her down, weeping, and rested beside her, sobbing into her body. Across the square, men were pouring into the National Gallery, descending the steps into the basement vaults and hidden rooms, following the passage that extended beneath the square to the hall in which a spiral staircase rose up into the body of the tower. The count had little time to make his decision. He could save himself or die with her. Gazing into her lifeless eyes, he could not imagine going on alone, forever running. Then beneath his knees he felt a vibration, heard the unbolting of locks. He turned, ran a hand over her face, closing her eyes. Then, running across the platform, he hurled himself into the air and fought furiously upwards to where the air was thinnest. He was gone.

Netta slammed the book down and pressed her hand against her racing heart. She had not wanted the countess to die. Secretly, she had a desire to be just like her, but without the biting and flying.

❦❦❦❦❦❦

With little else to do other than return to the house and to the horrible secret that stagnated within it, Judy was at a loss. She wandered across the heath, saw the servants at the Ranger's House prepare the grounds for the Winter Ball, watched the great firework display being prepared with its gigantic bonfire and turned in the direction of the tea hut.

The proprietress was pinning up a notice. She shook her head at Judy and pointed to the new street lamps. 'I preferred the dark,' she said. 'It's not natural, all this light in the evening.'

Judy leaned in to look at the notice.

'I suppose your sister will be guest of honour? I'm surprised they don't let her chop his head off herself.'

The page announced the hanging of Blackheath's infamous murderer before the firework display.

'I'm expecting to make record takings,' she confided. 'Between your book and her evil, Blackheath has become a goldmine.' She pointed to the shelf inside her hut where six copies of Judy's book sat waiting to be sold. 'Arrived this morning, can't put it down. Oh! Here she comes, look!'

They turned to see Maggie, nose in the air, riding past in a royal coach.

'I don't know what she thinks she looks like!' the proprietress said, shaking her head.

Chapter 26

The doors to the great hall opened. Outside, the streets were crammed full of people wanting to witness the spectacle. Father Henry Legge and a large mob of churchgoers with placards were barring the path of worried ticket holders, chanting angrily, preaching the Bible at them, ordering them not to attend, warning them in no uncertain terms that the devil and all of hell lay inside the doors.

'By letting these women open up the forbidden, they are exposing you to evil. You are inviting Satan into your souls. You are dismissing God and allowing evil in. Evil will fester within you. You will go to hell.'

'Oh for goodness sake!' Netta snapped, pushing through them to force a gap through which people poured, covering their faces.

'We will drive you from this village,' the vicar shouted, shaking his lantern, foaming at the mouth with rage. 'You have brought disrepute to Blackheath. They are throwing women such as you into the asylums across the country. I will see to it that you will join them.'

Netta pulled people past him. 'Wherever there is excitement you'll find the clergy there craving attention,' she shouted at him. 'Always damning someone or other to get your voice heard.'

Carriages were pulling up into the chaos. People were pushing away others to get to the doors, thrilled to be the first to have secured the hottest tickets in town, the occasion heightened even more by the spectacle all around them and the sight of the priest screaming at them to turn away.

Inside the hall itself, the atmosphere was a heightened mix of nervousness and excitement. Most were frightened, some were dismissive but each and every ticket-holder was eager for the evening to begin and thrilled that they had a place. They waited with their nerves on a knife edge, looking around at the dark brown walls with their dancing oil lamps, at the candlelit stage, and at the others as privileged to share the evening with them. This would be an evening that would go down in history and they all felt it's importance.

Mrs Walters walked to the centre of the stage and looked out, waiting for the noise to subside. It fell to silence quickly. 'Ladies and gentlemen,' she announced. 'We ask for complete silence throughout this evening's sitting. We also ask you to remain in your seats until the curtains close at the end. Miss Margaret Cloak is now preparing.'

The atmosphere became exhilarating. Murmurs here and there were met with cries of 'Shhh!' until all was still and they waited expectantly, already frightened. The long black curtains opened, revealing nothing but a simple chair, a row of tall candles and a tall table on which stood a wooden box with a small closed door. Around the auditorium, staff extinguished the lamps, plunging the room into darkness. Four hundred people drew their breath.

When a moment had passed and eyesight had adjusted, Maggie appeared suddenly on the right of the stage. She was unrecognisable, towering tall, long-limbed and spindly, her face white, a blot of red exaggerating the centre of her lips, her eye sockets darkened with blue, her nails long and white, her bonnet a parody of fashion, tight and fussy and tall and barely touching her head. She walked to the first of the tall candles and squeezed the flame between her fingers, then, extinguishing one after the other until just a solitary lit flame remained, she looked out at the crowd, able to make out just the slightest glow on faces in the little light that remained. They followed her movements nervously. For a moment she simply stood staring, then she took the remaining candle back to her chair and, sitting, she extinguished it. The room was in total darkness.

Maggie listened to the silence, the shifting, the frightened sound of a woman, the cough of a man.

'I hear you!' she shouted.

The room fell as still as it would be when empty.

She let her mind clear, closing her eyes, unhurried. Then she saw a spark of light which drew her eyes to the right – the fifth, maybe sixth or seventh row back. She stood, wandering in the darkness towards that side of the stage, noticed another spark and another.

'The spirits are here,' she said aloud, 'I see three of them scattered amongst you, wanting to draw my eyes to them.' Her exaggerated footsteps echoed through the room and the box on the table was opened. From it poured a blue light as she took out a lit lamp. Then walking back to the right of the stage, she stared at a nervous couple, pointed to them, held her finger out for a long moment and said:

'There is death around you. You have just lost someone. Your mourning glows around you like a fog. Your mother, is it? An older woman. She is just there, at your left shoulder. I don't like it when they stand to the left. It's like they want to tell you bad news but they are doing it via some sort of code.' She peered out. 'I'm not here to crack codes, woman, come forward.' Her eyes followed something down the aisle and she climbed down the stairs to it. She stood in silence, looking into thin air, then climbed back up. 'She says you are to keep your son indoors for one month or there will be an accident and you will lose him too. He must not set one foot out of your house – no school, no friends. Once thirty days have passed he will be safe. Don't try to put it to the test. Not if you want to keep him.'

She looked out towards the back of the auditorium. 'Gentleman, big man, very big. Fat.'

A man raised his hand.

'No, bigger than you.'

A large man, almost taking up two seats raised his hand.

'Nine months to live,' she called. 'Heart. It can't cope.'

The hall was outraged.

'You can prevent it, but you won't. You know what you have to do.'

The man was furious, but Maggie had given up caring about what people wanted or didn't want to hear. She was being told things she didn't want to know and if she had to accept it, so could everyone else.

She turned to a woman in the front row. 'You borrowed that dress.' She addressed the man with her, 'If you had changed jobs like she told you to, she could have bought a new one. The bottom is going to fall out of your business within two months, move on now or you'll go down with it.' She turned and climbed back up onto the stage.

'Quite a few affairs going on in here, aren't there?' She had no idea if there were, but the idea of throwing it out there amused her.

She moved to the chair and sat. 'Who has a loved one that they would like to speak with?'

A dozen or so hands were raised and she surveyed them. She pointed to a woman in the front row with her hands firmly in her lap.

'Where are you from, dear?'

'Winchester.'

'Have we met?'

'No.'

'Then turn around and pick a hand.'

She chose an elderly man.

Maggie nodded, 'Come up. Bring him a chair, please.'

Netta hurried on with a chair and helped the man up the stairs to it.

Maggie was already in trance, her head hanging, a light snore coming from her. The man sat facing her, watching nervously. Maggie's snoring grew louder until a laugh from the audience roused her. She looked up, looked at the old man and smiled lovingly, tilting her head from one side to the other, and in a weak, loving northern voice she said, 'It really is you, isn't it?'

The man blinked incredulously.

'You came all the way here, all these years on, for me!'

He was self-conscious, but the voice was unmistakably hers.

'Grace?'

'Hello, lovey.'

'Oh good lord! Is it really you?'

Maggie smiled, her head lolling. 'You never stopped loving me, not for a moment. And now you are here! In London! Fancy that, London! And you came here to find me.'

He was shaking, a hand reaching out.

'I miss you, Grace. I miss you very badly.'

'I know you do, Ronald, but you must be patient. I am waiting for you.'

'When will I see you again? Will it be soon?'

'There is some time yet. But I am with you. You still fold your shirts like I taught you and you are still house-proud. You're a good man.'

He nodded. 'I just wish you could come home. I think about you every day.'

She smiled and, reaching out, caressed his face. 'I love you, Ronald. I will always love you. Since the moment we met, right up until now, we are for each other. I am waiting for you and if I am sleepy when you arrive, you have to remind me, but I will remember. As soon as I see you I will remember. Please be happy, please be strong. Do lots of things that you can tell me about when you come. I love you Ronny Ron Ron.'

Maggie fell limp in the chair, remaining motionless as Netta escorted the man back to his aisle. He was distraught, crying and refused to take his seat. Instead, he allowed himself to be walked out of the auditorium to the foyer, where she gave him a seat and made him some tea.

Suddenly from within the auditorium, there were cries, horrified objections. Maggie was seated, talking to the audience in a man's voice, shouting at them, warning them that they were not welcome.

'You are tampering with the dark arts. You are crossing all sorts of lines. These women are building a bridge between the devil and your own souls.' Suddenly Maggie jolted. She screamed hard, and as she did, a white bubble grew from her mouth.

The crowd let out a gasp of shock. The bubble grew larger, falling from her mouth to her lap, tugging with it long lengths of the doughy grey mess causing her to retch. It hung, pouring, feeding the ball. The crowds were horrified and fascinated. Then, what had first caused many to shake their heads in disbelief had become something else. It was now horribly apparent that it was not any contrived movement of Maggie Cloak's legs shifting and rolling the thing, something was rising inside the doughy mess, it was big and round, it filled the shape out to that of a rugby ball, then something poked from the centre, an inch or so in length and the curved shape began to alter, become a little more square, and dents appeared above and to the sides of the middle protrusion. Beneath it, a hole opened, around which lips formed. The crowd was aghast. Cheekbones became evident, then a brow, and next, a horrible and shocking surprise, the eyelids lifted and pale white eyes with darker pupils stared out at them. There were screams, people looked away while others leaned forward to see the thing clearer in the darkness. Netta hurried onto the stage with a lamp, slowing down to look at it, and as she passed, the pupils followed her. The crowd screamed with horror as the pupils looked back at them and the mouth, like that of a baby, dry and unused to movement, opened and closed. Inside it, a tongue moved. At the back of the auditorium, several distraught couples were leaving, hurrying away before anything further happened.

Maggie was sprawled back in her chair, breathing heavily, letting what had left her body pull itself slowly back inside. She retched several times as it withdrew into her but it was not as traumatic this second time. When it had been swallowed and she felt suitably recovered, she took a glass of wine and sipped it for several minutes, plunging the room into macabre silence.

Outside, in the street, those who had left were accosted by crowds, eager to know what was happening inside.

'It is evil!' they gasped. 'She is bringing back things from the dead and we could see them.'

The crowds were wide-eyed, exhilarated. Many raced to the doors to beg for the now vacant seats, offering to pay triple the ticket price, but Netta refused. 'The atmosphere is set. It cannot be altered by new arrivals.' Instead, the crowds turned, shoving Father Legge and his parishioners aside to follow the outraged couple into the pub where they found themselves the centre of attention.

'I have only tried this at home,' Maggie told her audience, rising up at last. 'But I am prepared to try it here for you tonight. It might not work. It is a new thing that the spirits taught me. It requires all of my concentration and energy. After it, I might not be awake for your appreciation so I bid you goodnight now, just in case.' She took another gulp of wine and nodded to someone off stage.

In the background two men brought in a large deep wardrobe. Maggie finished her wine and asked someone with rope-tying experience from the audience, a ship's captain or a policeman, to secure her to the chair. Two men hurried onto the stage and spent a few minutes binding her feet, then her hands to it.

'Now please carry me and put me on the chair inside the wardrobe and close the door. But please, do untie me when it is finished.'

The men nodded and with admirable agility for men of their advanced years, lifted her into the wardrobe and closed the door. They returned to their seats.

The audience was nervous. The evening had already exceeded their expectations and most were not sure they could take anymore horror or spectacle, but then there was a scuffle inside the wardrobe and the room fell silent. Two minutes passed, then three, and although the wait was uneventful, it held the room's full attention. Suddenly a confusion broke out, people became suddenly aware that they were cold, that their breath could be seen, that their noses were red. The temperature had fallen almost within minutes from warm and stuffy to frosty and cold. Then there was a muffled sound from within the wardrobe. Maggie could be heard mumbling, her voice growing louder. 'I can see you,' she said.

'I can see you too,' a much older woman's voice said.

'You must go out.'

'But I am frightened. Where am I?'

'You are with friends. Take a look.'

The handle on the wardrobe turned.

In the audience, several women recoiled, buried their faces in their hands, or into the shoulders of their husbands. Several more people made a bolt for the exit. The wardrobe door inched open. Suddenly, an eye came into view, looking out at them. There were cries of horror from the front rows as both men and women braced themselves to face whatever it was. The door inched open a little more and the outline of a figure appeared. The screams could be heard outside until even Netta had to hurry in to see what was going on. The wardrobe door was opening and a ghostly white hand curled around it, a little white foot stepped out onto the stage and peering around the door, a ghostly figure stepped into view. The crowd was groaning under the weight of nerves, making involuntary anguished noises that they were unaware of. More hurried from the auditorium to escape into the street, pushing past Mrs Walters who covered her mouth and asked 'How is this possible?'

On the stage, the figure, a female, old and decrepit, gaunt and barely strong enough to stand, put one unsure foot in front of the other. It was not a pleasant sight. Her body appeared in the throes of advanced decay. It was timid, frightened and unsure of where it was or what was going on. In the spotlight, shielding herself from their screams as if they were throwing things, she walked on painful feet to the front of the stage, where she stood and looked at them.

'It's the medium,' someone said, 'It's not real.'

The ghost turned its head to look at him and walked very slowly away to the side of the stairs to look up at those seated on the balcony. They stared down at it, shaking their heads in horror. Just then from the wardrobe there was a groan and a knock. Everyone's heart stopped as the door, creaking forward on its hinge, revealed Maggie, tied and unconscious, her feet shuffling, her arms jerking against the restraints, her head lifting and falling back, her mouth open. Watching her, the ghost moved slowly back to the wardrobe. It stepped inside, and with a last look out, pulled the door closed. The crowd was shocked into silence.

Mrs Walters hurried down the aisle, climbed the stairs noisily and rushing to the door, put her hand on the door handle, too nervous to open it. She crossed herself and swung the door open. Maggie was still asleep, tightly bound.

'Someone untie her!' she shouted, and the men who had tightened the knots lifted the chair out onto the stage and inspected them.

'She could not have left the chair,' one of them announced. 'My knots are too tight. They are as I left them.'

The room was reeling with loud horror as Mrs Walters hurried to the front of the stage.

'Ladies and gentlemen, Miss Cloak will need to sleep now. Thank you for attending. Goodnight.'

Chapter 27

Monday morning brought the papers, the front page of which Margaret Cloak dominated. There were outcries from priests, medical concern over the women who had fainted and had been carried out, reports on the apparent rise in church congregations in the area, with people feeling the need to throw themselves back into the arms of the Lord. A blow-by-blow account of the evening was laid out for the feasting eyes of excited readers, paragraphs littered with warnings and exclamation marks.

In the foyer of the hall, Mrs Walters had the owner cornered. With the following Friday's hanging bringing Maggie to the attention of an even larger public, demand for tickets for a second night was stronger than the first, and now she had a plan. She wanted to pay him less, a lot less, and that was not the end of her demands. She wanted stagehands, staff, and the hall for several more Saturday nights, starting with two and continuing until the demand dwindled. He had at first put up a protest, mistaking the little lady for being little more than a little lady but she quickly corrected him and walked away with everything she asked for.

She hurried through into the hall to tell Maggie who was in another of her new outfits and looked horrifyingly macabre. She was staring out at the auditorium, frozen, her face painted white, her eye sockets brilliant red, head tilted, listening. Netta stopped dead in her tracks.

'There is some sort of conspiracy,' Maggie shouted down at her from the stage.

Mrs Walters waited quietly.

'My father. There is something about my sister, something she knows that I don't.' She leaned forward, peering menacingly at Netta, focussing on her eyes. 'Do you also know something I do not?'

Netta waved her away. 'I don't know and I don't want to know.'

She turned and walked away leaving Maggie staring around her into the room.

'MOTHER!' she shouted, 'Why is it that you are now so slow in coming forward too?' Her eyes fell on the doorway, catching sight of her sister. She glared and hitched up her skirts, storming noisily down the steps and up the aisle. Judy was startled by her appearance and frightened by the force and speed with which she was being approached.

'GET OUT!' Maggie screeched. 'GET OUT!'

Judy turned quickly to escape but then stopped herself and turned to face her, which was not easy given the horrible, clownish violence that was bearing down on her.

'NO!' she shouted back. 'I want to talk to you. I demand to talk to you.'

'You demand!' Maggie laughed genuinely surprised.

Judy held firm. 'I will be in the Hare and Billet waiting for you. Wash that stuff off your face and meet me there. This is important. I am worried about you, Maggie.'

'I think perhaps you are more concerned about my success.'

Judy shook her head. 'You are changing.'

Maggie laughed. 'I am not changing, you silly girl. I am changed. And you changed me.'

꙰꙰꙰꙰꙰꙰

At the Hare and Billet, Judy drank some wine tucked away at the window, remembering the times spent there with Maggie, the Maggie that had once been so timid that she dared not venture into a restaurant, the Maggie with whom she had been poor and with whom she filled her glass from a bottle in Maggie's coat pocket beneath the table, while putting the world to rights. But now there was a new Maggie who ripped out her hair and retched and screamed out such obscene blasphemies that Judy questioned the safety of her soul.

She was lonely and unsure. The future was upon her and there was no one other than the man she wanted to marry to talk it over with. She had always had Maggie on her side. She considered Africa, the great Dark Continent where the skies were low and endless and there were giraffes and lions and hippopotamuses and elephants and where she would be involved in the building of a great lodge which visitors from all over the world would visit to see them.

What had once been a life of poverty had long gone. Opportunities had opened up all around her. The only path not available, it seemed, was the journey back to what had been before. Perhaps Maggie had been right, perhaps the simple life had been enough. Everything, it seemed, was now suddenly possible. 'The world is a great big adventure,' Christopher had told her as they cuddled beneath the great telescope looking out into space. 'We will be in Africa for four years. Perhaps we will fall in love with it and never return, but if you miss London so terribly, we will come back to settle.' And she believed him. As far as she could see, there was no choice, staying meant being alone, enduring Maggie's one-upmanship and hatred. She shook her head at the irony of it; by making them a success, she had driven them apart and herself out of Blackheath.

She was lost in her thoughts when the sight and spectacle of Maggie storming into the room and ordering port threw her into a state of panic. She considered slipping out unnoticed while there was time but as she rose her sister's voice pushed her back down into her seat.

'I hear you are to be married,' she said, with a tone of disgust.

Judy reddened, intimidated by her.

'I am considering it.'

'What is there to consider? You have nothing here – no job, no income. I suppose there is that silly little book. Although it must drive you to distraction that I am the star now. Even on your big day it is I who was summoned by the queen herself. Everyone wants me and you're just fading away unnoticed. How does that feel?'

'I am not in competition with you, Maggie. I am pleased for you.'

'Pleased for me!' she spat. 'You are green with envy.'

Judy sighed. 'Is this how it is to be now? We argue and compete until one of us wins and the other is pushed aside?'

'Different when the shoe is on the other foot, isn't it?'

'I didn't write my book to beat you in some way. I didn't force us to open the shop for me. I made us do it because we needed to change. We were starving. We had nothing.'

'And now we have it all – money, food, success, clothes. Are you happy?'

She looked away silently.

'You see, Judy, I think we were happy before. Before you opened all of this up.'

'Well if you were so happy with having nothing, being cold and hungry with nothing to look forward to, why don't you just go back to it?'

Maggie glared, the fury wild in her eyes. 'Because I can't! I am changed! I had to keep up with you or be left behind. You forced me to face things that I did not want to know the answers to. You moved the boundaries. Have you seen what I am capable of? What I can do? I can raise the dead, Judy. I can talk to demons. I see them around me all the time – spirits moving, watching, trying to grab my attention, asking me to contact people for them to pass on messages. They wake me in the night, they gather around my bed. They are there when I wash, when I am walking through the streets. It's become so blurred that sometimes I cannot tell which are spirits and which are people. Something inside me has broken and it won't repair because I broke it with such force.' She swallowed some port. 'And all because I watched you in your new clothes with your abilities and all the people fawning around you and I did not want to be the useless one. I wish I had accepted my place but now it is too late.'

Judy nodded to the seat opposite her. 'Please sit with me.'

Her sister shook her head with scorn.

'You have no idea, do you, Judy? Life is still simple for you. Everything has its place and now, now there is love again,' she knocked back her drink and stormed out of the door, the wind hurling her skirts up around her. Judy followed; pushing into the gale 'Wait!' she shouted, giving chase.

Maggie pushed on, steadying her bonnet that threatened to be torn from her head by the wind.

'I *will* talk to you!' Judy demanded.

'Talk to me about what? About love, about how I will now lose another one I love to Africa?'

'Maggie!'

'They are all around us now, Judy, look at them!' she pointed, sweeping her arm around in the wind that lifted her hair and skirts around her. 'They tell me things, and not just things they want me to tell the people they have left behind. They tell me what goes on there, in the afterlife, what is to come for me, what is beyond. And it's not nice, Judy. It is not the fluffy clouds and heavenly gardens I was once so happy to dismiss as religious nonsense and neither is it final, the end. God, I miss my old naiveté. What I would give to be that stupid again, to know nothing.'

Judy held on to her scarf as it tore away from her in the wind.

'There are towering walls in which spirits are contained, there are those great dark planes that Netta told us of. There are tests and trials and depressions. There is fear and panic and many, Judy, many turn to me asking how they can escape, if I can help them. And now I know all of this and soon I will know what is beyond the next barrier, beyond what these people I can talk to at the click of my fingers do not yet themselves know. It's coming, I feel it. I am starting to see into the next part of the afterlife. And I don't want to know but I have no choice. It is there, opening up to me. And do you know what, Judy? All of this knowledge I am accumulating,' she hammered her finger maniacally against her head. 'All of this pollution building up in here, I will never be able to get rid of because of you.' She stared at her, letting out a scream of frustration. 'I know where I am going and what it will be like when I die! It won't be all fresh and new for me when I die. I can't blind myself with optimism and walk towards it with the innocence of a lamb to the slaughter. I know how it unfolds. I am ruined. I am damned, and you ruined me.'

Judy was crying, reaching out, holding tightly onto the hand that tried to wrench itself away.

'Maggie, I am sorry. I am sorry!'

'And now I am to watch you fall in love with someone else, endure all your girlish excitement and your dreamy sighs and see the sparkle in your eyes when your thoughts turn to him!' She snatched her hand back. 'We were settled, you and I, growing old together. Life was calm. It suited us. I did not need to fear growing old alone. You promised me that we would grow old together. And now I am pushed away again, forgotten.'

'People cannot help falling in love, Maggie.'

'I forbid it. I forbid you to see that man again. If you say that I mean so much to you, then you will refuse his hand and we will grow old together, as you promised we would.'

'You are making me choose? Maggie –'

'I do not want to be left in that kitchen on my own as I get frail!' she screamed. 'You made a promise and I am keeping you to that promise.'

She watched her sister with disgust. 'But I see that you have no intention of putting me first.'

'Maggie, please. There are alternatives, compromises.'

Maggie snarled. 'Look at you! Look at the pathetic ways you try to get all that you can.'

'I cannot help that I fell in love.'

'Cannot help? Are you so terribly disabled that you are no longer in control of your own mind?'

'I love him!'

'You have known him five minutes. Go to Africa, Judy. I do not want you any more. You are no longer a sister to me. When you are gone, I am going to begin forgetting you. And if you enter my head, I will think of you as someone long gone, someone that I once liked, someone that died. And when enough time has passed you will be just like all the others that have died. The pain and the outrage and the mourning and the loss and the loneliness that you left me with will fade and you will be erased.'

Her sister stared at her.

'I am the biggest name in London, Judy. I have people fighting for seats, paying whatever I like, just to be in the room with me. I am filling grand halls. Night after night, there aren't enough seats and, it seems, not enough nights. Now go to your new man and forget me. It will make dealing with the guilt of abandoning me even less bothersome to you.'

※※※※※※※※

Christopher found her red-eyed and distraught in the little cottage. He lifted her chin and kissed her. 'Sisters have the most ferocious arguments but these things can always be repaired.'

'Not this time, not ever.'

He smiled. 'Give her time, she will miss you. She will miss you sooner than you think.'

Judy nodded tearfully.

'Sometimes you just need to keep chiselling away at people until they break and give in, then everything is fine again.'

She doubted his words and considered how optimism could sometimes conveniently shelve anything that needed putting aside. Perhaps she was more guilty of that than most.

'Let yourself off the hook for the evening and tomorrow you can wade back in.'

She smiled.

'Now, do you think you could bear to take my arm and escort me to the Ranger's House Winter Ball?'

He produced two tickets from his pocket. 'I did have to battle hard to get them. I know how much you wanted to go.'

She smiled.

⚡⚡⚡⚡⚡⚡⚡⚡⚡

Mrs Walters was looking at her reflection in the mirror in the back of the shop. How old she looked now. How strange that despite all the effort she had made to preserve her looks, all the preening and styling and plucking and moisturising, there could be no halting the decline of the body. She lifted the loose skin of her cheek and let it drop, frowning. In the background Maggie raged, damning her sister to hell, accusing her of ruining her life. Mrs Walters had stopped listening long ago. She pulled an alluring face at herself in the mirror and caught Maggie's angry stare.

'Are you listening to me?'

'No,' Mrs Walters replied, 'not to a bloody word of it.'

She turned to one side, posed, a glint of optimism sparkling in her eye. Perhaps, after all, things were not so bleak. Her eyes were still young and her lips, although not as full, still had the allure that could draw the eye. Maggie stared furiously at her as she picked up her bag and pushed past her.

'Do you know what, Maggie?' she asked. 'I have been waiting for this moment for decades, and it has finally - finally arrived.'

With that, she left the shop.

An hour later, Netta pushed open the door to the hair salon. She sat, smiling curtly at the hairdresser, who unpinned her bun and with surprised eyes, walked backwards across the room, unrolling her hair for some distance. The hairdresser was keen to suggest all the hairstyles of the moment, lifts and swirls and sausage curls, even those unsuitable for a woman of her years, but Netta shook her head. She had the style in mind; she had had the style in mind since the days she had rocked herself to sleep in the belly of the great ship. It would be tall, it would be as tall as it was when the judge shouted guilty and, just as before, by God, it would be impressive.

She held up a drawing. 'I want this. Exactly this.'

༾༾༾༾༾༾༾༾

Inside the gates of the Ranger's House, scandalous whispers were nodded in the direction of the dance floor where Christopher Benedict and Judy Cloak swirled to 'Sauteuse in D', hardly able to look away from each other. Perhaps they were a little too open with their affection for such an early hour. Indeed they appeared to have even shaken themselves free of the formalities of the dance and were instead adding very little to the overall choreography of the room. 'They are like logs swirling in otherwise peaceful waters,' commented Lady Dartmouth, biding her time before questioning Judy Cloak about how her name had come to be included in the novel that everyone she knew was reading. The shock of her own appearance in it had driven her from her bed in the early hours to brandy and palpitations and a rage that lasted a whole day. She sobbed over her ridiculed reputation. She had read, over and over again, the pages in which her breasts and body were discussed so liberally, then turned the page to find herself fornicating with a vampire. Feeling herself redden and noticing eyes wander her way, she left the room.

Judy was living her dream. She was at last at the ball in the Ranger's House. Every year she had watched it from afar and stared devotedly at the great ladies and lords arriving in all their finery and now, turning and gliding to such wonderful music, she was lost and happy and in the arms of a man that made her heart race and her mind confused and eager and . . . she pressed her head against his chest, raising the eyebrows of other women.

'Perhaps she imagines herself to be one of the liberated characters of her book!' one of the women giggled.

'Perhaps,' her companion wheezed, 'there will be an orgy!'

'Oh I do hope not! Not again!'

'No. I have enough mouths to feed as it is!'

They rolled back into their seats suppressing laughter,

'It is a good thing that the princess is not here!'

'Indeed!'

The women's eyes turned to Lady Dartmouth who swept across the dance floor and, with a bow, allowed her hand to be taken by Christopher Benedict. The women stamped their feet with hysteria.

'It is true! He is the count. Poor Lady Dartmouth, do you suppose she realises what is about to happen to her?'

The laughter rippled across the room so rapidly that those unable to control themselves found themselves with no option other than to rush from the room and down the stairs to the servants quarters where they gasped and let out loud shrieks into their hands.

When Judy and Christopher were together again, he noticed something in her eyes, tucked away behind the affection was a haunted look that concerned him. He ushered her outside, where they could be alone.

On the small side lawn, with her girlish dreams fulfilled, Judy looked towards the house that she had grown up in, at the window of her room where she and Maggie with their heads full of dreams had stared across the heath to the lawns on which characters, just like she and Christopher, stood and talked and sometimes shared a romantic kiss.

'There is something wrong,' he said, taking her hand. He suspected that his proposal was to be met with a gracious refusal, or at the very least an explanation of why she could not leave London and her writing. It was a magnificent time for her and he realised what he was asking her to give up for him.

She was silent and, before all was broken, she kissed him and pulled him tight.

'I cannot leave her,' she said. 'I cannot abandon her when she needs me the most.'

He was silent, her words changing everything that that he had hoped for.

'I love you but I cannot leave, and I cannot marry you.'

He nodded.

'I have no choice.' She felt her stomach turn.

He composed himself with a slight cough and turned to face her. 'All of my family's investments are tied up in a piece of land in Kenya. The building materials are in place, the staff are employed and the land is being cleared even now.'

She clung to him, hating the moment, angry at her sister and the responsibility of looking after her.

'Could you wait for me?' he asked.

She nodded.

'Perhaps you could visit. I will come to London and you will come to Kenya and the years will pass quickly and . . .'

But they both knew. And with everything already said, she watched him leave through the gate and disappear into the darkness without a backward look. The enormity of her mistake enveloped her as immediately and completely as the news of the death of a loved one eradicates all hope, and the empty days that lay before her beckoned her back into their unwelcoming arms.

At her feet a shadow stretched from the lighted doorway and she turned hesitantly to see who had been standing there watching and listening to them. Her eyes met the formidable stare of Lady Dartmouth descending the steps. In this brief moment, Judy felt something she had not experienced in some time, the smallness of her place in the great scheme of things. For so long she had bathed in the lights of attention and adoration that she had forgotten her previous position, that of a small, unimportant woman, a mere shopkeeper who had dreamed of an invite to the ball in which the rich and powerful moved and in which Lady Dartmouth was a permanent feature.

The woman smiled politely at her. 'I think we shall take a walk.'

Judy nodded, the horror of the situation and of her wrongdoing rising to stifle her throat.

Illuminated like a brilliant white swan in the small dark garden, Lady Dartmouth moved graciously out of earshot of the other guests. Judy followed anxiously, dreading the moment the woman would stop and turn to face her. Then the moment was on her.

'What you have done to my reputation is unforgivable.'

Judy stood silently, her cheeks reddening, her head bowed.

'You have described to the whole of society, my body, which, even if incorrect in your description, has brought their imaginations to imagine it. I am a reasonable woman, Miss Cloak. I understand the flight of fancy that accompanies the creative mind but you have brought shame to me and to my family. You have offered me up as a vulgar spectacle to the masses. You have placed me at the centre of gossip and ridicule.'

'I am sorry.'

'We are beyond the point where your apology has any value.'

'I insisted that the names were changed –'

'But they were not changed, Miss Cloak. And although people do not dare to broach the subject with me, I am aware of the ridicule that surrounds me.'

'I will make a retraction, I will stop further –'

'Miss Cloak, you and your sister have trespassed against Blackheath without any consideration for anyone other than yourselves. You have terrified and brought ungodly scandal to the people of this village. Indeed it appears to me that you have done your utmost to destroy it. The princess could not possibly attend this evening with the furore of infamy you have brought her and then of course, there is the betrayal of her trust when she specifically asked it of you. You could barely contain yourself to add her pregnancy to your work of gossip. Let us walk to the gate.'

Taking her arm for the sake of appearances, she escorted Judy past the doormen to the heath and stood looking out at it.

'This is where we part. Such a shame that you turned down the hand of Christopher Benedict, Miss Cloak, because you will find soon that the whole of Blackheath will turn against you and you will no longer find yourself tolerated here. Enjoy being the flavour of the moment, my dear, but I am still Lady Dartmouth and I think you will find that Blackheath is very much mine.'

The woman turned and walked past the flickering lights up into the rippling blue glow of the doorway and Judy's dream of attending the Ranger's House Ball was completed.

Chapter 28

The gallows stood empty, lit from below by flickering fires and torches. Around its fence, people were squeezing in to get closer to the spectacle, pressing up against the elbows of those who struggled to keep their positions. The excitement of a psychic leading to the capture of a murderer had brought publicity like London had not before witnessed for a public execution.

Below the gallows, inside the enclosure and seated, the murdered girls' families, defiant and angry, awaited justice. They wanted to see the fear in his eyes. Even those who had never shown any interest were now drawn in and bayed for blood. The outcry for justice in the locality had been too overwhelming for the authorities and crown not to bring the hanging to Blackheath. In some ways, the girls' parents were also aggrieved that he would not be subjected to life in the most horrifying of Victoria's mental institutions with its tongue clamps and iron maidens and unimaginable tortures but drawn in by the atmosphere and the anger of the crowds, they now felt the right decision had been made. Silently they waited, experiencing emotions closer to fear than satisfaction. The nauseating expectation of what was to come filled them with unease.

Maggie was tucked away in the shadows of a doorway opposite the great hall above which her name in tall letters flickered in the gaslight proclaiming her as *the woman who brings back the dead, live, tonight.* She watched the passing crowds stop to take it in, their conversations becoming excited. She would watch the execution from a distance, and joined the march to the heath dressed in her old clothes, hidden and plain and unimportant. She had not intended to watch, but a new curiosity had stirred within her.

The scene on the heath took her breath away. The crowd stretched as far as she could see and were noisy, excited and cold. In the distance, men guarded the towering bonfire and hurried about with large fireworks, seemingly oblivious to all else. Maggie mingled with the crowd unnoticed, rubbing her hands against the bitter chill of the evening. She waited with her head down, experiencing the chaos that she and her sister had brought to London.

Finally the police coaches appeared and the gallows were illuminated. A roar of excitement spread through the crowd. The parents of the girls glanced at each other for support, steeling their nerves to look into the face they were not sure they wanted to see.

Policemen surrounded the first coach bracing themselves for the crowd's anger and the condemned man's possible attempt to escape, not that it was likely – it would be a far easier death to swing by the neck than be torn apart by a furious mob. From the second coach, a figure stepped into view. He was burly and masked and walked without any hesitation to the gallows, where he climbed the steps and took his place, surveying the crowd silently. Father Henry Legge followed with a worried expression. Then the door of the condemned man's coach was opened to the hysterical screams of hatred and excitement and, carefully, the thin hooded figure stepped out and down onto the road.

He was pushed forward and made the first faltering step towards the gallows. The fingers that guided his shoulders dug into his muscle, deep and purposefully. Every few steps he felt himself shaken off course for the amusement of the crowd and finally, amidst a deafening roar, he was stopped. He stood, swooning a little, feeling his hot breath fill the hood. Words were spoken into his ear and, following instruction, he lifted his left foot, sought out the step and found it. He rose upwards again and again, stepping blindly before the noise. A firm grip stopped him and steadied him and he was turned in the direction of the deafening cries of hatred. A rough snatch tore the hood from his head, tearing out his hair with it. He winced, his eyes adjusting to the light, gazing out at the crowds and down to the parents.

The parents dared to look back, to meet his eyes. The anger they expected to feel was missing. He did not appear as they had imagined. They had pictured a ferocious character with wild eyes but he appeared meek, calm and surprisingly ordinary.

He was shaking. The feeling of calm resignation he had maintained was now overwhelmed by fear. He put a clumsy foot forward, twisting it against the frame of the trapdoor and let out a weak cry of pain that was lost beneath the crowds laughter at it. The noose was placed over his head and tightened at his neck. He closed his eyes, felt himself shaking, heard himself gasp and the deep fast thudding in his chest. Behind his back his fingers intertwined, clinging to each other, his fingertips digging into his knuckles. He heard the mutter of a prayer, footsteps move forward and he gasped a last breath as he plummeted down.

Hidden in the jeering crowd, Maggie closed her eyes and tried to find him, wanting to feel the spark of transition, his entry into death, but there was nothing. More often than not, the dead slept for the first few days, but she had to try. She shook her mind free, negotiated her way out of the crowd and walked to where the heath was darkest and most empty. He would surface soon enough and then she would have to face him again. Behind her the fireworks began popping in the sky, celebrating Guy Fawkes Night but they held little interest to her so she began walking and kept walking until she was in the dressing room of the great hall.

Locking the door, she urgently threw off her clothes and pulled on the black and purples, filling her sunken eye sockets with blues and blacks and painting the centre of her lips a small round bloody red, a disgusting parody of all that was attractive and fashionable, turning it ugly and confrontational and sour. She pulled the cocked bonnet, which barely fitted, onto her head, tilting it. She tightened her corset, too tight, pulled up her ribs to accommodate it, looked just once in the mirror and walked furiously onto the stage to rapturous applause.

'What can I give them,' she wondered, 'that they could not, will not, ever be able to forget? I will begin with it!' And clicking her fingers, two stagehands wheeled a coffin out before the horrified crowd. They tilted it upwards, facing them with it and, at the nod of her head, removed the lid, revealing a horribly withered dead man.

The audience was appalled.

'I see you, Arthur Crabtree,' Maggie shouted angrily at him. 'NOW WAKE UP!'

There were cries of alarm and already the sound of footsteps hurrying to the door.

'I said, 'WAKE UP!'

Something in the casket began to shift, shadows of hands lifted and grabbed at the sides of the coffin. The crowd grew uncomfortable.

Across the face of the corpse a darkness was spreading. Maggie sat, transfixed by the room's reaction. The corpse appeared to develop two faces, one that remained lifeless and one, barely visible, that moved and opened its eyes. Slowly, unsteadily, the shadowy shape pulled itself up, stepped from the box, confused and bent over in pain. The crowd were alarmed, the people in the front rows turning to each other, preparing themselves for immediate escape.

The auditorium was cold and silent. Only the thing on the stage moved, swinging its body to help each leg gain momentum as it struggled onward. When it had moved several feet away from the coffin, it strained to look down at the front row, the dark eyes tightening. Then, turning, it looked at Maggie, looked at the coffin, the body exposed there for everyone to see, and it moved back to it, peering in closely at the face, then turning again to the audience. Then it cried. It cried because it could not bear seeing its body lying there exposed for everyone and it cried at seeing that it was dead.

The crowd was appalled. Many left but the majority remained, frightened and sickened but unwilling to miss out on whatever the madwoman had in store for them next.

Outside the hall, an already exhausted and traumatised Father Legge stood with his protesters listening to outraged reports. When Mrs Walters appeared in the doorway, her giant hairdo concealed under scarves, she watched the protestors' expressions growing angrier. When they noticed her they resumed hammering on the glass, refusing to stop until either she or the hall owner came to speak. The hall owner pushed Netta forward.

'They will destroy my theatre!' he yelled at her.

Mrs Walters stepped outside, closing the door behind her.

'I will see it for myself or I will close it down,' Father Legge demanded.

Netta stood up against their fury defiantly.

'You will not!'

The rage of the crowd brought them lurching forward towards her until she found herself falling backwards. She scrambled to her feet, alarmed and facing the spittle-flecked lips of the priest and the fury of churchmen who ordinarily wouldn't say boo to a goose.

'You are bringing damnation to Blackheath. That is a matter that concerns everyone, not just your pocket!'

'Burn it down!' some wild woman roared. 'Drum them out.'

'Very well!' Netta shouted, trying to catch her breath. 'I will allow you two seats at tomorrow's performance.'

'NOW!' Father Legge boomed.

Mrs Walters held up her hands. 'The evening is coming to its end. Tomorrow, you have my word.'

Father Legge nodded. 'It will be your last night.'

Netta turned, unlocked the doors, let herself in and sat out of view. In a mirror, when she pulled away the scarves, her hairdo looked so odd she barely recognised herself but she reminded herself of its purpose and was jolted from her thoughts by the excited crowds that poured out from the auditorium. She let them out chattering excitedly into the midst of the priest and his group who chanted at them with contempt.

When the hall had emptied, she made her way backstage and sat down, for the first time feeling the danger in what they were doing. Maggie had become out of control. She was capable of things that she herself dared not imagine. She had not dared watch the remainder of the performance for fear of what Maggie would produce next. The stagehands were whispering, unaware of her as they manoeuvred the coffin out through the doors back to the funeral carriage, confiding in each other that they worried for their souls.

Perhaps, she considered, it was also her time to move on and leave all this madness to Maggie, who was so crazed and strange and beyond comprehension that it did not matter what abominations she summoned to frighten others. But the draw of the money was too strong and she knew she was trapped.

In the background, Maggie had returned to the stage. She stood there, staring out at the vast empty auditorium and lost again in her own personal madness.

'Father! Show yourself!'

✷✷✷✷✷✷✷✷✷

The steamy air of Greenwich Market was thick with curling white smoke, aromas of spices, roasting piglet and sickly-sweet boiling toffee, drawing the hungry to feast and the penniless to thoughts of crime. Judy was seated at a table from which a queue curled and excited women, dictating their names to her quill, questioned her about the count. Behind her, greasy chinned and sampling the leg of a rather large fowl, her publisher nodded with encouragement.

Her book, he had told her, was encouraging many women to learn how to read. She did not know how much truth there was in this but she could not deny its success.

'You shall soon have to begin writing your second,' he said, putting down the drumstick and lifting another stack of books to her table. 'Perhaps the story of the séance parlour? That would be a guaranteed hit.' But Judy had no intention of writing about that. That episode of her life she wanted to erase from memory, not celebrate.

As she shook her head her eye was drawn to the far end of the market, to the pillars at the entrance. There he stood, Christopher Benedict, watching her, lost in his thoughts. Then, catching her eye, he turned away, moving through the market towards an older gentleman, his father perhaps. Judy could not concentrate and her eyes followed him. She put down her quill and watched as he walked out of sight. She felt as if she had made the biggest mistake of her life.

For several hours her eyes scanned the crowds around her, hoping for another glimpse of him or for him to come to her and demand her back, leaving her no choice other than to agree, but he was gone and she returned home to the quiet little house to sit awaiting the hour for bed.

The big house at the centre of the heath sat emptied and silent, its staff dismissed, the keys on the tiled floor inside the front door. The last carriage had left several hours ago. When the police arrived, only the auctioneer remained, loading what had not been sold onto his cart. He had no forwarding address, the governess had been paid handsomely before the sale and had left. South, she had told him, though he doubted she had spoken the truth. At the back door a group of boys with wicker baskets had gathered and been shooed away. Miles away, in the dull grey mist of Liverpool dock, the governess carried the young child up the gangplank onto the ship that for months would sail up into the icy seas of the Barents and through the Karskoye and the Laptevykh towards the towering cliffs where she would raise it as she had raised the count and countess. Her cabin was spartan: just a bed, chair and table would see her though. Beneath her in the hold, the house sat packed into crates. She had survived worse.

When the ship had made a seven-hour distance from Britain and night was over them, she locked the sleeping child inside the cabin and hurried out onto the deck with her lamp, peering into the darkness. The count would scan passenger lists heading north, watch the seas for her signal, race along the coast to find her, and, when he did find her, she would smuggle him into her cabin for as much of the journey as was possible.

Somewhere below, men laughed and shouted, the sea smashed and rolled and she waited, shielding herself from the spray and the winds but that night and every night along the way, he did not appear.

Judy climbed the stairs. In bed she imagined the room to be on a large ocean-going ship sailing across deep black water into to the unknown – to Africa, that strange-shaped continent with its great horn and mysterious eye in which its untamed animals and wild jungles and rivers full of snapping horrors awaited her. Where everyone she would see and speak with would be black, and white faces were nowhere to be seen. A place where the gossip would be of a whole new calibre. 'Imagine!' she thought to herself sadly, 'me in Africa.' When she closed her eyes, she could almost feel the ship rock.

She imagined saying goodbye to Blackheath, to everyone and everything that she had always known, to the shops and the neighbours and the kite fliers, to the familiar faces and smells and the fierce winds that battered it. Years would pass and Blackheath would be renewed again, she realised, over and over it would be reinvented. It would forget all about the Cloaks and Mrs Walters and the princesses and ladies. All the shopkeepers and miners and windmills would fade into the past along with the scandals and celebrations, and newness would replace everything. The séance parlour and her book would be forgotten, just as they themselves were forgetting about Blackheath's highwaymen and its slave-trading roots. There would be fairs and circuses and generations replacing generations until she and her sister and what their lives amounted to was long buried and forgotten.

But there would be no ship and no Africa and no goodbyes and there would be no Christopher.

ᗡᗡᗡᗡᗡᗡᗡ

Beyond the rattling of her bedroom window and past the wind that tore up Camden Row spilling out onto the little green before joining the great gusts of the heath, Father Legge, his overcoat flapping behind him, surveyed the spot on which the great church was being built. It would be spectacular, a giant structure towering against the smallness of the shops and houses. When he closed his eyes he could see himself pressing the body of Christ onto the tongues of those who knelt before him, he could hear the congregation singing his favourite hymns, he could feel the thrill of the very first service.

He turned and strode across the great dark expanse, his mind preoccupied with the task at hand, that of reasoning with Maggie Cloak, of making her see sense. But as he opened her gate and knocked on the door, he felt his determination weaken and prepared himself again for the ferociousness with which she would contradict his every point. The house was in darkness and there was no reply. She had not yet arrived home which, for a moment, filled him with relief. But resolved to deal with the matter without any further delay, he stood vigilant at the gate of her house determined to wait, despite the weather, until the devilish woman at last returned.

From this corner of the heath, to which he rarely ventured at night, he watched the growing traffic of Shooter's Hill Road beneath the new gas lamps and considered the shifting trends in society. This new age worried him and did not work in religion's favour. There was a nonconformity to it, a looseness of thought which brought with it wild imagination and recklessness. Those who had previously avoided worship had feared divine and societal reproach but now appeared able to do so with little more than a tinge of guilt; and even those moments of guilt appeared to be easily swept aside.

Maggie and Judy Cloak with their own separate horrors appeared to be aiding this migration, at least in his own parish and especially amongst women, at a tremendous speed. And soon, he imagined, there would be others in their wake, those too nervous to break out on their own who now had a path to follow.

He had been standing for about forty minutes when the rustle of skirts drew his attention and he found, rushing towards him, Lady Dartmouth. He nodded to her and returned her smile.

'Lady Dartmouth.'

'Father Legge. Good. I had intended to visit you tomorrow but

284

perhaps it is best that we speak now if you have some time.'

'Certainly, what can I help you with?'

'Would you care to join me for tea, out of this frightful weather?'

The man shook his head. 'I am here to see Margaret Cloak and I do not mean to allow her to slip past me.'

The woman nodded without expression. 'It is the Cloak sisters I mean to talk to you about.'

'They are quite the pair.'

'Aren't they? Well if we must talk here, so be it. Father Legge I have . . .' she paused, choosing her words carefully. 'I have made enquiries into the laws regarding such monstrous abilities apparently now held by Margaret Cloak. It appears they are nothing new. Indeed, the Spanish, particularly within the Catholic faith, have quite the history of these women and seem fully equipped to dispose of them with minimal effort.'

The priest watched her apprehensively.

'Indeed I am surprised – with all due respect, father – that you have let this blasphemous carnival progress so far within your own parish. You are, are you not, soon to be the leading voice of Blackheath's new church just yards from the doorstep of such profanity? Am I to take it then that you are a more lenient man, who has perhaps not yet grasped or is little suited to the enormity of the trust that will be placed in you by the good people of Blackheath?'

'On the contrary, my good woman,' he replied sourly and a little too eager to put her in her place. 'I am here to do precisely that.'

She smiled.

'That is reassuring. I would regret, in my various meetings with dignitaries, not to be able to support you, especially with so many other priests eagerly watching the progress of the church here. We are, after all, a rather rich borough with much to offer. Quite the prize, or so it seems.' She looked across the newly flattened heath to the Ranger's House. 'The princess will not be returning to Blackheath. It seems that the other Cloak sister succeeded magnificently in driving her away. I can only wonder what it is that exalts these two vulgar women so to the public. Perhaps they represent a world without religion. Perhaps it is the chaos they bring that leaves the pews empty. Perhaps it is in Blackheath itself that religious abstinence shall begin.'

She held her arms and shivered. 'Well Father, it is too cold for me now, I shall leave you to speak with your friend.'

At the centre of the heath, hidden in the darkness, Maggie Cloak pulled her hood over her head and watched. Father Legge was pacing, rubbing his hands and stamping his feet. She sighed angrily to herself. He was the last person she wanted to see, having drunk her way through a bottle of port prized for its potency. But with his mind made up, it was pointless hoping he would go away any time soon. And then watching him disappear into her garden and return dragging a large plant pot under which she hid her spare key, which he overturned and sat on, she cursed, hitched up her skirts and marched furiously towards him.

'Margaret,' he said, standing as she approached.

Maggie eyed him irritably, lifted the pot and placed it angrily back in its position with a loud tut.

'We need to talk.'

'I am tired. It has been a very tiring day.'

'Nevertheless, we must talk, now.'

She turned the key in the lock, huffing her disapproval and let herself in.

'Margaret?'

'Well, come in then! I didn't leave the door open for the benefit of my health.'

He followed unsurely, watching her light the lamps and set flame to the tinder beneath the kettle.

'I assume you'll be wanting tea?'

'That would be very kind.'

'Yes, I know,' she mumbled, wiping two cups and setting them down. 'Well, get on with it.'

'Margaret, you know why I am here.'

'Of course I do. You want things your way, I want things my way. You want to be the all-important man of the borough again and I'm ruining your fun.'

'Margaret! The way you speak of late . . .'

'It's the modern age, Henry, Why use two dozen words when you can get straight to the point?'

'It cannot go on. There are complaints, people are frightened. The tide is beginning to turn against you.'

'I thought you liked them frightened. Isn't that how you round them up and force them to give you the money they can't afford? Pay up or I'll send the devil round.'

'Margaret!'

'Oh come on, Henry, people say something you don't like and it's blasphemy, they say something you do like and usually it's because they are obligated to. You live in an ivory tower. You're detached from reality. It's your job to terrify people with your threats of hell and burning souls and paying your way into the big pearly gates. And what do people take from it? An hour of singing and feeling worthy followed by a week of stealing because they can't afford to live. If the Church wanted to follow in the footsteps of Christ they'd be handing out money, not taking it from the poor so you can afford your housemaid and the men at the top can live like kings. '

'And you are providing your sittings and your performances free of charge?'

'No, but at least I'm honest and tell them that every penny of what they are paying is for me.'

He drew his breath.

'Margaret, I need you to consider me now as a friend, someone who has known you since we were children. Someone who is looking to protect you. I realise that is a tall order.'

'I don't consider it any sort of order at all.'

'People want you stopped.'

She poured the tea into the cups, deliberately giving him significantly less. 'People wanted to believe that the world was flat, Henry. We didn't give in to them and I'm not giving in now.'

'There is a movement amongst the ruling classes to have you stopped. And they will use the Church to accomplish it without a second thought. Margaret, what have you left to prove? You have shown everyone spectacles that will never be forgotten. You have accomplished what you set out to do.'

She set the cups down and leaned back into the armchair opposite him.

'I have not even started. What people have seen so far is just the tip of the iceberg. Henry, I am discovering things that shock even me. All the messages and voices, that is like child's play now.'

'And what will you do, when you pull these demons out for all to see and find yourself being arrested and thrown into the cells of Bedlam? Because that is where they will put you, Margaret. They will condemn you either as a fraud or as a woman in the turmoil of mental illness.' He set down his cup and leaned forward in the armchair, fixing her with his eyes. 'Margaret, you are in very real danger. You must stop before you are stopped.'

She studied his expression and, lifting the cup to her lips, replied. 'No.'

Chapter 29

At four, Mrs Walters opened her wardrobe and took out the canary yellow shoes and the canary yellow dress that had seen her through the horrors of her engagement to Norman Clegg, through her trial and the nightmare of gangplanks and prison ships. Brushing out the wrinkles she turned to confront herself in the mirror. She was older, less busty and less attractive but it didn't matter, because her hair was impressive and massive, just as it had been, exactly as it had been. She threw her keys into her handbag and headed to Covent Garden.

He had left his house at five promptly every single Sunday without fail. First he dined with friends at Rules restaurant on Maiden Lane, then in raised spirits they would make their way to the Lamb and Flag. At ten, he wandered back drunk and content to his wife. There were no surprises; life was in order for Norman Clegg. It was interesting for Netta to see what her life might have been like had she married him.

She arrived at the end of his street at a quarter to five, with plenty of time to spare. Her reflection in one of the windows startled her. It put her in mind of some great bird or circus performer, still she was fashionably ahead of the time even though decades had passed. The startled looks and giggles that had accompanied her there this evening left her in little doubt that since the days of her wild youth, fashion had taken a conservative step backwards.

To her surprise, she felt nothing. She had imagined that this over-rehearsed moment would be filled with rage or fear or such seething need for revenge that she would not be clear-headed at all. She clenched something in her pocket, running her finger along its blade.

At two minutes to five, as expected, he stepped out of his house, turned left and walked up the street. Mrs Walters stepped into view standing at some distance, directly in his path so that as he walked towards her, his eyes studying her, he would be in no doubt as to who she was.

At first he looked at her without interest, then he looked again, and as he got closer, his walk slowed and he came to a stop, his face filled with shock.

'Hello, Norman,' she said.

He was speechless.

'It's been a long time.'

His blood ran cold.

'You don't look very happy to see me.'

'Netta? Netta Walters!'

She smiled.

'But you were hanged! You . . .'

'That would suit you wouldn't it? Everything gone, no evidence.'

He squared up to her angrily but his face showed nothing but fear. 'You leave me alone. You walk away from here and you do not come back or I will call the police.'

'Oh I've no doubt that it would suit you to let it all be a thing of the past but that's not going to happen.'

'What are you doing here, Netta? What do you want?'

'I want an explanation and I want an apology.'

He stared at her.

'You didn't hang around, did you? Married, a son, nice house and money, all settled.'

'Did you think I was going to wait?' He watched her, enraged. Behind them a door slammed and someone laughed. He looked around, took her arm roughly and pushed her into an alley out of view.

She stared angrily at him.

'What games are you playing?' he shouted.

She walked further down the alley, leading him away from escape. Her mind twisting with anger, her knuckles white, her fingers clenching the handle of the knife in her pocket. They were out of view, no one would see. But first there were things to say.

'You killed that girl and you stood there in that court room, and you watched, you and your parents, you watched them frame me, you allowed it. You let me take the blame. You let them take me away to be hanged.'

He stared at her. 'Have you gone mad?'

Her face twisted with fury. 'Don't pretend that all these years have

290

taken away the memory of what you did! Time has not taken away a single moment of it for me. I have relived it and relived it and I have waited for this moment to hear you admit it to me. So I can let it pass too.'

He grabbed her arms and shook her, looking at her hair and her dress. 'What is this? The same hair, the same dress? Is this supposed to scare me? Because it's working. It does scare me, Netta. It does frighten me that a woman capable of such a violent, jealous, horrible murder is back on the loose. They should have hanged you. They should have given her parents what they wanted. What we all wanted.'

She screamed and tried to break free.

'You killed her, Norman!'

'No, Netta! You killed her! You were so jealous when she told me she was carrying my child, you could barely breathe.'

'You were seeing her behind my back!'

'I stopped being with her because I met you. Because I fell in love with you!'

'You got her pregnant!'

'Before I met you!'

She stared at him.

'I don't know if you are crazy or if you are deluded or if you have lost your memory but you killed Alice, Netta. You killed that woman and you killed my child inside her. And now you come here accusing me?'

He paced the alley, his fists clenched. 'I loved you. I loved you with everything I had in here,' he thumped his chest. 'And I have been over and over it inside my head, all these years, thinking of how it might have been, with you, even though I had a daughter with Alice. I even dreamed about you liking my child, about how despite everything, we lived with the situation and made the best of it. I even dreamed you came back and I forgave you. That's how much you meant to me!

'I was even prepared, before you did that, for us to just run away, the two of us, abandon Alice and the child, pack up everything and move away, to the seaside, open a café, or a hotel, and never see my child again. I also imagined that I did finish things with you and that I went back to Alice, that despite the little we had in common, we made it work and we raised our girl. But you took that away from me too. I think about these things, Netta, every year of my life that you ruined. I wake up thinking about the horrible state of that murdered woman and my murdered child and what might have been, over and over and over.'

He stared at the ground, paced and turned angrily at her. 'So what are you doing here, Netta? What *are* you doing here? Is this your way of asking for forgiveness, putting the blame on me? I did not murder Alice or my child Netta. You murdered them and you made one hell of a mess of them.'

Netta stared, blinking. She looked at him, at the garden gates, at the stretch of alleyway and she turned walking quickly towards the street, listening to the sound of him hurrying after her.

'I don't want to see you ever again. Do you understand? And I do not want you anywhere near my wife or my son or my parents. If I so much as see you in the same street, I will kill you, Netta. I will stop you before it's too late. I will stop you from doing it again.'

She was not listening. Her mind was numb, confused; memories were surfacing, the wood, the girl, the argument, the screaming. She walked as quickly as she could, her canary yellow heels clicking against the pavement.

Hours later, she found herself standing on the stage. The crowd were watching her, confused by her silence. She was aware of them, aware that she was there for a purpose but her mouth would not move. Her eyes came to rest on Father Legge who watched her nervousness with relish, assuming it was his presence that had plainly disturbed the woman.

She mumbled through her words, explaining to a rowdy audience that there would be a delay, that Maggie had spent another afternoon with royalty at the palace, that she had now arrived and was preparing. The audience was impressed enough to bide their time without complaint, so with a nod, she left the stage. Looking directly ahead she moved past the audience to the front of the building and sat out of view, not daring to think. But the thoughts came, violent and sickening and filling her with fear.

She didn't notice Judy who stood watching her with concern and when she did, unable to stop herself, she stood and hurried to her, bursting into tears. Startled, Judy hugged her close.

Father Legge's presence cast an unwelcome gloom on the audience who feared appearing eager in front of him. Maggie was aware of this as she peered out at them, tucked away at the side of the stage, her eye against a hole in the curtain. She would not tone it down, she would muster something more shocking than they had ever imagined. She laughed to herself, imagining Henry Legge's expression when she plucked his parents from beyond the grave and paraded them around in front of the whole of Blackheath. The curtain lifted and she walked out to deafening applause.

Netta was shaking, her tears soaking Judy's shoulder.

'Many years ago I did something that was so very awful,' she sobbed, hardly able to draw breath. 'But I can never tell you what it is.'

Judy stroked her giant hair and pulled her close.

'And there is another lie. There was never a Mr Walters.'

'Then you are a Miss and not a Mrs?'

Netta nodded tearfully, allowing Judy's warm concerned eyes to soothe her.

'The past is gone. You must let whatever it is fade away with it.'

Mrs Walters shuddered against her.

'I must leave London. I am sorry to let you down.'

Judy looked at her.

'Is it so bad?'

Mrs Walters nodded.

Behind them the doors to the great hall crashed open and a couple hurried out to the street. Two elderly women followed. Letting go of each other, Judy and Netta moved to the door to peer in and saw, standing centre stage, in the dimmest of light, the figure of a stern, uniformed little girl, her mouth open wide, spewing out a deafening, non-wavering note. In the audience, people covered their ears, watching the abomination as it stared down at Father Legge who endured it with indifference and shook his head in disgust. The girl's head rose and looked out at the room, then ending her scream, she swallowed and announced in a deafening wail, 'Cholera is coming. It will claim you.'

Behind her, in the wardrobe, Maggie Cloak hung forward, swaying, bound to her chair, her mouth foaming. The girl moved awkwardly on pointed toes, taking one last look at the room with angry suspicious eyes and closed the door on them. The audience sighed with relief. When the door opened again, Maggie was retching, thick white mess pouring from her open mouth. The stage hands picked up the chair and carried it to the centre of the stage, setting it down and illuminating her with lamps. Her nostrils flared and dripped with the white foam that formed long prongs and reached out, testing the coldness of the air. From her eyes too, tears of sticky white string appeared to force themselves out. Maggie hung forward, the large white mess moulding itself on her lap, suspended like a puppet.

Father Legge closed his eyes. He had not imagined anything so foul as the devilish circus he was witnessing. For the first time in many years he felt the overwhelming need to summon, under his breath, the protection of God. Around him, disbelieving screams and gasps were accompanied by the leaning forward of heads studying the spectacle with incredulous fascination as the puppet in Maggie's lap stirred and fought while Maggie herself groaned and choked and swayed like nothing he had witnessed before.

Father Legge was as frightened as he was outraged. He found himself suddenly standing, shouting out his objection. But the show continued around him, his words drowned out by screams as the thing took form, sprouting arms and little kicking legs, its head turning and its mouth opening, and the sound of a baby echoed around them. The crowd was troubled, watching it lose shape and rise back up into her. Father Legge, wild with outrage, climbed angrily onto the stage. He reached out, grabbing the form, pulling it, and then, with a look of horror, he let it go, stared at his hands. His shock reaffirmed in the eyes of those who watched him, what they had wanted to believe, that the phenomenon was real. But with sleight of hand, he dropped something from his pocket next to Maggie and stepped back. Then as if having just noticed it, he stooped and picked it up, turning to the crowd to show them a mixture of flour and string and paper that gave explanation for the horror they had just witnessed and inviting people up to examine the evidence.

When Maggie came around and was untied, she was shocked to find people around her. She jumped back, clutching her heart.

'You are a fake, Miss Cloak!' Henry Legge shouted.

He pointed to the floor.

'Your deception has been found out.'

She was confused, reaching down to examine the things before her and picking them up. Then she laughed.

'Oh Henry, really! Do you imagine that I could do what I did with fresh flour and string and batter?'

He turned to the audience. 'You have all been deceived by light and string and trickery.'

Maggie was outraged.

'Then let me see you do it. Show us all how it is possible.'

The audience was on her side. She knew it. She also knew that even if it had been trickery, they would still pay to come again.

Father Legge refused angrily. 'I will play no part in this.'

'Then take your deception and leave or return to your seat!' she hissed. 'Reserve your judgement until I have finished.'

She sat, resting for a moment without taking her eyes from him and shook her head disappointedly, seeing in his eyes a determination to put an end to her reign. She closed her eyes, nodded and mumbled. For a moment there was nothing, no movement, no sound, and then she swayed dramatically to one side, almost falling from her chair. Then sweeping upwards, she rose, her arms spread out before her as if she were blind. She walked across the stage, negotiating with difficulty the stairs and then, to the crowd's horror, she was wandering amongst them, her arms raised at the elbow, delicately moving as if dancing, as graceful and light as a bird.

She moved through the rows, touching faces, hands, then stopped before a young woman. She stood motionless, the smile falling from her face. Then, opening her mouth, she screeched down at her, so loud and so relentlessly that in a shocking moment, the people in the rows around them fell over each other to escape. The seated woman covered herself with her arms, blocking her out, turning into her seat.

From the aisle, Judy hurried across, grabbing her sister, pulling her away, forcing her into the aisle.

'What is it?' the seated woman cried out after them. 'What does it mean?'

But there was no answer. Maggie had thrown her sister aside and was already climbing back onto the stage. She hurled the chair into the wardrobe and sat on it, summoning the stagehands to tie her. They were frightened, flinching at her every move as they hurriedly bound her tight and closed the door.

'Come to me!' she screamed from within it. 'Come to me now!'

Those gathered in the aisles ready to flee at any moment, turned. There was a long silence. Nobody moved. Then suddenly, a thud from within made the whole wardrobe sway. Netta and Judy stared, unable to look away. There was another heavy blow and the wardrobe lurched forward, unsteady on its legs. From within there was a loud grunt and a third crack, knocking a hole that splintered through the wood. The front rows began to stand and move towards the aisle as a series of thuds and moans grew in intensity, and suddenly another punch-sized hole shattered through its side. A deafening crash sent the door splintering out across the floor of the stage. The audience was screaming, staring at Maggie who hung, bloody and battered from her chair as it fell outwards and crashed down onto its side.

Judy hurried to her, screaming out to the stage hands and the men in the audience for help until reluctantly, they came to their senses and struggled with the knots that bound her and a knife was brought to cut her free.

'Is she alive?' Judy cried, taking her hand, reaching out to her battered face.

One of the men nodded and turned to the audience. 'Is there a doctor?'

She was being lifted, carried towards the stairs. But as the men reached the bottom step, she began to stir, looking around her, startled.

'Put me down!' she demanded. 'What are you doing?'

'Maggie, you are hurt,' Judy told her. But the sight of her sister only enraged her further and she fought herself onto her feet, pushing her aside.

'You!' she said turning to Father Legge, 'should never have touched me! Do you see what you did!' And holding on to the backs of seats, she pulled herself up the aisle and out into the night.

Father Legge turned to Judy and Netta. 'She is in danger,' he said. 'She must be stopped. I have tried but she wouldn't listen. It is now in your hands. If you can't stop her, prison will. We had better find somewhere to talk.'

∞∞∞∞∞∞

In the Hare and Billet, wiping the blood from her face with her handkerchief, Maggie drank. She had cleared the half of the room in which she sat, the customers frightened away from her. She ignored them, summoning more port with the click of her fingers.

'I am not a fraud!' she bellowed. She turned to see Judy being hurried in by the landlord and shook her head.

'Oh here she is! Wherever there is limelight, she'll come hurrying along to be in it.'

Judy, trying her hardest not to appear afraid, walked up to her.

'Can I sit?'

'Why not? Let's hear what you have to say. Let's all hear it.'

But the pub had emptied and only they remained.

Judy sat, her concern and fear palpable.

'Maggie, look at me,' she said softly. 'I am your sister and I love you. It doesn't matter what you think, or what you say, I love you and I am here for you. We must end this. We have to stop it now.'

Maggie laughed. 'Had a bit of a scare, did you?'

'They are going to force you to stop. They are talking about hospitalising you at Bethlem, Maggie – Bedlam.'

'They wouldn't dare. Do you know who I spent the day with, little sister? Do you? The queen. We talk like old friends. Queen Victoria, Judy. Do you think she will allow them to lock me up? I have not even shown people half of what I can do.'

'There will be no more evenings in the great hall. It has been stopped.'

'I don't need the hall. I have the shop, your wonderful Blackheath Séance Parlour.'

Judy rose and poured herself a glass of port from behind the bar then took the glass from Maggie's impatiently waving hand. Some habits could survive anything, even hatred and trauma. Judy filled it to the brim and put it in front of her, listening to her grunt.

'Try to remember before all of this. When we used to sit here and imagine –'

'Oh spare me the nostalgia. I am a success, you are to be married, everything is new.'

'I have refused him.'

She grunted out a mocking laugh. 'Then you are a fool because I do not want you. I do not want you now and I never really did want you.

You were always in the way as a child, forever forcing yourself on me and on our mother, driving her to distraction in the shop. She used to complain about you all the time. Did you know that? Eager but always ruining everything that you turned your hand to, that's what she thought of you. And she was right.'

Judy shook her head, in no mood for so much as even the sound of her sister's voice, let alone her ranting.

'Be quiet!' she shouted. 'I have no interest in how much you would like to hurt me. You have dominated my life for long enough. You demanded that I turn down Christopher's hand in marriage and I did. You have accused me of ruining your life – well you have now ruined mine so we are equal! And I will return to the shop tomorrow morning and if you cannot work with me, then you can leave because I am going nowhere!'

Maggie stood up, throwing back her seat. 'It is my shop!'

Judy stood up, mimicking her angrily. 'This is my shop! He is my father! Mine, mine, mine. Not everything is yours, you silly woman.'

'You cannot bear that I am more –'

'You are right. I cannot bear. I cannot bear you at all! And as for our father –'

'Yes, our father. Tell me, what was in that note you slipped into his hand before he ran for the ship? I have seen it. I've watched you curl his fingers around it, don't think I haven't.'

Judy was surprised. She had not thought of that moment for so long.

'Were you telling him not to come back? Is that why he was forced away from us?'

Judy stared. 'You do not know anything about that man!'

Maggie turned, seething. 'I knew it! I knew you had to be the reason.'

'He was my father too, Margaret. Do you imagine that I had another tucked away somewhere or that I simply didn't need one? What is it that allows you to dare to imagine that he was entirely yours?'

'He didn't care much for you,' she said with a sly smile.

'I was young, I was a toddler. Of course he had more in common with you. He had yet to learn who I was! It was you who took him from me! You used up all of him that there was, and pushed me away. There was no room for me. And what good has this fixation done for you in life? He did not love me, or our mother or you!'

'How dare you talk about him like that!'

'Do you want to know what happened to him, Maggie? Do you?' she shouted. 'Then follow me. Let us have all of your temper. Let us see it all at once.'

She marched out, pushing through the crowds gathered outside the door and turned down into the village, towards home, aware of Maggie's struggling breath following her. She turned into her row, through the garden and opened her door. She had lit the lamps before Maggie had even reached halfway up the path and stood with her hand resting on the door to the room, shaking with anger. She had sworn that she would never, not under any circumstance, show her sister what waited inside. It would break her.

'Well,' Maggie demanded, stepping inside angrily, 'what is it that you are hiding away here?'

The spite in her voice drained away the last of Judy's compassion.

'I was never going to show you this. I wanted to spare you the pain, but you deserve what little heart you have in you to be broken.'

She stepped aside, watching her sister's face soften and fill with excitement.

'Is he alive?'

'No.' she replied. 'He is dead.'

Maggie opened the door.

Inside the room, towering stacks of furniture, boxes and crates confronted her. Maggie looked at it, confused. There were chairs and cushions, paintings and portraits, cupboards and chests, clothes and toys and kitchen utensils and blankets and shoes and hairbrushes. There were books and furs and jewellery, children's clothes and children's seats and carpets and other expensive things, all piled high in the centre of the room.

'It arrived the day I came to live with you,' Judy said coldly. 'A lawyer from Brighton turned up. I was expecting a summons and suddenly he was talking about father, telling me that you and I were his sole heirs.' She joined her sister in the room, looking at the full horror of what had made living there unbearable. It had turned her world upside down and promised to do so again now, but this time with complete devastation.

'I don't understand. What is all of this?'

Judy pointed her to a large chest, inside which Maggie found paintings and framed sketches. There were drawings of the family home, of herself and her sister. Maggie's hand rose involuntarily to her lips at the sight of her mother smiling up at her from a chair in the garden.

And then there were drawings, sketches of Blackheath and of herself at the windmill, of the kitchen which had changed hardly at all since the day he had drawn it, of her grandparents, of the ship to Africa. Maggie drew her breath, tears welling in her eyes: there she was, small and crying, standing at the dock, waving up to him as his ship sailed away. He had seen her and he had loved her as much as she remembered he had. She studied it; her mother and Judy were mere blurs but the detail he had put into capturing her was astonishing; the eyes, her little desperate loving eyes and the tears that begged him to come back . . . She let out a sob.

'Why did you hide these from me?' she asked, genuinely confused. Judy watched her, dreading what was about to happen. 'There are more.' she said softly.

There were sketches of the enormous deep shafts with their diamonds, of slaves and chains and beatings and lions and fences and of his humble home there. And then on thicker canvas, there was an entirely different collection devoted to his journey home, to another woman, to the birth of a boy, a garden she did not recognise. There was a little girl, playing on a sandy beach, a portrait of him with his new wife and family, seated in a lavish home. Maggie stared, looking at the pictures over and over, at first confused and then angrily.

'They all died together, last year,' Judy said wanting to console her, 'some illness for which there is no medicine. They lived in a rented house in Brighton. Apparently there was no record of us, nothing at all. The lawyers eventually traced his history back to the ship and found us there in the paperwork.'

Maggie came to the final pictures, more muted and strange and fragile as if drawn by a much older, unsteady hand. A twist in the Thames, the crumbling windmill on Blackheath, and Maggie, ten or so years ago, seated in a pub, idling away the time, not recognising him or not having noticed him or not realising that she was being drawn.

Maggie nodded, unable to speak, surveying the room and noticing in the far corner, a wire cage with a floor of straw in which uncollected eggs sat in nests and a semi-circle of hen feathers covered the carpet. Judy looked away, embarrassed.

'You had no right,' Maggie glared, turning to her sister, her face sour with rage. 'No right at all to keep this from me!' She climbed angrily to her feet, confronting her, 'He was my father!' She heaved up the box of pictures and pushed past, storming out of the gate and was gone.

Chapter 30

In the dark, fire-lit kitchen, Maggie sat motionless at the table. Her bruised face was swollen and grotesque but she refused to acknowledge the pain. The spitting and fizzing wood in the grate sent up fountains of sparks that drew her eyes momentarily but she closed them again and swayed in her chair, tired and spent and empty but the pictures and their faces refused to leave her in peace.

Rising, she lit a table lamp and dragged the box across the room, placing the paintings side by side before her and opening a bottle of bourbon. She pulled up her chair.

'Father!' she shouted. 'It is no good hiding now. I have found you.'

She studied his face, the sincerity of his smile, the hand that rested on his new wife's hip as they cooed around their new children. He looked the same as she remembered him, a little older, more moneyed, but behind the disguise of a moustache and glasses, the same. She shook her head, leaning in with the lamp to find answers in his apparent happiness. What had it been that this woman and these children had given him that she and her sister and mother had not? The woman was prettier than her mother, she admitted guiltily, perhaps also a little more refined, but it was hard to tell, perhaps in that expensive gown with her hair and nails and skin so pampered, her mother too would have looked as beautiful. In the children she saw a spark of resemblance, her eyes in the boy, something of Judy in the little girl but her eyes returned to her father's face again and again.

'Father!' she shouted, 'Explain yourself to me!'

She looked at his new home, at the pretty dresses on the girl as she frolicked in the sand and, reaching for a knife, she drilled it into her. 'This should have been mine! All of this! It was mine. You were my father, not hers! You abandoned us!'

She tore through the girl with her hands, hurling her, frame and all into fire. Then with stab after stab, she took out the eyes and mouth of the boy, cutting through the canvass into the table beneath.

'Show yourselves!' she screamed, and looking up she saw flickers coming into focus in front of her, small, frightened faces pulled into her world. Maggie rose, screaming, staring at them.

'You stole my father from me! You took him! He was mine!'

The children were confused, looking at her and to each other for reassurance. Behind them, a taller figure appeared – female, reaching out, protecting them. Maggie's rage was uncontrollable. 'You!' she pointed, 'You stole our father from us. You took him and we waited and I waited and every day he didn't come back and every day he was with you. You ruined everything!'

The woman and children were unaware of her, looking around the room until Maggie, mustering everything she had, shouted, 'You will look at me!' and they did, all at once.

'Where is he?' she demanded. 'I demand that you bring him to me!'

And suddenly they were gone and Maggie fell down into her chair, crying against the picture of herself.

When she rose, her arms and face were smudged with paint. She moved around the room, hurling things at the walls. She would wipe him from her mind. She would force herself to forget him. He was worthless, one of life's magpies, always out for himself. He should have respected the rules, been disciplined enough with his emotions not to ruin the lives of those who loved him. Instead he had become nothing more than a selfish man who destroyed others because he could not say no to the fancies he had an eye for on his journey through life.

She climbed the stairs, threw back the sheets and climbed into bed. She would sleep, sleep through the night and the following day without waking. She would regain her strength, let her dreams take away the burden of Judy and her father and her damaged reputation so that she could prepare for the fight ahead with a clear head.

❦❦❦❦❦❦❦❦❦

At a large house at the bottom of Hyde Vale, Judy stepped from her carriage and composed herself.

She was nervous. There had not been a day during which she had not relived every minute of her time with him, laughed at the easiness of their rapport and teasing. There had not been a single night before sleep she had not relived the memory of his words and the tenderness in his eyes and her excitement as he went down on one knee and proposed. And there had not been a single day where the disappointment and hurt on his face had not haunted her. In her heart she did not expect forgiveness. But she at least had to try.

She opened the gate and climbed the steps, knocking quickly, not allowing herself further time for thought, readying herself to apologise and beg him to take her back. She waited, listening to the sound of footsteps coming towards her. Perhaps it was too late, she realised, perhaps she had hurt him too deeply and his pride was too bruised, perhaps he would immediately dismiss her. She would know the answer at his first expression, when she looked into his eyes. She had been tempted to look in the ball, to foresee it all, but had refused herself the easy route. Life was for living; life was about surprises.

There was movement, the sound of a chain, the unlocking of the door and the struggling with stiff hinges, then the surly face of a butler peered questioningly at her.

'It's all right, Lawe,' a voice from the stairs called to him, 'I will deal with this.' And suddenly he was there, looking at her, shaking his head gravely.

She smiled nervously.

'Are you aware, Miss Cloak, that you dismount carriages like a man?' he said.

'And are you aware, Mr Benedict, that you are shoeless and improperly dressed to receive visitors at your door?'

'Where I am going I won't have the stuffiness of social etiquette to trouble me.'

'And in the presence of wild animals and danger, it is perhaps more suitable that I dismount like a man.'

'You are assuming that my offer still stands?'

'Does it?'

'I shall have to think about it.'

'When?'

'I am doing so now, please wait.' He pulled a serious face, wrestling with smiles and frowns, then said, 'I'm afraid, after careful consideration, that it will have to be a no.'

'And why is that?'

He looked at her earnestly, his voice becoming serious. 'Because I am frightened that you might change your mind again and break my heart a second time.'

'I don't intend to make a mistake of that proportion ever again.'

'And you are sure? Really sure?'

She nodded.

He considered her in silence, watching her look back with sorry and frightened eyes.

'Then I am the happiest man alive.' And he closed the door on her.

She stood confused, unsure of what was to happen next, then hearing him laugh, saw the door opening and his grin appear from behind it. She laughed as he stepped out and swung her around him under the scornful eye of passers-by who knew what was proper and what was scandalous.

'I watched you, at the market, looking for me but not seeing me. I knew you would come.'

She kissed him.

'But you do know that I must leave in under a week? Are you prepared for that?'

She hugged him. 'The sooner the better.'

❧❧❧❧❧❧❧❧

Mrs Walters swept through the shop and struggled to close the heavy door. The sagging frame that held it in place had dropped even more and it now took a major effort to wedge it shut. Upstairs Maggie was shouting, conversing with some spirit or other, rehearsing the next abomination she would unleash. Netta did not want to know what madness she was plotting but took a deep breath and climbed the stairs.

'Do not interrupt me!' Maggie shouted.

'I have something to tell you,' Netta insisted.

Maggie sighed and turned to her, half listening. From her expression, Netta knew her attention was little more than pretence. In her head she was elsewhere, her eyes continually shifting and her expressions changing from annoyance to preoccupation.

'I am giving you my resignation. I will leave the shop this Friday.'

Maggie waited, her eyelids tightened, her head tilted. She was listening to something else.

'Did you hear?'

'Yes, yes,' she said irritably and turned away. Netta shook her head and walked back down into the shop. Outside, a group with placards, who usually saved their energies for the evening performances, had assembled. It was the second time that day. Netta stepped out, ignoring their taunts and threats and, locking up after her, slipped the key in her pocket and walked quickly up the hill towards Lee. There was trouble brewing and she wanted to be free of it before it began. Since Judy had left, the parlour had become a madness to which she was drawn each day and from which she fled hoping to find some semblance of normality at home. It was no longer the exciting adventure she had enjoyed; instead it resembled a battleground in which Maggie fought for and had won supremacy. All that it could have been had been achieved, it had surpassed that, but now it was moving into realms that she did not want any part of.

Over the past week, Father Legge had taken to timing his walks along this route to coincide with her journey home and each evening she dreaded him. He questioned her faith, questioned her past, criticised her motives, sometimes even prayed aloud, inviting her to join him as he accompanied her, and when she took an alternate route or delayed her journey, she would rise the next morning to find him waiting in the road outside. His very existence had become another unbearable weight. But the most unbearable weight of all came from the memories she fought to keep suppressed. Those that would no longer remain contained. More and more the sickening recollections flooded back, and the more they came, the more she wondered about what else her mind had hidden from her.

In her hand she clutched a letter to Norman. She would post it; she would not make him face her again. In it she promised that she would never contact him again, that she was sorry and that he need not fear her. She would be leaving London forever. She owed him that.

❧❧❧❧❧❧❧❧

Maggie paced the room, peering impatiently out of the window down to where the newspaper seller awaited delivery. She could barely wait to read the review. When the papers arrived she hurried out, snatching one up and tearing it open. She stared, slammed the door behind her, spread it out on a table, devoured it. The spread was bigger than usual. It branded her a fake, a fraud. There was talk of the string and flour and a comical drawing of her vomiting up a rabbit in a top hat.

'Beneath the darkness of inadequate lighting and the glow of sulphur, it is possible to make anything appear real,' Father Legge was quoted. 'She operates within a world of hope, in which people want her to succeed and want themselves to believe. Her trickery might satisfy those eager for titillation in the darkened curtain-swathed parlour and on stages where sleight of hand has traditionally amused all for hundreds of years but I put it to her that in front of scientists and priests and non-believers all of her tricks will quickly come to light.' Maggie laughed. She had expected it. She had predicted it and she was ready to prove them wrong.

She set to work on her reply. In it she demanded that the newspaper retract their accusations. She offered herself up to those who did not believe. 'Bring whoever you like: priests, scientists, men of medicine, journalists and also whatever means of testing me that you choose. I am not a fraud. I am Margaret Cloak, the world's most powerful medium. You will see that I have nothing to hide and then you will retract these accusations that tarnish my name,' she scribbled and hurried out to catch the penny post.

As she passed through the village, she saw a commotion at the entrance to Camden Row. Crates were being delivered and assembled in the street. Her sister's garden was full of activity. Maggie stormed towards it and into the house where she found her sister packing.

'What is all this?'

'I am leaving Blackheath.'

Maggie was unmoved. 'And I suppose you imagine that you are taking all of father's things with you?'

Judy shook her head. 'I mean to leave all of it to you. Or to whoever wants it.'

Maggie pushed past her into the room, rummaging through boxes and thrusting jewellery and journals into a basket.

'These belong to me.'

'Then take them. Take it all.'

Maggie struggled with a basket towards the door.

'Are you not even curious about where I will go?' Judy called after her.

Maggie turned and looked savagely at her. 'No'.

⚡⚡⚡⚡⚡⚡⚡⚡⚡

Late in the evening, a knock at Netta's door signalled the dreaded prospect of another visit from Father Legge so she peered carefully through the curtains, and was relieved to see Judy waiting patiently. She hurried to let her in.

Judy stepped inside looking around at the bare rooms. Netta had moved many times, it was not new to her. She knew how to clear a house quickly and travel light but still she felt the nervousness of leaving it all behind and starting afresh. In what remained of her kitchen she brought tea to the table and they sat, acknowledging that very soon they would see each other no more.

'I am to be married,' Judy told her. 'And since my sister no longer acknowledges me, I would like to ask you to be my witness.'

Mrs Walters smiled and squeezed her hand, 'I would be proud to.'

'It will not be a lavish affair, a simple ceremony. We both agree on that. And later in the afternoon, we leave London.'

'For Africa?'

Judy nodded.

Both women felt the sadness of the situation, of their parting and their uncertain futures and of Maggie, who both, if they spoke their minds, were pleased to be escaping.

They sipped their tea in silence.

Later, in her cold little room, Netta rested her head on her pillow and looked at her open wardrobe with its four new dresses. It was all that she had bought. Her only extravagances, everything else had been put away for a rainy day and the day was finally approaching. She thanked the crystal ball for warning her. She would leave behind the bed and its threadbare pink eiderdown that had never been warm enough, even in summer, and would buy something luxurious for her new home, something beneath which warm, reassuring comfort could be found.

Before the séance parlour she had relied on the occasional tarot reading, some cleaning work and stitching to make ends meet. Now she would reinvent herself as a woman with considerable means. She also had an idea. She had seen, many years before, an advertisement which had always appealed to her and stayed at the back of her mind. It had read:

> BOOTH FOR RENT,
> SOUTHEND PIER.
> RENT NEGOTIABLE.

She pulled herself up onto her elbows and looked at herself in the mirror, old and tired and in need of a drastic haircut, but she was not without style, not without energy and according to her lifeline, nowhere near the end.

'Southend Pier,' she said to herself, listening to the sound of it. 'I do miss the sea.'

Chapter 31

On the afternoon of Netta's final day, her resignation fell again on deaf ears. Maggie was pacing, she had nodded but had not heard a word. She was engrossed in a letter informing her that her challenge had been accepted. A team of scholars, doctors and priests had been assembled and they required her to give a private performance in which her skills would be put to the test. She was to pack a bag and be ready. A carriage would be sent for her at five o'clock promptly. Netta shook her head, speechless.

'MAGGIE!' she shouted.

Maggie turned angrily.

'You are aware that this is my final day working here?'

Maggie stared.

'That from tomorrow, it will be just you. I will be gone.'

'Where are you going?'

'I don't know,' she lied. The last thing she needed now was for Maggie to follow her.

'But what will I do? I can't manage alone.'

'I told you on Monday, you didn't listen.'

Maggie turned away irritably.

'Maggie?' Netta asked at last. 'You do you know, about Judy?'

'Know? Know what?'

'Judy is to be married, on Sunday, before they leave.'

Maggie shook her head sourly. 'How quickly she throws around her affections.'

'She is your sister. Do you really mean not to go to her wedding?'

'She is nothing to me.'

'She is your sister!'

'Pfft!'

She was gone again, peering through the window, pacing, mumbling to herself. Netta sighed and went through to the kitchen. She had worked alone all week, contending with queues that could have kept all three women busy while selling the contents of her home piece by piece in her breaks. She hadn't complained, the extra money would always be handy, so every penny that went into her own pot was an investment. She reached up to the shelf for the money jar and poured it into her handbag. The remorse she had expected to feel was outweighed by Maggie's madness. There would be no teary farewell. She doubted Maggie would even notice she had gone. One day perhaps she would revisit, but now her mind was eager to move on. She would leave London on Sunday, take her skills to the seaside, rent a booth on a pier and reveal light-hearted predictions to those of a less serious disposition. Life would be simple, carefree and better than it ever had been.

Maggie was alarmed. She was rushing about the room, putting on her hat, checking her appearance.

'They are here!' she called.

Netta peered out at her struggling to open the door.

'Lock the door after you.'

'Maggie!' Netta shouted. 'It is my last day!'

Maggie turned. 'Right, well, all the best.'

She hurried out, climbing into the carriage, and was gone.

Netta stared after her.

In the carriage, Maggie was wild with excitement. How they would have to eat their words! How they would be forced to believe, and how defiantly she would demand that they redress the balance, putting her back in her rightful place in the public eye, as London's most celebrated *grande dame*.

The carriage took her through London, across Southwark Bridge. She had it all planned. She would begin with something magnificent, something that would astound them all. If they thought to brand her a fake then let them hunt for string and flour, let them hold it out to her as proof. She chuckled to herself and looked out as the carriage turned towards St George's Fields. Her smirk fell; she began to panic. This part of London was famous for one thing and one thing only. She looked down at the door for the handles but there were no handles. She could not get out. She hammered on the carriage wall to the driver but he ignored her as the carriage slowed and turned into the grounds. Maggie was frantic, shoving at the doors as Bethlem Hospital towered above her.

They were taking her to Bedlam.

'No!' she screamed.

Outside the doors, medical staff were already awaiting her. Maggie was furious. She knew all about this place. It was the stuff of legend. Within it, the mad screamed and were tortured. They even allowed the public in to view the spectacle of the cells, allowing them to poke and beat the patients with long sticks to enrage them into fights and screaming fits for entertainment. On open days, selected patients were even thrown together to perform sexually together for private onlookers. The experiments and tortures had titillated society dinner parties for decades. Tales of screaming women tied to walls to be experimented on, of blood-letting and brain experiments. Inside the walls of Bethlem, people surrendered the right to be human and became the playthings of the affluent and curious.

Maggie looked down at her hands; they were trembling. Judy had tried to warn her, Father Legge had warned her too but she hadn't taken either seriously. She shook her fear away. No, she would not allow it. She was Maggie Cloak, all she had to do was prove that she was not a fake and then she would be released, and if they refused her her rights, she would send word to the queen immediately. When she didn't return to the shop, alarm would be raised, Netta . . . Judy . . . Maggie began to panic.

The carriage came to a halt and the door was opened. A suited man held out his hand to aid her descent.

'Welcome, Miss Cloak,' he said. 'Everything is ready for you. Would you like something to drink?'

Maggie shook her head, relieved that she was not being manhandled or restrained. And when the man and his assistant turned to the door and walked in in front of her, with no attempt to ensure she did not make a run for it, she breathed a sigh of relief.

She followed him down a long corridor and up a flight of stairs that smelled of vinegar and soap. There were no sounds, no screaming. Perhaps, she considered, the lunatics were kept out of view of formal visitors like herself. Perhaps they were kept in another wing or down in the cellars. At the end of a short white freshly disinfected corridor she was shown into a small room.

'I will leave you to prepare,' the man said. 'The matron here will tell you what is expected of you and see that you are ready.'

Maggie Cloak nodded and heard the door close. She sat.

With the door shut, the nurses moved to her bag, tipping the contents on a table. Maggie was outraged; she pushed them away, shouting out her objections. Suddenly her hat was being taken from her head, her coat was being removed.

'Take your clothes off,' the matron ordered. 'Everything.'

'I most certainly will not!' She shouted.

The nurses moved in.

In a simple white smock, Maggie stood at the centre of a large white room. It was empty except for a long table, eight chairs and two nurses who stood guarding the door. She stared around her. The room was bright, too bright, the gas lamps high on the walls so numerous that there was not a shadow in the entire room. She waited. Shortly the matron returned. She spread a large cloth over the table and placed Maggie's bag at the centre. Maggie watched her suspiciously.

'Is there anything you require from your bag?' the woman asked sternly.

Maggie shook her head.

The matron nodded and looked up as the door opened again. Through it came five men, including, as Maggie had expected, Father Henry Legge, who looked apprehensively at her. She shot him a disapproving look as the men took their seats. At the centre, the doctor turned to the matron.

'Her clothes have been examined?'

The woman nodded 'There was nothing.'

The man nodded.

Maggie felt satisfaction. 'There will be no cheating, no trickery. I want you to be absolutely certain,' she said, her tone sounding less authoritative than she was used to.

'Please remove the smock.'

Maggie stared.

The doctor pointed to it. 'Take it off.'

Maggie looked in the direction of Father Legge who turned uncomfortably away. Nervously, Maggie lifted the simple white garment over her head and, placing it on the table, turned to face them – brave and defiant. The doctor moved forward, raising her arms, looking into

313

her mouth, inside her nostrils and ears. He turned her, examined her buttocks and, moving around to crouch in front of her, reached for a metal spoon. She bore it with silent rage.

'I am not a fraud!' she objected.

When he was satisfied that nothing was concealed, she snatched up the garment and covered her body furiously.

'Prepare yourselves. You will see all of it,' she boasted, attempting to regain control.

The doctor nodded.

Looking around at the men one by one, she identified them quickly: Father Legge, a keen but apprehensive scientist, the doctor and two priests, one young and one of much older years who appeared to know Father Legge.

'Please begin,' the doctor said.

She closed her eyes.

When she opened them again the men were waiting expectantly, not with expressions of dread or fear as she was used to, but of calm patience. Behind them, the room began to fade and darken for her and she saw someone peeking through the door, while others loitered behind. Figures were rising in the corners, dark and sly, watching her, multiplying around her as if she and the priests were appearing in the spirit world rather than spirits appearing around them.

The white walls and the white floor darkened around her.

'You must tell him.'

'You must find my wife.'

'Are you still in life?'

'My sons, please tell them I miss them.'

'My husband . . .'

'Tell her I am very angry. Tell her she must not remarry.'

'He must see a doctor.'

'They must not go there.'

'They are so sad but I am –'

'Enough!' Maggie shouted, startling the men who appeared back before her eyes with immediate clarity in the blinding white room. But here holding the spirits at bay was short lived, and she saw them beginning to rise again, heard the sounds of creaking, whispering and felt them growing in number in other rooms, attempting to find her.

She cleared her head, sought out the strongest, most adamant voice and listened to it. It came through at once, hurling its voice out into the room through her at deafening volume. The men jolted backwards. Maggie's eyes had altered and now cleverly considered each man in turn.

She turned to Father Legge.

A man's cough erupted from her and she growled.

'What is your name?' the voice demanded. 'You are familiar to me.'

'I am Father Henry Legge,' he replied.

'Of London?'

'Yes.'

'Son of Thomas?'

'Yes.'

'Thomas son of David, David son of Edward, Edward son of Charles, Charles son of John, John son of Edwin, Edwin son of Mark, Mark son of Clarence, Clarence son of Edward, Edward son of Matthew. Matthew son of . . . And you are Henry?'

'Yes.'

She stood and leaned in to study his face, her own creased with concentration, her eyes straining to see. She nodded. 'Yes, I see the similarity of features. It is diluted but I see.'

The old priest, far advanced in years with skin as transparent as wax and hair as thin and white as an old maid, lifted a claw like finger and turned his face, sagging with folds and lines, to study her.

'Where is it that you reside when you are not summoned?' he asked, considering her with an air of impatience.

'I am not familiar with it yet,' the voice replied. 'It is new to me.'

'But you are dead?'

'Dead to you.'

'And would it be dark or light where you find yourself?'

'I passed through the dark and light a long time ago.'

The priests exchanged concerned glances with each other while Father Legge, obviously unskilled in these matters in comparison, tried to fathom the meanings of their silent communication.

'Tell us who you are.'

'I find here that I have the thoughts of many people. I am joined.'

The old priest closed his eyes. 'And you are becoming less of yourself and more diluted with others?' he asked calmly.

Maggie shook her head. 'It is knowledge. It is comforting.' Her eyes moved around the room, 'What age is this?' the voice asked, her eyes focusing on the gas lighting. She moved towards them, looking up with fascination.

Suddenly Maggie found herself shaken free; she blinked, turned to face them, a little confused, and walked back to the table.

'Come, sit, be yourself a moment,' the doctor said, waving her to the chair before them.

'How do you connect with these other beings?' he asked.

Maggie considered him patiently, scanning his face for flickers of mockery or disbelief but when it appeared his question was in earnest, she let down her guard and spoke. 'It took a long time to learn how to hear them. At first I could only see them,' she said, eager to share her experiences with those of a more serious and analytical mind, 'then I started to pick up sounds and fragments of words but for the life of me I could not communicate back. When I finally started to talk with them I found that if I allowed their trust to become stronger, their voices became louder. I have no emotional interest in them, I am simply a door through which they can walk. Then they started to inhabit me without me even being aware of it.'

'Isn't that dangerous?'

'It can be. Sometimes it can be hard to get them back out but I am strong. I know how to stop them.'

'And how do you stop them?'

'I close them down, I think of other things. Eventually there is no room for them and they slip away.'

The man nodded. 'Let us continue with your demonstration.'

Maggie nodded then closed her eyes and waited. Within moments she began to swoon and an older voice came forth.

'Hello, boy,' it said, looking at the old priest. 'Look at how old you have grown. You are older than I was, I imagine.'

The priest was unmoved.

'Still a surly old sod. Still a man of the cloth barking orders? How old are you now, seventy? Only a few more years left, old chap. We're all here, waiting for you. It won't be long now.'

The priest stood. 'Miss Cloak, would you please come back to us.'

She shook the spirit away.

'None of this is new to me. I have had mediums up to my eyeballs over the years. If you are so very special then I would like you to draw forward a much older spirit. Something from somewhere more distant than you have ever reached before. The spirits you have brought forward so far are of no interest to us.'

Maggie nodded, 'But when they are very distant, sometimes I cannot understand them.'

'Just let them speak.'

Maggie obeyed, her eyes darting quickly behind her eyelids.

The men waited for several minutes during which there was no sound at all until, with a soft outpour of breath, Maggie rose from her seat, her mouth open. Her right hand, limp and flaccid, lifted before her, veering off to her right, then her left hand, equally as lifeless, rose and hung pointing across to her left. Her head lifted to the ceiling, then fell forward.

The old priest was outraged. 'What blasphemy is this?'

Maggie's head rose up from her shoulders, the muscles of her throat and jaw clenched in pain.

She turned, panicking, looking at her suspended hands, first one, then the other, and then at the men who studied her. 'What is happening?' she asked.

A whisper rose in her throat, overlapping her voice. Maggie froze.

'Where am I?' it whispered.

'Tell us who you are?' asked the younger priest.

Maggie tried to talk but the priest held up his finger to silence her.

'What is this place?'

Maggie was distraught. 'It is different!' she said, 'This is not –'

'Miss Cloak, please! Be silent!' the priest warned. 'Let the spirit communicate.'

Through her open mouth, sounds began to rise independently of her. Maggie was rising from her seat, her eyes frightened. She watched her hand as it reached out daintily to touch the younger priest's face. She ran a finger over the lines around his eyes, reached down and lifted his hand.

'It is skin,' the voice said with astonishment. Maggie's face lowered to study his hand, her fingers stroking it, feeling the bone beneath. Her hands wandered up to his face, felt his eye socket, his ears, lifted his lip and peered in at his teeth.

'It was real once. I am losing it now, the memory.' She slid a finger into his mouth, and he allowed it nervously, feeling her finger run over his tongue.

Embarrassed, he looked at the others.

'That is enough!' the old priest said firmly.

Maggie withdrew her finger. She moved around the table, stopping at the scientist and felt his hair. She ran a hand over his face, parted his lips, peered into his eyes crouching before him, and ran her hands over his body. The man was red with embarrassment.

'Miss Cloak!'

'There are ribs. There are bones. And blood?' she asked turning quizzically to the group. 'There was blood?'

Father Legge nodded.

'You are still here. Existing still. I was among you once. I think. I have the memory of it. Very faint. Like a trick,' she said and gazed lovingly at them.

Her hands fell to her frock and she rubbed it between her fingers, scratched at the wooden back of the chair with her nail, looked up at the ceiling and the floor. 'It exists?' she asked.

'There was a dark place and then a light . . .' said the old priest.

She nodded.

'You are back before the dark place,' she said, 'you are very far away.'

Maggie shook herself from it and stood, staring angrily.

'I do not want this. I don't want to do that again. I do not want to be conscious when it speaks through me.' She rubbed her eyes.

The older priest watched her impatiently. 'You'll do what we tell you to do. Bring it back.'

'You don't understand. It hurts.'

'That is no interest to me, Miss Cloak. Bring it back.'

Maggie stared furiously at him, following his hand as it rose into the air and he clicked his fingers. She felt a change in her, felt the spirit clawing inside her mind and her arms grow heavy and she swooned.

'No!' she shouted and shook herself free.

He clicked his fingers again, watching her sag lethargically.

'You are not the only person who knows how spirits operate, Miss Cloak.'

Maggie was mumbling, shaking her head, sinking down against her will.

'What is your name?' the priest asked, scribbling notes into a book laid out before him without looking up.

Maggie's eyes were closed. She choked, coughing up deep angry tones.

'What is your name?' the priest repeated.

'That is of no consequence to you, Father,' the voice shouted with a tone of authority.

The old priest began again. 'Do you come from the light or the –'

'Where I come from, Father Franklin, is none of your concern.'

'And will there be repercussions when you return?'

'There are always repercussions, as well you know.' Maggie lifted her hands, rubbed her eyes, shook her head angrily at him and tried to talk, but he clicked his fingers again and she was drifting, watching the events from somewhere, helpless.

'Tell us your name.'

The voice laughed. 'So young and so naive and yet how very wise you consider yourself to be. The simplicity of the old life, it was not without its charm.' Maggie was holding her jaw as if her teeth ached. She was shaken free again. Unsure of what had happened, then pulling herself up, she screamed at him, 'Stop it! Stop doing that! I cannot cope with it.'

The priest clicked his fingers again, and the voice roared back at him.

'You cannot summon me.'

'But I can. I did.'

'You will get no further than me. I am a sentinel.'

'What is it that you guard?'

Maggie leaned forward, resting her hands on the table, staring into his eyes.

'You already know, Father.'

The man stood, leaned towards Maggie, mumbled words that no one else recognised into her ear. Maggie nodded.

The priest sat, satisfied.

Maggie laughed. 'The little explorers. Discontent with your lot.'

'We have been further.'

Maggie nodded. 'We know.'

The priest mumbled again and watched Maggie shake her head.

'You did not like what you saw. Therefore it is better you go no further.'

'What is beyond that?' the priest demanded. 'We die, we sleep, we wake into darkness, time passes, there is light. What is beyond that?'

The voice laughed. 'Why do you fear what is so very far away?'

'It is human nature to seek answers.'

There was no response.

'What is there?'

'Patience, Father.'

'Take us there.'

'Not yet.'

'But you can?'

'Of course.'

He clicked his fingers, turned to the others and looked again at Maggie.

Maggie was blinking, staggering forward, her face confused. She stared at him angrily.

'I will not have you do whatever you are doing to me!' she shouted at him. 'I will not have it!'

'Would you please leave us for a moment,' he requested, dismissing her.

The nurses stepped forward, escorting Maggie who was still reeling and holding her head as if she was in severe pain out into the corridor.

The old priest sat for a moment and rubbed his hands. He passed an eye over his fellow priest who held his stare with a look of worry and looked down at the table as the old man coughed and addressed the doctor, the scientist and Father Legge.

'There is little doubt that she has the talent. What makes her astounding is that in the short time she has been indulging her passion, mere months I am lead to believe, she has reached further back than most other mediums manage in a lifetime. These women who meddle in matters that don't concern them are an infernal nuisance. And they are always of the same stock – gossips, greedy delusional gossips. Out to spread their rumours in the hope of finding meaning in their lives.'

'Could she be of use to us privately, Father?' the younger priest asked. 'It seems there is rare opportunity here.'

The old priest shook his head adamantly. 'This must be stopped before it goes any further. She must be made an example of.

'But Father,' motioned Father Legge, 'perhaps if she was to be guided away from –'

'Guided away?' he chuckled. 'Father Legge, there is one reason and one reason alone that she has been summoned before us today and that is to save the borough of Blackheath from damnation in the eyes of the church and for the sanity of its parishioners. I see little point in dragging this on any further than it already has. If she is to be stopped then let her simply be stopped. She need never leave this building again.'

'Father, I have a duty to her family.'

'Family, Father? I have been informed there is a sister. But I hardly anticipate much in the way of obstacle and objection from her when it appears that her own outbursts could lead her to the same destination. No. The Church has seen this before. She brings only the threat of disruption. That is why she must be stopped.'

Much to the old priest's irritation, the young scientist chose this moment to assert himself. 'As a man of science I have seen nothing here that proves anything other than this woman has imagination and can project accents. I would like to see more.'

The older priest considered him irritably.

'If the newspaper reports and word of mouth are accurate,' agreed the doctor, 'then I think we should see the whole performance. We won't be able to judge until we have seen it all.' His eyes rested on the face of the old priest who now motioned impatiently for him to call her.

'Whether you keep her here to play with or you keep her here under my authority is of little difference to me. What is of the utmost importance to me is that she doesn't leave.'

'Father . . .' interrupted Father Legge urgently, but Maggie was already entering the room and his words were waved away.

At the head of the table Maggie stepped forward. She knew what was expected of her. 'I cannot summon certain spirits without my cabinet,' she said 'but I can bring them forth in a more basic form.'

The doctor nodded. 'Let us see them.'

Maggie bowed her head, catching sight as she lowered her eyes of Father Legge glaring at her and shaking his head as subtly as he could.

She ignored him.

'There is no need,' Father Legge interrupted. 'I have seen it and found it to be false.'

Maggie lifted her head and looked at him. 'Perhaps it is you that needs to be observed more closely, Father Legge.' She looked away and remained motionless for several minutes until, at the corner of her eye, next to the tear duct, a small white bubble began to rise and inflate, it reached a pea size, then fell forward, dangling down her cheek on a white thread that seemed to pulse of its own accord.

'We must take a sample,' the scientist said, rising.

Father Legge shook his head. 'It must not be touched. It does not come away. It appears to be part of the body.'

'Not so false after all, Father Legge?' the doctor ventured. He returned his gaze to Maggie, as fascinated as the scientist next to him.

Extending from her face, the strange substance took the form of a long stick which rose and fell and searched about the room, not unlike the trunk of an elephant, thrilling the doctor and scientist to the point of rapture.

'If it is a free ticket for the stage show you require, doctor,' Father Legge interrupted, 'I'm sure –'

'It is not, Father. I am a man of science. I seek only to prove or disprove.'

The old priest, casting a wary eye over Father Legge, spoke. 'That is enough. No more.'

'No, let it continue,' insisted the doctor.

'That is enough, Margaret!' insisted the priest.

'No, she must be allowed to –'

'I forbid it!' shouted the priest.

The doctor cleared his throat. 'Might I remind you, sir, that this is a medical establishment and your authority has –'

'My authority, doctor, extends to everywhere and everything. Now, if you will excuse me, I would like to talk to Father Legge privately.' He stood, turning to the younger priest. 'Bring her around, see to it she remains awake while we are gone.' And, moving to the door, he took Father Legge's arm and escorted him through it. They walked some moments silently down a long corridor which sloped downwards into the bowels of the hospital.

'What is your issue here, Father?'

Father Legge looked at him. 'Duty.'

'Your borough wants rid of her. They turned to you for help but it appears you were not effective. Would you have me release her? To let her encourage all of London's boroughs to explore the realms of the paranormal and turn their backs against God? Science, Father, is little more than a licence to separate men from God's teachings. It gives licence to blasphemy but at least it removes these mad women from society where they are intent on wreaking havoc.'

'But what if she could be stopped?'

The old priest stopped walking and turned to face him. 'You have seen this woman, you know her. You know her ambition. She has renounced the Church. She has turned her back on you. It is quite apparent she has no respect for you or your position.'

'Father, she cannot be locked up here. She must be left to me.'

'To you?'

'She is my parishioner, my responsibility. I cannot fail my parish.'

The old priest peered forward into the dark corridor, from which moans and cries were becoming audible, and turned Father Legge around, walking him back in the direction they had come.

'What is it that drives you to protect her with such enthusiasm? Come, let us go back. Let us finish the examination.'

When they re-entered the room both men jolted at the spectacle that confronted them. The doctor, scientist and young priest were standing, moving back from their seats towards the door.

In the centre of the room, like a figure covered with a sheet, Maggie stood, the milky white ectoplasm covering her from head to foot like a cocoon. She was motionless, only swells of the sticky fluid rippled over her.

Father Legge stared, moving aside as the old priest moved forward and touched her shoulder. 'Wake, child,' he said. 'Wake now.'

Slowly the liquid began to rise, like a skirt being lifted. It sucked and gurgled appallingly at her throat and was still retreating as the nurses escorted her from the room to the bed of the waiting cell.

'And you suggest we unleash that back into society?' the old priest asked Father Legge. 'We will resume the examination in one hour. Let us take time to collect our thoughts.'

'Perhaps now would be a good time to talk about our donation,' the doctor said quickly following the old priest from the room. 'We are keen to acquire her. From a scientific point of view she is most valuable.'

With the other men absent, Father Legge kneeled and let the silence envelop him. He closed his eyes, clasping his hands together in prayer and asked for guidance.

There were often moments during prayer when he felt something more than just his own conviction was present. Usually, when he asked for advice, his own reasoning took the place of a heavenly voice to provide the required reply, but occasionally, just occasionally there was something else at play within his mind. And now, that something was with him. He stood up, let himself out through the door and, dismissing the nurses that stood guard outside Maggie's cell, he let himself in.

Maggie was recovered and sitting on a wooden shelf, that, should she be condemned to stay, would more than likely be her bed. She looked up at him and shook her head, ready to gloat.

'Margaret, it is important now that you listen to me,' he whispered. 'You are in great danger.'

She rolled her eyes.

'They mean to keep you here, Father Franklyn means to charge you with ...'

'I shall call on the queen.'

'Oh Margaret, she will not dare interfere. The doctor and scientist are fighting to keep you here to experiment on you. You are at the centre of a tug of war and whichever side wins wants to keep you in here. Margaret!' he shouted as she looked away, uninterested. 'They mean to keep you here.'

'And that would suit you.'

'If it suited me do you think I would be in here trying to protect you?'

'You aren't,' she said bluntly. 'You are here to trick me into condemning myself. So that you can go back to Blackheath and tell everyone you were right.'

'Margaret, you must renounce everything that you have achieved and you must let it become a thing of the past.'

She shook her head. 'Do you remember when my stupid sister dragged me into that church after so long? How you gloated, standing up there at the altar, preaching away for your own benefit, applauding yourself that you were right and the Cloak girls had come back to the church after all these years, just as you predicted. It was you who drove us away from God to begin with. You and your stubborn pride and the value you placed on yourself. You made it sickening for us to come to worship.'

'Then it is my duty to rectify –'

'Oh your duty. Always about you.'

He paused, considering how he could change the balance of trust. How in this moment he could convey how much faith she needed to have in him now, but she was thrilled by her certainty that she had defeated him.

'No one here doubts your capabilities, Margaret. You have astounded even those of us who have seen such phenomena many times, but even those with a fraction of your abilities that came before you were stopped. And that is what this evening is about, stopping you.' He stared at her, grabbed her shoulders and made her concentrate on him. 'You can go no further.'

'I have a lot further to go.'

'Margaret, you are not safe. If you do not heed my advice you will find yourself remembering this conversation and wishing that you had listened to me. Listen to me now not as a priest but as Henry Legge, the man you think of only with contempt, the man you cannot bear. I am trying to help you.'

'Will you stop at nothing to have things your way?'

He sighed and shook his head in despair. 'If you have ever had a flicker of friendship towards me, I ask you to recognise my friendship towards you now.'

She studied his face.

'We know what you see. These men, Maggie, are very powerful. They are experts in this field. You have brought yourself directly into their paths and you are standing at the outer circle of something that will drag you to its centre and dispose of you without a second thought.'

She shook her head.

'You must refuse any further part of it. Denounce yourself as a fraud. Do whatever it takes to stop them from examining your talent further.'

'That would suit you, wouldn't it, Henry, for me to be nothing and

Blackheath to be all yours again?'

'Blackheath will be mine whether you cooperate or not. But if you listen to me, Margaret, you will live past this.'

'Are you threatening me?'

The priest's attention was drawn to the sound of the men moving towards the room and he rose to his feet.

In the examination room, Maggie was brought before them again and stood silently considering them.

Father Legge stood up. 'Margaret has agreed that this is perhaps the wrong path to have followed. She has announced to me that some aspects were fraudulent and –'

'I said no such thing!' Margaret snapped.

Father Legge closed his eyes.

'Your loyalty to Miss Cloak is commendable, Father Legge,' the old priest said, 'But we have made our decision. Miss Cloak is to be charged with heresy.'

Maggie stared at them, panicking.

'But it is not heresy! It is real!'

The doctor turned towards the door.

'I shall have a room prepared.'

Father Legge was about to speak again but the old priest rested a hand on his arm.

'It is out of your hands now, Father.'

He turned to see Maggie's foolish eyes look at him.

'I will not be locked up! I shall call Queen Victoria! I count her as one of my personal –'

But nurses were entering, taking hold of her, forcing her arms down and turning her so she could be secured.

'You will find here, my dear, that a lot of the patients claim the very same thing,' the doctor replied.

Maggie stamped her feet.

'I have not finished yet.'

'We have seen enough!' Father Legge shouted at her.

'Have you indeed?' she shouted back, pulling herself free from the hands that restrained her.

'You demanded to see far, far back.'

The old priest stopped and considered her.

Maggie, wild-eyed, hurried to a seat, threw herself almost immediately into a trance and beckoned the old priest, her mouth barking out a language she did not understand.

'I can tell you everything that you want to know,' she whispered.

The old priest motioned everyone else out of the room and closed himself in with her.

౿౿౿౿౿౿౿

In the cold hours of the night, Maggie paced a damp cell at the bottom of a sloping corridor. From this holding room, she could hear the other inmates of her new home wailing in the distance. Her lips were tight with fury. She was outraged. She meant to call the newspaper, call the palace, and summon the people of Blackheath to come to her aid, all the influential people that had visited her séances privately would have something to say about this.

She kicked some straw bundled in a corner and dislodged a family of mice that scattered in all directions then sat down with a thud on the shelf, looking around her. The walls were decaying, the paint and the plaster crumbling to reveal the red brick beneath it. Scratch marks ran the entire length of the door, though they were mostly concentrated around the locks and barred window. From time to time someone would look in on her, blocking out her only source of light. She was not sure if it was a nurse or lunatic so muffled were their remarks.

After an hour or so, a nurse opened the door and motioned her out into the corridor. Here before her were two large men, nurses or guards prepared for trouble. Behind them Father Legge stood with his head bowed, unable to look at her.

She glared at them and demanded to leave, putting up a fight as hands clenched her arms and marched her deeper into the bowels of the hospital.

'You will have your own room tonight,' the nurse said, 'but from tomorrow you will share with some others. You will soon get used to it. The medication will help you relax.'

'I do not need medication!' Maggie objected proudly. 'I demand to be released. This is a mistake. I am not a lunatic. I am not a madwoman.'

'None of them are, dear,' laughed the nurse, 'not even the six Jesuses and the fourteen devils. All want to go home to their own beds. Don't even know their own beds were sold to pay for their keep here.'

Maggie twisted in their arms, turning to look at Father Legge. 'You must do something.'

'I tried, Margaret.'

'You must do something!' she repeated.

The nurse turned to him and handed him an oil lamp.

'We will take her from here, Father, Best you don't see if you are a close friend.'

He nodded.

Maggie was distraught, fighting against the hands that dug into her arms and turning to face the light of the wide corridor that opened up before her with its cell doors and screaming, fighting sounds.

'Henry!' she screamed. 'Father, you must do something!'

'Come along now. I'm sure he will visit you sometime in the future.'

Henry Legge turned and walked back in the direction they had come, listening to Maggie screaming after him.

In the doctor's study, sipping brandy on the sofas, the men, tired from the ordeal, reconvened before departing. They looked up as Father Legge entered.

'You all right, old man?' asked the doctor. 'Quite traumatic when they first get taken down. Here, let me pour you a brandy.'

Father Legge nodded.

'Quite the livewire,' he said, handing him a glass.

'Quite something indeed,' said the scientist. 'I look forward to examining her further.'

'It is an ability that has grown out of control. That is all it is,' Father Legge said. 'It can be put to sleep again. What we saw was spectacle, nervous energy, illusion.'

'It is not the spectacle that worries me,' the older priest said. 'It is the knowledge, the path she has begun down.'

'We once had a man who claimed he could predict the future,' the doctor said, making himself comfortable in his armchair next to the fire. 'He passed all of our tests blindfolded. Guessed every symbol we held up, without hesitation. Correct every time. It turned out he had an enlarged temporal lobe.'

The scientist nodded. 'There is always a scientific explanation.'

The old priest shook his head and waved the words aside.

'Do you mean to tell me that you believe our very thoughts are a mere movement of chemicals in the brain? That the mixing of one chemical with another creates words, knowledge, aspiration, dreams, the drive to build cities'

'I believe that if an action is repeated several times then that action forms a series of minute connections in the brain. Rather like holding a board on which a drop of water is resting and tipping it to the right repeatedly. Eventually there is a wet path for the next drop to follow and there is now an association with that action.'

The old priest laughed. 'Are we to believe then, that according to science we are all thoughtless empty beings, simply reacting to the varying strengths of the dilution and swills of chemicals? That in fact, there is no point to our existence other than to supply these chemicals with the actions they desire from us? That there can be no universal spirit, that there is no soul, no consciousness, that we are simply receptacles that move like the stars on their courses? And that within us, the need for knowledge, to learn and appreciate life, to enjoy music and art is there merely to satisfy the requirements of shifting of liquids?'

The scientist moved uncomfortably in his seat.

'Even the madwoman that we locked up this evening believed in more than that, and we charge her with heresy.'

'She is a good woman,' Father Legge said absent-mindedly, 'I have known her all my life.'

'We all have to make sacrifices, Father. It is part of your duty,' the old priest said, motioning his young companion to top up his glass. 'You said yourself that she had to be stopped.'

'But not this way,' he replied. 'She is a family friend. We have been through much together. Her life has been hard but she has a good heart.'

The old priest nodded. 'So much harder when they are known personally to us.'

'But she did deny God,' the doctor interrupted, offering up his glass to the young priest who now carried the decanter from person to person.

'She did,' the old priest laughed. 'What were her words? I do not believe in a God, but I do believe in the soul. The soul . . . how did she say it? The soul is never-ending and I have proved it. Souls are not the creation of God, souls are the things that priests gather like foxes steal eggs.' He laughed. 'You must hear things every day that make you laugh in this hospital.'

The doctor nodded, 'Where there is madness there is genius.'

'I can stop her,' Father Legge blurted passionately. 'She will come into the arms of the Church, under my guidance. I owe her family that much.'

'Father Legge . . .' the old priest groaned, content with his brandy and the thought of home.

'A decision has been made.'

'There is an opportunity for true redemption here. Father, I am asking you now as a personal –'

The man shook his head, exasperated. 'You are a fool, Father Legge. She is too strong-willed. You will not tame her.'

'She will renounce herself publicly.'

'Even if she does, you cannot guarantee that she will stop.'

'I can contain her. I will take her under my wing. Bring her into the Church. Stop it from progressing further.'

'Let her go, Father. Let sleeping dogs lie.'

Father Legge looked earnestly at him. 'I can't, Father. She is my parishioner. I cannot fail her. I will turn her away from this obsession. She will denounce herself to the public as a fraud. She has felt the power of this place, seen how things will turn if she does not seek out a simpler life.'

The doctor stood, pouring the last of the brandy into his own glass.

'Gentlemen, it is late. I suggest you sleep on it. It will do her no harm to spend a night contemplating her sin if your decision needs further discussion. Although I will express my disappointment if she is removed. You will understand that I am curious to test her further.'

The priests stood.

'We will return tomorrow morning, doctor,' Father Legge said firmly, shaking his hand.

The old priest sighed.

'So be it.'

࿔࿔࿔࿔࿔

Maggie was sitting bolt upright. She had passed through the terror of her predicament and now that her anger had subsided, her mind was firmly stuck in a state of complete disbelief. There would be absolutely no way she would allow them to keep her there, but in the meantime, she marvelled at the opportunity of seeing the inside of a cell in Bedlam. She could hardly wait for the experience to end so that she could tell others what it was like.

Standing with her eyes peering through the bars of the cell into the torch-lit glow of the wide, sandy corridor she listened to the screams and foul-mouthed shouting. They, like herself, were demanding to be let out, insisting that a mistake had been made, assuring the emptiness that they were fine, upstanding community people, tax payers, churchgoers.

Maggie grimaced and flopped down on the shelf.

'Everyone really does say the same thing,' she said to herself.

For a moment she imagined that she had just woken on another day in her cell, that she had been there for several years. Today she would probably be injected with drugs, force-fed gruel and scrubbed with brushes by thick uneducated women glad to have employment. She growled her disapproval.

Outside frenzied screaming and hammering was met with the howls and screams of others and she rose again to the door to peer out. A cell was being unlocked. Two men, nurses as strong and threatening as jail keepers, were shouting, reaching into the open door and shoving someone about, ordering them to stop making so much noise. Behind them, roused, the woken inmates in other cells were hammering at their doors, chanting and howling like dogs.

The person in the cell the nurses had opened was begging to be freed. He rushed forward, trying to pass them but was caught in their arms and he sunk to the floor.

'I am not mad. I do not belong here. I am being set up by someone who wants my position at work. He can have it. Please, just turn me out. I will not go back there. I will leave London.'

A nurse reached for an instrument hanging on the wall, one of many devices that until now Maggie had not noticed, while the other opened the prisoner's mouth. Together they pressed between his teeth a large flap of leather connected to a metal strip that covered his mouth and chin and secured it tightly at the back of his head with buckles. They bound his hands behind him and listening to his terrified cries with complete indifference, dragged him back into the cell and slammed the door.

'If anyone else wants the same, speak now!' one of the guards cried furiously.

Maggie lifted her hand, looked at her knuckles, then knocked loudly on her door.

A moment later a set of eyes peered in at her.

'You think it's funny, do you?' the guard roared. 'Have the devil inside you, do you?'

Maggie stood and peered back at him. 'I do, and since I won't be stopping, I thought I might as well have the full experience tonight.'

The guards stared at her, unamused.

ഇഇഇഇഇ

At first light, before the opening of the doors to the public and the doctors descended below to carry out inspections, the guards entered her cell again. Maggie was chained to a wall, her mouth gagged, her legs splayed in metal cuffs, her arms stretched above her head and secured to a wooden block, water dripping down on her head.

'Was it worth it?' they asked as they pulled the soaking leather flap from inside her mouth and tossed it aside. She swallowed and coughed. Then feeling her arms fall next to her devoid of any feeling and her legs finally able to move from the spot, she manoeuvred herself to the bed and shrugged.

'I've had worse.'

They laughed.

Father Legge and Father Franklyn, both a little worse for wear after a night of overindulgence on fine brandy, met again in the grounds of the hospital at seven fifteen to discuss, briefly the predicament of Margaret Cloak.

Neither man had slept well; Father Legge through over-rehearsing what he had to say now and Father Franklyn troubled by the revelations Maggie had told him when they were alone together.

'I have been thinking,' Father Legge said, his breath hanging before him in the cold morning mist that always seemed to envelop this part of London.

'I had imagined you might,' the man replied. 'But before you speak, Father, I would like to say one thing – my mind has been made up. My decision is made.'

Father Legge nodded. Then he spoke.

'There is an opportunity here, Father. A public admission by her that it was all trickery will be a shock to society, an embarrassment to those who were duped and made fools of. Those who promoted her to friends and colleagues, declaring her a genius and her performances as proof, will look foolish to one and all, and thereafter treat all such phenomena with contempt. If Margaret Cloak publicly denies there was truth in any of it, even those most determined to believe cannot argue. But Father, if we lock her away, they will say that she was stopped, that she was genuine, that we were afraid. They will honour her. And people will go on searching for the next medium, and in her wake there will rise, another and another and another until the Church is not dealing with one but hundreds. They will grow in numbers because people will believe it has to be true. Why? Because you and I took her from society. It is like an admission on our part. The threat of Bedlam might dissuade other mediums from rising for a while, but ultimately we would have created a legend: Margaret Cloak will be heralded as the most famous and prestigious medium in history. They will write books about her, she will become the stuff of stories and exaggeration. We cannot, when we have this opportunity in our hands, pass it up. Her denial will discredit the paranormal and even if she chooses to retract her statement later, the damage will have been done. No one will dare to believe her. It is by far a worse punishment than keeping her locked up in here where – trust me, Father – they will generate more publicity for her and take the money they charge people to see her for themselves. Maggie Cloak must be released and she must be made to renounce her beliefs.'

Father Franklyn, his eyes firmly set on Father Legge's face sighed angrily. 'For God's sake, man, are you in love with this woman?'

※※※※※※※※※

After a night surviving a dripping, stinking, deafening and terrifying hell in which embracing madness seemed easier than remaining sane, Maggie watched Father Legge and the doctor walking towards her cell and sighed irritably. Her mood was not alleviated when the guard, a seemingly useless fat thing, took an eternity trying different keys in the door to get to her.

'Come on man, for God's sake!' Maggie shouted. 'I haven't got all bloody day.'

The door swung open and she marched towards them, pushing him aside.

'Am I in or out?' She demanded.

'If you announce yourself as a fraud, you leave now. If not, you stay, for good.' Father Legge said.

She eyed him furiously.

'I mean it, Maggie, there are no other options.'

'Not even leave Blackheath, become rich and famous in Paris or . . . No, I shan't like it there, it will have to be Blackheath.'

'You will make an announcement that everything was simply a stage performance and that none of it was true.'

'People will want to kill me!' she said.

'I'm sure you will stand a better chance of fighting those off than the patients in here.'

She sighed.

'Well?'

༺༙༙༙༙༙༙༙༺

Maggie stood on a raised platform on the site of the new church in Blackheath before a crowd of villagers and newspaper men who were gathered there at Father Legge's insistence. She looked a state and was not happy. Her make-up had been removed. Her tight strange outfit had been replaced with a simple moth-eaten dress from her wardrobe. And being forced to stand on the exact spot where Henry Legge's church was being built was rubbing her face in it.

Before the whole of Blackheath, she studied the pages on which her signature was required.

'Do you see now how you trespassed against God?' Father Legge demanded theatrically.

She stared angrily at him.

'These documents declare that you agree that under medical and scientific conditions our findings have exposed you as a fraud. That you admit you were misleading the public and that everything they saw was nothing more than parlour games and sleight of hand.'

She gritted her teeth and signed, mortified at the shocked murmurs coming from the crowd.

Father Legge held up the sheet to the crowd.

'She has signed it. Do you declare yourself as a fraud?'

Maggie glared down at her feet.

'The people cannot hear you.'

She looked him square in the face. 'I do!' she shouted, far too loud and aggressively.

Father Legge stared, annoyed at her, as the crowd shouted abuse at her.

'This is your declaration that you will not pursue these activities in any form again,' he shouted, waving another form to the crowd. Maggie snatched it from him and signed, moving to one side as if she was about to leave the platform.

Father Legge waved another before her. 'You will sign and declare in the name of God, that you will return to the Church and attend once a week and renounce your sins.'

She stared at him, seething.

'And you will give the land and your shop to the Church as an apology.'

'I will do nothing of the bloody sort!' she said defiantly.

He marvelled at her. Even now, with her life on the line, her spirit astounded him and he wanted to laugh, but he remained stern faced. He took the document away.

'Bloody pushing your luck,' she mumbled, climbing down the stairs and fighting her way through a crowd, whose jeers were silenced by the fury on her face.

'Out of my way!' she snapped. 'And don't think for a bloody minute of giving me those looks.'

'Family shop taken away and given to the bloody Church!' she exclaimed to herself, storming through the doors of the Hare and Billet. 'Over my dead body!'

As it was she might have to murder Father Legge to reclaim any sense of justice.

She slammed money onto the counter. 'Fill a very big glass with gin. NOW!'

'I hear you made all that stuff up, then?' ventured the barman.

Maggie snatched her drink from his hand without taking her eyes from his.

'Do you want me to kill you, sonny?'

Chapter 32

The following morning, in the vast empty expanse of St Alfege's church in Greenwich, dressed in a simple ivory gown, Judy Cloak became Judy Benedict before the watery eyes of Mrs Walters and a small group of others. It was a big day for all three of them. Within hours, London would disappear behind each and new lives would begin.

Judy had hoped she would turn during the ceremony and see her sister but only the closed doorway had met her glances. Mrs Walters hugged her, beaming up through tears into her eyes.

'It was beautiful and you look lovely and Maggie will regret it.'

'I won't get to say goodbye,' Judy whispered, trying not to let the heartache ruin the occasion. She swallowed, her eyes spilling tears onto Mrs Walters dress. The woman smiled and wiped them away with her handkerchief.

'Come on, chin up. You are Mrs Christopher Benedict now. What adventures will that bring, eh?'

Judy nodded and let her friend take her arm and steady her climb into the carriage that took them up the hill to the small restaurant on Royal Parade. Stepping out of the carriage, she crossed her fingers and dared to hope that Maggie would turn up and make things right.

'A toast,' Mrs Walters said, rising when the meals had been consumed, 'to my very good friend, whom I will miss . . .' – she paused, aware of the quaver in her voice – 'very, very much, and to Christopher, her husband. May you both be very happy and lucky enough to escape the jaws of lions and the feet of elephants. I hope that we will find each other again one day, and in this life.'

The small crowd raised their glasses.

When they stepped out on to the heath, Judy and Netta's final hug had them both in tears. They clung to each other tightly and Judy, peering over her shoulder, looked out at the heath, hoping to see her sister watching from afar somewhere, but she was not. And then, kissing her new husband, she climbed aboard the carriage and was gone.

Mrs Walters stormed across the heath, her fists clenched, her anger driving those who walked towards her from her path. She swung open Maggie's gate, hammered on the door and then, heaving the large pot onto its side, she thrust the key into the lock and entered the house in no mood for Maggie Cloak's dramatics. She found her in bed, furious that Mrs Walters had let herself in.

'Your sister cried her eyes out at her wedding because of you!' she shouted.

'I told you, she means nothing to me,' Maggie replied angrily.

'Well you meant a lot to her!'

'Have you not seen what she has done? She ruined my life!'

'You! You ruined your own life. She is not your mother or your husband. You do not hand someone responsibility for yourself! She did what she thought was best and you made it difficult for her every step of the way. You are a spoilt, spoilt woman, Maggie Cloak, and you have a sister that not only put up with you but somehow, loved you. That woman turned her head a hundred times at her own wedding, hoping that you would arrive but, no not you! Why should the great Maggie Cloak put herself out for anyone other than herself?'

'Get out of my house.'

'I am not going anywhere until I have said my piece.'

Maggie glared angrily.

'You have convinced yourself that you can just throw her aside. No wonder no man will ever love you. No wonder at all.'

'You will not speak to me like that.'

'I will speak to you as I damn well please!' she shouted.

'Did she tell you about how she concealed the truth from me!' Maggie shouted, 'How she lied to me about my father?'

'Your father! Oh your father! We're all bloody tired of your father! What she did Maggie was try to stop what he'd done to you from breaking your heart. She carried that burden for you. She let you go on believing because she knew how much finding out would hurt you. That's what your sister did for you.'

She stormed around to the side of the bed, tearing back the sheets from her.

'Get out of bed! Get out of bed this instant! You stupid, stupid, selfish woman.'

Maggie pulled herself up, reaching for her housecoat but Mrs Walters snatched it away and threw it back.

'You get out there. And you find your sister before she gets on that ship and it's too late. And you tell her that you love her. And you tell her you are sorry. And you mean every word of it. It cannot end like this. I will not have it.'

Maggie stared at her.

'NOW!' Mrs Walters screamed.

The walk home through the village was filled with many memories but Netta was not sad to leave them behind. She stopped suddenly, staring at the séance parlour on which the words 'Closed forever' in Maggie's hand, were painted inside the window. She smiled. Perhaps it was for the best. Maybe now Maggie would reopen her dreadful chocolate shop or something else. Something that mellowed her back into the boring woman she had once been.

With the last of her bags loaded and her savings safely secured to her person, Mrs Walters closed her front door for the last time and stepped into her carriage. How many lives, she wondered, could she squeeze out of this one and, lifting her crystal ball onto her lap, she peered inside, then changing her mind, put it away and looked out of the window at the children who ran alongside, screaming and pointing with laughter as she and her giant chocolate gorilla headed south.

ᘏᘏᘏᘏᘏᘏᘏᘏ

On the bumpiest road that Maggie Cloak had ever had to put up with, she rattled at tremendous speeds, leaving London behind her. She peered out of the window at the endless houses and shook her head.

'I don't remember any of this!' she said with annoyance, tapping at the roof and opening the window.

'I have been to Southampton before!' she called to the coachman, 'Are you sure you are on the correct road?'

'Yes, madam. When did you last travel there?'

She closed her window, ignoring him, then opened it again.

'How long now?'

'A long way yet, madam.'

'I've been in this thing five hours. Can't you go any faster?'

He shook his head at her and closed the window on her himself.

She tapped her foot and folded her arms irritably.

'A heretic!'

'I'll show you heresy, Henry Legge. Just you wait until I get back. If you think you are taking a shop from a Cloak woman, you are in for a surprise.'

She looked out of the window at even more houses. She didn't recognise any of those either and opening the window told the coachman so.

𝄢𝄢𝄢𝄢𝄢

When she arrived in Southampton, Judy was in a lighter mood. She watched her new husband organise their crates. Huge cranes and hundreds of men clambered over the ship, lowering the massive containers down into the holds. Their belongings were to be locked away until they were delivered to her new home, whatever that might be, in the wilds of Africa.

He hurried back to her.

'I think, perhaps, a drink,' he said, 'to steady your nerves.'

'Oh really?' she smiled. 'And not yours?'

He shook his head, puffing out his chest, 'Not mine. You will find mine to be very steady.'

'I see.' She held out her hand, watching it quiver.

He looked. 'How many drinks might that take?'

She shook her head and shrugged. 'Several, I should think.'

He smiled, leaning down to kiss her and they moved off in the direction of one of the less rowdy taverns that lined the docks.

In the tavern, on their second drink, Judy remembered the first time she had met her new husband and how, looking into the ball, she had peeled away his garments, layer by layer to find what was distracting her until she reached his fashionable and shorter than usual undergarments. She looked at him as he carried back their drinks from the bar and wondered if he still sported that fashion. Her mind recalled a drunken conversation with Maggie in the kitchen when they had discussed lovers and how Judy's previous husband had proven to be rather lacklustre in the bedroom. She felt a nervousness rise and her mind race to the chapter in which Lady Dartmouth received the count and allowed him to see her naked and at how, even though she had little confidence in her body, he had made her relax and enjoy every caress.

'Did you ever,' she asked, as he seated himself next to her and smiled, 'read my novel?'

He shook his head, 'Only the parts that were in the newspaper.'

She smiled weakly.

'Might you?'

'You told me that it was more suited to women.'

'It is, it is, but I think it important, since we now are married, that you at least read some of it.'

He smiled. 'I will read it all on this journey.'

She returned his smile, wondering if there was a way in which she could divert his attention to that particular chapter first, perhaps before dinner, before they retired to their cabin, maybe even before the ship pulled away from the dock.

꙰꙰꙰꙰꙰꙰

Maggie was furious, screaming out of the windows at a farmer who herded cattle across their path at such a slow pace that she thought her head might explode or she would be forced to reach for the coachman's pistol. She opened the door, stepping out, heaving her way through the stupid brown beasts to reach the daydreaming dawdler that was ruining her life.

'You!' she spat. 'I am very short-tempered and I am in a hurry. I've already had enough ordeals to kill a lesser woman and had to change horses several dozen times and you, you do not want to be on the receiving end of this temper.'

'Cows are cows, madam. They won't –'

She snatched his stick away, turning to the animals and beat a frenzied channel through them until the carriage squeezed through. Then threw the stick back at the farmer, shaking her head and, pulling up her skirts, climbed back on board, bouncing from one side of the seat to the other as the carriage sped onwards.

She let out a breath, then thinking back to the cows' terrified faces and what a sight she must have provided to onlookers, she did something she had not done in a long time: she laughed.

❧❧❧❧❧❧❧❧

The deafening ship horn blasted through the building and set Judy's heart racing. The moment was here. Hurrying his drink, Christopher stood, taking her hand and, with a small bow, pulled her up. She curtsied, giggling, and they opened the doors, shielding their eyes from the brightness of the sun and walked towards the giant vessel that would be home for several months. They stepped at last onto the gangplank, their feet leaving English soil.

Inside the ship, Judy was surprised to find it quite modern and realised that, until this moment, she had paid the vessel very little thought at all. She had half imagined one great communal hall, in which sleeping spaces were allocated, so she was hugely relieved when they followed one of the crew along several passages and came to a door marked number 6. On entering, she found herself in a small but perfect little room with a bed and a cupboard and a table and chairs, and their cases placed neatly at the foot of the bed. Without thinking, she wished that Maggie could have seen it too but she shook the thought aside and clapped her hands, turning to kiss her new husband.

Outside the horn blasted again, calling the stragglers on board, announcing the urgency of the looming departure. She fell back on the bed, looking up at the porthole and went to it. Outside on the docks, families and sailors and workmen were hurrying and she recalled when they had waved away her father.

Four years, she thought. After four years, would she return?

He pulled her to him.

'Mrs Benedict.'

'Mr Benedict.'

❧❧❧❧❧❧❧❧

Maggie had arrived in Southampton, her heart hammering and her hands trembling as the carriage negotiated the streets and headed to the docks. She didn't remember any of this either. She hated the way everything changed. Suddenly the distant sound of the ship horn blasted and ten minutes later blasted again. She was shouting, urging him to drive faster, opening the door and jumping out, running towards the crowds, screaming for them to let her though.

'I cannot miss her! I cannot!'

And suddenly, she could see it, gigantic in the water, the dock workers climbing down, steam pouring from the great chimneys, hundreds of faces peering down at her as the doors began to close. She fought her way down into the crowd that tried to block every step of her way but she would have none of it. The engines let out a roar.

'No!' she screamed and battled her way towards the front row, staring up at the faces, screaming out her name. 'JUDY! JUDITH!'

She finally broke through to the front, stopping almost too late, finding herself teetering on the edge, with her hands clawing out midair. She rocked, feeling hands grab and pull her back and she fell against families that complained angrily at her.

'JUDY!'

She recognised none of the faces that looked down at her. In an instant she remembered herself as a child, searching out her father. And suddenly there was a great swill of water, a churning down below and the horn sounded again and she screamed out at it angrily, her voice lost beneath the sound of the engines.

On the deck, Judy, with Christopher's arm around her waist, looked out at Southampton. Her last memory of England would be Southampton beneath an orange and pink sunset, and they would stay there watching until it was a dot on the horizon. The ship vibrated beneath her feet and she marvelled at it, feeling the tremendous force that would keep them afloat. And then, as the engines grew silent for the ship to saddle out sideways in the water, as she turned to squeeze Christopher's hand and look up at him for the hundredth time, she heard her name.

'JUDY CLOAK!'

She ignored it. It would not be for her, and then she heard it again, unmistakably angry, and she ran, pushing through the crowds to see, her heart in her mouth. It could not be Maggie, Maggie would never, she wouldn't even know how . . . She stared at the crowds, frightened that she had raised her hopes and would see someone else calling out to her namesake. And then, bold as brass, at the front of them all, in her tired old clothes, there was her sister. Judy jumped back in shock, covering her mouth, letting out a gasp.

'JUDY CLOAK!'
'MAGGIE!'

But Maggie was looking the wrong way and then she looked up but did not notice her and looked past her and past her again and Judy waved frantically, calling out to her.

'I AM HERE! I AM HERE!'

The ship was turning and time was running out and, tearing off her bonnet, Judy hurled it down in front of her sister as the ship began to move The crowds pointed to it, laughing, and then she saw Maggie's head lift from it to her and in that brief moment, both women stared at each other, their lips trembling and their smiles ugly with emotion, both unable to take their eyes from each other.

'I am sorry!' Maggie shouted. 'I am really, truly sorry!'

Judy's face crumpled.

'I love you!'

Judy was shaking, nodding, trying to swallow so she could call back, her hands trembling against her mouth.

'I love you too!' she shouted.

Maggie was mouthing something urgent but the ship was moving further away and her words were getting lost beneath the roar and cheers but the woman would not be defeated and in the last moment, as the sound of the engines lowered to a purr, she shouted.

'Please come back to me!'

And her sister nodded, watching the tired little woman left standing on the docks as the ship moved away and she lost yet another to Africa.

Chapter 33

Suffering from a ferocious cold, Maggie Cloak pushed her home-made draught excluder against the door and threw another log onto the fire. She had barely ventured out for weeks but since the storm seemed never-ending, she doubted she was missing much. She picked up her sister's book and pulled a shawl over herself, toasting her toes before the fire.

'It really is appallingly written,' she said aloud, pouring the little port that remained into her glass and picking up where she left off.

Mr Boedeving, curator of the Hall of The Extraordinary, escorted the crowd through the exhibition. He moved past the bearded lady, the tattooed man and the giant who nodded to them politely and towered three feet above even the tallest of men. They stopped to marvel at the Siamese Twins and looked in horror at the German Pig Man with his dribbling snout, bulky pink face and violent unpredictable eyes. At the front of the crowd a smartly dressed man placed a reassuring hand on his son's shoulder as the thing shook at the bars of its cage and snorted aggressively at them.

At last they came to the magnificent curtained centrepiece.

'Here is an odd creature,' Mr Bodeving said facing the crowd, 'It was discovered just ten years ago, shot down from the sky in the centre of London. The story has it that she was one of a pair, creatures that inhabited the London suburb of Blackheath. At night they would fly over London, swooping down and plucking unsuspecting Londoners from the street to drink their blood. Some say that they were of royal blood from some far-off land and moved from city to city, fleeing when discovered. Behold, the winged lady.' He reached to the thick gold cord and pulled, opening the curtains to reveal a vast water-filled tank in which, naked, the countess hung on a frame, her hair floating around her, her wings stretched taut, her magnificent eyes replaced with painted glass balls.

The boy looked up at her and turned to his father who closed his eyes and looked away. The crowd marvelled, children giggled at her nakedness and walked around to the back of the tank to inspect where the wings met the shoulders.

The man and his son remained before the tank long after the crowd had moved on, and as the sun began to sink outside and cast long shadows across the hall they turned and walked out into the narrow streets of Prague.

A knock at the door pulled Maggie grumbling from her chair and when she saw who it was, she grumbled even more.

'Oh, I should have seen this one coming,' she said, letting him in.

Father Legge stepped inside, blowing his nose into a hanky.

'Come to lecture me about God knows what again?'

He frowned at her.

'I brought you the brandy you sent for and to bring you communion.'

'The communion was a way of getting this delivered,' she said, taking it. 'Well, sit down if you're stopping or get out.'

He kicked off his boots and hung up his coat, sitting on the spare chair next to hers to warm his hands.

'I have a proposal,' he said.

'Not another one. You have too much time on your hands.'

She tapped an extra glass with the brandy bottle and he nodded.

'Sometimes, people who have lost everyone or have no one, even those who are not believers, turn to the Church for comfort and friendship.'

She sighed. 'You do exhaust me.'

'I just thought …'

'Do you know what I see when I close my eyes, Henry? Do you? When I pretend to be in prayer?'

He took the glass.

'There we have another thing in common. I also have the weight of knowledge.'

She shook her head. 'I think I win that one, don't you?'

He reached into the fire and turned over the log. 'I often find myself considering you. You are one of life's enigmas, my life's in any case. All the way through, you've been interesting and challenging but overall annoying.'

She eyed him.

'Why did you never marry, Henry? Was God really enough?'

He smiled into his brandy. 'I was too busy. And you?'

'It is impossible for any man to find me attractive in any way.'

He laughed.

'It's not funny, Henry. It broke my heart.'

They sat for a while in silence, watching the flames twist up into the chimney.

'To a casual observer we might appear like an old married couple,' she said.

'If I am honest, women rather frighten me.'

'Do I?'

'No, you never frightened me. You were the one I enjoyed fighting with.' He paused. 'Margaret there is another reason I am here.'

She froze. 'You're not going to ask me to marry you, are you?'

'No,' he replied, watching her breathe a sigh of relief.

'It's something else.'

'Don't spoil things, Henry.'

'I'm afraid I must, but you can say no. There is a bursary, a fund.'

'I don't want charity.'

'Enough to pay for your passage to Kenya, to Judy. That is why you came to mind, because it is Kenya.'

She shook her head.

'She will be back.'

'The trip is for one year. Missionary work.'

She rolled her eyes.

'I just thought that perhaps . . .'

She shook her head again.

'She will be back. She promised.'

'You are a proud women, Margaret Cloak.'

She eyed him and topped up his brandy. Then, reaching for her sister's book, she flicked to the last page and motioned to him. 'Listen to this.'

Professor Klaus Van Dayne stood before the firing squad and pulled off his blindfold, looking directly at the men who were about to kill him. He saw the first flash, heard the shots and felt a sting. Heat tore through his chest and he felt the movement of the bullet pushing through him, as if, just for that moment, time was slowed. And, as all thoughts flashed through his mind, he felt the exact spot, the nucleus of where death had begun in the body and he felt it spread, invading him. His mind slowing, his body weakening, he turned to face the cliff, looking out at the sea, and he ran, throwing himself headfirst

into the air, opening his arms, feeling the wind around him as he soared over the waves and he felt what it was to fly.

She slapped the book closed.
'How on earth that rubbish was ever published, God only knows.'

Acknowledgements

The National Trust, The Ranger's House, The Royal Observatory Greenwich, Neil Rhind (Blackheath Village & Environs), Lewisham Council, Greenwich Council, iinet.new.au convict list for NSW, with special thanks to the real Lady Dartmouth – M Brand.

Why I wrote *The Blackheath Séance Parlour*

The idea for the Blackheath Séance Parlour came to me one evening when a small shop became available in the village and I wondered what it was that Blackheath needed. It is a fiercely independent village, the sort that drums out Starbucks to make way for a proper old fashioned fishmonger or truffle emporium. I kept mulling the idea around in my head then came up with the one thing that Blackheath would have an absolute fury about, a séance parlour. Though, I do think that if I opened the actual shop today it would do phenomenally well.

Blackheath is a great exposed common overlooking London, it's prone to crazy storms, battering rain and knee high snow, which often comes as a surprise to those venturing up from a more sedate, neighbouring Greenwich. It is often so dramatic it lends itself to imagination. The count and countess story was born on a night I was being hurled about in a gale crossing the heath. To have the ability to throw yourself up into the gusts and wide black sky and to enjoy being battered by it appealed to me and the little lit windows breaking up the darkness made me curious about what it would be like to live in fear of what lurked about on the heath in a different age. But I didn't want to create some bog-standard vampire; I wanted something more intelligent, something deliberately constructed with a mind that didn't just want to kill and give evil looks to camera. I love the scene in which he seduces a much older woman and she is forced to let go of her nervousness and insecurity and allow her body to be viewed and touched by a man two thirds her age.

Fortunately the heath is punctuated by a pub; I think more people run in there to escape the elements in winter than intended to go there in the first place. It's warm and snug, usually with old men reading novels or doing crosswords scattered about it. It's a great place to write. So really everywhere I turned in Blackheath inspired one scene or another. My book opens with a storm, Maggie Cloak struggling against the gale past the Hare and Billet pub. She continued onward, but on the

night that scene was born, I went inside the pub and wrote it.

The book attempts to be as factually loyal to Blackheath at the time as I could make it, right down to the names of the people who owned the shops back in 1842 and the building of the iconic church. It also clears up the misconception over the name Blackheath, which contrary to popular belief, is nothing to do with the Black Death; disappointingly it got its name because the soil was darker.

As I started to research Blackheath properly, incredible stories began emerging, the history and importance of the place is astounding; golf was invented here, weather forecasting, the rules of rugby were decided in the Princess of Wales pub, Dick Turpin reigned terror, a suspect in the Jack the Ripper case resided just off the heath, powerful slave traders and ship builders dominated Dartmouth Row's huge houses, providing neck and ankle irons to the world. As well as the history of the observatory, Blackheath was the playground of royalty, The Princess Sophia Matilda who resided in the Ranger's house, and appears as herself in two versions in the book was probably the most dull princess there has ever been. Police were being introduced, street lighting... There came a point where I had to draw the line for fear of losing the novel to Blackheath's history.

There is a mix of gothic horror, humour and the historical in Séance Parlour that I've not come across elsewhere and wanted to create. While maintaining a feel of the historical, it also has a streak of modern day sensibilities to appeal to the modern reader. The People that have read it so far seem able to discuss different parts of it at length with a passion but all come back to talk affectionately about the main characters and how much they love Maggie and Judy.

The Victorians were obsessed with vampires, ghosts and death. Within the Blackheath Séance Parlour, Judy Cloak's novel within a novel celebrates this but as the serialisation in the Illustrated London News begins to gather momentum and starts to bleed into real life it shows up the very real monster at its centre.

I love strong female characters; I find them easier and more exciting to write than men and the women in Séance Parlour are magnificent, giving every man a run for their money. Maggie in particular has a singularity of mind that made her exciting to write. Whenever she walked into a scene, as a writer I pretty much sat back and listened to what she had to say. She pretty much wrote herself, so when forced into a role that she despised it became apparent that it would not be long before she ran the entire show.

The mid-1800s was an age where all was new and unfolding. Without the means to scientifically scrutinise mediums, sleight-of-hand was far more convincing. Visiting a medium or attending a séance was the equivalent of stepping into dangerous and unchartered territory. It was, by far, the height of sophistication in entertainment. Of course, the majority of mediums were exposed as frauds. In darkened rooms where things were barely visible, the spirits conjured to walk around the guests and touch them were usually friends covered in net curtains; the ectoplasm they produced from their mouths and nostrils was linen or tissue caked in flour and water, surreptitiously moulded by hand to resemble vague shapes. Spirit voices usually came from someone hiding in the next room throwing their voices. I wanted to do away with all the trickery for this book and deliver the real deal. I've read too many books where at the last moment the psychic reveals it was all false and as a reader it was like being slapped across the face. Maggie puts an end to that quite firmly in the Blackheath Séance Parlour, she makes it clear from the outset that she will not be putting up with anything misleading and that if a job is worth doing, it's worth doing properly. If she'd known her abilities would spiral out of control at such a horrendous speed, leaving her the victim of it and terrorising everyone around her, she might have changed her mind, but then, there's not a lot can control Maggie.